THE DEVIL'S MINE

ELLIOTT G ALLEN

ISBN 13: 9781499251012
ISBN 10: 1499251017

Table of Contents

CHAPTER 1

Sketches in the Night

The earth is *talking to me. The sky and the stars confide in me their woes. The stones share their story with me alone. Today the boiling sea spoke of many things, few of them good. I listen, and I feel, and my worry grows. Would the stones lie to me? No; they speak truth, as ever.*

It was still dark when Jack woke up abruptly. Shadows hovered and clustered in the room, and in his mind. He knew by the feel of his body, its tightness, the tension in his head and back, that he had slept only lightly. He lay still for a few minutes, then reached over and fumbled for the switch of the bedside lamp. Its light showed him what he did not want to see: over the bed and on the floor were scattered numerous sheets of paper, while broken in pieces around him were bits of pencils.

He lay back and tried to loosen his taut limbs. So it was happening again. He shouldn't be surprised; he knew the pattern well enough. What was it his father had said? "It's just stress, Jack, just stress. Everybody has their own way of dealing with it. Only with you, it's a bit different." *Why* did he have to be different? Why couldn't he be like any other teenager? He rubbed his head, got out of bed and went over to the desk, taking one of the sheets of paper with him and carefully laying it flat in the circle of light from the lamp, where he could see it properly. On the paper, executed in quick, heavy pencil strokes, was a drawing. He turned it this way and that to make sense of it, then, having done so, he sat quite still. The picture was of a building, or perhaps two separate buildings, one with a finger-like projection from its roof that might have been a chimney. It seemed to be made of stone, roughly the shape of an old chapel with narrow lancet-like windows. The building clung to the edge of a plunging cliff that descended to meet … the sea? Yes, surely, for there were choppy waves and maybe some gulls.

Thoughtfully, he put the drawing aside and reached for another sheet. Here just one building, again with its stumpy chimney, was sketched alone and disembodied in the middle of the paper. Dark, formless shadows, drawn with vigorous cross-hatched lines, hemmed it in and loomed over it as if poised to pounce. Quickly he gathered up the other drawings. They all had the same distinctive buildings as their subject. Then he opened a drawer to reveal a pile of similar such sheets, made as if to put the papers on top of the pile, then thought better of it and left them lying on the desk. From another drawer he produced a bottle of pills, which he set on the desktop and regarded for a while as if it were an enemy. Then he relented: he didn't want *the other* to happen. Shaking out two of the pills into his palm, he padded across the landing to the bathroom, sweating, fearful in case ... but perhaps not, after all. He shouldn't be so negative!

In the bathroom Jack swallowed the pills with some water and stood staring into the cabinet mirror. His haunted face stared back: dark eyes deeply ringed with tiredness, black unruly hair whose long locks lay tangled on his forehead, high cheekbones and thin cheeks. Again he tried to relax ... "It's stress, just stress!" But as he bent to rinse his face, he froze. What was that? Was it ...? Echoes ran around the bathroom, the trace of a whisper, in the pipes, behind the mirror, under the floor, in – his head? No, please, not *that* voice! He pressed his hands to his ears to try to shut it out, but he knew in reality that it was useless. The voice was within, not outside. Steeling himself, he continued with washing his face as if nothing had happened, letting the cold water waken him up, shake him out of it. And the whispering slowly receded, then tailed off, its indistinct syllables dying away without resolving into anything definite.

Jack Tyack had been hearing voices in his head, on and off, ever since he was a small boy. Sometimes it was just background noise, indecipherable murmurings. Sometimes they would tell him to do things, harmless, trivial things: what to eat, what to wear, when to go to bed. Or to do things in a certain order. Sometimes he obeyed the voices, sometimes he didn't. Once, however, when he ignored them something bad had happened. That he had slipped, and fallen, and broken his arm, might have just been coincidence but Jack thought not. He was convinced there was a connection and he'd never disobeyed the voices since. Now he took medication and the voices had largely gone, or were muffled at worst. Until recently.

He patted his face dry with a towel and took a few deep, measured breaths. Yes, recently one voice had begun to intrude again. *That* voice, he called it. It didn't tell him to do things, in fact there were no intelligible words at all. Yet what it spoke of was not pleasant. Since it had started he'd felt bad: drained and weary. He padded back across the landing, trying to feel normal. It never occurred to Jack that he was in any sense ill. There was Jack Tyack, a seventeen-year-old, and there were the voices, and now The Voice, which were different and not him, not really to do with him at all. As for the family – well, his parents never seemed to want to talk about it much, something he had learned to live with, too.

The drawings were different. They had started later, much more recently. He was never conscious of producing them; they were always done in his sleep. The doctors had said he must always keep a pad and pen by the bedside; it was just a natural outlet. But now there was this particular drawing, over and over again. What did it mean – if it meant anything?

He decided to go downstairs. The Tyacks' house was large, stylish and modern, and was built using a split-level approach. On his way down to the kitchen Jack noticed light streaming from the fractionally open door of the study: his father, at work already, as was increasingly his habit of late. Jack knew better than to disturb him. The study was strictly off limits. He passed on.

Most things happened early in the Tyack household. In the kitchen, his mother had just returned from her morning run and was perched at the breakfast bar eating a yoghurt. She was a petite woman, her physical trimness all the more evident in her tracksuit. Her blonde hair was drawn back in a tight little pony tail high on the back of her head. Now she looked at him inquiringly with dispassionate grey eyes. "Up already Jack? What's wrong?" Her eyes narrowed, instantly detecting his discomposure. "Not another bad night?" Increasingly, it seemed as if Jack's issues were an irritant to Mrs Tyack.

He looked down. He wanted to divulge, to share it all, but at the last minute checked himself. "Nothing Mum. I just woke up early, that's all. Did you have a good run?"

Her gaze lingered on him for a little longer, penetrating, then she looked away, gave a quick shrug and carried on eating. "I'll be going to the office in a minute. I don't know what you've got planned for today but *please,* Jack, try to spend some time looking for a job. You know you need to." She threw the empty yoghurt pot into the recycling and reached for her mobile. "You only get one chance in this life. Don't waste it. Now, I must get my shower and be off. I'd be *very* grateful if you could walk Terry later."

"Yes Mum," he said, to her receding back. Then, feeling hungry, he helped himself to some cereals while staring out at the wide, landscaped garden bathed in the early morning light. His headache was still there, but at least the voice had gone. He glanced over at the clock. Seven a.m. Suddenly Jack felt very alone. He wanted to show someone the drawings *now*, to share them. He started to climb the stairs, then hesitated, unsure as to what to do. He could distract himself by walking the dog, or ... He made for his bedroom. The drawings were still scattered on the floor where he had left them. Or had he? That was funny; he felt sure he'd gathered them up in a pile. Perhaps a draught, or perhaps his memory was playing him tricks ... or maybe those drugs?

He gazed at the trees through the window, listening to the birdsong, the whole system of nature rousing itself for another day. The encounter with his mother had left a bad taste. His parents had become so remote, both of them – preoccupied with their work. Yes, they owned and ran a successful company, which was bound to take up their time. The business flourished, but it never used to be as bad as this. They were closer once, but that had all changed. His father, increasingly closeted away, all work, work, work; his mother, colder, harder, more impatient. At bottom, Jack knew he was officially a 'disappointment' to them. His problems – the voices, the drawings, their impact on his mood – were glossed over, rarely discussed, as if the whole lot would magically disappear of its own accord. Meanwhile, his studies slipped and the goal of academic excellence, so prized in Tyack circles, drifted further out of his reach. But what to do? Things were getting worse, he couldn't deny that. There was perhaps one person he could turn to, whose advice he could trust, who could be relied on to have his best interests at heart ....

He picked up the nearest drawing and scrutinized it again. The harsh, jabbing pencil strokes and frenzied deep shading now looked more alarming. The picture exuded a dark, troubled atmosphere, something *other worldly*. He made up his mind. His friend would know what to do. He would ask him as soon as possible – today, if he could – and see what he might suggest to sort out this mess. He put the drawing down, picked up a towel from the airing cupboard and went back to the bathroom, hoping a shower would somehow wash away all these complications. He made it as hot as he could stand, until the water stung his skin and the steam wrapped around him in dense wreaths. But the strange, alien atmosphere of the drawings lingered in his mind hauntingly.

⅄

The person whose advice Jack sought was not of his own age but was older, in fact, than his father. Richard Attlee and his wife were long-time friends of the family. Jack couldn't remember a time when they had not been on the scene. He had always got on well with the eccentric Attlee and a special bond had grown up between them, somehow transcending the difference in age. It was to this man that Jack now decided to turn for help.

The Attlees' house was within easy walking distance of the Tyacks'. It was located down a private, leafy road and approached via a gravel drive that wrapped itself around a green island of turf, in the centre of which was a mature oak tree, stately and ancient. That tree had no doubt been there for hundreds of years. Many tall beeches rose serenely on the margins of the spacious plot, making it all very private and secluded. The house itself was a substantial cottage with numerous angles and extensions. The roof was steeply pitched and mossy, the eaves low and welcoming; the whole effect had a touch of the fairy tale about it.

Jack was welcomed in by Miriam Attlee and shown through to the kitchen, where the lean figure of her husband was seated at the table, the weekend papers spread before him, gloomily regarding the back garden over the tops of his glasses. His iron-grey hair fell over his forehead in a Fuhrer-like flap. "Ah, Jack, greetings. Would you like some tea? I was just thinking what a mess that mole has made of the lawn. I've tried sonic deterrents but they're a complete waste of money. Are you any good at mole catching?"

Despite himself Jack laughed, "Sorry Richard, I can't help you there."

"Interesting things, moles. Nobody really understands much about them. You know, their tunnels stretch for miles underground. I believe they go much deeper than people used to think. It must be a totally different world. They stay down there for weeks on end, just surfacing now and again to ruin my grass!"

"Can't you trap it?"

"I'll have to, I suppose. Don't like killing things though." He pulled a face, then got up to make the tea. "Well, summer's here at last. What have you got lined up for these disgracefully long holidays you youngsters get?"

"I've got to look for a job. There might be one going in the coffee shop starting in a couple of weeks. You know, the one in Amersham on the corner. And I need to do some studying, too."

"That doesn't sound very exciting." He noisily clattered cups and saucers. "You wouldn't have caught me studying over the summer."

Jack knew Attlee well enough not to be offended. "Well, what did you do in between your A levels?"

"Went travelling. Hitchhiking around Europe as a matter of fact. Quite adventurous for those days. I left home with twenty pounds in my pocket, and that was enough to keep me going for a month! It took me three days to get to Switzerland – there were no motorways then, of course. Then on to Germany, Austria ... I wanted to learn some German, you see." He brought over the tea and a packet of biscuits.

"Where did you stay?" asked Jack. "Hotels?"

Attlee made a sound of unbridled contempt. "Certainly not. Nothing pampered, not like youngsters these days. Cheap hostels, railways stations, subways …." He looked rather evasive and diverted his gaze down the garden. "Fields, now and again." Knowing Attlee's tendency to exaggerate, Jack was about to inquire further but he quickly changed the subject.

"So, how are things at home? Is everything okay?" His eyes narrowed shrewdly, eyeing Jack's bag which contained the drawings. Attlee was no fool.

Jack hesitated. "No … not really. Can you ... look at these for me?" He produced the drawings and set them out on the table. Suddenly he felt almost too choked to speak. "It's started up again, but worse. I did them last night. In my sleep. I just wanted you to see them, that's all."

Richard Attlee, who more or less knew the score with Jack, barring a few details, adjusted his glasses and started leafing through the pictures, calmly and analytically. "Ah. You did *all* of these last night, yes?"

Jack nodded. "They were all over my room when I woke up. And the voices have come back. Or one voice, anyway. I don't know what I should do–"

Attlee smiled sympathetically, still looking closely at the drawings. "Well let's see, I'm sure there are some clues in here somewhere … These buildings are all of engine houses, you know?"

"Er, no. I thought it was some sort of factory. What sort of engine houses?"

"In this case, I would say a sort characteristic of Cornwall. Hold on a minute." He disappeared into the hall and came back shortly with a small booklet which he waved in front of Jack with animation. The cover proclaimed the title *Tin and Tin Mining*. He flicked through it, found the page he was looking for and flattened it out on the table so they could both clearly see it. "Look at this." The black and white photograph showed a picturesque but dramatic view of steep cliffs dropping down almost vertically into the sea, with some small buildings clustered at their foot, doused in the spray of a breaker. "Now look at this–" and he placed one of Jack's drawings alongside for comparison. The similarity was immediately obvious, and quite uncanny. "All these drawings essentially depict the same thing, I'd say: Cornish engine houses, used in the mining of tin and related ores through the nineteenth century and well into the last one. The question is, what's put these into your head just now? Have you been looking at any mines recently? Seen anything on the TV? Have you been studying the subject, or reading about it?"

Jack shook his head, feeling steadied by Attlee's rational tone. "I definitely haven't been anywhere like that. I don't remember reading or seeing anything about them either. Anyway, even if I had, why would I be drawing them compulsively in my sleep?"

Attlee inclined his head a little sceptically. "Well, you say that Jack but the subconscious mind is a funny thing." He pursed his lips and gazed vacantly out of the window. After a while, Jack broke in on his thoughts.

"There's something else. Okay, the buildings are engine houses. What are those, then?" He pointed to the various shadow-like shapes that appeared to flit and cluster around some of the buildings.

Attlee looked serious. "I know. Those shapes are more than just abstractions, wouldn't you agree? Some of them, if you look closely" – and here he held one up to the light, at arm's length – "some of them have distinct features and *appendages*, quite subtly drawn in fact."

"So?" Jack had a nasty feeling his fears were about to be validated.

"I don't want to alarm you but to be quite frank they look like representations of some kind of demon. All cultures have their own form of them, of course – Hebraic Moloch, the Greek Gorgon, Belial in Judaism, Mara in Buddhist mythology, and so on. What's interesting is how distinctly you've drawn them here. Not just vague shadows, but with real differentiation."

Jack looked again at the sketches and, yes, he could see what Attlee meant. The shadows suddenly looked more concrete, more real and individual than they had earlier. Why hadn't he noticed that before?

Attlee sat back in his chair. "The real question, as you say, is why on earth are you drawing these things? Each on its own would be unusual, but the two together like this seem *so* incongruous ... I don't know. Jung has theories about the collective unconscious of course ...." He trailed off, leaving the chain of thought incomplete. "And you definitely haven't recently seen anything to do with these?"

"No. Definitely. Look, what have – *demons* got to do with it? You don't think I'm ...." Jack lowered his voice, not wanting to say it. "Not *possessed*?" But Attlee remained silent, and just looked puzzled.

They both gazed out of the kitchen window for a while, listening to the birdsong, watching the pigeons meanly oust the sparrows and wrens from the bird table and gobble up all the food. Upstairs, Mrs Attlee could be heard hoovering. Eventually, Jack rejoined, "So what do you think I should do next? It's obviously getting worse."

Attlee continued looking perplexed, and said, "It can't be irrelevant that the pictures are of Cornwall. An actual, specific location, not just a general evocation. Those buildings on the cliff are known as the Crown Mines, and they're right down at the bottom of the peninsula, near Land's End. You know, Jack, you could do worse than take a trip down there. Treat it as a holiday." He sucked in his cheeks thoughtfully and glanced down again at the drawings. "I'm serious! It's a lovely part of the world. The change would do you good and – who knows?" He gave an enigmatic smile. "It might just exorcise some of these demons."

CHAPTER 2

THE CROWN MINES

AND NOW WE *see these same disturbances become more frequent and volatile, according to their unruly nature and as is the way when Strife has ascendancy. As is truly said, having seen a small part of life, swift to die, men rise and fly away like smoke, persuaded only of what each has met with as they are driven in every direction. Now those troubled souls are newly stirred in the heavens, restless in their wanderings as their sins pursue them. My rain gauge registered 6cm by lunchtime. One would have to return to the first week of last October for similar conditions.*

A curious lone figure shut the door behind him and headed to the cliff top where he had earlier viewed the storm with growing concern. Now it lay menacingly in the distance, the electrical activity flickering and lighting up the base of the towering, black clouds which jostled together in the vast currents of air before metamorphosing into mighty forms and shadows. Yet its dark energies were not uncontested; a warm weather front had swept in from the south and appeared to be pushing the storm back out to sea. The clouds that shrouded its distant epicentre now marched in a defensive line against the clear skies that were directly overhead. The visible divide between the two fronts ran parallel to the cliff tops as far as the eye could see. Sharp, violent gusts of wind plucked at the window panes of the house and made the nearby flagpole rattle and vibrate in frenzy before they abruptly subsided. The figure stooped to inspect intricate equipment contained in a small shuttered box, then straightened and surveyed the heavens again. Satisfied that the worst of the storm had passed, it retreated into the house that seemed to grow out of the cliff, both seeming lost in the vastness of the sweeping coastline and wide sky.

⅄

"Running away from your problems won't help." His mother's words were still fresh in Jack's ears as he stepped off the old bus that had coughed and spluttered its way to the town square. St Just was a small market town in the furthest south-west of the Cornish peninsula, on the opposite side to Penzance. He looked around and took in the place. The whole area was entirely new to him. The square was fringed with shops and pubs, faced in a craggy grey stone, which seemed to lean in around him as if to take a closer look. A church steeple rose up behind their lichen-stained slate roofs. In the middle, where the bus had dropped him, was a little triangular island, where a grubby looking, solitary, bearded character lounged on a bench and was now staring at Jack with open curiosity. The man had been browsing through a local newspaper that rested loosely on his lap, pages fluttering in the light breeze. The church clock chimed: seven p.m. The summer sun was still strong, although the shadows lengthened. The bus pulled away in a cloud of fumes and peace descended on the square again.

As a reflex, Jack pulled out his mobile and fiddled with it. Maybe he should give home a quick ring. The man on the bench continued to regard him with interest. "You won't get any signal round here," he said presently, a note of satisfaction in his tone. He was right, the phone was useless. "You see," he leaned forward conspiratorially, "we don't *do* gadgets like them things. Nothing like that works properly here. So you'd best forget it." And he nodded briefly, as if that was the end of the matter.

Jack smiled weakly and tried to orientate himself. He was already wondering if he had done the right thing in coming down here. The trip was hardly the most attractive prospect but Richard Attlee had been remarkably insistent about its likely benefits. In truth, Jack had become so desperate at the appearance of his nocturnal drawings that he was willing to try any expedient, even this. There was a largish building with tall Georgian windows to his left – the Commercial Hotel, where he had booked a room for his trip. It was cheap enough. Again his mother's voice echoed in his head: "Go if you like, it's up to you. Just remember, all this costs money. If you want to spend, then you need to earn too. You'd be better using the time to find a job. You get nothing for nothing, in this life." He screwed up his eyes, as if by doing so he might blot out that dismal discussion. This place, St Just; the sea; the three hundred miles or so between him and home ... with luck these things would combine to overwrite the memory of it. Seagulls wheeled and cried mournfully above as he hefted his suitcase and, carefully avoiding the gaze of the bearded man, crossed the square to the hotel.

Inside, the Commercial Hotel had a well-worn sort of feel to it. It was dark and not exactly immaculate, yet friendly enough. It had probably seen better days. But as Jack checked in and was shown up irregular flights of stairs and along uneven corridors, he rapidly started to feel more alive. This was *his* holiday, *he* was making the decisions now. He suddenly felt he'd done the right thing after all in coming here. A sense of relief swept through him, along with a new lightness.

After leaving his things in his room he descended again to get a snack and something to drink. The building was clearly very old and the bar had a low, timbered ceiling with irregular plastering over its walls, dark red carpet, nooks, crannies and old prints here and there. It was empty except for a group of a dozen or so locals drinking in one of these nooks. Their conversation was loud and clearly well-lubricated by beer. Jack turned his attention to the bar where the landlord, a large and rugged rugby type, had now appeared. "Now young man, what can I do for you?" Jack cast his eye over the bar snacks menu and ordered some sandwiches. The last part of his order, however, was drowned out by a peal of explosive laughter from the group. He stared over to see one of them, a middle-aged man in a scruffy yellow cagoule, half rise to his feet as if to give a little speech, then collapse again in helpless mirth, his beer spilling in all directions. "Don't you mind them," said the landlord in a friendly tone. "That's our local conservation society. You'll usually find them in here of an evening."

"Oh. What do they conserve?" asked Jack, mildly curious.

"Old buildings, old engines. Plenty of them down here, you know, what with all the mines."

Jack gave the group another quick glance. They had quietened down now and seemed immersed in discussion about a more sober matter. "Are there any mines near here?" He thought he would get the landlord's account of the matter even though, taking his cue from Richard Attlee, he had done a bit of research on the subject.

"Certainly. Cape Cornwall, just on the headland there." The landlord waved across to his left. "Or you can walk a bit further round and get to Crown Mines. Worth a trip, that. They're famous, you know."

Jack nodded, thanked the landlord and perched on a stool while he waited for his food to arrive. Idly he regarded one of the pictures on the wall to his left. It was a black and white photo, clearly very old, showing a dray horse and cart delivering barrels of beer to the hotel. In the background, the town square looked very much the same as it did now. There was even the same bench in the middle, on which the bearded man had been sitting. Jack already felt that the march of progress had been slow in these parts. Somehow he liked that. He glanced up and saw that one of the members of the conservation society was looking at him. The look was not exactly hostile, but when his plate of sandwiches and his drink arrived Jack nevertheless preferred to take them back up to his room. Besides, the long journey had tired him and the idea of spending the rest of the evening alone, watching TV and having an early night suddenly seemed very appealing.

Back upstairs, he settled himself on the bed, switched on the television and took a swig of his drink. Again he felt a wave of relief, exhilaration almost. He had already decided he would not leave out the pen and paper by his bed that night. Something told him they would not be needed, something perhaps connected with the fact he was now following his inner impulses. Soon he felt drowsy. As luck would have it, though, his room was directly above the bar. As he lay on the bed, flicking through the TV channels, he could hear the murmur of voices below, sometimes swelling into gales of laughter, sometimes subsiding to snatched mutterings. Like the sound of the sea, he thought; the sea, that must be only a mile away at most. He would go to it and see it tomorrow, for the first time since he was a boy. Thinking of its wide expanses, strange life forms and cold tides, he drifted into a dreamless sleep.

⅄

Jack woke early, at six o'clock, and made the immediate decision to get up and washed and to set out as soon as possible to find the mines. This was action at last, the antidote to the denial and stifling accumulation of tension of the past weeks. Thanks to Richard Attlee, he really did feel he was on to something important, something that could lead him to the root of his problems, something to help him to help himself. With this in mind, he swallowed down his tablets with a glass of water (avoiding a strong impulse to skip them), then packed a rucksack with a water bottle, energy bar and the ordnance survey map of the area that, on Attlee's advice, he had previously studied and brought down with him. After glancing out of the window, he donned a waterproof and woolly hat, laced up his trainers and made for the door, pausing at the mirror to see what sort of a figure he cut. Inside his head, all was quiet. He felt it would continue to be, at least for now. He was doing what The Voice wanted, even if it couldn't tell him directly.

Quietly, he let himself out of the hotel and surveyed the little town square. Conditions were not good: a mist hung heavy in the moisture-laden air and the place had a leaden, shrouded feel. Seagulls wheeled and flapped disconsolately overhead and strutted on the pavements, picking at stray chip wrappers. It was distinctly chilly for the time of year. A part of him wanted to retreat back to the warmth of his room. As soon as the thought entered his head, he felt a palpable recoil, as if a rein were being tightened in his mind, pulling him back. He should go; he *must* go. He set out down the road to Cape Cornwall, shouldering his rucksack in what he hoped seemed a professional, determined manner.

The road led down between Georgian terraces before crossing a golf course. A narrow footpath cut off to the right between hedges. This Jack took, noting the sign to Botallack, three miles. The path wound down a valley and past a ruined arsenic works before climbing again and finally emerging on the cliffs. And here at last was what he had been waiting for: a panoramic view of the restless sea. Yet visibility was not good; though the wind was up and the mist blown away it had been replaced by a driving, murky drizzle. He stopped and breathed deeply, clearing his lungs and mind, allowing the last traces of home to be blown away, imagining them coursing down his neck in the rain, running away like waste water. After some minutes he set off again, following the path along the coast, seeing no-one, emptying his mind, concentrating only on his goal: the Crown Mines.

During the next half hour's walking Jack witnessed the gaunt shells of disused mine buildings rise out of the rain and murk on his right like ghosts, their crumbling stonework green with moss, then recede again into the past behind him. In such an atmosphere, his imagination began to work overtime. He tried to resist the idea that things were coming out of the mines, inclining to follow him, and instead he focussed on the path ahead, making sure he kept well away from the cliff edge to his left. Below, the sea boiled and heaved, throwing up briny fingers of foam that stretched up the beach, probing blindly. It would have been all too easy to slip and fall. He pressed on for another hour or so, beginning to regret that he'd missed breakfast. Surely it couldn't be much further? Without a phone signal, and with no gps, he was thrown back on simpler resources. Extracting the map from his rucksack he struggled with it against the buffeting wind, then gave up. He knew he must be near. And indeed, now the path branched, the left fork running down the cliff steeply. A battered wooden signpost pointed that way to Crown Mines. Jack paused to wipe the rain from his eyes, then began to descend. The sea birds (what sort were they? – he couldn't say, and suddenly felt ashamed of his suburban ignorance) cried above in their strange, desolate way. And then ahead there loomed into view a vision. Rising out of the rocks, apparently growing from them and perched at the very edge of the coastline on a small promontory, was his goal: a partially ruined cluster of stone buildings standing out grey and forlorn against the turbulent sea and washed with spray.

He stopped again. It was the very scene from his dreams, the view he had drawn again and again in his sleep. It brought him up short: so familiar, yet so strange and alien. He stifled a reluctance to approach nearer and continued his descent, his feet slipping on the loose gravel and sending little cascades of stones rattling down ahead of him. Soon he was standing directly above the mine buildings, looking down on them. Straight ahead and at the very edge of the rocky outcrop was a tall, narrow structure, partially unroofed and with a stark chimney seemingly rising out of the foaming sea, just as he had drawn it. This was the pumping house, containing the equipment that would have kept the mine dry. Except for the chimney it resembled some old religious building, a chapel, for instance. It looked as if it was about to fall into the sea. Above it, and to its right, was a similar but larger building, with no chimney, which had also partly lost its roof and through which the spokes of a great wheel could be seen. Nearby the remains of other structures were apparent, little more than foundations, mere ground plans.

Again something held him back, but it was no good. He had to find out. Neither the awful drop below, nor the slipperiness of the rocks, nor the indefinable fear of the grim and lonely relics of the mine's surface remains could make him turn back now. He continued his descent. When he arrived at the first of the ruined foundations, he saw they were barely waist high, but even so they provided some protection from the elements. How, he wondered, could such buildings have been erected in such a place? How did they get the stone down there, for a start? Surely there were easier places to mine for tin, or copper, or whatever it was?

A further, rather better preserved, flight of very steep steps took Jack down to the threshold of the pumping house, and there he paused again, sheltered from sea and wind. Now the buildings could be seen to be much larger than they had appeared only a few minutes ago. The walls were tremendously thick and towered above him. At the very top of the wall facing him half of a gigantic, rusting iron beam projected from a hole in the upper storey. From this beam a thick rod of timber plunged down and into the black mouth of a well at his feet, disappearing into the depths. The well was partially covered with a metal grill, as if someone had carelessly replaced it. Attached to this grill was a streaked sign warning of 'danger'. Another sign reading 'Danger: keep out' was placed on the wall just to the left of the small arched entrance. A rickety wooden fence laced with yellow and black tape ran across the front, making the point. Jack eyed it uncertainly, then made up his mind. He'd come too far to turn back now. He clambered over and, feeling a strange reverence, went inside.

Despite the glassless windows and partly open roof it was comparatively quiet within, the sea's roar and the howling wind muted. His eyes adjusted to the poor light. All around was the stilled, shadowy anatomy of a huge machine. Rods emerged high above from the darkness, and plunged down through the floor at his feet; pipes coiled like plants around vast supporting columns and arches, and crept up the walls like tendrils before entering tarnished brass gauges the size of large clocks. Ahead, in the gloom, was the outline of an enormous cylindrical vessel that ascended through the ceiling. Jack craned his neck back and, taking out a torch from his rucksack, let the beam play over the strange forms of machinery. Contrary to his expectation, it didn't look that decayed at all. He ran a finger down one of the rods. There must be … oil on them, yes! And yet he had assumed the whole place was disused?

He stood in front of a tangle of levers and brass wheels, many of which were strangely scrolled and engraved, as much works of art as machine. The arms of these levers soared up out of sight and onwards to connect with other machinery high above. A tide of terror washed over him. What was in the shadows that gathered so deeply in the corners and arches of this place? He'd known those shadows before, from his dreams, and they had life. Slowly, the thing he had been dreading, the sibilant whispering in his head, stirred and murmured. But was it only in his head? Did it not run down the levers of the machine, and rustle up its columns? He pressed his hands to his temples and let himself down onto one knee. *What was it saying?* The sense of a unique moment overpowered him.

Feeling his actions were no longer his own, he jerked back up to his feet and moved to inspect a sort of plate or plaque fixed on the cold stone wall, playing the light from his torch over it. It bore an engraving, some sort of animal or something. He peered more closely at it. Etched on the plate was quite clearly depicted a coiled serpent, its tail in its mouth, and underneath, just discernible through layers of dirt, the inscription *In my end is my beginning.* As he read, the whispering in his head strengthened. There were still no words, just jumbled syllables, but for the first time it felt like something, some message, was on the brink of resolving itself.

Turning away, following instinct or direction, Jack mounted the iron stairway running up one side of the building to the upper floor. At the top, the space was long and low, and partly open to the sky. Rain was lashing in through the hole where part of the roof had once been. Someone had tried to effect a makeshift repair with some plastic sheeting, which flapped and tugged in the wind like a struggling live thing. This upper floor was dominated by one half of the huge beam that was visible from the outside. The end nearest to Jack rested on massive wooden stops. He stood and stared, fearing the vast thing would move, his heightened senses roving for the key to whatever it was that had plagued him in his dreams.

Then he was back below, in front of the oddly shaped levers on the ground floor, from which the engine would have been controlled by its masters over a hundred years ago. He was on his knees, shining his torch through the metal grating on which he stood. Underneath was a large chamber, filled with black water that lapped sluggishly, inches below. The rods and pipes from above disappeared under the surface, where lurked barely discernible submerged vessels and other structures, all part of the vast organism of the pumping engine. A slow dripping from some tap or cistern was clearly audible, otherwise there was only the booming of the sea in the background. The shadows commanded him now. The grating was hinged; it squealed as he lifted it. A ladder disappeared into the depths. He must descend. He turned to go down backwards, his trainers sloshing on the first submerged rung, the icy water rushing into them with a cruel chill. And at that precise moment, the fragmented syllables that had been jostling in his mind finally clarified themselves into a repeated, strangled mantra.

⅄

Where does the corporeal end and the incorporeal begin? From above pressed down a colossal edifice of energy and geology, fused into a single, incomprehensible barrier. Below, a tiny speck, a single soul, lay extended, drawn taut like a wire, tuned to the highest pitch of agony. A Soul that sensed, understood and suffered. The millennia lay before it, an endless road uncoiling ahead through which it must continue, with no end and no hope, no prospect of redemption.

Physical suffering is only the shadow of true pain: the pain of loss, betrayal, avoidable error replayed through eternity, perpetual mockery, the panic of drowning rehearsed again and again for all time. An amputee feels pain in the lost limb: in the same way, the Soul writhed its burned and blackened lips, as they seemed to it, in a vain attempt to moisten them, arched its bleeding torso to find release, surveyed with lidless eyes the steaming coals over which its entrails lay strewn, popping and crackling. The sense of its lost body lingered on, grafted to its pain.

The air was thick with a jeering babble of laughter that spoke to the Soul of its folly and vanity, stupidity, failure and loss. This cacophony would never cease; there was no escape, ever. And all the while some vast, intangible greater Thing surveyed the Soul with the tiniest part of its wider consciousness, and stooped to feed off it with a cold eye, drained the Soul repeatedly to the dregs, paused for it to slowly recover itself, then bent to its feast again like a giant parasite.

The Soul had a small fragment of awareness that remained its own, capable of being detached from the pain of the moment and applied independently to other objects. With this fragment it sensed something far above it: a column spiralling up and up to air, light, life, perhaps peace! If only it could reconstitute its lost voice, gather its strength into one mighty cry – there was life up there, and kinship. There was a consciousness like its own, a being of its own blood. Secretly, it saved up small portions of itself, tiny parcels of energy that, somehow, the beast overlooked. And then at one time – there were no days, no weeks, nothing to mark off one point in the continuum from another – it hurled its message upward.

⅄

Save me, save me ...! Release me! Save me! – endlessly repeated, like an SOS signal. Somehow, Jack knew The Voice had neither energy nor power for anything more than those stark anguished phrases. It was almost as if his contact with the cold waters, *these* waters in *this* very place, had been the enabling medium through which at last the message could get through. He stood quite still for a full minute, the water up to his knees, allowing the words to flow through his mind, surrendering to a rising wave of sadness, compassion and horror. *Release me!* Then, without warning, there was a deafening crash, a shriek of large parts convulsively moving. The sound filled the whole building, ringing and reverberating from top to bottom. Ripples spread on the black surface of the water. Jack had a vision of a chain reaction of many parts and links, spiralling down into the depths. He felt a terrible sense of foreboding. *Release me!* Snatches of mocking laughter echoed all around him in the dark corners of the building, sinister harbingers from a remote portal. With feet slipping on the slimy rungs in haste, he breathlessly clambered out of the pool and threw himself on the floor, head in hands, moaning. After some minutes lying there, too frightened to move, wishing he was anywhere else, he slowly struggled to his feet and made for the door, legs dripping.

Outside, the weather had indeed worsened. The light was very poor and the rain came in steadily off the sea, mixed with spray, in dreary diagonals. Jack briefly stood to collect himself, gazing up at the black beam silhouetted against an iron-grey sky. Then he ran as best he could, up the stone steps, away from that place of ill omen. On his right he passed the ruined winding house, roofless, the spokes of the enormous winding wheel exposed, framed against the expanse of the grey skies. Only when he had reached the top of the hill did he stop, turn, and look back breathlessly. The buildings were huddled on the rocks below him, again the same view as in his dream-drawings. Only the analogy was closer now, for as he watched dark shadows seemed to cluster and dance around them with a life of their own. In that moment, Jack had a powerful sense that something had been released, by his mere presence. And that something, whatever it was, would have been better left undisturbed.

CHAPTER 3

SPIRITS IN THE SHADOWS

The room was in deep shadow, its dark recesses concealing only the vaguest shapes. A tall clock stood like a sarcophagus in a corner, its pendulum swinging in slow, resonant arcs. In the grate of the hearth flames from a coal fire licked and played, joining the light from two candles set on a side table to provide the only source of illumination. Seated in front of this fire was the shadow of a brooding figure, lost in its thoughts, staring pensively at the glowing coals while its hands clutched the arms of the chair as if it were poised to rise. But rise it did not, and as it continued to sit and to think a brutal, larger shadow slowly detached itself from the dusky margins of the room and approached, mummy-like, with slow deliberation. Towering over the seated figure, it paused for a moment and then craned down in an attitude of deference. Slowly, delicately almost, something was proffered – dark shapes held reverently on some sort of tray. The smaller figure closed quickly over them like a spider. The two forms briefly merged; only the woody ticking of the clock and the rattle of the storm at the windows could be heard.

The mummy shape retreated into the depths of the room, blending with other silhouettes until it became lost as a distinct entity. The man twisted around in his chair, seeming to make a motioning movement as if beckoning, or perhaps caressing, something. There was a pause and then a new, soft light sprang up, suffusing the area around the chair with a play of flickering colours. From the figure came a long sigh of satisfaction. The kaleidoscope continued for some minutes more, its source still not clear. Then the shadows deepened again, closing in on the figure and his fragile light source as if he were a hunter in a forest at night, having lit a small fire to fend off nameless wild things. A light draught blew through the room, a mere breath, cold and dank, redolent of the tomb. Behind it came a sound: a distinct sobbing, from far, very far away – another world. No ordinary sobbing, this, though – not a quiet, introspective sound, but a long, muted wail of despair and desperation, the product of long ages of pain, a lifetime of suffering.

Now shapes arose, shimmering projections against the darkness, baroque patterns of barbed tendrils, slitted eyes, things that were whole being ripped asunder, hunched toad-like gargoyles lurching across the walls, swelling and receding, accompanied by a faint and cruel laughter. There was something, some action, repeated over and over: a plunging, stabbing gesture. And all the while could be heard the long, drawn-out sound of lamentation swirling through the air, now louder, now softer.

Presently the shapes diminished, the sounds faded; the room was quiet and still again. Last of all, the glow around the seated figure receded and he was left in silence: a lonely shadow sunk in thought.

CHAPTER 4

At the Commercial Hotel

And now a singular thing: the stones tell me that someone with Affinity has come to these parts, this last day, or two. It could be they will be our salvation and defence against these gathering dark forces. I think I can guess the answer to this riddle ... but for now – we wait. All will become clear and what, after all, are a few more weeks when set against the cosmic rhythm of the Vortex? Wait, and see.

Piano for one half hour at 7 o'clock. Memo to practise further the fortissimo passage in the E flat Nocturne. It should be less staccato.

One of Mrs Attlee's favourite sayings was that sleep is nature's greatest healer. It was this precise aphorism that popped into Jack's head as he awoke from a particularly heavy slumber. Light streamed in through the hotel bedroom window; across the square the clock chimed. What had happened that morning had unsettled him at some deep level, as if a buried portion of his mind had reached out to, and found, its dark counterpart in the Crown Mines. With every step he took back to the hotel the feeling receded and he felt more in control again. Almost as soon as he got to his room, which fortunately had been made up, he knew he needed to give in to the overpowering desire to sleep, even though it was only late morning. And now, he raised himself on an elbow and looked out of the window at the church clock across the square. Five p.m.: he'd been out cold for six hours!

Jack quickly ran over events at the engine house and squeezed his eyes shut momentarily. So: the words of the voice were clear for the first time. *Save me, release me!* The sinister mantra lingered in his head. He hadn't disobeyed the voices for many years but how could he obey now? Who should he save, from what, and how? Again he felt strangely moved by a tide of compassion for an entity as yet unknown. Was that possible? Jack coughed and rubbed his eyes. The Cornish air was stirring things! One thing was certain: he was getting closer to some core truth and the mine, the domain of The Voice, was at its heart. But where should he go from here? Whatever the case he knew he would not be going back to the mine. No; that terrible laughter, those shadow forms his visit had released … He wondered with a shudder what might be happening there now.

Reluctant to pursue this train of thought, Jack showered and changed into fresh clothes, hoping thereby decisively to draw a line under the morning's events. He decided to do something about the overwhelming feeling of hunger that had come over him. One energy bar all day wasn't enough!

He walked over to the window as he towelled his hair dry. At last the clouds were lifting, the sun was struggling through, and with it the promise of a fine evening. Across the square directly opposite the hotel, sandwiched between an art gallery and a pub, was a fish and chip shop. Perfect. He stuffed his wallet into his back pocket and made his way downstairs. On his way out he passed the bar, glancing in as he did so. There, in their usual nook, was a small contingent of what looked like some of the very same locals who had been making such a noise the previous night. One of them, holding forth about something or other, caught Jack's eye with the questioning look of the local for the stranger. Then he was out in the fresh air, the low afternoon sun blinding him, stomach rumbling importunately.

⅄

Back inside the bar of the Commercial Hotel, the quartet of members of the Woolfe Society, dedicated to the preservation and conservation of Cornwall's mining heritage and the greater glory of one of its most ingenious sons, a certain engineer from Camborne named Arthur Woolfe, discussed the merits and demerits of their newest member, the mysterious Peregrinus. They were a small and select band, as they themselves saw it: all locals, all dedicated to the cause. Their driving force, even if some of them wouldn't readily admit it, was their secretary Morgana, a woman born and bred in St Just, who organized the Society, fund-raised, published its pamphlets, promoted and publicized it with a demonic energy.

She had been successful, for sure, in her mission to increase the range and effectiveness of the Society's achievements … yet this new man was her idea. In reality, he'd been on the scene, in a handyman sort of capacity, for over a year – but that counted as 'new'. His influence seemed to be profound, if subtle. For example, the obsession with draining the Crown Mines at Botallack – that had all started since *he* came on the scene. And although Morgana had partly won them over to that plan, with all the time and resources it was absorbing, it seemed a mark against her that she hadn't shared her decision making. Since she never attended their informal meetings in the hotel bar, the others could discuss the matter freely and had been doing so for several months, in various combinations, without tiring of it.

In truth, they could not make much sense of the newcomer, whose manner was as enigmatic as his name. This Peregrinus was usually polite enough, but remote. Occasionally he was capable of cutting asides or sarcastic put downs, which was enough to alienate him from the other members. He seemed preternaturally aware of what was going on, frequently anticipating the others' movements and sometimes even thoughts in a most unsettling way. Very little had come to light of his background. He claimed to have local roots but declined to expand on that statement. His very self-sufficiency provoked suspicion. It was this suspicion that the scruffy, bearded Derek Ballard was voicing as Jack passed by in the hallway.

"And all this money and time, gone into draining that there mine, and not so much as a proper discussion about it.

It's all come from 'im. If he *is* local, why doesn't he come out and say where, where was he born? And then he says he's got mining in the blood. So I asks him, direct, if his father was down the mines, and he gives me a strange look, turns his back on me and he walks straight off! No civil answer to a civil question!"

"I wonder," said Carole Banks with a little smile, "where Morgana found him. She won't say, but I don't see why it should be a secret." Carole, like the others, was a paid-up member of the Woolfe Society, but not a local in the 'true' sense. She was different in her attitude and it was common knowledge that she had something of a soft spot for the newcomer. She settled her glass on a beer mat as she spoke, rotating it thoughtfully.

"Someone said he used to work in a *circus* or something," put in Tom Bradley, articulating the word incredulously, "though I can't rightly remember where that came from."

"It were me," returned Derek Ballard, clad in his customary dirty waterproof, even indoors. The others stared at him, almost accusingly. Carole said urgently, in a low tone, "He told you that? Why? When?"

"Why not?" returned Derek, sullenly, taking a casual swig of his pint. Since he seemed disinclined to say more, Carole modified her tone. She really had to find out.

"Well, you're the only one he's said anything to. Come on, Derek, what did he say?"

Derek insisted on completing a laborious, spun-out trip to the gents before he would be drawn. "It were last week.

I was standing at the bus stop and he were next to me. We was waiting there an' he wasn't saying much ...." Carole suppressed a smile; she could hardly imagine there had been much in the way of conversation between two such disparate characters. Derek continued, "All of a sudden one of them great trucks comes past, from the circus, with the dodgems on the back, you know. They'd be on their way to Penzance, I suppose. Anyway, old Perry, he just stares after that truck as if he'd seen a ghost. He sort of froze, and stared." Derek produced a comical impression of goggle-eyed amazement. "So I asks him if he'd ever seen a circus before, as a sort of joke, see. And he looks at me in the strangest way and says, 'I've seen one. I used to work there.' You could have knocked me flat. So I asks him why, and when, and what he did."

Derek was well into his stride now and clearly enjoying the attention of the others, who were hanging on his every word – although Carole suspected the possibility of embellishment. "Well, he carries on staring sort of through me, until I felt quite funny about it. Then he mutters, like, you know how he does, 'It was a long, long time ago,' and I'm sure he said 'before your time'. Well, 'scuse me but that there Peregrinus can't be more than forty odd wouldn't you say? So I asks him to come again, and he ignores me and doesn't say another word. Bus comes, he gets on after me and sits as far off as he can, rude little beggar!"

Denny the fuel merchant gave a low whistle. "Well, well. And nothing else, not even when he gets off?"

Derek gave a slow smile. "Yer. He gets off when I does, and we're standing on the pavement in this 'ere square, and

I says, 'Been down to Botallack lately?', and he just smiles. So I says to him straight, 'You seem to be spending an awful lot of time there, don't you? Why's that then?' He shrugs, and says something on the lines of, 'That's none of your business,' and stalks off."

The other two men were outraged: "Cheeky so-and-so!" "What a nerve–" "What does he mean?" But Carole held her peace.

"That's it," said Derek Ballard, with a grim smile. "It's all coming from him. Proof positive, as we thought."

Carole nodded, apparently unsurprised. "Well, what have you said to Morgana?"

"I'm on my way there now, after this," and he nodded at his near-empty glass. He downed the remainder of his pint in one, stood up unsteadily and looked around at his companions. "What's needed is a trip to Botallack – all of us, mind, the whole group – and she can give us a run though of where all our money's going, and why!" Tom and Denny nodded vigorously. "But if you'll mark my words, that Peregrinus is behind it all. There's more to come out from that quarter, I'd be willing to lay money on it and it'll come out any day now. And so I'll bid you two gentlemen and lady good evening." He wiped his mouth with his sleeve, made his way to the door with a perfunctory wave of his hand and was gone, leaving the others to ponder the new, if meagre, revelations about Peregrinus.

CHAPTER 5

Wheal Owles

Morgana Trevose, Secretary and Chairwoman of the Woolfe Society, was sitting in the Wheal Owles engine house before a pile of papers. She liked to use the building as an administrative centre for the Society and could frequently be found there. A small woman in her sixties with straggling grey hair, shapeless dark clothing that had a home-made look, and a generally eccentric aspect, Morgana preferred to keep on top of the accounts side of things. She had appropriated a small outbuilding, annexed to the main structure, as her office. Documents of all kinds were piled high on sagging shelves. A few planks of deal laid across brick supports served as her desk; a little window looked out to sea, somewhat alleviating the claustrophobic feel of the 'office'. In one corner, a locked cupboard suggested perhaps more papers and files within. Before her stood Peregrinus, the 'newcomer', idly prodding here and there at various engine-related parts – a pressure gauge, an oil glass, a plastic container full of bolts – that were strewn around the interior. His sinewy form was clad in jeans, t-shirt and a leather jacket that was too short in the arms and from which his thickly haired hands and wrists protruded in a vaguely simian way.

Morgana pushed back her glasses onto her forehead and gave a long, stress-laden sigh. "I don't know what we're going to do about these accounts," she muttered, listlessly flicking through the papers in front of her. She gazed over at Peregrinus with a tired eye. "You know, the books here used to balance wonderfully, until you came along. I sometimes wonder what on earth we're doing … Every penny's soaked up in that Crown Mines project of yours at Botallack. It wouldn't be so bad if I could see some return on the whole business" – her voice rose in agitation – "but here we are a year on, still spending, the pot's nearly dry … *I don't know*," she concluded, trying to sound emphatic.

Peregrinus continued to circulate around the small room, probing and prodding in a mildly curious way, showing no sign that he was listening to her. That in itself, so typical of the man, was irritating! She watched him uncertainly. Eventually, as if satisfied everything was in order, and taking his time over it, he fastidiously seated himself on a stool opposite and from under low brows looked across the desk at her, gnawing a fingertip as he did so. He said quietly, "You should have more faith, Mrs Trevose." He always used her title and surname, whether out of respect or in sarcasm Morgana was never quite sure. "Did I ever say the Crown Mines could be drained overnight? Or in a few weeks. Did I?" She nodded slowly in agreement, more placid now. "This job is nearly done" – he leaned forward a little – "and it will be a success. You shouldn't let money get in the way of grand projects, Mrs Trevose. If you ever need more, I can get it easily enough."

She tried to rouse herself from the passive haze that had come over her. He'd said the bit about money before, several times, and it made her uncomfortable. She said faintly, "It's not that, I just – don't like these things dragging on. The members, you know, they don't like it." Heaven alone knew where Peregrinus would get the money from; she didn't want to think. He certainly didn't seem to have any for himself. Maybe it was from that 'special friend' of his he sometimes referred to.

He had sat back again and was regarding her under slightly lowered lids, hardly with the demeanour of the factotum he was supposed to be. "Well, just remember that. Money!" He made a dismissive, snorting noise. What was he really thinking? She wished she knew. There was something … *animal* about him; sometimes he seemed as if he might have no thoughts at all in his brain, as if he was simply pure, sharpened *perception.* He could seem so uninterested, so distracted. And yet he didn't miss a thing. She watched carefully as he got up again and began circling the room, prodding and inspecting stuff, as if to make clear the subject was closed.

"What *is* this thing you need from the mines?" she cautiously inquired. "We've sacrificed a lot for it, you know. Time, resources – not just money."

Peregrinus smiled a thin smile. She noticed for the hundredth time the vague impression of deformity his small, wiry figure conveyed; nothing specific … or could it be a slightly hunched back, perhaps? Too long a neck? Or all that low hair on the forehead? She really couldn't say. Nor, for that matter, as to his age, though certainly he was a good deal younger than her, for sure.

"That's good!" he returned ambiguously, with what might have been sardonic enthusiasm. But when she looked closely she saw his eyes had lit up with an inner fire, a genuine animation. "That's as it should be! You'll need to bear with me a little longer, until it's recovered, then everything will be clear. And in any case," he added, "you get the mines drained, don't you?" He inclined his head inquiringly. "And that's a good thing, surely, a good thing for a society that conserves these mines?"

Morgana didn't dare contradict him; it had long gone past that. She tried another tack. "You know they – the members – want a group visit there? To the Crown Mines. Yes, they all want to go along together and make an assessment. I can hardly say *no,* can I?"

Peregrinus thought for a few moments. "I'm not sure that's wise," he said, eyeing her carefully.

"Not wise? What do you mean?"

"To visit the mines. All the members. Not just now."

"I'm not sure I have any choice! How could I put them off? It's been a group enterprise, after all."

He stared seawards through the window, inscrutably. Just when she thought he might have fallen into some sort of a trance, he gave a quick shrug. "Well then. Let them. Everyone can see what a useful project it's been – and how much work and dedication *you,* Mrs Trevose, have put in to rescue this piece of heritage. Everyone can go, and be pleased with themselves. You will go along too, and they will I'm sure be pleased with you as well, and want to recognize you – in some way." He returned to the stool, cupping his chin in his hands. He sat there like a little ape, smiling. "And if I find what I'm looking for, then remember, your reward will be great."

"Well, if you say so," she said, uncertainly, greed and circumspection alternating rapidly in her mind. So much was still confused. She *had* to get some clarity. "Tell me, though," she pursued doubtfully, her voice sounding unfamiliar in her own ears, "*why* do you want it? *Why* will this special friend of yours be so pleased?"

Peregrinus stopped grinning and suddenly looked serious. He spoke reverently now, without any trace of sarcasm, his eyes sparkling. "Recovering this object, which may seem an insignificant thing to you, is *not* insignificant. It may be the difference between the triumph of justice over injustice. Now the time has come to retrieve it. And when we have done this thing, no-one in this Society will be forgotten, of that I assure you." Peregrinus smiled agreeably, then added with a somewhat less agreeable undertone, "But for now, as I've said, that's between ourselves – if you don't mind. Our secret, and *not* to be shared with the members."

There was a long silence while Morgana took in this little sermon. Its implications would need to be digested later. "I see," she said finally, trying to appear matter-of-fact.

Then she rose to her feet and pulled a ring binder from the shelf behind her. It was time to reassert herself. "Now, on a different matter, while I sort out that visit you can be getting on with a bit of maintenance work they need doing down at Geevor. It isn't a big job, replacing some transoms, but they'll need a hand. I'll tell Terry you'll be on the way tomorrow morning." She looked up, forcing herself to meet his eye. "Yes?"

Peregrinus had stood up too, the fervour and truculence all gone, and was nodding submissively.

"Certainly, Mrs Trevose, I can get on with that."

"Good. Close the door when you leave, would you?" He moved to go. "Oh, and Peregrinus. You haven't seen Carole recently have you? I can't seem to get hold of her at all." She looked at him in what she hoped was an accusing way. "She seems to be very tied up with something or other these days. If we're all going to Botallack then I really think she should come too .... Perhaps you could tell her – if you see her?"

He stared back evenly at her. "Yes, if I see her, I'll tell her you want her. Thank you, Mrs Trevose." And he left, shutting the door very quietly and respectfully behind him.

CHAPTER 6

A Skull and Old Tomes

"There is nothing *like looking, if you want to find something. You certainly usually find something, if you look, but it is not always quite the something you were after." I like that. One must find time for a certain amount of relaxation, amid all the haste, and so I come across these things. Fact: if every phenomenon was known fully down to the last atom then every event could be predicted. Yet we have free will.*

6pm: Jacob brought me tea (rather too weak for my taste, though he should know) and lit a fire. I feel the damp more than ever of late and it is cold for the time of year.

Jack's second night at the Commercial Hotel was not as successful as his first. For one thing, having gone to bed earlier in the day he found it difficult to get to sleep. The events at the mines ran again and again through his mind. But it was when he woke up that his problems really began. The room looked as if it had been burgled: bedding was strewn all over the place, a chair had been overturned and his toiletries were swept off the chest of drawers. And there was worse: in his sleep he had emptied the remaining contents of his suitcase all over the floor, presumably to get at the pad and pen he had brought down with him. Now there were drawings, drawings everywhere – on the bed, under the bed, in the bathroom, all over the floor. With trembling hands he reached for the nearest and squinted at it.

Filling most of the sheet, shocking in its immediacy and bold execution, was a sketch of something different, something new, something far less welcome than the previous enigmatic mine pictures. Jack stared at it for some moments in disbelief: the grinning depiction of *a skull*. Then he pitched forward, head in hands. Again! What did it mean this time? He tried to scrape together his thoughts into something approaching an explanation. Perhaps, just perhaps, this was not the setback it seemed ... Loose ends of threads, seeking connections, jostled in his mind.

He got up and took the drawing over to the window, looking at it more closely. It had obviously been done very quickly, but even so there was something subtle, something individual about it; this was no simple anatomical rendition of a type. The eye sockets were deep and dark, the mouth not so much the typical skull's rictus as another thing. Yes, there was a subtle individuality, almost an expression, written on its face, for all the lack of flesh. A chilling, *personal* expression of ... what? He thought of The Voice: *Save me! Release me!*

Jack scanned the room, picking up other drawings at random. Most were of skulls, with the same haunting undercurrent of individuality about them. Some were solely of mine buildings, some juxtaposed skull and mine buildings on a single sheet. And the mine buildings – well, he knew what they were about now. There was no doubt in his mind that it was Crown Mines that were represented.

He lay down on the bed and let a profound sense of disquiet wash over him, succeeded by the same strange feeling of compassion he'd experienced the previous day. Tears pricked at his eyes. He was way out of his depth. What was he to do now? He wasn't going back to the mines, not for anything. Yet the answer to at least part of the mystery seemed to lie there. The drawings were telling him the mines were linked to – a skull? A *particular* skull at that, he felt sure. The mines, the skull, The Voice. He looked at his watch on the bedside table. Nine o'clock. The day stretched ahead, now looking bleak and uninviting. Well, he would fill it with something useful, and not mope about. There must be a library in this place, presumably stocked with information about local history. There, at the least, he could find out more about the mines. There might just be some nugget of information buried away in old records, some clue or clues to set him on the right track.

He tidied up the room (God knows what sort of a noise he must have made in the night, and what his neighbours in adjacent rooms must have thought!), gathering up the drawings in a neat pile that he placed in his suitcase. Then he showered and dressed, trying all the time to banish the impression of those dark eye sockets from his mind. Breakfast first, then the library. On his way out he noticed his bottle of tablets. He looked at it for a few moments, undecided. Then he took it into the bathroom, tipped the entire contents down the toilet bowl and flushed them away. A new certainty had come over him about the whole 'medication' business. He wasn't ill, and never had been. Whatever was trying to communicate with him was real enough, not a figment of his supposedly diseased imagination. And it wasn't going to go away.

⅄

The library, Mr Greenaway the landlord informed Jack, was very close: just turn left out of the hotel, head down towards the beach and it was on the right. It was a low, modern building that despite its small size turned out to be well-stocked with books on local history and also had a couple of internet terminals. But, unusually for him, Jack was drawn to the books. He'd never been a great one for reading, let alone 'research'; in fact the whole business reminded him of school and of his mother, who was always nagging him to spend more time at his studies. Plus he could never concentrate for long. Yet now it was different: he felt curious, *impelled*. The local history section was at the back, where he settled himself in a quiet corner. The librarian, a boffinish-looking man of middle age, initially drifted over, perhaps to offer assistance, but at close quarters drew back as if he'd seen a ghost and left him alone. This worried Jack; he didn't look that bad, did he, after his terrible night? The only other person in evidence was a slim young woman in a tracksuit hovering at some shelves on the other side, searching here and there for something or other.

After leafing through several dull tomes on various types of ore and different mining techniques that tested his new-found enthusiasm, Jack picked out a slender, academic-looking book *The Crown Mines at Botallack,* by J. Peters BSc, MA, PhD. It had a blurred black and white lithograph of the mines on the front, which served to heighten their romantic and dramatic setting. It, too, looked heavy going. But as Jack read, getting into his stride, he became more and more drawn into the extraordinary story of the Cornish mines in general, and the Crown Mines in particular. He was strangely gripped by it. It seemed that the mines went back thousands of years, but hadn't really been systematically worked until about 1720. The turning point was when steam power became available, from which time the tunnelling increased dramatically as ever deeper shafts and adits could be drained. A contemporary description of the Crown Mines touched a chord:

> *Surely, if ever a spot seemed to bid defiance to the successful efforts of the miner, it was the site of the Crown Engines, where, at the very commencement of his subterranean labours, he was required to lower a steam engine down a precipice of more than 200 feet, with a view to extending his operations under the bed of the Atlantic Ocean! There is something in the very idea which alarms the imagination; and the situation and appearance of the gigantic machine, together with the harsh*

jarring of its bolts, re-echoed from the surrounding rocks, are well calculated to excite astonishment.

Jack read on, making a few notes as he did so, suddenly feeling quite scholarly and enjoying the engagement of his mind, which at least distracted it from dwelling on his latest nocturnal drawings. The whole mining business sounded quite interesting on its own account:

The lode could be seen cropping out in the rocks beneath the engine, the ore being the grey and yellow sulphide of copper, mixed with the oxide of tin ... Mixed with the grey sulphide, a purple copper ore, called by the Germans "buntkupfererz" was frequently met with.

Maybe he could get into geology, become a geologist! And so he continued, sometimes merely skimming and sometimes reading more thoroughly, through bewildering passages about metals and ores and precious and semi-precious stones with evocative names: jasper, arborescent native copper, jaspery iron ore, arseniate of iron, sulphide of bismuth, haematitic iron, the hydrous oxide of iron in its prisms terminated by pyramids. Clearly, the entire coastline around here was riddled with potentially lucrative deposits – and what the old miners wouldn't do to find this holy grail!

Something flickered into Jack's field of peripheral vision. The girl in the tracksuit had moved closer and was now browsing the local history shelves too, her back to him. Her dark hair was pulled up in a pony tail; she looked trim and athletic. This was annoying, a potential distraction. As if in unspoken acknowledgment of the thought, the girl paused in her searching and half turned towards him. Jack saw the fine line of her jaw, the flicker of long eyelashes, the crease of a faint smile around the mouth. Then she moved away again, wandering over to one of the computer terminals on the far side of the library. Resisting the temptation to stare after her, he returned to his book.

There was no doubt that this Peters man was a master of his subject. Jack had now reached the section devoted specifically to the Crown Mines. As the descriptions became more detailed, Jack felt a resurgence, in muted form, of the terror he'd felt the day before while exploring the engine house. Another Victorian visitor to the workings was quoted:

> *The workings of this mine extend at least 70 fathoms in length under the bed of the sea, and in these caverns of darkness are many human beings, constantly digging for ore, regardless of the horrors which surround them, and of the roar of the Atlantic Ocean, whose boisterous waves are incessantly rolling over their heads.*

But he also felt a flicker of excitement. His pulse quickened; he had a strange feeling that, amid all this history, he was on to something. At the same time, he felt amazement at his facility to absorb all this theoretically very tedious stuff. He bent low over the book. The story of the mine was a study in frustration, it seemed. When it stood on the brink of closure in 1835, someone by the name of Stephen Harvey James stepped in with a rescue plan, but it continued to struggle until a remarkable find of rich copper lodes in 1842, and the new owners became wealthy men thanks to the 'great copper find'. Through the rest of the century, the mine's fortunes were uneasy and fluctuated as tin took over from copper as the principal quarry. And then a new shaft was made, "one of the most remarkable and famous shafts ever sunk in a Cornish mine", as Dr Peters put it. This tunnel, Boscawen Shaft, consisted of a raised tramway above the surface that plunged down diagonally down like a huge roller-coaster from a great height and vanished into the blackness below, continuing all the way down to the sea bed. And it was with the construction of this shaft that the Crown Mines suddenly became a national, in fact an international, tourist attraction.

Once the spectacular diagonal shaft was operational, people came from far and wide to travel down on tourist excursions into the ocean depths, let down in a railway wagon by the winding engine that had resided in the higher, taller building that Jack had seen yesterday, with its stark and ruined roof and still visible winding wheel. (He shuddered at the recollection – a bleak and ghostly place!) There was even a royal visit. For a few years, the mine was famous. It was during this period that a curious episode occurred, that shocked not only the local community but also made national headlines.

Jack now felt instinctively that he was approaching something of special importance. It was almost as if some external impulse was pushing him on, pushing him to read. Quickly he turned the page. It seemed that a small party consisting of three directors, a couple of visiting politicians, a Mr Pencarrow from Hayle and a seventh person from London, not named, entered the mine on a late autumn morning. The book quoted from the *St Just Gazette* of November 1878, which took up the story:

> *Once the visit was complete, the established practice was for the leader of the group to communicate to the engine man via the cable tell-tale when the party was ready to ascend, and the wagon would be wound up the long incline to the surface. This being the case, Mr Meyerstein gave the signal and the party duly returned up the shaft as described. It was only on disembarkation that it was noticed that the visitor from London was missing from the group. Mr Meyerstein and Mr Allen both vigorously asseverated that he had been present when the signal to ascend had been given, and no-one in the party could account for his absence. Immediately a search party was sent back down Boscawen, but no trace of the unfortunate visitor has been found and it must be presumed that he became lost and has perished.*

Without the slightest expectation of it, Jack felt a surge of sadness come over him, mingled with fear, confusion and … something else. It was as if he had opened a door on a new space, a vast expanse of pain and worldly suffering that had no precedent in his own small playpen of experience. What was wrong with him? Whisperings jostled for attention in his head. He blinked hard and looked up from the book, wanting to ground himself in his immediate environment. The young woman was nowhere in sight. The librarian was standing outside his office, staring over at Jack. How long had he been like that? Then he started to walk over, slowly, deliberately. When he was at Jack's table he stopped and looked down at him, eyes swimming through thick spectacle lenses. Clearly he had overcome whatever initial impression of Jack had repelled him earlier. "You seem very interested in that book?" His tone was inquiring, not unfriendly.

"Er, yes, I'm … researching a project on it."

The librarian seemed entirely uninterested in the truth or otherwise of this statement. "Well, you might like to know that Dr Peters, the author, is giving a talk tonight. At the civic centre, just opposite the library." He waved vaguely in that direction. "On Cornish mining. You might like to go." Had the man been spying on Jack? How had he known what he was reading? He bent lower, and said in a confiding tone, "There's nothing Dr Peters doesn't know about that subject. Nothing. I'm sure you'd find it interesting."

Jack nodded slowly. "Yes, I'd like to … go, thanks." Then, feeling that something further was required, he added, "Quite a coincidence – that he should be here, I mean, tonight."

"Coincidence?" said the librarian. "There's no such thing!" And with that he quietly padded back to his office.

Jack stared after him, not knowing what to make of this exchange, trying to resist the (probably mad) thought that he, Jack Tyack, seemed to be part of some vast plot in which everybody apart from he himself knew what was going to happen. Still, he should go to that talk at the civic centre. It seemed – *providential.* He knew he was on to something; he just had to follow the thread, and here was a lead that could not be ignored. As he reflected, Jack gradually became aware of a change in the interior of the library. It was more a question of atmosphere than anything tangible. A darkness came over the place, though the lights were still on. Shadows gathered; the angles of the walls seemed to shimmer and blur … A storm was brewing outside and no mistake! This was the calm before it, a high pitch of tension. Something was about to happen. A noise exploded to his left, piercing the silence. Jack shot out of his chair in fright, actually trembling, his head whipping round to find the source.

There on the floor lay, not a bomb crater, not the wreckage of shelving, but simply a book. It must have been poised to fall, disturbed when he took out the Peters volume, and finally some small vibration had dislodged it. It lay there, small and insignificant; but as Jack went over and stooped to pick it up, he felt it was anything but. The cover of the book was plain, a blotchy dark red. No doubt it had once had a dust-jacket. Jack clumsily opened it, looking for the title page. As he did so, something fluttered out, as if with a life of its own: a small, yellowed square of paper, stiff with age. With a quick movement Jack caught it and, knowing beyond doubt that here was something of special significance, took it jealously back to his desk. The quiet in the library had become complete, expectant, like the silence in a theatre just before the start of a performance. The place seemed quite empty; no doubt the librarian was in his office, and the young woman had probably left some time ago.

Disregarding the book, Jack flattened out the piece of paper, which had been folded in two, on the table before him. It was an old newspaper cutting of what appeared to be an obituary. Since the obituary had been at the top of the page, the name and date of the paper were included in the fragment: the *Chesham & Amersham Times,* 28 November 1878. Jack read:

> *Register*
>
> *It is with regret that we record the disappearance and presumed death of Mr Owen Tyack of this parish, earlier this month in a mining accident in Cornwall. Mr Tyack, a surveyor, mining engineer and entrepreneur well–known in this area, had long evinced an interest in the extraction of tin and copper lodes from Cornish sources, and had been visiting the celebrated Crown tin mines in Botallack, in the parish of St Just. He was lost in the course of an underground tour of the mine, of the kind that has become fashionable recently, and which are not without their dangers, as to which several incidents over the past year have testified. We extend our condolences to Mr Tyack's family and colleagues.*

When he finished reading, Jack remained absolutely still, witnessing almost with detachment the stray threads in his mind knitting together. Owen Tyack. The Crown Mines. Presumed lost. *The same name as his own*, and an unusual one at that. The same profession, even, as his father! It was surely an ancestor. Lost, lost in the mines ... In that moment he intuitively knew, without the need for more research or further evidence, that The Voice, *that* voice, was connected with this man, long dead though he was; that the drawings, too, somehow came from the same source; and that the mines, Crown Mines, held a secret that bound them together. He stared sightlessly at the cutting. He weakly perceived an entity, lost, far from Jack in space and in time, veiled by many layers, hidden deeply, pitted against all conceivable odds – yet despite all, with an extremity of effort, reaching out as best it could to him, Jack Tyack.

He didn't know how long he sat there, looking into other worlds as it seemed. When he came back to the present, one or two locals had come into the library and were engaged in quiet conversation. An elderly man, smelling of beer, had settled down opposite Jack with the day's newspaper. Jack briefly glanced at the red-covered book that had contained the cutting. It was a guide to the wildlife of south Cornwall and clearly had nothing to do with the subject in hand. Its 'purpose', surely, had been to deliver the cutting, which clearly belonged in the other book. It must have been misplaced at some time. Feeling that, despite the revelation, he needed to finish the history of the mines, he turned back to Dr Peters' account. What remained was not an eventful story. The disappearance of the visitor, now clearly identified by the cutting as Owen Tyack, cast a shadow over the enterprise, the fortunes of which once again entered a downward cycle compounded by falling tin prices and terrible winters with extraordinary floods that overwhelmed the pumping engines and rendered the mines unworkable. The mine was put up for sale and its material assets auctioned off. Dr Peters provided a bleak conclusion:

> *In such a fashion the pathetic remains of the once mighty Botallack were broken up, while underground the unchecked waters steadily rose and drowned the workings where generations of miners had laboured to win the rich deposits of tin and copper.*

However, there was a postscript to this sad story. In 1906, a modest revival of the tin industry occurred, with a rise in metal prices and new demand. A limited liability company, The Cornish Consolidated Tin Mines Ltd, acquired a lease of the Botallack sett, with its directors and head office being based in London. A new shaft, Allen's Shaft, was sunk and drainage began. But it was a false dawn; only poor quality ore was recovered and in 1914 the pumps were stopped for good, the waters rose and flooded once and for all the labyrinth of underground tunnels that stretched for over a mile beneath the ocean floor. According to Dr Peters, there had never been any further activity in the mine since.

Jack flicked to the front of the book and looked at the date on it. Three years ago. Whatever restoration work had been going on there had to be recent, then. Really, the Crown Mine should be derelict! He closed the book and stared through a skylight above at the stormy, darkening sky. Rain was falling, creating a consistent drumming sound against the glass. He gathered his things and headed for the exit. By the door the librarian hovered, as if waiting for him. He looked at Jack significantly and smiled. "Seven o'clock this evening," he said. "You'll find it interesting."

CHAPTER 7

Woolfe on the Beach

It was one of those long summer afternoons that seemed as if it would never end. Cape Cornwall's wide bay spread out in a generous arc, the half-tide sparkling placidly in the low sun. Orange-billed choughs, the distinctive emblem of the Cornish peninsula, launched themselves indulgently from the cliffs, wheeling and swooping in the light wind. In the rock pools Oystercatchers waded and strutted, their beady eyes searching for the next morsel. On the pebbly beach a couple of small red and blue fishing boats were pulled up, their sides strewn with a tangle of nets and floats, empty lobster pots lying around them like lanterns. The occasional young family was packing up rugs and picnic things, gathering up wayward toddlers, thinking about heading for home.

Outside a semi-derelict stone hut with a streaked yellow slate roof two dozen or so members of the Woolfe Society stood around and chatted amongst themselves. On the opposite side of the bay stood silhouetted the stark ventilation chimney of the mineshaft, proud on its tall promontory, while the sun sedately made its way towards it. It lent the scene a pagan sense of mystique so that you would not be entirely surprised to see an animal sacrifice being made there and then on the beach. A small figure could just be seen leaning against the chimney's base, motionless, perhaps surveying the glorious view from that special vantage point. The Society members paused in their conversation and stared with reverence at this symbol of Cornish industrial heritage. They all felt proud to be part of the fabric of history that it embodied. Presently, one of them disappeared into the old hut and emerged with a pile of hessian sacks that he distributed to the other three, along with pairs of gloves. Then they began to shuttle to and fro, keeping close together at first, picking up the litter that visitors had dropped and the tide had washed in, strewn in damp clumps over the rocks. For the Woolfe Society was a public-spirited body whose activities extended beyond conservation of the past. As they worked, they continued their conversation.

"Dirty lot, some of these tourists!"

"It ain't just tourists. The locals can be as bad."

"There's enough to keep us here all evening," said Carole Banks.

"Aye, we could do with some help." This from Derek Ballard as he prodded a dubious pile of sodden magazines with a wince. "Eh, what we need is some help from that there Peregrinus. He's fit and strong enough. Never around when you want him, always popping up when you don't."

"He'll be busy spendin' our money on them Crown Mines. That's what he cares about, right?" said someone else sardonically.

"Right enough," wheezed Derek, struggling already with the effort of bending.

Carole Banks said nothing, but began to trace a wider arc towards the water, leaving the conversation to the others.

"Hey Carole, there's plenty 'ere, still."

"No, I'm fine, there's all this lot near the water, see?" And so they continued their work, gradually returning the beach to its unsullied state.

An hour later and the last family had left the bay. The older Society members straightened up and stretched their backs, resting, drinking in the early evening air, listening to the calls of the birds, the sounds of the tide sucking at the pebbles. The sun had finally reached the promontory, silhouetting the chimney against a dramatic disc of orange. Long shadows took possession of the harbour; a chill entered the air. The incoming waves slapped noisily against the boats, which rattled and tugged at their painters. Morgana Trevose now appeared from along the beach, hurrying, conscious of her lateness. For on the Society's schedule this afternoon, after litter-picking, was a group visit to the Crown Mines engine house, to assess progress just as the members had petitioned her. She paused to catch her breath. "Well, it's a little late for litter-picking, isn't it? But I see someone's been doing a good job!" She smiled at them benignly, aware that she should really have been there to help. "I'm sorry I'm so late, I got a little delayed. But no matter. Are we ready? It's a fine evening for a walk!" They returned their bulging sacks to the hut, to be emptied later, and filed off in a line along the beach, Morgana at the head. As they did so, a figure left the high ridge to their right and descended obliquely down one of the paths to intersect with them. When it was about fifty metres away the figure stopped and stood quite still, watching, listening. It was noticed.

"Eh! He's here!"

"That's him."

"Peregrinus!"

"Now you come down here!"

Peregrinus declined to come any further, though, preferring to hover at a distance. But Carole Banks at this point detached herself from the group and forked off up the path to join him, as if in response to an unheard summons.

"Eh Carole! You not coming with us?"

"You'll miss the mines ...."

"What are you playing at?"

"Oh leave her, she's off to his tonight!"

Carole paused and gave a tentative little half-wave to her fellow members, then resumed her progress towards Peregrinus. The others continued in their little column, now wending their way in a zig-zag up the cliffs until they joined the coastal path. Behind them the two silhouettes of Peregrinus and Carole receded, then blended with the early evening shadows and were lost.

⅄

The members of the Woolfe Society filed along the coastal path towards the Crown Mines, circling the bay in a great arc. Then they began their descent to the dramatically sited mine buildings. As they did so, each and every one of them had a growing feeling that something was not quite right. Admittedly, it was rather late in the day to be visiting; the broad washes of pinks and darker reds on the horizon testified to that. Conditions were fine, the sea calm and placidly glittering in the late evening sun. And yet …. Morgana looked down at the engine house below her. What was wrong? The shadows seemed to cluster there rather too thickly; was it that? Again, the place seemed unusually free of the seagulls that normally swarmed noisily around it, perhaps it was that? Whatever it was, she and the others were all aware of a most uncomfortable sensation as they approached, and a corresponding reluctance to get any nearer. Yet nobody said anything, thinking it to be some private phenomenon and not wishing to invoke the scorn of the others.

Now they were all standing at the chevroned yellow and black tape that fluttered and twisted in the evening breeze, cordoning off the way into the engine house. A premature night had descended on the place; all their senses were muffled, turning their minds inward to probe unexpected fears. They hovered on the threshold undecided, each reluctant to take the plunge. Eventually Morgana asserted herself, trying to adopt a matter-of-fact tone. "Well then, let's see what progress Peregrinus has made, shall we?" She laughed uncertainly, a thin and hollow performance that fooled nobody. Yet she led the way, and the others filed in after her one-by-one, through the blackness of the arch-headed entrance until the chapel-like walls enclosed them all.

They were gone for some time. From outside, a few lights, the lights perhaps of their torches, could be seen within. The sun had long since dipped below the sea when they finally emerged. Yet, strangely, the place seemed lighter than it had before, at last truly reflecting the length of the summer evening. As they processed up the path and homewards in little knots of twos and threes, the atmosphere of the mines quite changed, and the seagulls and other sea birds that had been so curiously absent flocked back, wheeling and crying and perching with renewed nonchalance on the stony parapets of the old buildings. The visitors were specks crawling along the path, lost in the immensity of the coastline. And each now carried something inside them, for the darkness that had only recently shrouded the mines had found a new home.

CHAPTER 8

Delving Deeper

If the divine *exists, it is a living thing; if it is a living thing, it sees; it sees as a whole, it thinks as a whole, it hears as whole. And in psychology? The dark things, they go under, into the 'id', crushed down, banished, lost – but never completely. They are always there, deep down, and they surface in strange ways. So what to do?* Reconciliation. *Let me speak to Jacob again about the bath – it's happened again, water everywhere. The part needs replacing.*

"Then we come to the well-known, terrible accident. November 15th 1894." The speaker paused, looked around his small audience as if for dramatic effect and blinked myopically a few times before flicking to the next slide. A ghostly image of a vast wheel-like structure wrapped in lengths of cable appeared, trembled uncertainly on the screen for a few moments, then vanished. The man tutted and fiddled with the laptop leads. The picture reappeared and he continued. "Eight men were being wound up, and it was bad weather, with a violent storm. Not that the weather would have had any effect, mind you ... Ahem. Anyway, suddenly the engine started to run away, and the engine men knew something was wrong because it had no load on it. The cable whipped up in through that aperture you see there" – here he ponderously adjusted the focus on the projector, striving in vain for a sharp picture – "with no wagons to be seen. It had snapped clean through. You can imagine what it must have been like for those men being hauled up. They plunged the full length of the shaft all the way down to the bottom, all the time picking up speed. When they eventually found them the next day, it was a terrible mess. Bodies everywhere, some of those poor men had been decapitated in the accident." He paused again, ruminatively. "The mine was closed for a while – and it took a lot to do that, because it was lost revenue – and it was all over the local press. It made the national newspapers too, because the Crown Mines were such a tourist attraction. Remember, this was only a week after a royal party had been down there." The speaker looked at his watch, surveyed his audience again and abruptly said, "And that, ladies and gentlemen, was the end of the mines, commercially speaking. They never recovered from that terrible tragedy, and never made significant revenues again. Thank you."

A minor ripple of applause ran around the room, along with the rising murmur of conversations breaking out and much shuffling of feet. The speaker gave an awkward little bow and blew his nose on a spotted handkerchief. Jack, seated at the back, began an extravagant yawn then quickly smothered it as the man caught his eye and began shouldering his way through the half empty rows of chairs towards him. Approaching Jack, he awkwardly shook his hand and said, in a quiet, nasal London twang, "You must be the young fella researching the mines, yes? Oh, don't be surprised – I know everyone in this room except you. Brendan said you'd be coming along." He blinked rapidly, as if in a nervous spasm. No fossilized retirement relic, Jim Peters looked about fifty. Despite being indoors, he wore a yellow waterproof, shorts and heavy boots, as if he had just wandered in off the cliffs. His greyish, gingery hair was drawn back tightly in a pony tail; a straggling beard of the same colour strayed over his face like moss. He cut a chunky figure. Jack was reminded of a mature, benign hell's angel, without the bike.

The evening talk had contained a lot of tedious stuff about winding gear, 'man engines' and mining economics. Jack's unexpectedly productive session in the library earlier in the day, along with the librarian's mysterious-sounding hint, had spurred him to come along. Now he was wishing he hadn't. It had been hard going and he felt self-conscious and out-of-place, crammed in this stuffy village hall with these local types who were all thick as thieves. He replied, "Yeah, I'm not really researching. I was just … checking one or two things."

Jim Peters looked as if Christmas had come early. "Ah! What sort of things?"

Jack hesitated. He might as well take advantage of having an expert on hand … but what more would Dr Peters really know, about the bits in the story that really mattered? "You said just now that Crown Mines were pretty much finished after the accident. But in your book you said that someone went missing down there too?"

"Ah yes, my book. I see you've been doing your homework. Someone did indeed go missing, a visitor. They had these tours, you see. And that was a contributory factor. The Botallack mine closed for several years, never really prospered again. That was a tough one to bounce back from."

"Oh, I see. And this person who got lost down there … Does anybody know anything about them?" He said nothing about the obituary in the newspaper cutting, and its positive identification of Owen Tyack as the missing man. In some strange way, *that* seemed like private, special knowledge – knowledge destined for Jack alone.

Jim Peters was looking keenly at Jack. "No, there's not much information on that point," he said, carefully.

"But," Jack persisted, "I remember reading in your book that it wasn't the end, and someone tried opening it again a bit later." Instinctively he lowered his voice as he spoke. A couple of middle-aged men sitting in the row directly in front stopped their conversation, stood up and filed out, turning to look at Jack as they did so. All of a sudden he felt like a fugitive, somebody with a secret to hide.

Jim Peters, who had come right up close and was standing uncomfortably in Jack's personal space, looked pleased.

"You've got a very good memory," he said. "That's right. Some gentlemen in London got together and formed a company, the Cornish Consolidated Tin Mines Ltd. They bought out the mine, and had another go. Didn't last long, mind you. Once the Great War came, that put a stop to it. They did sink a new shaft."

Jack's curiosity was stirred. "So who were those people?"

Dr Peters was staring at the floor, sucking in his cheeks and looking pensive. "As a matter of fact I've been doing some research on that very point. That's where the book needs a good update, you see. The chairman of this company was a bit of a mystery – I was always interested who was involved. Anyway, I've turned up that it was a gentleman by the name of Tyack. This chap, John Tyack, headed up the board of the company, and with Sir Lewis Molesworth and a General Carew they got things going for a bit."

Tyacks again! This was beyond coincidence. The words of the librarian suddenly floated into Jack's head: *There's no such thing as coincidence.* He had a sudden hallucination of a family tree, branching out underground, growing into seams and shafts, full of dusty ancestors and grinning demons. What, he wondered, was the true extent of his family's involvement in these mines? Jim Peters was rattling on, "It's a funny thing, tin mining. You never know where you're going to find a lode. Take coal. It's laid down in seams, so you can follow that seam and know where you're heading, and where more is likely to be. But tin and copper now, that's different ...." He rambled on for a while, forgetting Jack's presence so it seemed, then concluded significantly: "It's strange, I couldn't see the point of reopening the mine in 1906 and nor could anybody else at the time. It didn't make sense, economically speaking. Very odd. I'm surprised it lasted as long as it did."

A Tyack missing in the mine. A Tyack behind the reopening of the mine ... What was going on? Surely Jack's father would have mentioned it, knowing about the pictures he'd been drawing? What sort of connection was this? Cautiously he asked, "So how long was that, the reopening of the mine?"

"'Til 1914. Eight years, then the war came along. They put a fair old bit of money in there too, and lost it all, so far as I can see. There was some talk at the time, though, that this Tyack character was after something else. Some sort of crack-pot scheme – at least, that's how it was considered."

"But I thought that all they could get from the mines was tin and copper?"

"Oh, surely. I just turned up odd references, half hints, you might say." He screwed up his face. "Something about a new form of energy in that connection. No records from Tyack himself, mind you, just allusions, so to speak. There's nothing direct from this Tyack, in his own words." Then he squinted and sniffed. "People are always searching for some kind of answer, aren't they?"

"But he was the chairman, you said?"

"Oh yes, set the whole thing up when the mine reopened. You know, we could make a historian out of you, young man, with your curiosity! Yes, there's only tin and copper of any value in the mines. Mind you, there's tremendous geologic interest around here. The composition of these rock strata is fascinating. You'll find unusually high concentration of hydrous oxide of tin, for example. Now that's very interesting ...."

Jack was completely engaged in his own thoughts by now. So, it had been worth coming after all. A late goal! The question now was what to do with it. Everything was bound up with The Voice and the drawings. He was sure of that. He alone was the one who held all the threads. He would question his father about the whole thing when he got home. He wasn't mad, he wasn't ill, he didn't need medication – but he knew he was a part of something much bigger. The answer to what that might be was surely connected with the Crown Mines and the mysterious consciousness that was trying to reach out to him.

Jim Peters had talked himself to a stop and was now looking intently once more at Jack. Not exactly directly at him, but almost *around* him, as if flies were buzzing round his head. It was thoroughly unnerving. He said, in a somewhat different tone, "You know, there's history – and I'm a historian – but there's more to the past than just that."

"What do you mean?"

"Well, legend, for instance. As a historian, I like facts, demonstrable facts. But I've got an open mind, too." He paused, as if considering whether to say something. "These mines. They're not to be taken lightly, you know. They're not just the stuff of dry histories. No, that wouldn't do them justice at all. They should be treated with ... *respect.*"

After such a cryptic comment Jack hardly knew what to say. There was an uncomfortable silence while the historian, still too close for comfort, continued to stare at Jack. Then he said quietly, "You're not in some sort of trouble are you, young man?"

"Er – no. Why should I be?"

Jim Peters seemed about to say more, then changed his mind and abruptly handed Jack a little card. "Well you just be careful. Here's my email address, if you've got any more questions. If you let me have yours, I can let you know if I turn anything up about the missing man, since you're so interested. That's good, thanks. Now," he glanced at his watch, "I've got a bus to catch in thirteen minutes." He went off to gather up his laptop, shouldered his rucksack and, giving Jack a kind of awkward salute, wandered off to the nearest fire exit. Before leaving he turned and said, "Remember, you can email me at any time if you need help." Then he was gone.

The civic centre main hall was now quite empty. It was getting dark outside. Someone had turned off the main lights and only the fire exit signs and a small fluorescent strip glowed. Quiet laughter came from a side room; stragglers, no doubt. Jack stood for some moments and reflected. So, the script was slowly unfolding. The Tyacks and the mine. The voices and the mine. The drawings and the mine. The mine reopened. *Some new form of energy*. He was tired; the possibilities played out in his mind fruitlessly. There was nothing for him to do just now but go back to his hotel room, watch some TV and get some sleep. He could order a sandwich from the bar. He yawned. The background laughter, low and incessant, was getting on his nerves. It had a jeering, jangling quality. Suddenly annoyed, Jack went across to the side room to find the source. He put his head in but the room was quite empty. Now the sounds had shifted their source and seemed to be behind him, mocking and insidious. He spun round but nothing was there. The acoustics of the civic hall must be playing tricks and the laughter was coming from outside, much further away – a pub or gathering somewhere. The room shimmered and swam a little before his eyes; he felt cold and clammy and inexplicably frightened, like a small child. Taking one last look around, Jack shouldered his bag, left the civic hall and crossed the square to the Commercial Hotel.

Outside, rain glistened on the pavements and streaked the shop windows. Nobody was about except a lone figure under a street lamp, swaddled in a waterproof. Feeling this person's eyes were on him and fearful of a growing paranoia, Jack went straight to his room, turned on the TV and tried to empty his mind. He lay on the bed and momentarily closed his eyes, his earlier confidence suddenly evaporating. What an idiot he'd been to throw away his tablets! What had Jim Peters meant, "If you need help?" Was there more to that offer than met the eye? He turned on his side. From the bar below came voices and laughter. But whether they truly were downstairs or – the thought he dreaded – inside his head, he felt he couldn't say for sure.

CHAPTER 9

Not Alone

While the sea air and rugged coastline invigorated Peregrinus, the mines awakened much more profound feelings in him. As soon as he came anywhere near a ruined engine house, with its dark slits for windows, its toppling chimney and straggling ivy-covered walls, he was deeply moved. He came alive merely at the sight of such buildings. And now, at last, thanks to his job with the Woolfe Society, he could be near them all the time, soaking up their energy, tending them, loving them … and working, always, towards that deeper goal that dominated his every waking moment. At last, everything was coming together!

There had been many, many long years of drifting, scraping a living doing the most menial jobs – dossing, even, when all else failed. Through all had been a haze of amnesia, cloaking strange and vague recollections that seemed from long,

long ago. And then came *The Awakening*, as he liked to call it. Clarity, realization, purpose, his slumbering power stirring again – and with all that, his new 'alliance' with the Society. It was perfect. What had started as a general odd-job man role had grown into something more responsible and varied, just as he had planned. He would do various routine jobs for them, a bit of polishing here and small-scale fixing there, he would even maintain and repair both the engines and the subterranean structures below them: the man engine, the well-shafts, sump pits, pump rods, and so on. He wouldn't get much in the way of money, but he could live comfortably enough and it was not, in any case, money that motivated Peregrinus. His material needs were few. No; this Woolfe Society was his chosen instrument, his route *back*. Now he could control them with relative ease, via Morgana, in whom of course he had had to confide to some extent. Everything, in short, was coming together: the access to the mines, his ascendancy over the Society.

The Crown Mines at Botallack were special. It was here that much of Peregrinus's energies were concentrated, here that the vital, immediate goal lay. All kinds of memories were stirred in him by these mines, for which he had a stronger attraction than any other. Memories very old, very dark ... Down he must go, deep down, in his quest. But it was difficult work. First, persuading the Society had in itself not initially been easy, and it was not an enterprise he could accomplish entirely alone. Then, all but the uppermost part of the workings were flooded and progress was slow. The mines must be drained, the ancient machinery set to work again. He had become accustomed to clothing his sinewy frame in a wetsuit and descending into the claustrophobic, murky depths with a powerful torch and a set of ultra-compact aqualungs. It was an eerie scene down there. He would guide himself by gripping the pump rod, down 150 metres below the level of the sea to the sump, while the black mouths of crossing shafts would gape out of the gloom, briefly yielding a few yards of their mysteries to the beam of his lamp before receding into shadow behind. Shoals of little fish would start to follow in Peregrinus's wake as he got deeper, intrigued by this alien intruder and not a bit shy of either him or his lamp. This was their empire, after all – at least now its creators had long since abandoned it.

A little while after his talk with Morgana, and after the Society's self-important visit to the Crown Mines, Peregrinus returned there for the first time in some while. His task was to replace the retaining bolts on the furthest portion of the pump rod. It was a chill day, more like November than the summer. His sharpened senses, his intuition, had warned him days ago that something would be *different* there. Quite what, he couldn't say, but he had sensed the change. Something – energies of some kind – had been released, he felt sure. Sure enough, at any rate, to see that Carole had no part in a group visit. Now he would find out for certain.

As soon as he began his descent down the steep and grass-tufted path to the mines, he knew without doubt that something was wrong. He should have come sooner! He sniffed the air as he approached. Along with the brine was another tang: metallic, acrid, carried on the wind like a warning. Ozone? What had they done? Now he saw the engine house doused in spray below, clinging to the rocks precariously. He paused on the threshold. The warning tape fluttered in the breeze, the flimsy fence tilted in a new direction. Peregrinus's features settled into an expression of intense concentration; he scanned the building's exterior, up the mossy walls, the stubby chimney, searching for what no other eye might see. Then, warily, he moved through the arch and into the hallowed space beyond. A whiff of burning lingered in the air – the engine, or something else, something subtle? The shadows parted as he advanced, the machinery looming all around. He stood in his own pool of light. Everything looked normal enough. And *yet* ... He stood still for some minutes, listening, smelling, feeling. The Society? Someone else? He remained there, alert, motionless for a full five minutes, pondering the change in the atmosphere of the place, what seemed like unmistakable signals. Then with a jolt he roused himself. He had work to do! Reluctantly putting suspicion to one side, he prepared himself for his descent, which would be to the deepest part of the mine.

Two hours later, Peregrinus emerged from the dive with no small relief at leaving the icy waters. He retreated from the well-shaft back into the shelter of the engine house to strip off his wet suit and towel down, out of the fine rain that was falling. It was cold and it was misty, not a day to tarry outside. He could not rid himself of a sense of intrusion, yet all below had been as he had expected. But then, nothing could possibly disturb him *there,* remote in the depths of the flooded workings. His own world. The light was fast fading when, as he stood inside, pulling on his jeans while staring through the arch of the entrance at the mouth of the shaft, he thought he heard a noise from that direction. It was a noise that he really should not be hearing: the sound of bubbles rising, as of air being blown through water from down inside the shaft. Dismissing it as an effect of the wind, he was about to turn away when the sound was repeated much more distinctly, a sloshing now very near the surface. Surely it could not be!

A mesh grill covered the entrance to the shaft, a grill that Peregrinus had only just carefully replaced, as he always did, on emerging from below. Now, as he looked on in amazement, this grill began to rattle and grate. Were those *fingers* he could make out in the gloom, poking through? The mesh gave a final rattle, then was lifted clear from underneath. Out clambered ponderously the giant shadow of a man. Peregrinus, frozen in astonishment, could make out only a little detail in the deepening gloom, but enough to assure him that this apparition wore no wetsuit and had no special equipment. Certainly, it had no breathing apparatus. Gods! Was this possible? He drew back behind a column, fearful of being seen. Dripping, the form deliberately lowered itself onto the turf then very precisely and methodically stooped to replace the grill, just as Peregrinus had done before him. Then, without turning in the direction of the engine house or looking back, it strode off up the hill and was swallowed by the dusk.

Peregrinus was not one to be easily unsettled. He had seen many things, many of which had only recently come to consciousness from the remote reaches of his past, and some of which made him shudder as they had crystallized in his memory. But the sight of that unwieldy shadow-form rising out of the shaft, the fact that only minutes before he had been down there himself, presumably close to it, and the inhuman fact that it appeared not to need to breathe – these things thoroughly unnerved him. What did it want from the flooded depths? He shook his head. His earlier misgivings, and now this– The mine was changing, or *being changed.* Something he had not foreseen ... Something that made his work there, surely, the more urgent. He turned away into the darkness of the engine house, lost in contemplation.

CHAPTER 10

A Tooth and Old Stones

We are all vigilant, and all play our parts. Jacob is my eyes and ears, as ever. And I have sent my precious jewel to place the stones – we will have news soon!

The Reverend McDowell, vicar of St Mary's church, St Just, was enjoying his morning stroll. Whatever the weather, the cliffs around Cape Cornwall never disappointed and today was no exception. There was a wildness about the area, a primal feeling to the coastline, that energized him in a surprising way he would not have thought possible. For the Reverend, the move to these remote parts from a small living in Surrey, so familiar and so close to home, had been a big step, a challenge. But life was what you made of it. He used to ask God for help many times, but all he seemed to face were greater challenges. Then he realized: the challenges were God's way of helping him, and each time he faced, and surmounted, one he became stronger. God *was* helping him! He was still a young man, with a career before him. Moving to St Just was an opportunity not to be missed, even though the place was so different from his old parish. Different in what way? he asked himself. He pursed his lips and breathed the sea air deeply. It was hard to escape the conclusion there was something ... *heathen* about the place. Was that the right word? Well, very ancient, in a pre-Christian, Celtic sort of way. Take that preservation society, for instance. He was hardly a seasoned man of the world, but he'd be surprised if there weren't some strange practices going on there. He knew they were stand-offish. No, more than that: hostile. But that was probably no more than a reflex reaction to a newcomer. These small, rural communities were always suspicious of strangers. He could break that down, he felt sure; he could establish a bond of trust, the first step along God's path to redemption.

It was a beautiful morning. The vicar climbed a small rise and the majestic outline of Wheal Peevor came into his view, perched high adjacent to the coastal path. These old mine buildings had a religious flavour, he thought to himself. The chimney so like a steeple, the arch-headed windows looking out to sea like the east end of a chapel. But ruinous, decayed – no model for God's house there! Outside the engine house clustered a small band of folk. Ah, the Woolfe Society, no less. And there was that woman, the secretary. The Reverend fixed a smile to his face. This fine morning, what a perfect opportunity to reach out to them, all of them. He strode purposefully up to the little group, radiating (he hoped) compassion and love for all. "Good morning! What a lovely day it is."

⅄

Nearby, in the confined space of the annex to the old engine house, the original purpose of which was long forgotten and could not now be conjectured even by an expert like Dr James Peters, a pair of eyes gazed unblinkingly through a narrow aperture in the stonework, surveying the scene unfolding on the grassy slope beyond. They were the strangest eyes: impassive, dead in their camera-like detachment. The view through the slit was restricted, yet enough was visible to build up a picture of what was happening. The woman – yes, she was known; the woman commanded, the others obeyed. The figure in the middle – yes! he was different, not one of them. *An Outsider*, known too, known from the followers of the Other Way, the church in the village. He was a leader too, their vicar. And they all talked, the vicar smiling, nodding.

A cloud passed overhead and darkness filled the annex; shadows rippled over the coarse grass and gravel of the coastal path. Darker energies gathered in the spaces of the old building, and around it. Not that the eyes cared for those, or that the mind behind them could feel such things. They continued watching, recording. *See, see what happens, so you may tell him all.* Those eyes, eyes with neither whites nor irises, gazed with greater keenness. The people talked, then the talk stopped. Now the vicar was in their midst, the others had made it so, and they were ringed around him. There was shouting and laughing, like a game. They were all playing, playing like a game. And the others were moving in on the vicar, and he was lying down, curled up in a ball. Like a ball.

They pushed and kicked the ball. It rolled slightly to one side and was hidden by the masonry of the engine house. Calmly, methodically, the unwieldy dark form inside the annex shifted its huge bulk a little to one side, bringing the scene back into the view of its blank stare. The group closed in on the vicar, pulling him out of his ball and up to his feet. He stood there all ruffled looking. The watcher's eyes momentarily lowered, as if in mimicry of reflection, then fixed again on the drama being played out in the circle, unemotionally scanning, registering each and every detail. The woman stepped forward while the others held the vicar, reaching out, his head back, and she had something in her hand, reaching out, to his face, in his face, in the mouth. *Howling, howling noise, like the animals*, and the woman held up something from the mouth. A tooth! There was stuff running down the face. Much blood. And now the vicar had rolled up again, in his ball, hands at face, blood streaming. They stood back, the others, waiting, waiting until the man slowly got back to his feet, and they let him pass, let him run off down the slope, away from them.

⅄

The sun came out. Denny Gedge brushed some earth off his jacket. Derek Ballard lit a cigarette. Morgana pulled back her hair neatly out of the way, gripping a hair clip in her teeth while she did so, and fixed it there. Trudy from the playgroup perched on a stone and tilted her face skywards, drinking in the warmth like a sunbather. Others variously composed themselves and chatted in twos and threes. Derek sidled up to Morgana, blew smoke in her face and gave her a tarnished grin. "I reckon that there vicar knows what's what now, eh?"

Morgana smiled slightly, resettled her glasses on her nose and gave a little nod. She had some blood on her hand and was wiping it on a tissue. "I'd like you to have a good look at those accounts for Wheal Jane. We need a little more in the way of funds for the loft restoration. Nothing major." She stopped wiping and looked around, as if for the first time seeing where she was. "Well, it's such a fine day I think I'm going to get some washing out when I get home. Perfect for getting the sheets done!" She gave them a little smile and set off down the path, back to the town. They watched her go, then gradually themselves began dispersing, relaxed and in good spirits. It really was such a lovely day.

Once again the figure in the annex shifted in its hideaway, adjusting its view. It would stay there until they had gone, all of them. Then it would leave. And it would remember.

⅄

The painting was in the style of someone he'd been studying at school. What was the guy's name ... Hodder, or something? It showed a peaceful Cornish scene of an estuary bathed in light. A yacht was tacking cheerfully in the foreground and a serene, inviting-looking whitewashed house rose from a sandy beach on the far shore. The composition exuded poise and tranquillity. Jack bitterly contrasted it with his own experience of Cornwall on this short visit. He scanned the other pictures in the gallery window. All the same sort of thing: all bland, all with that soft sunlight. There was nothing showing the *dark* side of the place. But he'd seen that, hadn't he? He should have known, coming down here, pursuing those drawings – what did he expect! He pulled back a bit from the window and watched in it the reflections of pedestrians behind him, coming and going across the market square. For some reason, they made him feel nervous, even furtive. A journey to Cornwall … and somewhere darker, for sure. And yet, and yet … He moved on, circling the limited selection of shop fronts and cafés, reluctant to face facts. And yet, something worse lay in store: *going home*. Whichever way he looked at it, and despite the 'darkness', this trip had in many ways been a liberation. He'd had real freedom, not just freedom to do things, but freedom *from* things: from the endless nagging, or – worse – silent reproof, of his mother; the whole medication regime; the stifling repressiveness of family life. He'd got away from all that and it had been like a sort of awakening.

Jack went into a small coffee shop-cum-art gallery (how many such galleries *were* there in this tiny place?) and sat with a Coke and a chocolate brownie, thinking. A liberation, then ... but maybe a liberation for something else, too, something that would have been better *not* liberated. He briefly thought of the mine buildings and the shadows, not entirely formless, that had clustered evilly around them. Hurriedly he turned his attention back to the problems that lay ahead. As if on cue, those dismal parting words of his mother's came back to him: *Running away from your problems won't help*. And *was* he running away from them – or facing them? He frowned and with his fork pushed his brownie, which was stale, around the plate. All this unresolved stuff: job, school, his studies, the medication (what would he tell them about that?), and now this. *Some new form of energy* – now it was Jim Peters' voice he could hear. *You're not in some sort of trouble are you?* What a mess! Jack honestly wasn't sure what to do now. As he stared out of the café window the colour drained out of everything: the early morning ramblers, the locals pottering on their rounds, the delivery vans, the tourists, the clear blue sky itself. All he knew was that he hated being at home. But today, his last day in St Just, was funnelling him remorselessly closer as the minutes ticked away. There was no escape. He looked at his watch. Still an hour to go until his bus was due. He needed to pack and check out of the hotel before then.

Suddenly a powerful new feeling came over him. He wanted to run, to hide, just get away from it all, parents included; to *disappear,* preferably permanently. It would make everything way, way easier. But there was more to it than that. Cautiously he scanned the interior of the café. At the back there was a young mother with her two small children, faces smeared with chocolate. Then a respectable looking gent, reading his morning paper. A couple of walkers were stoking up with a cooked breakfast. All entirely normal, and yet he had this constant awareness of … what? Some presence or other. What a cliché: he *felt he was being watched.* Something he could sense, but not see or hear. It was as if there was a shadow in the corner of his eye, like an eyelash, but as soon as he turned it had vanished. Well, at least the voice had gone now. Just that final moment of clarity in the mine, then nothing – apart from what he now knew to be imaginings. Had he just exchanged one problem for another, though?

He paid up and went across to the hotel, still turning over his problems. The basic question remained: where did he go from here? Not just with the whole voice and drawings business, but with *his life*? Again he felt his options draining away. Maybe he could simply stay down here, at the Commercial Hotel, and not bother to go back at all. Back in his room, his eye caught the empty bottle of pills, still in the waste bin. Again he felt a nagging doubt about kicking his medication. Should he own up to that, when he got home, or just lie? But then, to be trapped in a web of lies … not good!

Collecting his remaining things, Jack clipped together the retaining straps in his suitcase, checked he had everything and snapped the lid shut. The corner of a protruding sheet of paper caught his eye. The drawings. He could take them back, show them to Richard Attlee. He might have some more ideas. After all, it was thanks to Attlee he was down here in the first place. Consumed by a wave of gloom, he manoeuvred his case off the bed and onto the floor, dropping his phone as he did so. As he bent to retrieve it, he noticed several small objects under the bed. What were those? It was strange he hadn't seen them before. On his hands and knees, he scooped them up, went to the window and held them in the light. Three small stones, beautifully polished. Each was quite distinct: one dark green and flecked with little veins of grey, one a reddish brown with white crystals blooming in clusters on its surface, the other entirely black with no mark of any kind. Thoughtfully, Jack weighed them in his hand. They couldn't belong to the hotel – what would they be doing down there? But then, he was almost certain they weren't there when he arrived, since he had tried to squeeze his case under the bed to get it out of the way. Impulsively he slipped them in his pocket, feeling they would somehow be better with him than left behind; a small piece of Cornwall he would take back with him.

Once outside, he trundled his case over to the bus stop, sat himself down on the bench and waited. Around him locals came and went, gathering in little knots to chat, smoke, go about their business in a typical weekday morning scene. Just before his bus arrived, however, there was one disturbing incident. From a side road opening on to the square, the road leading to Cape Cornwall, Jack saw a figure running towards him. It was a youngish man, wearing jeans and a light sleeveless coat, in distress and clutching at his face. As he came nearer Jack noticed the dog collar; the man must be the vicar. Blood was spattered on his hands and down his chin. He ran, like a wounded animal, straight across the road without looking, across the central island right in front of Jack and down the road to the other side that led to the church. Despite the fact the man was obviously in distress, and staggered and lurched drunkenly, nobody moved to help him during all this. An old man walking a dog paused and stared at him neutrally, that was all. Then the vicar had gone and the bus, belching its clouds of fumes, drew up. Jack got on along with a couple of others, stowed his case in the luggage rack and got settled. He found himself wishing he could have left a few minutes earlier and missed that disturbing scene. With a grinding of gears the bus pulled away.

He twisted back in his seat, taking one last look at the market square. As he did so, a veil seemed to be pulled aside. He winced. There was a blast of heat, charred forms writhed briefly before his mind's eye in silent agonies. Then the veil fell back in a puff of smoke and left only the echo of that awful, drawn-out cry: *Save me!*

CHAPTER 11

The Waters Recede

As he walked along the cliff path to the Crown Mines, Peregrinus reflected. He had felt relatively confident about progress until the disconcerting appearance of 'the apparition', as he privately referred to the monstrous shape he'd seen emerging from the shaft on his last dive. And then there'd been the sense of intrusion, the intangible awareness of violation. It didn't bode well but he would get to the bottom of it. On his right, he approached and passed the ruined engine house of Wheal Jane, all tumbling stone work and straggling ivy. Peregrinus surveyed it with a reverent eye. Presently he came to the steep descent to the mine itself, down which he strode purposefully. He kept all his equipment in a locker within the engine house, allowing him to travel to and fro without much baggage, inconspicuously.

As he entered the engine building, he put his reservations aside. Today was a special day. A very special day. For the first time he could discard his wetsuit and breathing gear, for the mine was now drained. The old engine, restored to working order by his efforts and those of the guileless Woolfe Society (thinking they were pushing forward the frontiers of conservation), had flexed its giant limbs day and night until the waters receded. Now he would descend to the bottom by climbing, not diving. He felt his pulse lifting, his instincts quickening, at the thought of success, and what it might bring.

After donning his waterproof gaiters, hard hat, gloves and packing his backpack with some light tools and a powerful torch to supplement that on the hat he moved aside the grill, swung himself over the lip of the well shaft and began to descend using the rusting iron ladder clamped to its walls. Soon the sea's roar receded and Peregrinus became enclosed in a narrow sleeve of darkness. He reached up and flicked on the switch of his helmet lamp, which threw a cone of light on to the wall of the shaft immediately in front of him, and continued his descent. The pump shaft at the Botallack mine descended to the deepest parts of the workings, as indeed it must, nearly 200 metres vertically down. Directly at his back and running down the centre of the shaft was the streaked pump rod itself, made from sections of stout timber spliced together. Relentless in its activity over the previous weeks, now it was stilled, its work done for the present.

As the sounds above diminished, the dripping noise of hundreds of tiny rivulets running from lateral tunnels and crevasses became louder until it dominated. The ladder was damp and slippery; great care was needed on each rung not to slip. Peregrinus climbed past the black mouth of a side tunnel, the initial few feet of which were briefly illuminated by his lamp. The whole substrata were riddled with such tunnels, relics of previous pursuits of the elusive tin lodes before the miners were forced ever deeper underground. Down he continued, steadily, evenly, until eventually the shaft flared out into a wider chamber. There the pump rod terminated in a box-like construction that was the pump itself. Peregrinus's boots sloshed in a pool of ankle-deep water; he had reached the bottom. Now he produced his LED torch from his backpack and swung it to and fro before him, as if warding off evil spirits. Facing him was an archway leading through to a series of chambers. These he had explored already in his diving gear; they did not reach far before ending in blind rock. He turned around and was faced by another tunnel, reasonably wide and brick-lined. This tunnel sloped gently upwards from the horizontal; its purpose was to feed the sump through a groove-like channel in its floor, now covered in puddles and deeper pools. It seemed to beckon, invitingly. This way he had yet to travel. And somewhere, somewhere in the black beyond, the mines held a secret, a secret that he needed to locate, a secret the recovery of which would be a single, giant stride towards the realization of the Great Project. He was tantalizingly close now ... On the face of it, the task seemed impossible, like searching for a needle in a haystack. But he knew his instincts would guide him to the place, sooner or later. He set off.

Peregrinus's lamp pierced the darkness to about ten feet ahead of him and then abruptly failed, the beam dissipating in the blackness. The tunnel maintained its modest upward gradient and was periodically choked with rockfalls and mounds of silt, as well as deep pools of seawater up to his thighs that he must needs wade through. It being principally designed for drainage, there was little evidence of subsidiary workings. He glanced at his watch. He should be mindful of the life of his torch batteries; without that torch he was lost. After ten minutes or so he diverted to briefly explore a side tunnel. It extended for only about ten metres before ending in a blind wall. He turned to go back but as he neared the junction with the main tunnel he stopped. Peregrinus's highly developed instincts, animal-like in their intensity, prompted him to switch off both his torch and his helmet light, and to stop and wait, in silence. Something was coming, he felt it.

Sure enough, as his eyes accustomed themselves to the blackness it became apparent that there was, in fact, a faint light outside in the main tunnel. Presently this light grew stronger, and stronger, accompanied by a scraping sound, until its source was almost at the mouth of the tunnel. And as Peregrinus watched in amazement there slowly hove into view the shadow of a massive figure, hunched in the small space, shuffling past with stooped gait. In the feeble light it was hard to discern much detail; he observed that the legs flailed through the deeper pools of water in an uncoordinated, spasmodic sort of way. One huge hand held a large lamp that twitched and wavered as the creature floundered on. The light reflecting back off the murky ground water created a curious halo effect around the head. The features were a dark blur: deep crevasses and ridges, almost like the surrounding rock itself. Peregrinus saw enough to assure himself it wore nothing in the way of special equipment or clothing of any kind. He shrank back into his cave as the thing paused directly opposite the entrance, adjusted its hold on its lamp, then resumed its progress in the direction of the pump shaft. It was soon swallowed up in darkness, a receding sloshing and scraping echoing faintly in its wake.

It was a fearful sight, yet not entirely unexpected, given previous events. Peregrinus could only hope the giant would ascend directly and had no intention to return that way. It was some minutes before he felt confident enough to leave the side tunnel and continue his quest. The surprise of the meeting was one thing but his worse fears had now been borne out and inwardly he fought despair, despair that all would be in vain, that the other thing was on a mission, too – the same mission as his own. But no, he should pull himself together! That could hardly be possible … Trying to focus and clarify his senses for the purpose that he had in hand he moved on along the main tunnel, away from the bizarre intruder.

Peregrinus's instincts did not fail him. Remorselessly they led him on, through semi-flooded gullies, past treacherous spars of rock, under rough low ceilings in which the veins of the ores showed up in his lamplight in fluid, alien patterns. He found it eventually, just when he was beginning to doubt that success was possible. Two hours later he was back on the surface, in the engine house. Safely in his bag, swaddled in layers of cloth, was his prize, that little piece of priceless history recovered from the world below. A sense of relief suffused him: all the long work of drainage had at last been vindicated. He completed changing back into his normal clothes, shouldered his bag and glanced outside at the darkening sky. It would soon be time to move on, on to the next stage in the plan, time to leave these Cornish skies for an altogether bigger purpose.

CHAPTER 12

Back In Amersham

Jack was exploring a pit, which was also the lower part of a building. Filling the pit was a vast structure of metal, a huge engine of ancient design. There was an enormous, streaked iron cylinder and, high above, a gigantic beam. The machinery blended into the structure of the building around it and pipes sprouted and threaded their way through arches and apertures. A rod the thickness of a tree trunk descended a shaft into dark depths below. It was this gaping shaft that breathed fear. Its walls fell away, lined with bricks, and much water below covered the lower part of the machinery. These submerged structures held a nameless terror. He moved slowly through this machine, tentatively, fearfully. Snakes coiled around the columns and pipes, their tongues and eyes flickering evilly in the weak light. Sometimes, from above, one would dangle its head in his face, then slither away into the shadows. Feeble light bulbs hung low from remote anchorages above. If only he could turn back the clock, never have come to this treacherous place! It was too late now. Then came a slow tide of terror from the pit below, gradually rising like smoke. The first wisps enveloped him, but the greater fear was deeper, rising, rising, and with it came words, a whispered fragment: *Release me! Release me!* repeated again and again, building to a hoarse shriek. Soon he would be engulfed, and then ....

Shouting, Jack emerged from the dream into wakefulness, bathed in sweat. For a few moments he was disorientated, not knowing where he was, what was true and what was dream. Then the familiar surroundings of his bedroom one by one registered, calming him: the light through the curtains, the ticking of the clock. He held his head in his hands, despairing. It was not the first such dream he'd had since his trip Cornwall. And yet – he scanned the room warily. The pad and pen by his bed remained unused: there had been no more drawings, and no more voices, save those in the dreams. He flopped back on the bed and stared sightlessly at the ceiling. Whatever had been causing them had somehow shifted. *Their* message had been delivered. Now the thing behind them had taken on more reality. No longer speaking through drawings, nor mutterings in his head, it had somehow detached itself. A new shadow followed him. It was as if something that had been trapped had acquired a tenuous freedom. He shuddered, converted the shudder into a stretch and twisted round to see his alarm clock. Nine a.m. – probably time to get up and find out what people were up to.

Running a hand through his hair and letting the residual sense of disturbance from the dream recede further, Jack swung himself out of bed and gulped down a glass of water that had been standing on the bedside table. No more tablets; he'd stuck to his decision to ditch them – secretly, though. So far as his parents were concerned he dutifully followed the doctor's orders. And that's how it would have to stay. Next to the glass, in a little group, were the three rather beautiful, polished semi-precious stones he'd found in his hotel room in St Just and brought back with him. His gaze settled on them. There was something unaccountably compelling about these stones. Sometimes he carried them around with him, though he couldn't say why. He always had to look at them there, on the bedside table, in a strange little ritual before he could get up and get on with the day. Maybe a new facet to his 'problems'? He frowned.

Jack shuffled down the staircase and made his way to the breakfast room at the back of the house. Through the tall patio windows the wide expanse of garden was visible, curving around in a generous arc and containing benches, a gazebo, an elegant and large central pond and a summer house. Early autumn leaves blew across the grass. At the long breakfast table sat Jack's parents. David Tyack was reading something, no doubt the news, occasionally glancing at his watch. Joanne Tyack was at the opposite end. She was wearing her 'posh' tracksuit, as Jack called it, to distinguish it from the ones she wouldn't be seen out in. Stylish glasses were pushed up on her head. Her slight figure was bent over a laptop on the table in front of her, at which she was staring intently. Plate, toast rack and cutlery had been pushed to one side to accommodate this activity. Despite it being a Saturday, work never stopped, these days, for Joanne. She glanced up briefly as Jack entered and directed a wintry smile at him before returning her attention to the laptop. "Morning Jack," his father said, without looking up from his reading.

Jack helped himself to cereal while gazing vacantly out into the garden, trying at the same time to remember more details of his dream. What exactly was it that was coming up out of the pit? The fear had gone now, but had left a kind of unfocussed anxiety when he tried to think about it. He could almost see it, the thing that was rising up … He felt something soft brush against his leg under the table. "Hello Terry, good boy." The family's Airedale Terrier snuffled and gave a friendly wag of his tail before drifting over to see his mother.

"Not now Terry," said Joanne impatiently, prodding the dog away with the point of her toe. She furrowed her brow and then rubbed it with a forefinger. "Spreadsheets! There must be a better way. Why isn't this adding up?" After a long sigh she fixed her son again with her extraordinary, grey eyes, always unnerving in their detachment.

"What are you up to today, Jack?"

He shrugged guardedly. "Not much at the moment."

His mother's gaze sharpened. "Have you taken your tablets?"

With an effort to look frank and matter-of-fact he met her eyes. "*Yes!* Why do you always ask?"

She said sceptically, "Just checking. It's only for your own good, Jack, you know that. And how about a job? Have you got any further?"

Did she know? Jack struggled to control his response. Confrontations with his mother were never successful yet he felt ever more resentful of her relentless questioning. "I've got an interview later this week, at the café. Just waitering, but they'll train me on the tills." He felt a bit of him die as he said it.

She held him with her gaze a little longer, then briskly turned away as if it were of no consequence. "Well make sure you wear a suit. Even for that. It all helps. Now, I've made a list that I've stuck on the fridge. You know we've got the party here tomorrow evening. I need everything to be in order and I don't want any mess. As well as walking the dog at some point can you have a look at that list and see what you can do? It would be a big help."

Jack knew there was little point in resisting despite his hatred of the chores list that regularly found its way onto the door of the fridge. But he had jobs of his own to do today: getting a passport photo (something he was dreading), getting his hair cut, buying some new trainers (the old ones having been ruined by salt water in Cornwall). He wandered over and cast an eye down the list to a backdrop of renewed cursing from his mother. "Now why won't this formula paste? Oh, I don't know!" Mrs Tyack slammed shut the lid of the laptop and pushed it away from her as if it were a plate of inedible food.

"David, I'm off for my run now, and then I'll be meeting the girls for coffee in town." She glanced sharply at her watch, produced a band from her pocket and deftly twisted her hair into a pony tail with it. Then she stood up and briefly stretched. "I'll see you both later."

"Bye Mum"

"Bye, Jack" she called over her shoulder. The front door slammed.

David Tyack, who had barely stirred from his reading throughout all this, finally looked up and surveyed the scene before him as if for the first time. He smoothed his hair back pensively then started fiddling with his mobile. "Look Jack, can you walk Terry as your mother says and make sure you at least make a start on some of those other things? Katja will be giving the place the once over tomorrow but we'd really appreciate your help today." He strode over to the sink and began meticulously removing a stain from his shirt with one hand whilst making a call on his mobile with the other. "Hello Alan? Alan, its David. Yes. About the gamma file–"

Jack turned away and wandered off to his room, the unsatisfactory fragments of those unsatisfactory conversations and a thousand like them circulating aimlessly in his brain.

⅄

Two hours later and Joanne Tyack was sipping a skinny latte in the coffee shop in Amersham with her friends Maddy and Jemima. There was a pleasant bustle in the café; these places always did well. Although all three women had just finished demanding exercise routines of one sort or another, and were all wearing tracksuits, none of them seemed particularly tired or sweaty. They were in their mid-forties, but looked considerably younger. Maddy, sitting with her legs flexibly tucked up under her, was in questioning mode. They were reminiscing about their university days.

"But surely it must have been *gruelling*, Jo? –Another year on top of your degree, full time, very intensive as I hear. I've always wanted an MBA but I must confess I don't think I could do it now, not with Sebastian and the yoga too. Yes, I should have stayed on like you, and done it then, straight after my degree."

Joanne Tyack stared into her coffee cup and shrugged. "Well, I didn't find it particularly hard. It was quite intense, I suppose. And I have to say it's been very useful."

"I always say," put in Jemima, smoothing an eyebrow, "that anyone who wants to be anything in business should have an MBA." She was another slender, super-fit looking type, with no ounce of spare flesh on her. Joanne was her role model. "It really is essential for a serious business career. It's helped you, hasn't it Jo?"

"Oh yes," said Mrs Tyack carefully, looking up from her coffee now and giving them a thin smile. "I couldn't have started Geothermal without it. Nor without David of course – I suppose," she added as an afterthought, to snorts of laughter. "No, it wasn't hard, intellectually speaking, but it did take a disciplined approach. I was fortunate to have a good lecturer. That helps. Yes, we got on very well, as a matter of fact." A fainter smile played on her lips, as she remembered. "You could still do it, Maddy. Sebastian's old enough to sort himself out now. You should get on and do what you feel is right for you. You only have one life: live it to the full, as *you* want to. It's not too late, you know." Her clinical stare fixed her friends each in turn.

Maddy reflected briefly on this while dropping two extra sweeteners into her latte. "Well, I'm sure you're right. Maybe I should look into it. What do you think, Jems?"

Jemima nodded emphatically. "Agree with Jo. You said you've always wanted an MBA. Do it. Nothing falls in your lap in this life – go out and make it happen, that's what I say. You could do it in two years, part time. Why don't you?"

Maddy deflected further urging on this point by returning to her original tack. "You've never told us that much about your university days, Jo. Southampton, wasn't it? Were you and David in the same year? Was it love at first sight?" She smiled ironically.

Mrs Tyack briefly reflected on the events of over twenty years ago. Episodes of crystal clarity, as if yesterday, alternated with periods of vagueness and disorder, as if the sequencing had broken down. How time played tricks! She had met her husband when they were both undergraduates. They were in different faculties and studying quite different subjects. He was one of the brightest geology students in his year, while she was pursuing a degree in economics.

"Yes, we were in the same year. I don't know about love at first sight ... I suppose we were attracted to each other. We were both very young of course, but felt terribly grown up. You must remember what it was like. Several friends were getting engaged – it seemed the natural thing to do."

"And then, happily ever after, eh Jo?" said Jemima with an exaggerated wink.

Mrs Tyack shifted in her seat with a trace of discomfort, and said coldly, "You might say that. David got a good job straight after graduation. I stayed on and did the MBA. Then we got married. It all worked out perfectly well."

"Well one thing's for sure," interposed Maddy, anxious to smooth things over, "after everything Jo went through she deserves a medal for setting up Geothermal. Not just for setting it up, but making it a *success*." She ended on a rising note, as if to underline the nature of the achievement. It was common knowledge that "everything Jo went through" referred to her illness. For Mrs Tyack had been ill, grievously ill, in the period before they'd known her, when Jack was small. Indeed her life had been despaired of. She'd been away, down in the West Country pursuing yet another vocational qualification at a local university, when disaster had struck. After weeks of intensive nursing in hospital she had pulled through, to the admiration of all, and gone on to yet greater heights. But older friends and family, and no-one more than her husband, had noticed a change since then; she'd become more distant, inscrutable, unfathomable. And from that period dated the obsession with her health and appearance: endless exercise regimes, eating next to nothing, the minutest attention to her clothing, even those regular sessions in the tanning salon that imparted a year-round bronze glow to her skin. In all of this she encouraged, with missionary zeal, her friends to follow her example. She was an inspiration.

Jemima realized her blunder, inhaling some of her latte in her haste to rectify it. "Oh, *of course*! I meant, happy ever after *in the end*. Nobody else could have done what you did Jo, not after being so terribly ill. I just don't know how you managed it."

Joanne inclined her head slightly in acknowledgement. What was to be her finely judged response was pre-empted by her phone ringing. "I must answer that, it'll be David." The others continued the conversation while she turned to the side, blocking one ear with the palm of her hand to better hear her husband above the noise of the café.

"David? Yes. Where are you? Let's go through it now. The office, yes. OK, I'm just finished here, I'll be over in quarter of an hour." Joanne slipped the phone into her bag and turned back to the others. "I must dash – I'm needed at the office." She rapidly drank down the dregs of her coffee and collected her things. "Maddy, you should think about that MBA. Remember, you only get one chance in this life." She gave them a quick smile. "I'll see you both at yoga." And with that, she was gone.

⅄

It was the face from a nightmare. The nose, large and inflamed, hooked down low to meet a rubbery upper lip that had partially writhed back from the teeth and was frozen between a leer and a lisping attempt at speech. Shadowy stubble strayed like moss over the lower jaw, appearing not stylish but only seedy. One eyelid drooped low over a drugged pupil while the other eye stared wide in startled apprehension. The head itself seemed continuous with the thick neck and showed neither jaw line nor any other redeeming contour. It looked like the end of a grubby thumb on which someone had drawn crude features in pen.

Jack looked around nervously, stood back from the booth and carefully put the passport photo in his wallet. Tears pricked at his eyes. Everyone took a bad photo in those things, he told himself. He needed it for his provisional driving licence application, and somehow knew in advance it was going to be bad. Still, the shock and despair were unmitigated when they came. It was all in his mind, he told himself, a symptom of the low self-esteem that had plagued him since his return from Cornwall. He surreptitiously glanced at the photo again. Surely he didn't look that bad? Trying to put it out of mind, he left the supermarket and walked round the corner to get his hair cut. Five minutes later he was looking at his reflection in the barber shop mirror, thinking that troubles did not come in ones. The barber, a young woman not much older than Jack himself, had temporarily sculpted his long dark hair into something like a mohican. He stared back at himself from under the ridiculous crest, feeling even more insecure.

"It's got very long hasn't it? Are you happy with your hair?" asked the girl, an accusing note in her voice.

"Yeah, just a tidy up thanks," Jack said, trying to avoid her gaze in the mirror. The girl made a resigned gesture, as of someone having tried and failed, and started cutting. While she trimmed away he scanned the bench behind him warily in the mirror. The shop was unusually quiet. There had only been one customer before him, just finishing when he arrived, and now the place was empty. After another five minutes or so, punctuated by the girl's desultory and unsuccessful attempts to start a conversation, another customer came in, picked up one of the magazines and settled himself on the bench.

Jack felt worried. His recent frame of mind was like a throwback to something more primitive: he was always on the lookout for a threat and every new face could spell danger of a nameless, intangible sort – the same danger that rose out of the pit in his dreams. For example, his immediate impulse now was to size up the customer behind him, almost as a reflex. Yet every time he tried, with a quick glance in the mirror, somehow the man's features evaded him. It was as if there was something *wrapped around* the head, a strange blurring, some sort of dark halo. At one point, when he was looking, the head tilted sharply up with unnerving quickness, as if sensing his gaze and returning it, yet again Jack could not make out anything distinct about the face. There was something primal in that quick movement that was extremely unnerving. A cold feeling of fear swept over him. Closing his eyes, he wondered if he could just run out, then and there, without waiting for the haircut to finish. When he opened them again, he was in time to see the figure rise to its feet, put down the magazine and walk out. Relief swept over Jack. What had made it go? Attempting normality and conscious of the sweat on his forehead he said to the girl, "He didn't have much patience, did he?"

She screwed up her face. "Sorry?"

"That man. He didn't wait for long."

"What man?" She looked at him doubtfully. "There's been no-one else in here since you came in?"

Jack said nothing more, simply waiting for her to finish and silently paying up. His very worst fears were coming true.

Back outside he glanced furtively around. The featureless figure was nowhere to be seen. Could it, just could it all have been in his head? He thought not; by now he had discounted any theories of his supposed 'illness' in favour of something very real, very objective, being amiss. Something, to be blunt, to do with the Crown Mines, something that had been liberated by his visit there, something that now had – how could he put it? – a sort of limited life and freedom of its own and would use that freedom to pursue him. Was that too fantastic? Jim Peters' voice came back to him: *Are you in some sort of trouble, young man?* Despite it all, though, and the various worrying pieces of evidence for his theory, he had made it a principle that wherever possible he wouldn't let them interfere with his normal life. And today, that meant resisting the temptation to scuttle back to his room and instead pressing on with the next job on his list, buying himself a new pair of trainers.

After the unnerving near-emptiness of the barber's it was a relief to enter the lively environment of the sports shop. The loud music, the knots of shoppers, the assistants everywhere helped make him feel less alone, more grounded – *safer*, if he was being honest with himself. Jack stood there and let it all permeate him. He relaxed. Yes, here he did feel safe. He drifted over to the footwear section and began to browse, absently. But he soon discovered that coming to a decision as to what to buy was almost impossible. He just couldn't focus his mind and found himself dithering pathetically. In frustration he pulled out his phone and checked his emails; this, at least, might help him feel organized. There was a short string of new ones but nothing that looked of interest: spam, more spam, one from Gareth about the football, spam, something from Leo about his party, then one from Charlie – could they meet up soon? The music's welcome beat surged up, cleansing his mind, pushing out the fears of the barber shop. He started to feel more normal. One more ... what was this? Jack didn't recognize the address of the sender. He opened it. "I have something more for you," it began. "I thought you'd be interested, since you asked me so many questions. It's good to see a youngster interested in the mines." Who ...? Jim Peters! Quite a coincidence! What could *he* want? Jack felt a spasm of hope. Maybe help was at hand. "You were asking about the tourist who went missing down there. I've been doing a bit more research. That man–" A sense of foreboding crept over Jack. He read on.

You seemed interested in him. It seems this missing visitor was from the same family as the man that got the mines reopened later. Owen Tyack, he was called. He was a surveyor and mining engineer from your part of the world, visited the mines in Victorian times, got lost down there and never returned. Now that's the same name as the gentleman who reopened the mines later, John Tyack. Interesting, I thought.

Well, so much for that. This much he knew from the old newspaper cutting in the library. But there was more.

I don't know much more so far as proper history is concerned. There is a legend I turned up. I just thought you might be interested? The visitor didn't vanish for ever in the old mine but came back to the surface and made a new life. It was said that something happened to him while he was down there, that he saw something devilish and made a pact with it. According to the pact this Owen would get supernatural knowledge and unlimited wealth, and that it might not necessarily be in the shape of tin or copper, but in return he'd have to give his soul back to the demon when his time came. Legend says that when he died he passed on his knowledge to his son, that same John who started the Cornish Consolidated Tin Mines Ltd and reopened the mine in 1906. You see? The idea was that they weren't really searching for tin or copper, but some special, secret thing, or energy, that was the devil's part of the bargain. But something went wrong, the pact was broken. And since that first visit of the father – local legend calls it 'The

Nightmare' – the whole family has been cursed and none of them will prosper. And Owen Tyack took some sort of terrible secret to his grave with him.

That's it. Good luck. You can always drop me a line if you need help.

Jim P.

Jack finished reading. The music in the shop, loud though it was, receded and he was in his own mental bubble. The implications of the email seemed too far-reaching to digest. Was Jim Peters spinning him a tall tale? But Jack had never told him, nor anyone else in Cornwall, his surname. Dr Peters would never have known there was the possibility of any relationship. No; extreme, ludicrous, absurd as the legend was – so obviously just that, a myth – Jack knew at that moment that he had come across something vital, something that could help him make sense of everything that had been happening. He wandered out of the shop heedlessly, trainers forgotten. And strangely, it was not thought of pacts, demons or curses that stayed with him but those plaintive last words of Jim Peters. Because Jack knew that if anybody ever needed help, he did, and now.

⅄

The Tyacks' slab-like black Range Rover pulled up sharply in the 'Reserved' parking space outside the large and modern offices that stood back somewhat from the Amersham to Little Chalfont road. With her customary air of total assurance, Joanne Tyack stepped out, still in her track suit, and forged through the rotary doors as if they were another component in her gym routine. The sign above proclaimed to visitors *Geothermal Ltd: Renewable Energy Solutions*.

It was only three stories to the top, where her husband's MD's office was located, but Joanne always took the lift. That short elevator journey provided the opportunity every time for the same reflection: her brief and justifiably self-satisfied survey of their achievement in founding and developing their own business. It had been such an act of prescience! David was without question an excellent scientist, and his geological and surveying skills were essential to the success of the company. But without Joanne's drive and business skills Geothermal Ltd would never have existed at all, let alone developed to its current size and prominence in the energy field. Interest in renewable energy sources was just starting to take off, Joanne had seen the opportunity and persuaded her new husband to take the risk with her and sink a large part of family money in the venture. The timing had been perfect. Throughout the 90s the company had invested in and pioneered techniques for deriving power from deep, thermally potent rock strata, as well as wind and wave sources. Geothermal, an early entrant to the renewable energy market, had performed outstandingly well, all things considered, and under the joint directorship of the Tyacks had gone from strength to strength.

The lift doors opened on the third floor. Joanne found her husband in their shared director's office, staring at a monitor. He glanced up at her, smoothing back his hair. "Ah there you are. I was just about to give you another call." David Tyack looked harassed. "It's the Chilean contract – I need a signature from you today to keep things moving along."

Mrs Tyack came and stood behind him, resting her hands lightly on his shoulders. He tensed himself, unnerved by the contact, a possible harbinger of … what? Anger? Irritation? Even mild impatience, from Joanne, was unsettling enough. She said quietly, "There's no problem is there?"

"Oh no. We're quite definitely in there, but they're insisting we supply hydrothermal reheating as part of the whole package, at no extra cost." He swivelled in his chair to face his wife, looking up into her eyes with an imperfectly steady stare. "I think we should."

"David. You know the rules about margins on projects now. It was signed off just on the wire. There isn't the scope for further concession without knocking a hole in the P&L and I won't have that at this stage."

"Joanne, please. We need the Chileans. That's point one – and they won't play ball unless we give a bit here. It's going to be a great foothold into South America, and what could be more important? Point two: the hydrothermal reheat technology is very new. This is going to be our first commercial application of it. They're actually asking us. What better opportunity to showcase all the investment we've been doing than here?"

Mrs Tyack had been frowning for some minutes. The frown intensified. "That's fine, they can have it, of course.

But they pay for it. Nobody else has this technology, we *do not* undervalue it by just giving it away. I've told you before David, we cannot just give product away and cut our margins in this way." Her tone became faintly more concessionary. "I know all the work you've put into this system. Let's make sure we reflect that in the terms of the deal, yes?"

Regarding the matter as closed, she went over to the coffee machine, inserted a cartridge and dispensed a coffee for herself. David Tyack sat staring into the space where she had been standing, reluctant to let the matter rest there, wanting to say more. He found himself thinking back to the old Joanne, a Joanne who was tough at times, yes, ruthlessly practical when necessary, but who yet had a warmth and playfulness that seemed to have gone now. Gone since when? Her illness? Certainly she'd never been quite the same since. Nor had their marriage. And she kept her distance, emotionally, even physically; it was a business partnership and barely more. Inwardly he winced. They never even slept together any more. He wanted to raise all this now, tie it into his dispute with her over the contract question, have it out with her once and for all. Yet habit and respect for his wife's business acumen prevailed and he held his peace.

Silence reigned for several minutes as Joanne sipped her coffee imperturbably. Presently she spoke. "What else?"

Her husband knew exactly what she was referring to. "Good. It's very good. I'll need to go down there in the next couple of weeks, sort some odds and ends out. But progress is good, considering how far we've had to come. You know," and he leaned back in his chair while narrowing his eyes and putting together his fingertips in a sage-like pose, "once we get this off the ground it's going to make hydrothermal reheating look like ploughing a field with horses."

His wife's frosty manner had rapidly transformed itself into a look of approval. Even so, her words were measured. "Well we're not there yet. It's certainly too early to celebrate, you know that. What about the triggering unit?"

David Tyack became hesitant again. "There are still problems there, it's true. But nothing we can't deal with." He looked down. There was nothing, no subterfuge, not the merest hint of misrepresentation, that Joanne couldn't see through. And not only with him; none of the Geothermal workers was safe from her probing inquiries and unerring ability to detect a deception, no matter how minor. He saw she was staring at him intently and collected himself. "If we can just sort out the trigger then we're home and dry with it. Believe me, Joanne, we're close, very close."

She looked sharply at him, seemed as if she were about to pursue the matter, then let it drop. "And what else?"

"Oh, nothing much. Well, one thing, possibly," he returned, uncomfortably. His wife raised an inquiring eyebrow. "It's Jack. You know how odd he's been since he came back from that Cornwall trip of his. Maybe it's connected with that – I don't know. Anyway, he's been asking about … *family history*. The ancestor."

He sensed her stiffening. After a pause she said, "I hope you didn't tell him anything?"

"No, not really. I just said, you know, he'd visited the mines once, had a bit of a fright down there when he got lost, and ended up with a quiet life as a vicar."

Joanne slammed down her coffee cup with frightening force. "You didn't tell him about the church?"

"No, I … I just said he lived out his life at Winslow – something like that."

For a moment she seemed about to explode. Then, containing herself, she simply gave her husband a smouldering glance and said icily, "Well, we'll just have to hope he doesn't go out there. Won't we?"

CHAPTER 13

In the Reptile House

Peregrinus was sitting at his desk, concentrating hard. He had found lodgings in a small apartment at the top of a peeling old Victorian terraced house in St Just, the faded relic of an earlier era, just affordable on his meagre earnings from the Woolfe Society. A fussing landlady lived below, but he kept to himself and gave her no trouble so she left him alone. Reading was one of his favourite leisure pursuits. After struggling with it for years, he had at last achieved the ability to focus his mind, and formidably so. Now he delighted in its exercise, turning to history (mostly of an industrial or technical kind), philosophy and occasionally poetry. He was at this moment applying himself to *Beyond Good and Evil*, racing through it with improbable speed, making copious notes. It was as if he were making up for lost time. In the corner of the room a battered old trunk stood half open. From it protruded various papers and old photographs. He had few possessions and liked to keep as many of them as possible in that one place: safe, secret, easily found. The shelves and cupboards in the small apartment were comparatively empty.

Although one part of Peregrinus's mind was immersed in his reading, another part was acutely alive to the world around him. He could, for example, if he wished hear the children in the local school playground on the other side of town: the songs, the games, the very words. A child fell and grazed her knee; Peregrinus heard her sobbing and he heard the actual footsteps of the teacher running to see what was the matter. Further afield, the seagulls cried to each other on the cliffs of Cape Cornwall; he heard those cries too, if he chose. Momentarily, he put down his pen and allowed the sounds of the wind soughing through the chimney of the old mines on the other side side of the bay to course through his mind, energizing him. Then, he could smell the bladderwrack on the beach through the open window – the wind must be blowing in his direction. He took up his pen and focussed again on his book. "With his strength of spiritual sight and insight the distance, and as it were the space, around man continually expands: his world grows deeper, ever new stars, ever new images and enigmas come into view," he read, and made a careful marginal note: *Not with O. He shrunk, the world closed in, despite it all.* Then he continued reading, devouring the pages at an alarming rate.

When, a little later, Carole Banks pulled up outside in her little hatchback, it was no surprise to Peregrinus. First, he had been expecting her; second, he had heard her coming, heard her even when she was two miles away. He knew the sound of her car (each one was entirely different). Nothing escaped him. He continued reading, waiting for the doorbell. Instead, he heard voices; Carole had obviously run into his landlady, Mrs Frisbee, who had let her in. He tuned in to their conversation.

"Yes, go on up, dear, he's in his room," Mrs Frisbee was saying.

"Thank you ...." The clatter of clumsy feet. "Oh, what happened to that lovely cyclamen, it was doing so well? Oh – and that rose?" Carole was keen on flowers and plants.

"Ah, yes, it's a shame, isn't it? All the house plants seem to be dying, I can't understand it. I used to have such green fingers, now I can't seem to keep a thing. I don't know what's happened!" Peregrinus smiled grimly to himself. What drivel these women talked! He returned to his book, and read: "That which evokes pity for this dangerous and beautiful cat 'woman' is that she appears to be more afflicted, more vulnerable, more in need of love and more condemned to disappointment than any animal." A grain of truth there, no doubt.

Then Carole was in the room with him, entering of her own accord through the open door. He anticipated her words correctly: "Wow, it's hot in here. You haven't got that stove on again have you? It's like a reptile house!"

He carried on reading for a few moments, then said, "You're late".

"I'm sorry. I got caught up with a few things." Her tone was genuinely apologetic, but she followed up with a more spirited, "Anyway, that's not much of a greeting!"

"Nor is 'it's like a reptile house'," he returned evenly. He closed the book precisely, shut his notebook and returned both these items to the trunk, shutting the lid before taking the weight of it to move it back against the wall. The muscles under his t shirt knotted and bunched as he did so, the tattoo on his forearm rippling with a seeming life of its own. Carole regarded the latter for a few moments, then fluttered the neck of her blouse pointedly.

"Honestly, it really is hot in here. Why don't we get out for a walk?"

"Cape Cornwall again?" He smiled, thinly.

"Anywhere! Just to get some air."

His gaze flickered to and fro, preoccupied, before settling on her again. Those eyes, with their intensely blue irises, for once seemed to be avoiding her. She never knew what to expect with Peregrinus, but she sensed a change. Setting aside her mission to get out, Carole instead went and sat on the bed. She realized that it was time to get it off her chest. She motioned to Peregrinus to sit beside her, to which he acquiesced with an inquiring look. She began earnestly, "Tell me, you don't have doubts, do you?"

He raised an eyebrow. "What sort of doubts?"

"Well, doubts about *us*."

"Of course not. Why?" He gave a nonchalant little laugh.

She sighed. Here they went again. But she couldn't let it rest. "You just don't seem … to *care*, that's all."

"Just trust me. There's nothing about this that isn't for the best. For," – he made the slightest of swallowing noises – "for *our* best."

"What do you mean, 'about this'? The best for what? You're avoiding the question!"

"Just trust me."

With a quick spasm she pushed him away and went over to the window, standing with her back to him, staring out at the street below. "How am I supposed to trust you when I don't even know anything about you? Every time I ask something, *anything*, about you, you put up a brick wall. You're so selfish … so *strange*." Her every attempt to get under his skin, to build up a picture of him, a three-dimensional portrait, failed miserably and met with the same stony silence, or curt response at best. So few clues to help her piece together the puzzle! Just odd hints of a dark and troubled past, or of turmoil, loneliness and conflict. Carole was the most self-sufficient of people; she didn't need more of that quality from someone else! She felt sure, though, he needed help, for all his apparent independence. She was certain she would somehow be able to heal him – if he would let her. She looked back at him. He looked almost crestfallen, hurt. Immediately she felt herself relent, and went again to sit by him on the bed. "I'm sorry. It's not just that at all."

"What, then?" he returned, a note of suspicion in his voice.

She considered. "It's the Society. I don't know what's got into them recently."

Peregrinus narrowed his eyes. "Why do you say that?"

She shrugged. "They've just *changed.* All of them. I can't really say. They've had a couple of meetings without me and that's not happened before. They don't discuss the Crown Mines any more, and you know how they used to go on about that so much. Morgana treats me like a stranger. It's as if they're all *distracted* by something. Surely you've noticed that too?"

Peregrinus remained seated on the bed, staring at the closed trunk, thoughtful. He'd had his suspicions, of course, as to what the Woolfe Society, that eccentric band of simple enthusiasts, might have come up against in its much-trumpeted group visit to the Crown Mines. Now he knew for sure, for this was confirmation. Keeping Carole out of that visit, *saving* her, was one small thing he could do, even if there was no long-term future between them. And he'd enjoyed their relationship, after all. Carole with her wider perspective, keener intelligence and heightened sensibility was always the one who was going to need more of an investment, more of his time. It had been a learning experience for him – and he was still learning. Yes, a small part of him would undeniably be sorry to go, even though his wider objective was achieved. Should he tell her now? He turned towards her.

Just at that point, there came a noise from the landing, the slightest of sounds, below the hearing threshold of the average ear. Quicker than a spider Peregrinus was at the door, arm extended. There was a little shriek and he dragged Mrs Frisbee into the room, watering can in hand, its contents slopping untidily over her apron. Letting her go, Peregrinus smiled politely. "Mrs Frisbee, is there anything wrong?"

"I don't know what you mean!" quavered the flustered landlady. "I was just watering these cyclamens on the landing here. Really, there's no need to go *pouncing* on people like that, Mr Peregrinus!"

"Well, I do apologize but as you know I'm a private sort of person and I get very nervous when I hear little sounds here and there, especially when I'm having a personal conversation. You see that, Mrs Frisbee?" His dry, respectful manner was almost comically at odds with his behaviour. The smile continued to play around his mouth, his eyes crinkling a little with what might have been enjoyment. "But don't let me keep you from your watering," he added. Mrs Frisbee straightened her apron in an attempt to recover her ruffled dignity, then self-consciously turned on her heel. He watched her shuffle off down the stairs until she was out of sight, and turned back to Carole. She, too, was smiling, in spite of herself. "You see what I mean?" she said. "You don't trust anybody. Even your harmless old landlady. Why are you so suspicious all the time? You never let up!"

He sat on the bed again, clasping his knees, back resting against the wall, and began speaking in measured tones. "It's been difficult for you, I know. You see, my childhood, the past – it was troubled, very troubled. I don't remember my parents, they died when I was young. I don't remember much at all. I had to – fend for myself, you might say. So it's not easy to talk about."

Carole came over and sat on the bed too, immediately engaged, sympathetic. "But you can tell me. You know I'll understand."

He nodded, his gaze flickering this way and that with the semblance of a hunted look. "So you see I never had a home life. The nearest thing I have to a home is round here." He made a sweeping gesture. "Cornwall, the whole area. But especially St Just. It's where I know I belong. So; I had to do all kinds of things when I was younger, just to make living, to keep independent."

Carole nodded, absorbed. "What kind of things?"

"All sorts." He gave a bitter little laugh. "I even worked in a circus, for a while. Anything I could get. I can't remember any of this very well. I've had a problem, with my memory. I was mugged, you see, and with a head injury – well, it's hard, hard to get back to normal. It's affected my recall. I needed help, I suppose. Eventually I joined the Society. It was everything I ever wanted – the mines, the support, the work. Being part of something. But I was still a mess. That's when I found you." He looked at her closely from under guarded lids.

Carole leaned closer and kissed him, caressing the lean, sinewy back. Then she rested her head on his chest. He had never been this open with her before. All would be well, she felt sure. Drowsy in the heat she let herself relax, listening to the steady pulse of his heart, and closed her eyes. When she opened them again they focused on the old trunk against the wall. Thoughts lazily drifted through her head. Did Peregrinus really have all his worldly goods in that thing? Something caught her eye, something trapped in the lid. She gazed across languidly. What was it? A piece of fabric, cream silk fabric with a distinctive blue pattern. It looked like ... a scarf, a ladies' silk scarf. She carried on looking at it, breathing regularly, while her thoughts slid away in a stomach-churning spiral. A scarf; another woman? With the sight of that little piece of fabric her new peace of mind melted away; she saw prefigured the fresh anxiety that lay ahead, and felt sick at the prospect. But Peregrinus's heartbeat continued strong and slow.

CHAPTER 14

Little Horwood

Beware the False *Magus. There is no profit to be had from those who would beguile with their false teachings. You will always meet them, yet their spirit is corrupt. They are not disciples of the True Path of Reason. Their teachings will disperse like mist at dawn and leave only division and hate, for their followers are all too easily seduced to the Path of Evil. Beware the False Magus: the Way of Truth does not lie there.*

"Ugh! That's a horrible thing!" Jack hefted the carving, a solid lump of lignum vitae, in his hand and turned it so the light threw its features into relief. The figure was undoubtedly ugly, with a bestial face, evil, slanting eyes and scythe-shaped horns, one of which had partially snapped off. It crouched as if to spring, its hunched back bearing the stubs of what looked like wings, taloned hands waving before it in a faintly ludicrous pose.

"What is it?" pursued Charlie. "Some sort of gargoyle?" But Jack continued to regard the ornament – if that was what it was – with quiet absorption, seemingly forgetting for a moment his surroundings. They were in a junk shop in the centre of the small market town of Winslow. Jack's motives for being there were, he had admitted to himself on the way over, divided. Of course, Charlie lived near Winslow, just a short cycle away, and yes, he wanted to meet up with her as she'd suggested. But there was also the chance (although chance was something he'd increasingly begun to doubt since Cornwall) of turning up something more about his shadowy ancestor. It was a long shot. Beyond confirming that Owen Tyack had a connection with the Winslow area, his father had been clearly evasive when Jack had questioned him. Hiding something? But what? Nothing – David Tyack had clammed up. But at least he had the clue of Winslow to follow. It was a relatively simple train journey, with his bike, from Amersham to Aylesbury, then the cycle out here: a welcome opportunity to burn off restless energy, try and settle himself.

What had drawn him into the junk shop he couldn't say, but Charlie didn't seem to mind. She was a pretty, blonde-haired girl with a hint of the Nordic in her appearance. Old junk and antiques were decidedly not her thing – she was more interested in fashion. But she was easy going and happy to have met up, happy to indulge Jack's whims.

A female voice close behind them said quietly, "Lovely thing isn't it? Part of a set, you see." The assistant had silently come up and was gesturing to a small group of similar such carvings, all equally hideous, clustered on the shelf before them.

"What is it?" asked Charlie again, pulling a face.

The assistant pursed her lips and smiled slightly. "I'd say," she replied with unexpected precision, "that is a carving of a medieval fire demon."

Jack looked across at her for the first time. "And what's that?"

"Oh, a relatively powerful malign spirit, conjured up by a magus to perform some sort of task. Destroying an enemy, for instance." Her eyes gleamed.

Jack swallowed. "You seem to know a lot about it."

"Oh, just a hobby." The woman looked back at the shelf. "They've been here for years. Cleared out of someone's house I suppose. Strange but nobody seems to want them."

Charlie, who did not think it strange at all, took the opportunity to drift off to look at some dusty paintings further back. Jack put the figure down quickly and surveyed the interior of the shop. It was a claustrophobic old place, junk piled high everywhere – old chairs, cabinets full of medallions, cheap jewellery and pointless porcelain stuff, carpets all rucked up on the floor, bookcases, brass things on the walls, ancient prints, maps and all sorts. Not much liking the look of the assistant, he gave a fleeting smile and slid past her to join Charlie, who seemed to have vanished.

To the rear of the shop was a doorway leading to a small, dingy room. Dim light came from an antique brass desk lamp that had been precariously placed on a stool. And there was

Charlie, flicking through a loosely bound book about 1950s fashions. She smiled at Jack when he appeared. "Look at this. I love the 'fifties. Take a look at these dresses, aren't they cool?" Jack joined her and gave the book a superficial glance. "Yeah. Charlie I wanted to ask you–"

"And these shoes – can you believe people wore this stuff? I'd love to study fashion."

"Yeah, Charlie I was wondering if–"

"Wow, and these hats!" Charlie, chewing rapidly on her gum in enthusiasm, had got quickly absorbed in the book. Jack watched her, and found himself thinking back to the library in St Just. The image of the blonde girl, browsing the books, floated into his mind.

Presently he himself drifted off, right to the back of the room. There was a corridor leading off from another doorway in the far corner. This corridor was unexpectedly long and its walls were lined with battered prints. As he looked along it, he noticed something seemed wrong with the perspective. The walls appeared to shimmer a little, and stretch. With a subtle yet at the same time dramatic reconfiguration, he found he now stood in a larger space. The high, Victorian ceiling sported ornate coving and weighty chandeliers; heavy velvet curtains of crimson red fell across tall windows and wing chairs in clusters of twos and threes filled the floor under yellow-shaded standard lamps. In these chairs, wasted figures lolled and gaped, some in dressing gowns, some in pyjamas, some in vague approximations of clothing from an earlier era. On the wall before Jack were clusters of old prints, some high, some low. A nurse came towards him, stared through him, and reached up to replace one of the pictures. She half turned back to him and the vision dissolved. He was in the narrow, dingy corridor again, colder now, staring at a print that occupied precisely the same position as that the nurse had replaced. He looked around. Nothing else had changed.

Shaken by the vision, Jack reached up and took the picture down to see it the better. The sepia photograph showed three men standing in front of a church, the vicar with his collar flanked by a waist-coated workman with watch chain and flat cap, and a mild, aristocratic-looking type in tweeds. Written across the bottom of the picture in a copperplate hand were the words: "St Nicholas, Little Horwood April 1900". Jack tilted the picture under one of the wall lights, to get a better view. There was something odd about it. He inspected the central figure more closely. The vicar looked old and bent, his face gaunt with its crooked smile scarcely concealing a deeper, troubled look. The aristocrat was presumably the local landowner. The workman, small and wiry, fixed the camera with the intense stare typical of Victorian photographs.

Jack reflected. Under close questioning, his father had confirmed Jim Peters' story that Owen Tyack had indeed survived his experience of getting lost underground. After his miraculous return to the surface he had foregone his profession as a mining engineer and turned to religion in later life, ending his days quietly as a vicar in the Winslow area. Jack thought again of the library in St Just, the providential way the newspaper cutting had made itself known to him. Then of the librarian's words, *There's no such thing as coincidence.* And now this photograph, and the vision preceding it. Could it just be he was looking at his elusive ancestor?

Jack scrutinized once more the figure of the vicar. The man looked as if he had seen a ghost. But there was something else. The three men were standing on a gravel path leading up to the south porch of the church. A large yew tree was on one side, while on the other gravestones intruded into the frame like unwelcome guests. What was odd about it? The sun must have been low-ish and to the left. The three men were not quite in a line, facing the camera but slightly staggered. The gravestones and two flanking figures threw long, clearly defined shadows on the turf and path. But not the central figure. The vicar had no shadow; its absence had given that strange but initially indefinable sense of imbalance to the photograph.

Jack remembered a film he'd seen in which somebody had done something very bad and was in some way *in the shadow of death,* in other words they were meant to die and indeed were very close to it. Their body had sort of thinned out, so light could pass through it. He checked his phone, searching for the email from Jim Peters. And there it was. He read: *Something happened to him while he was down there, he saw something devilish and made a pact with it. In return he'd have to give his soul back to the demon when the time came.* But surely this was all going too far? There couldn't be any truth in such legends … this was 21st century England! But the photo, and the haunted and haggard features of the central figure seemed to tell their own story. Jack felt a distinct chill. He put the picture back on its hook with his mind made up about at least one thing: he needed to take a look at that church.

Warily, fearful of further visions, he went back along the corridor. Charlie was now at the front of the shop, staring out of the window at the sunlit market square. She turned around as she heard him approach. "*There* you are. Why don't we get out of here and into the sun, it's a nice day?"

"Yeah, you're right, let's get out." He glanced over at the counter, where the assistant was sitting on a tall stool, holding a book but watching them keenly. She might have been in her late thirties, or perhaps early forties. Or maybe younger – Jack was never very good at ages. At any rate, on closer inspection this woman somehow failed to fit with her surroundings. She was smartly dressed, where a tweedy old man might have seemed more appropriate, and wore a close-fitting summer dress of knee length. Her body was young, her figure athletic and strong, yet the face also did not fit, seeming older. Jack gazed at the woman, who stared back in her turn. The cold blue eyes were timeless and penetrating. Yes, it was the eyes, set in that pale, ivory skin: they did not fit the face.

On their way out they had to walk past this woman, who directed at them a distinctly unsympathetic smile. "Sure you don't want to buy it?" she asked Jack, with what sounded like a faint sneer in her tone. "The picture you were so interested in," she elaborated, in response to his vacant stare. How ...? CCTV? She'd been watching him all the time!

"No thanks," he returned, as neutrally as possible.

The woman nodded curtly. She had put her book down; his eye drawn to it, Jack saw it was *The Complete Plays and Poetical Works of Christopher Marlowe*, an old edition with much decoration on the leather casing. She began lovingly stroking one hand with the fingertips of the other, a movement that was somehow both sensual and menacing. After a pause she inquired, "Interested in local history are you? Old churches, that sort of thing?"

"No, not really."

The woman smiled again coldly, and carried on stroking her hand. He felt Charlie's hand grip his arm, trying to pull him away, out through the door. But before he could leave, the coiled spring inside the assistant that seemed waiting to release itself suddenly did. Her face twisted into a remarkable impersonation of the medieval fire demon's and her voice took on a gurgling, slightly incoherent note crammed with hate. "Because *I* say it's a nasty photo and it's none of your damned business! *So get out of this shop and get on your filthy bikes and get away from this town!*"

Needing no further encouragement, Jack and Charlie shot out of the junk shop as if propelled by rockets, grabbed their bikes and were speeding away from the place within thirty seconds. Away from the central square and around a bend in the road they stopped, breathless and still shaken by the force of the woman's invective. Charlie was the first to regain her breath: "My God, what was all that about? I've never seen anything like it!"

Jack looked at her carefully. "I don't know Charlie. At least, I'm not sure …" They were both shaken by the shocking outpouring of venom, so unexpected, so at odds with the peaceful circumstances of the place.

"What did you say to her Jack? There must have been something to set her off."

"I didn't say anything. Honestly, I've no idea. She's obviously got a problem of some sort. Look, do you know where Little Horwood is? It's not far from here, is it?"

"No, about two or three miles. Why?"

"Do you want to cycle out there, now? It's – a nice day," he added, a bit lamely.

Charlie looked surprised, and pouted. "All right, if you like. But what do you want to go there for? There's nothing much there you know."

He smiled apologetically. "I wanted to see the church."

She threw her head back and laughed, then caught his serious look and quickly stopped. "All right, I don't mind. Might be a decent ride. Let's go, if you want." In point of fact, had Jack wanted to see an exhibition of Victorian snuff boxes Charlie would have willingly gone along with him, but to that fact he was oblivious.

They set off, along the curving and narrow street with its high-sided old buildings. A flabby man on a bench was cramming his mouth with chips from a greasy bag. He paused to stare at them in bovine fashion. A couple of young parents were squabbling angrily on the corner of the street corner as they rode by, their baby crying vainly in its pram. But

Winslow had little residential sprawl, at least on this side of the town, and they were soon in the flat, open countryside, pedalling along a straight but rutted single-track road towards a cluster of houses in the middle distance. Charlie, who was very fit and enjoyed triathlon, set a challenging pace at which it seemed that the hamlet would be only a few minutes away. Yet after ten minutes' hard riding it appeared barely any nearer. Jack pulled in and took a swig of his water bottle.

"I thought I was fitter than this!" he gasped

She looked at him with a smirk. "It's not that, it's just you've come all the way from Aylesbury already. It's definitely this way. Not far at all."

After another ten minutes' cycling they came to the village of Mursley. Charlie stopped as they passed the sign, and looked confused. "This is wrong! How did we end up here?" She shook her head, disorientated. "Anyway, never mind, it's very close now, just the next village." They set off again. Mursley was a tiny place, little more than a couple of farm buildings and a green with a pond and a few cottages scattered around it. A group of small children played with their ball in the road ahead. As they got nearer, however, Jack saw that they were in fact teenagers, tall and gangling, hotly disputing something or other. He felt their eyes boring into him as they cycled past. He concentrated on the road ahead, frustrated with his fragile emotions. Charlie had pedalled on effortlessly and was pointing at a church tower that had appeared over a low hill. "That's it – only a few minutes now!" The road coiled up a deceptively steep rise, giving a view of the wide plain to their right which stretched away seemingly indefinitely, peppered with more church towers, chimney pots and clusters of trees. It was a beautiful prospect, yet with a certain desolate feel to it. There was a slight haze in the air; the sun had a watery, autumnal quality. The whole of the Aylesbury plain was like another world, a land that time forgot, empty and strange. Things far seemed near, minor hills were not minor when you got to them, nothing was quite as it appeared.

The road curved abruptly and the whitewashed wall of a long and low thatched building appeared on the left, while a sign by the roadside proclaimed 'Little Horwood'. They pulled in. They were in front of a fine old pub, the *Shoulder of Mutton*, that rambled on and seemed to merge into farm buildings. Ahead of them, opposite the pub, rose a pleasant green mound on which stood the church, partly shielded by yews and other evergreens. Only glimpses of window tracery and roof could be seen through the heavy screen of shrubbery. A stone wall ran around the mound; steep steps led up to the gate. They left their bikes leaning against the wall – there seemed no point in locking them – and stood for a few moments, looking up at the green island. There was not a soul about and everything was quiet, apart from intermittent birdsong from the trees around the church. It was as if the church had been there first, and the tiny village had then grown up and clustered around it as an afterthought.

Charlie looked pleased. "So. Here we are. Shall we see if it's open? Might not be, you know," and she headed through the lych gate. Jack paused on the threshold, feeling a sense of foreboding. He suddenly had the urge to tell Charlie the truth about the whole business: the voices, the dreams, Cornwall, the Crown Mines ... But where would he start? It would just come out like rubbish, the ravings of an oddball. He felt so isolated. Suddenly he felt foolish for coming here at all; he would have liked to leave, but the need for knowledge drove him on. He followed Charlie.

The graveyard presented several uneven rows of jagged old tombstones, covered in moss for the most part, some almost obliterated by the ravages of age and weathering. The church itself was small and would have seemed homely and inviting were it not for the air of desolation and vague melancholy that hung over the whole place. Even close to, it was impossible to get a proper look at the entire building, obscured as it remained by the gnarled yew tree near the porch. The arch heads of the lancet windows of the chancel were jammed up against the eaves, indicating to the initiated that the roof had been lowered at some point. A St George flag fluttered from the tower serenely. Clearly, inescapably, this was the same place as in the photograph. It hadn't changed much, and the yew seemed to be conclusive. Which meant, taking into account the date of the photo's inscription ....

"It's open!" Charlie's voice broke in on his ruminations. Jack watched her disappear inside. Rather than immediately follow, he wandered around the graveyard. Randomly, he scrutinized the blurred inscriptions on the headstones for further clues. Most of them were well-nigh impossible to decipher. Something, perhaps moles, seemed to have churned the earth near one or two, although the piles seemed larger than a mole might make. Jack peered at the nearest tombstone, but could read nothing. He was about to turn to follow Charlie inside when he noticed three headstones in what seemed like a significant row. Approaching closer he saw that all were very weathered, being much overgrown with weeds and encrusted with moss. Something stirred in him, he felt cold; his stomach tightened. Looking at the eroded surface of the nearest he could just make out the words:

Owen Tyack 1840–1900
In memoriam
God rest my sinful soul
Hold me in thy love
Redeem me from my Nightmare
Spare me Oh Lord

And underneath, rather more clearly and almost as if it had been etched later:

Thou wilt not leave us in the dust
Thou madest man, he knows not why
He thinks he was not made to die
And thou hast made him, thou art just

Below this gloomy inscription a skull had been chiselled, from the mouth and eye sockets of which coiled and intertwined what appeared to be snakes.

"*Nightmare. My nightmare.* And he died in 1900," muttered Jack, and felt surprised to hear his voice, as if it were that of someone else. He stared at the tomb in silence, feeling overwhelmed by the striking and gruesome image, the stark force of the words and the spirit of fear they seemed to breathe. So here it was: the grave of Owen Tyack. He half expected to hear the sibilant whisper in his head, resolving itself into that chilling message first heard in the Crown Mines. But there was nothing. Only the desultory flurries of birdsong broke the silence. After some moments of communion with this most direct physical connection yet with his ancestor, Jack roused himself and turned his attention to the adjacent tombstones. The nearest was so decayed as to be largely illegible; but the word "Tyack" could nevertheless be discerned. The remaining one was evidently not so old, and bore the following testament:

John Tyack 1874–1914
Who died for his country in the Great War
Rest in peace
In the sweat of thy face shalt thou eat bread
Till thou return unto the ground
For dust thou art
And unto dust shalt thou return

Jack returned his gaze to the first tombstone, and continued to stare at it in silence. Proof, then, that Owen Tyack had indeed not perished underground. Here, too, was the son, the man behind the reopening of the Crown Mines, laid beside him. The man who searched, searched for something underground. And what was that thing? *Some new form of energy* … He felt almost drowned in sorrow by what he had seen, although he could not say why.

Presently he tore himself away and entered the porch of the church. The massive oak door sported elaborate hinges that fanned out in fantastic serpentine patterns, terminating in strange little dragon heads. He paused to listen. Were those voices he could hear coming from inside? Pushing open the door with some effort he found the interior dimly lit, musty and damp, much like any other local parish church. As his eyes grew accustomed to the light he discerned crude, canopied tombs set in the wall opposite the door, each bearing stone effigies whose hands were set in attitudes of prayer. A brass lectern glimmered near the chancel, its eagle's wings spread wide. Jack sniffed, aware of another smell, cloying and sweet, behind that of the damp. In the aisle to his right stood Charlie, staring at the north wall on which were the faded remains of a large painting. At her side was a scruffy little youth, his hair all tufted up in clumps, hands gesturing with rigid, awkward fingers at the painting, head on one side. He seemed to be in the middle of delivering a lecture, speaking in a loud, deliberate but halting voice:

"You see the different *layers* showing different *subjects* … they's from the 13th century on." Jack sidled up beside them, while the youth continued, unheeding: "That big one there, him in the middle, he's the main sin, he's *Pride*. See? Look! And you see those others, six more, around it. There's *six* more, that's ... *seven,* see. Deadly sins." He squeezed Charlie's arm in his enthusiasm and pointed to the top. "At the top there, that's *Gluttony*" – he pronounced it 'Glunny' – "he's drinking from a bowl offered by a, a ... *devil*, and below there's *Avrice*. See, he's got bags of money." Jack squinted up at the painting. Only faint tracery could be seen for the most part, but he could nevertheless make out the outlines of the huge figure of Pride, filling most of the wall, with the little pictures around it.

Charlie shot Jack a meaningful look, then turning to her self-appointed guide said, "Toby, this is my friend Jack." Toby, though, was entirely immersed in his subject and carried on regardless of the change in his audience. "You look at the bottom – carefully! See another there? That's *Lust*." Jack looked and saw two crude figures, man and woman, clasped in an awkward embrace while a shadowy third figure with tail and horns hovered over them, seemingly egging them on. The youth Toby went through the others with an obsessive thoroughness, rehearsing the descriptions with great care and satisfaction. "There on the right, that's *Envy* and there it says on that scroll '*is full of Envie*', see? And Envy has teeth–" For the first time, he looked over at Jack, giving him a friendly smile. Apparently reassured that he was paying full attention, he continued: "And that's *Wrath*, and that devil there's getting the man to stab him. And *last* – last is *Sloth*. But you can't see them well, ah? Because the plaster's gone." He took a step back and nodded his head several times, very rapidly.

Charlie asked encouragingly, "So how do you know all this?" Toby smiled and nodded, the tufts of his hair waving back and forth like antennae. He reached in his pocket and drew out a sheet of paper, unfolding it before them. Charlie noticed the tremor in his hands. "He's here! See!" The paper bore an elaborate sketch showing a reconstruction of how the painting must have looked originally.

"Did you do this?"

The boy looked uncertain, moved as if to speak, then shook his head in the negative.

An awkward silence fell. Charlie persisted, "So – do you show lots of other people the picture too?"

Again the look of uncertainty clouded Toby's eyes, almost a wariness. He nodded.

Feeling that some strategy was needed to wind up the discussion, yet uncertain as to what, Charlie asked randomly, "Who did you show it to last time, then, before us?"

The effect of this question on their guide was extraordinary. He flinched like a whipped dog, shrinking back before them, shot them both a fearful glance from under low brows and scuttled off to a dark corner, from which they heard him muttering "Nah, nah, nah," over and over again obsessively.

Jack raised his eyebrows. "What was all that about?" he asked Charlie.

"I've no idea. He'd been so friendly. Came up to me as soon as I came in. Told me his name, then started telling me all about that." She nodded in the direction of the wall painting.

Jack glanced across at the figure of Toby, all bunched up in a pew, hands over his ears as if trying to keep something out. "Poor guy. Something's obviously frightened him."

They left him alone for the time being and spent the next few minutes looking around the church, squinting at tiny carvings, examining the battered stone effigies, cricking their necks back to gaze up at the wooden ribs of the barrel vaulting, like a giant windpipe above. Aside from the wall painting, however, there seemed to be little else striking on offer. Through a heavy crimson curtain was what looked like the vestry, but there was little within of interest, just a cassock on a peg, a few file binders, some tea making equipment. A locked door might have led off to a store room of some kind, but that was it. Jack, in any case, felt he had seen all that he needed to in the graveyard. He looked over at Charlie to find her staring at him intently. She'd be getting bored by all this; yes, they should leave. Anyway, the atmosphere of the place – maybe the smell – was starting to get to him. He motioned to go.

On their way out his attention was briefly caught by a large painting that was hanging to the left of the door. He was casting an eye over it when, as if in response to some unheard summons, Toby was once more at their side, as garrulous as before. "Eh! I know that one. That's Adam and Eve, that is. That's *from Italy*, that! Now see, that on the left is Adam, and on the right, that's Eve. That's an *angel* above, showing them out of the garden. It's called a *cherub*, that. It's from the bible, this, Adam and Eve. You look."

While Charlie slipped through the door, Jack stayed, and looked. It was difficult not to be struck by the tormented, harrowed expressions of the two people in the picture. There was something especially disturbing about them, particularly that of Eve, who had thrown back her head and seemed to be howling like an animal. Jack shuddered. All the pain in the world seemed to be in that face, the knowledge of something infinitely precious once possessed and now lost for ever. His eye lingered for a few moments more on those tortured forms, then he suddenly felt impatient to be out of there. He made to go, then half turned back, awkwardly, feeling he should say something to the youth. "Thank you," he muttered, "Thanks – Toby." And Toby simply smiled back, the clouds gone now, pleased to have been able to deliver his little lecture. "Bye, mate."

Outside it was late afternoon and the light was beginning to soften in the sky. "That was interesting," Charlie said as she threw her leg over the saddle of her bike, not without a trace of sarcasm in her tone. Jack donned his rucksack and came to stand beside her. She looked very pretty, with wisps of blonde hair blowing across her face, her mouth playful. He wished he could tell her everything. Perhaps he should. "Yeah, that guy was a fair old mine of information. I wonder where he got it all? I wonder if he just hangs around all day waiting for the odd visitor to drop by?"

Charlie waved a guide book she had picked up. "It's all in here. He must have memorized it. Here you are – take it. You seem interested in this stuff."

He pocketed the guide reluctantly. Suddenly he didn't want anything that would remind him of the place. The visit had been a success of sorts; he'd found the grave of Owen Tyack, and his son, proving – what? He found himself reflecting on the tombstone's inscription, those fear-filled words. Then there was the reference to "my Nightmare". Coincidence again? What nightmare? The bizarre legend Jim Peters had alluded to? What had *really* happened to Owen Tyack? He felt no nearer to knowing now than before he came. The dismal atmosphere clung to him like a shroud, leaving him cold and empty. He wanted to get away.

"Are you okay Jack?" Charlie was looking hard at him, concern written on her face.

He summoned a smile. "Yes, fine. Let's get going." He swung a leg over his bike and pedalled off. She continued to stare after him thoughtfully for a few moments, then followed. The church receded behind her, disappearing in the shadow of the old yews, which were themselves soon lost from sight as she rounded the bend in the road leading out of Little Horwood.

CHAPTER 15

The Missing Link

Five p.m.: the clinically clean head office of Geothermal Energy Solutions Ltd, Amersham, Buckinghamshire. David Tyack at his desk, cufflinks removed and sleeves rolled up, sifting through documents both electronic and paper, ready for an early departure for home and tea … but not able to do so yet, no, not for some time. Deals to close, plans to draft, contacts to be phoned – and then this wretched meeting. Yes, the meeting … He paused, mid-spreadsheet, and leaned back in his chair, eyes narrowing. What a damned nuisance the meeting was! Set up by Perez. Why had he let himself be manoeuvred into it? Another hour at least on top of an already busy day; ah, he'd never get away! He glanced at his watch. Why the devil was the man coming so late? Why, in fact, was he coming at all? A hoaxer, a time-waster, no doubt. A fraud! He let his gathering temper subside. Because, despite his scepticism, there was something else. This visitor of his had known something so special, so private – commercially speaking – that there *had* to be more to it than a mere hoax. How could the man have known that? Well, he would soon find out. He leaned forward again and busied himself with his spreadsheet.

⅄

In the town centre, never very quiet, the traffic was building to its rush-hour peak. A light rain was falling, dampening pavements and roads but not yet heavy enough to cleanse them. A town of great affluence, Amersham: smart boutiques, all those cafés, charity shops containing immaculate, highly priced luxury goods, cast out for better ones. The women, so smart, so stylish and chic with their hard faces and single-minded consumer missions. And their men, pretending to be 'street', pseudo-shabby. Shoppers teemed in and out of food stores, getting in something for dinner (healthy, of course), while bookshops and fashion boutiques prepared to shut up for the day, politely edging their remaining customers out into the drizzle.

Through these knots of people there moved lithely and aimlessly someone rather different, an outsider. His dress was inconspicuous enough – jeans, t-shirt and short mule jacket; he might have been one of those faux-dilapidated partners of the posh-set women. But he was not. He could not have been more different and would easily have betrayed himself, had anyone bothered to watch him for long enough, by his quick and restless roving movements, brisk and yet without purpose; like a stray dog, miles from home, will trot quickly along, not knowing where it is going but only where it has come from and that it would like to go back there if only it could.

The man slunk into a coffee shop. Unable to bear the queue and the clatter of the place he was soon outside again, moving on, circulating, re-circulating. His reflexes were keen, yet occasionally his endless motion would bring him into collision with one of the shoppers, who would be momentarily stilled by the fleeting sight of the dark leathery skin and the intense blue eyes, the close-cropped hair: an apparition that simply didn't belong.

The outsider finally left the inner circuit of his perambulations and took a route that brought him past the library, down to the leisure centre and then across and along the White Lion Road. There was suddenly a purpose to his movements.

⅄

The cleaner emptied the bin, said "goodnight" and respectfully withdrew. Six o'clock; the evening security guard would now be on duty. He would be able to let anyone up – anyone, that is, who had business to come up. David Tyack had intended to press on working until interrupted by his visitor's arrival but as the time drew nearer he felt his concentration wavering. He glanced out of the window. The rain was falling a little harder now, audible against the glass, and it had turned rather dark. He switched on the desk lamp. He tried to go back to his spreadsheet but his mind had lost all focus and, giving up, he returned to the window, disgruntled at his lack of mental clarity. As he watched the rain descend in coruscating sheets a strange feeling, totally new, started to take hold of him. There was a slow, spreading edginess, radiating outwards from his core, a sensation of energy, yes, but coupled with a certain trepidation, the awareness via some long-unused faculty of the nearness of … of ... He straightened up as tall as he could, as if seeking to reassert control of his own office space. The feeling was still there. Something was coming, it was on its way up now, coming for him. Somehow he knew that whomever it may be (and it could only be his visitor, after all), it was completely focused on him, him alone. That sensation was almost exhilarating.

For some reason David Tyack kept his back to the door, even though he knew it was slowly opening, without any knock or preliminary. He shut his eyes and inhaled slowly. There was an unusual odour, an earthy smell. Tobacco? Damp wood? Resin of some kind? This was absurd! He turned around to meet his visitor. The man looked ordinary enough, in his jeans and t-shirt and loose navvy's jacket, a canvas rucksack on his back. His body was wiry and supple-looking, not tall, the skin tanned and weathered. His hair was short and dark, growing from low over the brow, as if he was wearing a fur cap. A sculpted face with high cheekbones and thin delicate lips. Their eyes met. His were not dark as one might have expected but blue, vivid blue – as blue as Tyack's own. They had already, with animal quickness, taken in every detail of the office and now they stared with absolute, unwavering steadiness back at its occupant.

Each man remained still for a full minute while David Tyack felt his newly sharpened senses expanding, reaching out like antennae to every corner of the room. The other continued to stand there, alert yet not in any way challenging, indeed almost deferential in his manner. Eventually, with an effort, the businessman motioned to a chair across from his desk. His visitor gave a faint smile and sat down, carefully removing his rucksack and laying it down by his side. Who was this creature who had wandered in off the wet streets like a stray dog? Tyack fiddled slowly with his cufflink, and said finally, "So, you wanted to see me? I don't know your name, Mr …?" He held all the cards – the office, the business suit, the status – yet he nevertheless felt disadvantaged before his scruffy guest. The man inclined his head slightly and maintained an enigmatic smile. There was a strange combination of roughness and delicacy about him. He remained silent. David Tyack tried again. "So, what can I do for you, Mr …?" He wanted to add that he was a busy man, but suddenly felt too disempowered to do so.

"Peregrinus," replied the man in a low voice. In the darkening room the man's face, illuminated slightly from below by the light of the desk lamp, looked shadowy and hollow. "I know you, Mr Tyack," and he emphasized the name in a most curious way. What was that accent? West Country? Irish? Galway, maybe? He seemed in no hurry.

David Tyack tried to recover the initiative. "I think not. I've never seen you in my life."

"Oh, but I do," returned the other, "even though you don't know me. And I know your family."

"What! I don't think so!" Had the man come to threaten him?

"Not your child. Your *other* family."

"What do you mean?"

"Your ancestors, I know them. I *knew* them," he corrected himself, while narrowing his eyes and gazing at the rain outside. "Yes, I knew them. You might say I am an old family friend."

David Tyack now started to suspect his visitor was unhinged. "What are you saying, man?"

"Just this." Peregrinus turned back to stare at him again, not hostile, not challenging, but with a new expression that was almost imploring, almost of – what? Tyack considered him again, trying to size him up. How old was this man? Thirty? Forty? Could he be older? "Just this," he repeated, as if reading Tyack's thoughts in his face: "I'm a firm friend of your family. I have served you well, and I will serve you well again. And to prove it, I have something for you, something I know you need." Still looking at David Tyack, he reached down into his rucksack and, by touch alone, very carefully withdrew a book-shaped package, wrapped in layers of cloth. The man held it delicately, with an air of reverence, as if it were some holy article. Then he proffered it. "Here, take it. Please. Open it."

Spellbound, Tyack reached out, took the parcel and placed it in front of him on the desk. As if in a dream, he slowly removed the layers of cloth until there lay before him a leather-bound journal that looked very ancient. The cover was quite plain, dark brown and heavily pitted. He raised it on its spine and saw that the edges of the paper still bore faint traces of gilt. In its day it must have been a luxury item. "How old is this?" he asked slowly.

The other was watching him closely with his penetrating blue eyes. "Over one hundred years. Open it. You will see the dates inside."

Tyack let the journal fall open naturally at the centre. The pages were yellow, the paper plain and unruled, the copper-plate hand that filled each folio was close and regular. At the head of one recto sheet was a heading, "October 12th, 1899". A diary, then ….

With a sudden movement, the visitor whipped around in his chair, half on his feet, shoulders hunched, every fibre alert, poised, listening. "There's somebody at the door!" he hissed.

"It's nothing, nothing … only the cleaner. I promise you."

Slowly the visitor relaxed and returned his attention to David Tyack. "Go on," he said, "turn to the front."

Tyack now opened the book at the flyleaf. Inscribed with a flourish was another date, June 1899", and underneath it the words, "Being the diary of Owen Arthur Tyack." He looked up. After a long pause he said faintly, "How did you come by this?"

Peregrinus was now fixing him with an eager, almost radiant expression. "Not easily. But now I have it, safe, for you. Do you see?"

"I don't understand!"

"No, perhaps you can't. Or shouldn't try. I might explain ... but look through it again, sir." Tyack wrinkled his brow in amazement at this form of address. But he did as requested and started to leaf more systematically through the journal. As he did so, a slow expression of intense absorption spread over his face. He quickly became transfixed, hunching low over the book. The lamp threw its small arc of light across the desk. The strange visitor faced him, also hunched, watching, like some sinister counterpart. There was a striking symmetry in the two men's forms. A phone rang. David Tyack ignored it and continued scanning the yellowed pages. Presently he put the book to one side and breathed deeply.

"This is extraordinary. I can't quite believe it. Extraordinary."

Peregrinus watched him closely and with evident satisfaction. Then he said, "You see, Mr Tyack, I know a lot about you, and I know what your need is. I can help. I *must* help, in any way I can. But first – *what progress have you made?* You can tell me everything. How near are you to it, Mr Tyack, how near?" There was urgency in his low voice.

Tyack closed the book and leaned back in his chair. He was aware of his mind opening and clearing at last; he felt a sudden reckless confidence in this bizarre visitor. After all, he had been as good as his promise: he had brought something of immense value that would have a huge impact on his work. But it was more than that ... he somehow *knew* he could depend on him. An hour ago he had never set eyes on the man; now, rather than feeling disturbed, he felt a rapidly growing sense of trust. Pray God it was not misplaced!

Peregrinus had also settled back in his chair and was staring inscrutably at the MD of Geothermal Ltd, ready to listen. Tyack made up his mind. To the drum of rain on the window he began. "You already seem to know quite a bit about me and my work. How, I've no idea. But believe me, you can't even begin to understand the struggle it's been to get to where we are now. My company Geothermal – this place – was successful enough, yes, and I have to thank my wife as much as anybody for that. Oh, we worked hard there! Yes, the market was ready for renewables; yes, we had the right backgrounds, each of us in our own way, and we had enough capital to put in. Even so, we fought for every penny we made. The technology was new, there were many mistakes. But we came through. I remember the first year we showed a profit … God, the exhilaration of it! I had a family now, and could provide for my child very well. I'd achieved my dream; I was a self-made man!" He paused and smiled grimly at the memory. Peregrinus was regarding him with a look of sympathy. "Geothermal had made good," he continued, "hence, this–" and he made a sweeping gesture around the office, finishing with a finger extended at the world map on the wall. Geothermal installations were dotted around it with red markers. He looked at his visitor sharply, confidence returning at the recitation of his achievements, while the other smiled faintly in approval.

"I have the strangest feeling," continued David Tyack, "that you know the next steps. I don't know how that can be, since we have kept the strictest secrecy – And yet, this!" He tapped the diary and shook his head, his voice trailing off in renewed doubt. Then he glanced at Peregrinus again, as if for reassurance. Whatever his visitor's reaction, Tyack was for better or worse set on telling the whole story now. He felt a compelling need to communicate the sequence of events. "It was the summer holidays. I went down to see my mother in Cornwall. I was helping her clear out her attic. She was moving, you see, and had all kinds of stuff up there. There was a box, full of family papers, some of it no more than junk. But in that box were other things, documents that were *not* junk. They were old – went right back to my great grandfather, Owen." Peregrinus was watching him very intently indeed now. "Yes, there were lots of them, hundreds, all packed tightly in that box. I'm a mining engineer, you know, and I could see there were a lot of scientific and technical plans among them, detailed descriptions of mechanisms. They looked as if they might be part of some wider plan. At any rate, they seemed of historical interest, if nothing else."

The room was quite dark. Peregrinus's eyes were gleaming like hot embers in the weak light of the desk lamp, willing the other to continue. "Well, I could see there was something scientifically viable being set out, some of it by Owen himself, and some by his son John, my grandfather. The papers were dated and signed, you see. I wanted to look at the whole lot more closely, get a proper handle on it. My mother – well, she'd obviously looked through them … I'd asked her on that point – but I don't think she had the slightest idea what it was all about. Anyway, the point is that, apart from her, these papers had lain there for years and I don't believe anyone had so much as looked at them. I took the box away with me; they were more use to me than to her. When I got them back I went through them all carefully, with my wife Joanne. It was then that I realized we were looking at detailed descriptions of a *device,* something totally new: a fantastic, extraordinary, incredible device." He shook his head in fresh disbelief at the memory. "I'd never seen the like of it, but the more we looked the more it seemed genuine. This device, it was like Providence – it could be a perfect extension of our work at Geothermal! The plans and papers showed how to construct the ultimate green energy generator. The descriptions were detailed. Think of it! A machine that could tap into a vast supply of never-ending, natural energy and solve the world's energy needs. My great grandfather had started with a small prototype; the plans for this were fairly comprehensive, yet certain key details were unclear. But it seemed to me it was feasible, though neither I nor anyone I've ever known or heard of could ever have dreamed up the initial concept. Where he got that first, great insight I will never know … Incredible. Anyway, after Owen's death it seemed from the papers that his son, my grandfather, tried to take the project forward on a larger scale, but with as much secrecy as he could manage. You have to see that this was a ground-breaking concept, quite ahead of its time. Clearly it was passed down from Owen to John, to be kept secret, lest the plans should leak out and competitors get in on the act. Had that happened, the Geothermal commercial advantage would have been ruined.

Yet, there was another reason for secrecy. There was something in those plans, some ingredient …" Here he broke off and looked highly uncomfortable. He licked his lips and his gaze floated nervously around the room. "Let's say there was an element in the experiments and the design that would not have been acceptable to the world at large: not in 1900, not in 1920, not now. Secrecy was essential, or the work would have instantly been stopped and who knows what would have happened to my great grandfather and his son!"

Peregrinus was nodding rapidly, as if to say "I know, I know, and understand". Reassured, David Tyack continued his narrative. "It looks like my grandfather John dressed the whole thing up as a conventional mining venture. To get the depth needed to tap into the 'geothermal' – to use a crude term – energy needed he concentrated his efforts at an existing, though defunct, mine in Cornwall. This he opened up again, under the guise of renewed speculation for tin – even though few believed there was any left there. And so was born the *Cornish Consolidated Tin Mines Ltd*."

At this, Peregrinus started forward in his chair and murmured: "The Crown Mines at Botallack!"

Tyack gave him a wild look, and said slowly, "How could you possibly know that?"

The other said nothing, but only waited for his host to continue. "Yes – the Crown Mines. Something had happened there, earlier, with Owen … But, in any event, the Great War came before the device could be started, the mine was flooded and shut for good, and my poor grandfather was killed in the fighting, still a young man. And then, if my reading of history is correct, the whole business was forgotten for decades, until I came across that box."

"And so what did you do?" Peregrinus had drawn up his knees and was hugging them as if in suppressed excitement. His whole manner had become more animated, more tense, as the story unfolded.

"Well, I thought the plans could work. Joanne and I decided to form a secret subsidiary of Geothermal. We called it *Parathermal*. We assigned a small number of our top scientists, all bound to strict confidence about the whole thing. The business goal was to validate a small prototype and then, if the results were favourable, begin work on the full-sized device as soon as possible. The rewards, of course, if we could get the thing working, would in purely commercial terms be immense – wealth beyond anybody's wildest dreams. I used revenues from Geothermal to fund the project: the shareholders have never known. So: we had a cash influx, a team of top men on the job, plans to work to and a tremendous drive in our little team. The natural energy stream which the device harnessed was given a name by my great grandfather: he called it *Gaia energy*. And so we had a name for the proposed device: we called it a *Gaia Reactor*. Parathermal was to create the world's first fully functional example! There would inevitably be physical signs of the work, so I got the idea from my grandfather of covering it up as something else, in this case an ecological experiment in simple geothermal energy capture.

"I have the strangest feeling you already know much of this history. But you asked me where we had got to with the project now. Well: several years' hard work and huge sums have gone into it, all in strictest secrecy. The great challenge is in the harnessing and converting of the Gaia energy to a usable form: for that is, in essence, all the reactor is – a mechanism to achieve that transformation. The plans and notes gave enough clues to know where to locate the energy streams themselves, deep underground. Do you see?"

Peregrinus now appeared to be in a kind of trance, mesmerized by what he was hearing and beyond responding to simple questions. He was like a cat being stroked in its favourite spot. Seeing this, David Tyack, caught up in his own story and having thoroughly discarded any qualms about confiding it to his visitor, resumed. "We chose a location for the reactor where the Gaia energy stream was nearest to the surface, concealed and remote on the Aylesbury plain: the place where this momentous apparatus was to be constructed." He rose to his feet, and started pacing in sudden agitation. "We made good progress. But then, after so much work, we came across a major obstacle. We couldn't achieve a large enough initial reaction to sustain the wider process. Our small prototype worked well enough but, when scaled up in the final thing, all we got were brief impulses. Do you see? Essentially, we have not been able to produce a viable starting mechanism. Some crucial element was missing–" He stopped pacing, returned to the desk and, remaining standing, stared down at the diary. "And now you come to me, heaven knows from where, and give me this!" Again he leafed through its pages, disbelieving. "The diary of Owen Tyack, containing his final experiments, the missing details. In all probability the answer lies in here … But why? Who are you?"

Peregrinus looked up at him. "A friend. Oh, I'll serve you well, Mr Tyack. I know your family. I can help you – See! You have the diary, I've retrieved it for you, haven't I? Now you have it, keep it – it's yours! The reactor – you *can* do it. You *must* do it. *We* can do it, working together. Take me on; together we'll succeed. I don't ask for any reward. The work's enough." His blue eyes burned fiercely.

David Tyack looked from the small, wiry man to the diary and back again, seeming to consider. "Alright. You've already shown your worth, with this. This whole project is utterly secret, for all of us who work on it." His eyes narrowed. "But you know that. I won't ask how you found me, how you knew… I believe you, Peregrinus. I can't guess at your motives, but I believe you do want to help. If you had wanted to betray me, you would have done so already." Slowly, he stretched out his arm and clasped Peregrinus's hand. He could sense the energy of the smaller man flowing through his grip like a charge. Peregrinus maintained the clasp for a full minute, staring at his new employer with a look of mingled humility and satisfaction. Then, with a quick, lithe movement he shouldered his rucksack and turned as if to leave. Tyack was amazed at his speed. "Wait! Where shall I find you? How … where do we go from here?"

Without turning, the other said softly, "I'll find you. I'll come to you at the church, leave that to me." Then he half turned so David Tyack could see the strong profile and jaw. "Keep the diary. Learn its secrets, share them only with the ones you trust. We *shall* succeed." Then he was gone.

David Tyack walked across to the window. Prematurely darkened by the rain, the evening was closing in fast now. He gazed out at the street below. After just a few seconds, Peregrinus emerged from the building. Ignoring the downpour, he set off at a fast walk and crossed the road, dexterously darting between the traffic. Tyack watched his bobbing rucksack until it merged with the other pedestrians and he was out of sight. He turned back to his desk. The whole episode seemed impossible. But the battered diary and the lingering aroma of earth and smoke remained to testify to its reality.

CHAPTER 16

STEAM AND A SPY

The blood-red sun descended serenely to the horizon and was then swallowed by a bank of dark cloud that slowly advanced like a ravening wolf. It had been a beautiful day and now the late evening sky was streaked with crimson and purple in a dramatic finale. The sea spread out below, concealing its dark secrets beneath a burnished, gently rippling surface. Solitary gulls circled and called, alerted to the approaching storm. Perched high on the cliff, overlooking all, the engine house of Wheal Owles was silhouetted against the darkening canopy, its broken chimney gesturing inquiringly to the heavens, its outlines merging in deeper shadows. Wisps of steam drifted up into the night air, to be caught and dispersed by the lightest of breezes.

Wheal Owles was one of a very small number of mine buildings that had been substantially restored by the Woolfe

Society, on occasion admitting visitors to working displays of its antique machinery. There were, however, no visitors at this hour, although lights now burned in the engine house. Inside, the smell of warm oil permeated the humid atmosphere. The chapel-like interior, with its arched windows and high ceiling, was dominated by the limbs of the giant beam engine around which the building was constructed. Tonight, the engine was very much alive, as testified by the slow pulse of background heat and the occasional release of jets of steam from leaky glands here and there. To the perceptive eye, a certain emblem was visible in discreet locations around the building. Engraved on the scrolled terminus of a brass lever, for example, was a tiny depiction: a serpent with its tail in its mouth. Again, the door to the engine house bore a plate with the same icon etched onto it; and more were to be found in various places.

Underneath the beam stood a dozen members of the Society, each clad in dark blue serge overalls, clustered before the seemingly insignificant figure of Morgana Florence Trevose. Most of the regulars were there, with the notable exception of Carole Banks. On a signal from Morgana, two of them made their way over to the engine's controls. Working as if to a choreographed script, slowly at first, they began to manipulate its levers in sequence until the beam above gradually tilted down with a deep roar from underground, paused, and lifted. Outside, a black pool of water churned and thrashed in sympathy with the subterranean motion, its depths stirred by underground currents. The two operators continued their motions, with increasing speed, until presently they stepped back from their task and the levers continued to drop, click and swing with their own logic. The beam fell into a slow and steady rhythm, rocking back and forth majestically.

Now the members formed a standing arc under the beam while Morgana, her hair wild and a crazed look in her eye, dragged an evil-smelling vat of old engine oil out from under an iron stairway and into their midst. She stood back and watched the thick, black fluid slop back and forth and slowly settle. The sucking sound of the steam intake, following the steady, longer roar of the pump descending continued all the while as a backdrop. Morgana, her movements rigid and unnatural, fixed the group with a steely glance. "As above, so below," she intoned. The group responded raggedly: "As above, so below." The phrase was repeated in a chant of gathering momentum for some minutes, while they fixed their respective gazes on the vat before them. Eventually, they dropped into the same rhythm as the engine, producing a curious fugue that trickled out of the engine house, through open windows and door, and drifted away on the evening breeze.

Then they fell silent. Morgana was again speaking, addressing them all in a ringing tone:

In my end is my beginning.
In my creation is my destruction.
In my demise is my salvation.
Life is death and death is life.
As above, so below!

This enigmatic declaration was followed by the whole group dropping to their knees, in a gesture of submission as it seemed, glazed expressions on their faces. Behind the noise of the engine a strange sound filled the place: multiple squeaks and echoes, as if a hoard of bats was flitting around the rafters. But nothing could be seen. Outside, the first drops of rain stippled the windows.

Absorbed as the Society was in these proceedings, nobody noticed a slender form concealed in the shadows behind a sturdy column. Had anyone looked closely they would have picked out a young woman hovering fearfully, watching, her dark hair pulled tightly back into a pony tail, her dark red waterproof and navy jog bottoms blending easily enough with the maroon livery of the engine. Yet despite her obvious apprehension, her calm gaze took in every detail of the strange ceremony with clinical efficiency. Even though she was a very young woman, scarcely into her twenties, there was something capable about her that was beyond her years. Keeping one eye on the bizarre ritual unfolding before her, she reached in her pocket and slowly withdrew a yellow velvet bag tied with a green cord. From this she extracted a handful of little stones, polished and parti-coloured. Her hand closed around them, as if for reassurance, while she watched events with mounting astonishment.

The chanting had resumed. Morgana's voice rose distinctly above the others, "*As above, so below*", louder and louder. She momentarily hunched over, appearing to search for something in a pocket, found it, and held aloft in a gesture of triumph the recently extracted tooth of the Reverend

McDowell. With the words, "With this token I join the realms," she proceeded to cast the tooth into the vat. Then she stood back, joining the semi-circle of her companions who were standing again and continuing their recitation with increasing fervour. All the while they stared fixedly at the vat of oil in their midst. With characteristic fluidity of movement the young eavesdropper drew back into the shadows, her eyes widening at what came next. First, delicate tendrils of steam rose from the surface of the oil. This continued for some minutes, an apparently harmless simmering effect. Then it began to heave and boil in sluggish black blisters that, on bursting, released bigger gouts of steam until a dense vapour hovered above the vat, entirely obscuring it.

At this point the onlookers stopped chanting and stood back vacantly, before one-by-one dropping to their knees again. The beam slowed to a halt with a final hiss, leaving in place of its regular beat only the myriad sounds of squeaks and clicks from above. The cloud of vapour floated ominously in the midst of all; within it, was it just possible to discern some kind of face coalescing among the swirls, partly formed, with sagging features and a crude, down-turned mouth … or was this only in the fevered imagination of the spy? At any rate, Morgana seemed to quail for a moment, hanging back as if something inside her rebelled. She paused, hand cupped to her ear, listening hard to the bat-like twitterings. Then, with renewed confidence, she strode up to the cloud and, head tilted back, appeared to spend some moments in communion with it, speaking quietly, conversationally. It seemed almost as if she were giving some sort of instruction, and quite detailed at that. Then she nodded in conclusion, stepped back and watched what happened next. Abruptly, the cloud began to disperse in little gusts, as if whipped away by a sharp wind, although no door or window was open. Soon there was nothing left of it. The vat of oil emerged again, its surface at first still. Then, with an unpleasant sucking sound, it convulsively heaved up and over the sides of the vat, spreading in thick waves across the floor. These parted around the onlookers in a sluggish brown tide that finally flowed under the door and out of the building, leaving not a trace behind it. There was complete silence in the engine house save the noise of pattering rain at the windows and the rising wind.

As soon as the conjuration had gone the group was transformed back to the semblance, at any rate, of normality. Morgana tidied her hair and pinned its errant strands in place with a clip. Someone moved the empty vat out of the way and stowed it in a cupboard. Somebody else boiled a kettle. Tea was taken, desultory conversation broke out. It was all as if nothing had happened.

With no sign of imminent further activity, and the rest of the Society members distracted by their private conversations, the young spy stirred from her hiding place. Waiting until nobody seemed to be looking she quietly crept from pillar to pillar, over to the iron stairway and finally to the cover of the large tool cupboard just behind the main door. But in doing so, her trainer clipped a spanner which rattled and rang on its hook. It was an insignificant noise, masked by the chatter of the others, but Morgana seemed to have preternatural hearing and spun around in its direction, her face contorted in suspicion, eyes beadily staring from behind her glasses. She remained glaring at the tool cupboard for several minutes but, when no further movement was apparent, turned back to resume her conversation. Seeing this, the young woman seized her opportunity and slipped from her hiding place and through the adjacent half-open door, out of the humidity and oily stench and into the clean, cold and now turbulent night air. Within seconds she had melted away into the dark.

⅄

Twenty miles away, in the cramped attic study of a small terraced house in Penzance, James Peters PhD was putting the finishing touches to an email:

"Furthermore, the indoor beam lintel supports you have used are wholly inappropriate for an engine of this period and type and I strongly urge you to examine the original plans, from which you will see that the six inch oak beams are the only authentic materials that you should consider using."

He sat back in his chair and gave his keyboard finger a rest. If only he had learned to touch type when he was younger! He pushed his glasses up on his brow and wiped the sweat from his eyes. It was a warm evening and the study was uncomfortably hot. Dr Peters squinted at the screen, struggling to review the large font type, and then replaced his glasses again and continued jabbing at the keyboard:

"Finally, I must draw your attention to the deplorable condition of the winding gear at the Crown Mines. This superb–" he squinted again at the screen, then hit the delete key. "This magnificent apparatus has lain derelict for so long that it will soon be beyond restoration. Yet even now it would be well within the means of the Woolfe Society to return it to its pristine state, if only you would show some dedication and initiative in applying yourselves to the task."

He paused and reflected. Was that too strong? She was a volatile woman, this Morgana Trevose. He didn't want to get her back up and yet he must convey, in the strongest language he could muster, the importance and urgency of the issue. He looked down at the keyboard and started prodding at it again, slightly less vehemently than before. "Of course, I would be more than happy to assist ..." Here again he reflected on, and altered, the text, "to be of assistance in any capacity I can. As you are well aware, I have a particular expertise in the area of winding mechanisms as applied to the Cornish engine and I am sure we could profitably work together on this enterprise to achieve a satisfactory result in restoring this magnificent apparatus to its former glory."

He stopped and picked at his beard pensively. That would probably do – no point in labouring the matter. This was, after all, his tenth email to the Society on the subject of the winding gear. He signed off, "Regards, James W Peters" and pressed the "send" button.

CHAPTER 17

CHARDONNAY AND CANAPES

3pm: I spent *one hour, by the taper, with her. As always I did what I could; she can neither hear nor see me, I know, but it was enough to be with her. I stretched out my hands and laid them on her and – oh! so cold, so empty. I can work miracles but alas! – not here. So I weep inwardly, and there is no period to my mourning.*

"I'm thinking of starting a women's network." Jemima Buffham looked over her spectacles, which were not needed for ophthalmic purposes, at the small group around her and helped herself to more peanuts. The Tyacks' spacious living room reverberated with the low hum of conversation from several such groups. Soft wall lights illuminated the variety of profiles, the cashmere jackets, the expensive necklaces. "A dedicated forum for women to share and surmount a spectrum of issues that negatively impact them in the workplace."

It sounded as if she was reading from a script. "Of course," she added more naturally, "it could also be used for a whole *range* of wider social reasons. A virtual space devoted to the specific essence of femaleness." She sniffed and deftly trickled some peanuts into her mouth. "We all need that kind of support, don't you think?"

Cordelia Graham, who had a managerial role at Oxfam, was sceptical. "Jemima, you don't have anything to do with the workplace. Have you ever been in one?"

Jemima was hurt, and looked it. "That's unfair. You must know how much effort I put in at the boutique." She appealed to the others. "Just because a person works part time doesn't mean they don't do anything. It's such a tiresome misconception."

"Well, I'd join your network," put in Maddy, anxious to smooth things over. Pretty and elegant, wearing a short black dress, she was sitting with her long legs crossed and balancing her wine glass on the uppermost knee. "The opportunities for communication are just fantastic nowadays. I wonder how we all managed with just a phone and writing paper."

"I'm not so sure," returned Cordelia. "You can have too much communication, you know. Don't you think we've lost something? Personal space, personal time – time to be left alone for a while. You can't go anywhere, do anything without someone wanting some of your time – and usually getting it. I keep my mobile switched off as much as I can."

The others stared at her sceptically. "Why?" asked Jemima after a long pause.

"I told you," said Cordelia. "All this communication, it takes something away." She seemed unwilling to expand further, but simply nodded towards a couple sitting on the short sofa in the adjacent group. Both were staring at their mobiles, heedless of each other's presence, seemingly.

Jemima still looked slightly flustered at this attack on her creed. The fourth member of the group, Joanne Tyack, had been sitting back in her easy chair and listening dispassionately to the discussion, occasionally glancing at her nails, missing nothing but not deigning to contribute. She too wore a black dress, but she was slighter and smaller than Maddy, and less striking. Her beauty was of a reserved and slightly severe kind, with a hint of the androgynous about it. Jemima took off her glasses and sucked the end of one side-piece. She was used to their host's withdrawn moods. "Well Joanne, what do you think? Will you join my network?" Mrs Tyack's tight-lipped expression broke into an ironic half-smile. "Yes, Jemima, of course I will. As always, you are full of good ideas. Cordelia, you need a top up–" she caught her son's arm as he was passing. "Jack, please get Cordelia more of the Chardonnay. It's in the kitchen."

The Tyacks' social gatherings were always good value: excellent wines, all the 'right' people, their elegant show-house of a home as a backdrop. Mrs Tyack was in the habit of requiring Jack's presence, on condition of his doing service as wine waiter for some of the time. He didn't mind; he quite enjoyed the people-watching aspect and liked to be a part of it. Plus, the opportunity to dress up somehow gave him a bit of lift. Tonight, he was wearing his newish charcoal chinos, white shirt and a black v-neck sweater. Only his old trainers let him down. But he felt good, and had even caught his mother looking at him with what could well have been approval. He scanned the lounge. There must have been at least fifty people there tonight. At the fireplace his father was holding forth to another little group, demonstrating something or other with exaggerated gestures. As he made his way to the kitchen the image of Jim Peters, somehow transplanted into this unlikely environment, popped into Jack's head. He smiled to himself, picturing the eccentric figure inserted into one of the groups: the shorts, pony tail, straggling beard and painful shyness. He could almost hear the flat, nasal twang reciting some piece of micro-information about Cornish mining, and see the baffled faces of his audience. Which reminded him, his return email to that gentleman had remained unacknowledged. He would wait a little, then send a follow-up, try and find out more about the bizarre legend of the mines.

Returning to the lounge, Jack dutifully topped up Cordelia before circulating to check if anyone else needed a refill. His mother, meanwhile, was addressing Jemima. "So, where will you host your network?" Knowing, as they all knew, Jemima's hopeless ineptitude with anything electronic, it was impossible to avoid the conclusion that Joanne was baiting her friend. In the face of the other's blank stare, she persisted, "You've thought of a platform?" Her strange eyes were unwavering, the eyes of a cold and careless intelligence toying casually with its prey. She slightly arched an eyebrow. "A platform, for your network?"

Jemima, flustered, reached out spasmodically for her wine glass and promptly knocked it over. "Oh I'm so sorry Jo, how stupid of me, I'm so clumsy." Red wine flowed liberally over the table and dripped onto the carpet. Joanne, however, was quite unperturbed.

"It's quite all right, Jem. I'll deal with that." She leant over to mop up the wine with her serviette, her wrist hovering over the naked flame of a tea light as she did so. "Oh, watch your hand!" "Don't burn yourself!" Joanne looked surprised and slowly withdrew her arm, on which had appeared a charred, sooty patch where the flame had licked it. She gave a small smile, "Don't worry, I have a high pain threshold. Jem, you need a fresh glass. I'll be back in a moment."

Meanwhile, Jack had drifted over to the group around his father, feeling curious. He was, now, perpetually on the lookout for any kind of fragments that might illuminate aspects of the family history and, hence, the complex web of events around the Crown Mines. Or so he hoped, since the two seemed so clearly linked. His father's evasiveness had itself been suggestive but, in the light of Jack's visit to Little Horwood church, seemed conclusively to point to a deeper secret. Those tombs, with their anguished inscriptions, were no ordinary ones; he was willing to bet on that. What he needed was … an *ally* in all this. He thought of Charlie – would she drop by as he'd hoped? Then he stuffed the thought quickly to the back of his mind. There was no point in getting expectations up. Making sure his father didn't see him, Jack hovered on the fringes of the group, appearing to be immersed in his phone messages yet alert to the conversation. David Tyack had been talking about mining, of the modern kind – no surprises there. A half-dozen guests, not all of whom Jack recognized, clustered around, drinking beer and wine, responsive and full of good-nature toward their host. A fire crackled and spat in the hearth, as if feeding off the energy of the discussion. "Now, the Brazilians," David Tyack was saying, "have good, solid, knowledge of the field and they are focussed. We all know what's going on with the economy there; it's an absolute beast and the opportunities are phenomenal. The problem is their technology – it's stoneage. And that's where we can help, and get in there with the hydrothermal heat exchange package. Test it out for ourselves, and give something to the South Americans that will give them a real boost." He paused and took a generous sip of his scotch, proceeding to gesture with the glass as he continued, "It really is too good an opportunity to miss. And that's what I love about the field: it's global, you see, truly global and there are no boundaries." At that moment he swung around in an arc and, seeing Jack, briefly caught his eye. What was it Jack read there? An immediate withdrawal, a veil of some sort … distrust?

An elderly woman, rather grave-looking and known to be religious, interposed, "You'll have to forgive me, David, but what is this hydrothermal business? I'm not very technically minded, you see," she added, with a self-deprecating smile.

David Tyack returned his focus to the group, happy to oblige. "It's always a pleasure to explain, Cynthia. Renewable energy from water sources. Deep down, you see, there is tremendous heat locked away in the planet. This sometimes issues in the form of superheated geysers and hot gases. Of course, if that energy could be harnessed it would potentially be entirely carbon-neutral – a truly green energy source, there for the taking. Now, such sources have indeed been used for years, but always with inefficiencies that have offset the green potential. My company, Geothermal, has developed an entirely new version of it – much more efficient, much more environmentally friendly than previous systems. We're ready to test it on a full industrial scale now." The fire flared up, as if to underline his enthusiasm.

Cynthia nodded approvingly. "Well, it's about time something was done to save the planet or we're all for it, if you ask me. We can't go on as we are, or we'll all end up drowned, or burnt to a crisp. I don't know why they don't just build more wind farms."

"Not that simple," chimed in a bullish-looking man with a moustache, cravat and oiled-back hair. "Your average wind turbine produces five megawatts of energy. Compare that to a coal-fired power station – what's that David? – two-thousand megawatts? Think how many windmills you'd need! Not to mention the mess they make of the environment, spoiling the views."

"Exactly, Brian," responded David. "And that's where the hydrothermal heat exchanger comes in. It's far more effective at capturing natural energy than any other method tried so far."

"Are you going to patent it then?" asked Cynthia, looking vaguely interested.

"I should think David's taken care of that," put in the moustachioed man "–or rather, Joanne, eh?" He looked around, chuckling, and glanced back at David. "Not one to miss a business trick, your wife, is she?" Jack could only see the back of his father's head yet he could visualize his expression, introverted, inwardly pained, along with something less decipherable. But David Tyack said nothing, and his lack of response was taken by the group to imply assent. "But tell me, Cynthia," continued Brian, "do you seriously believe all the climate doom-mongers? Do you really think we're heading for apocalypse if we don't mend our environmental ways?"

Cynthia nodded emphatically. "That's right, apocalypse – a very good word for it. It says in the Book of Revelation, *And the fourth angel poured out his vial upon the sun; and power was given unto him to scorch men with fire. And men were scorched with great heat.* Global warming – that's how we'll finish up. Personally, I think it's too late" – she inclined her head with a faint smile in the direction of David Tyack – "your heat exchanger notwithstanding, David."

There was an awkward silence, customary when people start quoting religion or politics in social gatherings. Cynthia continued, unperturbed: "We had everything, we were provided for with everything we needed for life on this earth. And we've messed it all up, with our greed. It's there in Genesis – it was greed that made Eve eat the apple. Look what happened – we were expelled from Eden and condemned to labour, to dig the earth in our greed for profit from then until now."

"Oh, really, that's just a story," said a stockbroker-looking type, who'd been following Cynthia's little speech with increasing irritation. "Technology has given us untold riches, solved untold problems. I'm sorry Cynthia, but it's just plain wrong to blame everything on human acquisitiveness. It's driven us to triumph over the world's biggest problems."

"Well, even if it's just a story, it's a good allegory. I'm afraid I have no hope for humanity at all."

"I'm afraid I disagree too," their host countered. "Look at my field: mining, originally. We – I mean humans generally – have moved on from scraping around on the surface to the great Elizabethan coal mining achievements, to all the progress in Cornwall and the tin and copper mines there with those amazing undersea workings. Now we can sink bore holes five miles down to tap into thermal energy that's going to help solve the world's energy needs. In South America, for instance . . . ." This triggered a general discussion about South American economics that everyone chipped into with enthusiasm.

Jack followed the discussion as closely as he could, interest in, and a certain respect for, his parents' achievements competing in his mind with ever-increasing suspicions of his own. It was hard, thinking back, comparing, but the company had unquestionably been absorbing more and more of their time recently, since … when? The last year? Two? Longer? They spoke less about it to him, yet invested more and more time in it. Were all families like this? Jack stared into the fire. He thought not. Why, then, were *they* so different? He returned his gaze to his father, who was holding forth again with quick movements and expressive tone. *Redeem me from my Nightmare.* What did that mean? Suddenly fed up with it all, the bragging and the false bonhomie, he turned away and made for the kitchen again. Before he had got half way across the lounge, though, he was stopped by a hand on his shoulder. "Off for an anaesthetic are you?" He turned to find Richard Attlee, clad in his customary tweed sports jacket and pea-coloured checked shirt, a glass of red wine in one hand. "Hello Richard, good to see you here." Jack was acutely aware that he owed Attlee some follow up from his Cornish visit. Attlee, who was after all the progenitor of the trip, would have been the natural person for Jack to share his experiences with, yet since his return Jack had barely seen him and had, moreover, felt a curious reluctance to talk about the St Just mines with anyone at all.

True to form, Attlee didn't beat about the bush. "I'm glad you're here. I've been meaning to ask you about that trip of yours. You haven't told me much about it. How did you get on?"

Jack felt at a loss, helpless in trying to sum it up. He shrugged in what he hoped was a casual way. "It was fine. It's quite ... an interesting place down there."

But Attlee was not to be deflected. He lowered his voice and drew closer to Jack. "That all? Surely more than that? Did you get any *benefit* from it – as regards the little problem we spoke about? Any more of *them* – the drawings?"

"Er, no. They seem to have gone. Nothing since, really." There followed an awkward silence, Attlee waiting for more, Jack intent on holding out, without quite knowing why. Presently Attlee relented and with a shrewd look said, "Well we should talk more about it. Perhaps" – he glanced around – "when we've got a bit more privacy. I should like to hear some details." His voice resumed normal volume. "But you look well, in good spirits! And there's certainly a decent turnout at this do. Ah, here's Jasvinder."

A large lady with an expansive manner swept up to them with a waft of perfume. Jack knew Jasvinder, a neighbour from a few houses away. She was a history lecturer who read a lot and could more often than not give Attlee a good run for his money. "Greetings Jasvinder, Jack and I were just talking about Cornwall. Know it down there?"

"Oh, a little, *you know*." This meant that actually she was quite an expert.

"Well, it's an interesting place," resumed Attlee, "especially the part you went to Jack." Jack saw that he was simply returning to the same question via a different tack. "That's where the industrial revolution really got going, there and the Midlands. Did you see many old mine buildings?" Before Jack could answer he was pressing on with increasing enthusiasm. "They're littered all around the place down there. You can't walk for more than a mile before coming across one. You know, I've always thought those buildings are an amazing tribute to the ingenuity and sheer enterprise we have in this country– or used to have anyway. Those chimneys and old engine houses are like monuments, really."

Jasvinder had been listening thoughtfully. She tilted her head back slightly and scanned the ceiling, an aspect she normally adopted when about to contest some point. On this occasion, however, she appeared in agreement, "Yes, it's almost like a forgotten realm down there. Mind you, I think people are finally waking up to it and getting some conservation work done. And not before time either. Last time I was down there those monuments you were talking about, Richard, were crumbling away pretty quickly. But I think there's some society that's taking them on now, isn't that right?"

He nodded. "Yes indeed. The Woolfe Society. They do a lot of good work. I always think it's amazing just how little pride we have in our industrial heritage in this country. What happened in Cornwall about, oh, one hundred and fifty years ago … well, it was quite extraordinary."

Jack gave a hesitant smile, drawn in despite himself. "That's not what our history teacher says. I thought one hundred and fifty years ago Britain was exploiting its empire …." His voice trailed off, while Attlee's became even steelier.

"Yes? Exploiting its empire, and?"

"Well, we just sort of sponged off other countries." Jack felt defensive.

"That's one interpretation you could put on it," replied Richard Attlee acidly. "Just think about it. Let's go back a bit further, to 1700 say? Technology was basic, living standards, by and large, miserable – except for a tiny few. Technology hadn't really moved on for centuries. Then what happens?"

Jasvinder chimed in, not to be outdone: "Devon. Dartmouth to be precise, chap called Thomas Newcomen; just a self-taught ironmonger. Basically he invents a workable steam engine just from experiments in his garage. How do you explain that? It *was* extraordinary. All of a sudden this massive leap forward. There's coal, there are mineral resources beneath the surface, there's initiative, there's enterprise, there's creative genius – Britain's never looked back since! Nor has the world."

Attlee took it up again, warming further to his theme. "You've got to realise, Jack, this really was a British achievement. Something amazing happened in Cornwall. The invention, just from thin air almost," he gestured expansively, nearly driving his wineglass into Jasvinder's face in the process, "of a machine that was applied to all the mines in Cornwall to transform British industrial output. All those chimneys and mine engines that you see littered around the place down there testify to that incredible leap forward. From that moment we led the world in industrial advances."

"And what's so good to see, Jack," said Jasvinder, regarding the younger Tyack benevolently, little gusts of perfume wafting Jack's way with her every gesture, "is your parents continuing in the tradition, driving forward progress."

Jack had never quite seen it in that light before. His parents: the inheritors of a great tradition? It somehow seemed unlikely. He thought back to his father's little speech on the new heat-exchanger thing. Perhaps *they* would go down in the history books too? As pioneers, innovators, all from their company headquarters in Amersham.

When he tuned into the conversation again, only seconds later, it had already moved on. Richard Attlee was in his stride on another subject. "I agree with you Jasvinder, that we all need ideals, symbols if you like. And of course the whole concept of The Fall is, as you say, very powerful in the collective unconscious, to use Jung's term …."

Jasvinder moved to stem the tide. "You know, I read an interesting book the other day. It was claiming that the earth is a sort of *consciousness*."

"Ah, well that's not new, of course. It was put forward in the 1970s that the whole planet functions like a single organism, and regulates itself in much the same way. It was dubbed the 'Gaia Hypothesis' by someone or other."

It so happened that Jack had recently seen a TV programme on just this subject, and so felt qualified to intervene. "Oh, I've heard of that! Some people are saying that if we damage the environment past a certain point the planet will just die, and won't be able to regulate itself any more. Do you think it's true?"

"Well, here's a point Jack," returned Jasvinder. "A short story I read once had people drilling into the earth, as part of an experiment, you see – to find out what lay deep down, really deep. So they constructed a shaft and gradually sunk it further and further into the crust. Then they reached a strange sort of gooey substance, and started drilling into that too." She paused.

"So what happened then?" Neither Jack nor Richard Attlee knew this story, and Jasvinder relished her moment.

"It screamed. The earth screamed, just like it was a living thing."

"Oh, very good!" returned Attlee, chortling. "And that story may have a point."

Jack was intrigued. "You think the earth *is* alive?"

"Could be. People aren't good at thinking at the macro-level. They tend to be too dismissive. And in any case no-one has drilled really far down anyway. Oil wells are the deepest we've gone. There's one in the Gulf of Mexico, you know, that's ten kilometres down. But even that's only a tiny fraction into the earth. It's an interesting thought, what would happen if you really did go further. We don't *really* understand what's down there. Nobody does. Who knows?" He was fiddling with his index finger, the end of which was swathed in a grubby plaster, which he proceeded to remove. He held the finger up theatrically. "Look at this cut. I did that chopping onions last week. Went in deep, too." He shoved it in front of Jack's face. "Got a bit of infection in it, as a matter of fact. But you'll see now – well, it's healed right over." He inspected the finger closely.

"Er, so?" inquired Jasvinder, sardonically.

Attlee looked at her sharply. "Well, just suppose the earth responds in the same way. It's violated, assaulted – and so it moves to protect itself. We've got antibodies, for example, to tackle infection. So might the earth, Gaia."

"Oh, you're joking!"

"Okay, but it might be true. Who knows? I've got some time for that theory. Anyway," he turned to Jack, "you should ask your father. He should know as much about that as anybody, given his line. And speak of the devil..."

David Tyack was passing them, on the way to the kitchen no doubt. Attlee grabbed his arm. "David! You've been busy, I've hardly had chance to say hello!"

Tyack senior smiled to see his old friend. "Richard, good to see you. How are things?"

"Good, very good thank you. Just a moment – remember that article you were going to lend me? I could really do with it now, I'd like to get it sorted tomorrow. Do you mind?"

The other appeared to hesitate, but Attlee's manner was quite firm. Reluctantly he replied, "No of course not. It's in the study, I'm sure. Won't take me long to find it."

"Wonderful. I'll be back in a moment, you two." He set his glass on a walnut occasional table. "Don't let anyone pinch my wine!" And the two men retreated into the hall, leaving a thoughtful Jack and a bemused Jasvinder.

CHAPTER 18

A Fine and Private Place

Night. The deep countryside. A Buckinghamshire churchyard, private enough in the daytime, now utterly secluded in the late hours of the evening. A milky half-moon shone feebly through the branches of the old yew, its pale face a patient backdrop to the slow passing strands of cloud. The last, late light shining in the rooms above the *Barley Mow* public house winked out. In these rural villages there is little in the way of light or noise pollution; the quiet was profound.

Yet it was not total. In the graveyard something stirred, causing a faint, dry scraping sound, repeated often. Between the dark crescents of the tombstones was another upright shadow, a shadow that moved. The figure was absorbed in some kind of task. A discreet observer, hiding behind the thick trunk of the yew, would have seen something very odd indeed. Around one of the graves twinkled a circle of coloured fairy lights, gleaming faintly in the near-blackness and in strange contrast to the sombre surroundings. Between them they gave just enough light to illuminate the ground inside the ring they enclosed. Within the magic circle stood the slight figure of a girl, a mere shadow. The figure held a trowel and with it was slowly, painstakingly, very quietly removing the earth from an area in front of one of the tombstones.

Every so often the girl, fearful of being detected, paused, wiped her face with her sleeve, looked around her from within her hood, then set to her task again. Then she paused once more and set down her trowel, which fell and clattered against cold stone with a ring that startled some creature of the night that had been hiding in nearby shrubbery. It broke cover and scampered off with a loud cracking of twigs that made the girl freeze for a full minute. Reassured that no-one was there, the shadowy figure reached for some heavier implement than her trowel, just visible on the ground in the dim light, and thrust it with a convulsive effort into the hole she had made. A sharp splintering sound was followed by profound silence. Now the girl crouched down close to the earth. Her arm disappeared into the ground almost to its full length, carefully feeling, groping for something within. She worked entirely by touch; she dare not use her torch, for such a strong light might be noticed.

Eventually, the girl gave a little sigh of satisfaction and slowly drew out something roughly spherical. She quickly placed it in a black drawstring bag she had brought with her for the purpose, putting it carefully to one side. She then proceeded roughly to kick back the earth she had dug out of the grave. When it was filled completely she hastily gathered up the little lights one by one and placed them in her pocket, and they faded and died as she did so. Quickly gathering up the black bag she padded quietly out of the churchyard, leaving it to the foxes and the hedgehogs, and the hoot of the owl.

CHAPTER 19

FLOOR ONE-AND-A-HALF

Let us see if she succeeds where Jacob failed me. It is a simple enough task, surely? Then, when she has it, she is to bring the boy to me. No more delays – the time ripens.

Joanne Tyack stared evenly at herself in the bathroom mirror. The grey-irised orbs stared back, unblinking, framed by the blonde hair in its fetching bob, the petite nose, the scattering of faint freckles, the hard lines around the mouth, the finely sculpted chin. The smooth, tanned skin was perhaps just a little too bronzed. She looked at her wrist, running it under the tap. The flesh was blistered; it would no doubt require a bandage in due course. She adjusted her short black dress and returned down the main staircase to join the others in the lounge, where the party was still in full swing. As she crossed the hall the doorbell rang. A late guest? Joanne opened the door to find a young girl standing there, clutching a bottle of something, nicely wrapped. Jack's little friend – what was her name? Charlie, that was it. Charlie was herself rather dressed up, smiling through teeth that chattered with the cold, or nerves. "Oh hi, is Jack there? He said he'd be in and I might like to come over." Mrs Tyack surveyed the girl silently. Unnerved, Charlie gestured to her bottle, "I've got something for the party. If there is one ...?" She trailed off.

"I'm sorry but Jack isn't in tonight."

"Oh. I don't want to be rude but – could you just *check*, please? He did say he'd be here."

"No. I'm sorry Charlie but he's gone out."

The girl stood there for a while, at a loss, then slowly turned to go. "I see, I – must have made a mistake. Sorry to bother you." She hesitated a moment longer, then vanished into the night, a picture of dejection. Joanne watched her go, then quietly closed the door and re-joined her friends in the light and hum of the lounge.

David Tyack's study was on a split level of the house, 'floor one-and-a-half' as he was fond of calling it. Situated at the back, it was private enough and had become ever-more important as his workload had steadily increased. Richard Attlee reflected on that point as he followed his friend up the stairs. He had seen less and less of the man lately. Their shared pints in the pub and their intellectual discussions, often over a whisky in the study itself, had more or less ceased. He hadn't been in the room for over a year, indeed. It was a shame, and he said as much. But David's initial bonhomie seemed to have largely evaporated in the short walk from the lounge and he made no reply as he bent to unlock the door. It suddenly occurred to Attlee that he had not wanted to be followed up there. "What's this David? You keep it all locked up these days! What have you got in there – state secrets?"

"Oh, not really. Just business-in-confidence stuff, you know." He turned seriously to Attlee. "Work's really taken off. We've got a sizeable turnover now. I can't just leave commercial stuff lying around for …."

"For what?"

"Well, for anyone to see. You never know," returned the host, defensively. "Anyway, the report's in here somewhere." Tyack looked around him with a bewildered expression, as if for the first time. Attlee noticed how tired he looked, as though layers of accumulated stress had suddenly caught up with him. He finished fiddling with the lock and entered. Attlee made as if to follow but was astonished when, with lightning speed, his friend shut the door on him. "David! What on earth are you doing?"

Tyack's voice came from inside: "I won't be a moment. Please wait." Attlee listened in disbelief. *Please wait.* Good grief, he wasn't a customer at the bank! What in God's name was the man playing at? Suddenly he felt worried.

After a good five minutes, during which time Attlee felt increasingly foolish and frustrated in equal measure, the door of the study opened by the smallest possible amount to allow

David Tyack to pass through. He hurriedly locked it again behind him after he had done so, turning, with a guilty sort of air, to confront his friend. He seemed openly confused now, uncertain of himself, so different from the party animal of ten minutes ago. "I'm … afraid I can't find it for you now Richard. Let's, er, go back down and I'll drop it by." He ran his hands through his hair in a neurotic sort of way. "Yes, let's go back down."

"Are you alright, David?" But the other appeared only to bite his lip, motioning for Attlee to lead the way. Whatever had happened to him to bring about this change seemed related to the study in some way; but it was clearly no use Attlee probing further at this stage. In silence they descended the stairs and returned to the lounge.

While they had been gone, most of the members of the group earlier composed around the fire had drifted off to engage with other conversations, leaving only a couple of men who appeared to be quite detached from the rest of the party. They talked quietly to each other, seemingly wary of other guests in general, occasionally looking around guardedly. When David Tyack returned, looking distracted, he joined this pair, and was soon immersed in close conversation again. The three of them drew around the fire, leaning in, wrapped in detailed technical discussion. Presently, as if to wrap things up, Tyack said, "So Miguel, are we all set for later?"

Miguel, who gave no indication beyond his name of being Spanish, responded, "Certainly. We've prepared a presentation for after the party, just as you asked."

The third man, a small and weasel-like character who, although perfectly well dressed, somehow seemed a misfit in the present context, added, "If you'd care to wait until then, we can go through it all in more detail. This will be particularly for Joanne's benefit, yes?"

David Tyack sat back and cradled his whisky glass thoughtfully. After a short pause he nodded, as if to himself, and then looked up at the others with an ironic smile. "Okay, that sounds fine. All will be revealed." He smiled briefly to the others and then rose to circulate among his guests.

All this Jack observed from a distance, while Jasvinder lectured him, oblivious to his distractedness, on some detail of the Mogul Emperors. He was suspicious of everything now. What was that discussion about, he wondered? Who were those men? And now his mother was there, having lightly come up behind him without him realizing. Her slight, boyish figure in the chic black dress contrasted almost comically with the amorphous bulk of the history lecturer. She laid her hand lightly on Jack's neck, half affectionate, half cool and detached. He turned at its cold touch. "You seem to be boring Jack, Jasvinder. He has *such* a short attention span. But would you excuse us?" The grip tightened a little. "Jack, I'd like you to help me with something. It won't take you a minute." And with that Jack was hauled off to the servitude of the kitchen. A little later, he saw his parents in fervent discussion in a corner by themselves, his father gesturing in his typically decisive way, his mother listening intently, then responding with quiet precision.

Meanwhile, Jemima Buffham had detached herself from her usual group and sidled off in search of other candidates for her women's network. She found them in the adjacent reception room, where a small group was clustered in the comfortable alcove of a bay window, around a long, low table promisingly littered with various snacks and mixers. Mrs Goddard, the head of the local primary school, was in intense discussion with some other ladies about something or other. She broke off as she saw Jemima approaching. "Ah, hello Jemima, do join us. If Jenny moves up you can just squeeze in here," and she gave her neighbour on the couch a decisive shove. "So how's the world with you?"

Jemima, making sure she had her glasses on, for authority, surveyed the others. "I was wondering if anyone would be interested in joining my women's network. It'll be moderated by me, of course. The idea is that we'll have a virtual space for women to articulate all gender-specific issues. We can have discussion threads based on 'topics of the week', you see, that people can suggest. What do you think?"

"Well," replied Mrs Goddard laughing, "you could start with Jenny's séances, for example!"

Jemima's eyes boggled. "Séances? Do tell me more."

"We were just discussing it. Go on, Jenny, tell her and see what she thinks."

The prim-looking lady in her fifties next to Jemima looked bashful. "I wish I'd never mentioned it. It's nothing really." But the others were expectant. She fixed Jemima. "Do you believe in *spirits*?"

There was a pause while Jemima reflected. "I've never really thought about it. I suppose I don't. Though you never completely know about these things," she added sagely, thinking it wise to keep her options open.

Jenny took a draught of her gin and tonic and nodded. "I don't either really. It's just that where I live – that's in Winslow, by the way – there's a woman who runs séance classes. I know it sounds silly but I saw them advertised in the local rag and thought I might go along. Winslow's so very dull, I thought it might be a bit of a laugh, that's all."

She paused, for effect, waiting to be implored to continue – which indeed she was. "Have you been yet?" "What was it like?" "You *must* tell us!" trilled several voices at once.

"Yes, I have been, several times. The classes run weekly. As a matter of fact, there's one tonight that I'm missing. Mrs Priestly – that's the medium – has us all round a table and we have to link hands, in a special sort of way like this–" and she demonstrated by taking Jemima's hand and clasping it with the fingers interlocked. "There need to be at least six of us or the spirits won't come, or at least that what she tells us. The room's darkened, and we just have candles." All eyes were on Jenny now, who was enjoying her moment in the limelight. She quaffed more gin and tonic and helped herself to nuts. "Well, we join hands as I said and just concentrate on … nothing. The minds have to be empty, you see, because the spirits are very delicate and get sort of fended off if there are other thoughts going on. So we clear our minds and wait, and after a little while Mrs Priestly says 'is anyone there?'" She paused again.

A stately and statuesque woman who had been standing in the background listening asked imperiously "And do they come?"

Jenny looked embarrassed. "I'm not sure … I can't say. I mean, it's all a bit of fun really. Mrs Priestly says someone or other is there – it's never anyone I know – and we can ask it questions through her. She answers in a sort of strange voice, not her normal one."

"What sort of questions, and what sort of answers?" put in Mrs Goddard, feigning indifference but clearly interested despite herself.

"Oh, things like *Where did you live?* or *What did you do?* or maybe *How did you die?* (although Mrs P says that's a rude question to ask a spirit). And they reply something like *On the high street* or *I got a fever*." She halted, having run out of steam with her story.

A severe-looking small woman, known as a fierce empiricist, snorted with laughter "Is that it? Sounds like this Mrs Priestly is having a bit of a laugh. She doesn't charge you for the classes does she?" It was clear from the ensuing awkward silence that indeed she did charge.

To smooth things over, Mrs Goddard tried to open up the discussion. "Well, what do other people think? Are there such things as ghosts?"

Jemima, who felt out of her depth when called on to discuss anything beyond the realm of the seeable and touchable, fiddled with her glasses, wanting to contribute but unsure. "I don't know, really. There could be, nobody knows, do they?"

"The thing is," said Cordelia Graham, who had drifted over and caught the end of the story, "if you believe in ghosts then surely you have to believe in God, and if you believe in God you have to believe in the Devil. I've always been surprised at people who say they believe in the spirit world but don't seem to have any religious belief. And we all know, let's face it" – she looked around at the others benignly – "that there's no such thing as the Devil."

"I'm not sure that follows," said Mrs Goddard. "You could just have a spirit world on its own. Is there really the need for an all-powerful God to make it work? I've always thought that if supernatural things exist, they do so within the natural world. Rocks, stones, plants, the earth itself. But then I always was a great fan of Wordsworth ...."

This was all too much for Jemima Buffham, and a long way from her women's network. Fearing exposure at any moment, she scooped up her glasses and, making an enigmatic gesture with her free hand, teetered off to find less challenging discussions in which to insinuate herself. A quick backward glance showed that the debate was still in full flow; it would continue for a while yet.

⅄

The night had drawn on. Jack looked at his watch. It was one o'clock in the morning. He felt tired, tired of all the interactions, the opinions, the suspicions and the egos. And he had drunk too much. His mother never bothered to regulate him on that point, at least at the parties, and was happy for him to have what he liked. Now, like a wounded animal he drew to one side, perching himself on a sideboard in the shadows under the stairs, a bottle of lager in one hand. In those shadows he felt calmer; it was all the light that was bothering him, perhaps. Again he thought of Charlie, and suddenly felt upset, lonely. He'd made a mistake to invite her, to stick his neck out. He wouldn't mention it again. In any case, he was probably just looking for support, and that wasn't fair. There he sat, listening to the rise and fall of numerous conversations like surf rolling in on the beach.

Eventually, the first guests started to leave, with many expressions of gratitude to their hosts. David and Joanne, joined by their son, gathered in the hall to see everyone off. It had been a pleasant evening. Cynthia would redouble her efforts to understand the Book of Revelation; Mrs Goddard would give the séance a try, just for a laugh; Brian McKenzie would check the power output of a wind turbine, so he'd be sure of his ground next time; Jasvinder was going to re-read *The Day the World Screamed.* Richard Attlee and his wife were the last to leave. Ever the one for accurate fact, he was going to verify the exact date of the invention of the Newcomen engine. Yet for Attlee, what would otherwise have been a pleasant after-taste was tainted by what had happened in the study. It was nothing too specific, to be sure, and if he were to tell his wife about it, for example, it would sound trivial. Yet something very odd was going on in that room, he felt convinced. He turned to Joanne with an air of mock exasperation. "You realise that the time taken to say goodbye increases with the square of the number of people present? It's all the various interactions, you see. Of course there are adjustments to the formula depending on gender difference; women just can't seem to manage a crisp, brief valediction."

Joanne laughed, familiar with, and appreciating, his banter. "Goodbye Richard. Goodbye Miriam. It's been so nice to see you." She coolly kissed them; David Tyack shook Richard's hand a little awkwardly and kissed Miriam. On his way out Attlee called behind him, "Jack – don't forget we need a proper catch up. Come over soon and you can tell me all about that trip of yours." Then they were gone and the Tyacks were left alone in the hall, the house finally quiet.

They stood standing still like puppets for a moment, then David said, "Well, I'd say that was fairly successful, as these things go. What do you think, Jack?" But Jack was preoccupied with his own thoughts. The silence closed in on him, now they had all departed, and became his new enemy.

CHAPTER 20

Embassy from the Church

As the last guests were leaving the Tyacks' dinner party, twenty miles away in Winslow dark clouds were gathering. The last member of Mrs Priestly's séance class, held rather later than usual, had arrived at her residence just as the first spots of rain, visible in the fretful penumbra of light from a mock-Victorian lamppost, were falling in fat drops on the pavement. It was a Georgian terraced town-house, located on the central square, with a modest frontage but nevertheless three and-a-half stories and some depth to it. It was, therefore, considerably bigger than it looked from the outside.

The atmosphere was agreeable enough inside. Mrs Priestly closed the front door, shutting out the worsening weather, and led her "pupil" (as she liked to call them) to join the others in the dining room at the back of the house. Despite Jenny Stoner's absence, the requisite minimum number of participants were there already, sipping sherries or cups of tea and catching up on a week's worth of gossip. In the grate a cheerful fire burned. The room was dominated by a large, oval mahogany dining table; above there was even a chandelier, a relic of more prosperous days.

Despite being driven to it initially by simple financial necessity, Mrs Priestly, a plump woman of sixty with a florid face, enjoyed hosting her séance "classes". They had been an ingenious solution to both her money worries and the loneliness of the life of a widow who had depended for too long on an authoritarian husband. Alec had always disapproved of her dabbling in spiritualism; but now he wasn't there to complain anymore and she could get on with it unimpeded. Mind you, she reflected, he didn't seem to be anywhere else either, i.e. in the spirit world, which just went to show what rubbish it really was. Still, it was a harmless bit of fun and her students clearly enjoyed it, too.

Mrs Priestly rearranged the curtains, ensuring they were properly closed. You could hear the rain dappling the windows; it sounded as if it would be a wild night indeed and would get worse before it got better. She turned to the others and beamed hospitably. "Now then, shall we get down to business?" Turning to the most recent arrival, who was standing self-consciously with his back to the fire and silently surveying the others, she said deferentially, "Oh, look, you've still got your coat on, do let me take it," and she bustled into the hall with the mackintosh. The group was a diverse cross-section of Winslow society. Old and sallow, Barry Holdsworth was the landlord of the *George & Dragon*. He had run the pub together with his wife, and ever since her death had been trying to contact her obsessively using various mediums and spiritualist groups of which Mrs Priestly's classes represented the latest attempt. They had so far not paid off. Then there were the two ladies who owned the tearoom and who had been regulars from the start. Rumour in the town had it that they were lovers. Mrs Priestly had her suspicions. Then there was Petra Kelly, a feral-looking girl of about twenty-five, very thin and pale with multiple nose rings and "self-harm" written all over her. At any rate, there were suspicious cuts on her wrists – Mrs Priestly didn't miss any details like that. Petra's was a case like Barry's, but sadder: her boyfriend had died in a motorcycle crash last year and the poor girl, distraught with grief still, only seemed to live for some sort of concrete spiritual contact with him. Mrs Priestly felt a little bad about this girl, but still, if the classes comforted her then surely there was no harm? And it was, indeed, high time that her erstwhile boyfriend 'came through'. She would see to that. Nice Jenny Stoner, her newest pupil, would have been there but was at a dinner do somewhere or other and so had sent her husband instead. What was he called? – Philip? Goodness knows what he'd make of it – his face spoke of ill-concealed scepticism. Nevertheless, the Stoners had paid for six lessons, so Mrs Priestly wasn't going to argue.

The final member of the group tonight, the late arrival, was more unusual. A dark, slim and tallish man of uncertain age (he could have been anything from thirty-five to late forties), quite attractive really, he wore a dark suit under his raincoat. He had not attended a class before and muttered quietly how sorry he was to be late. For Mrs Priestly, this man was a great catch: he was none other than the vicar of St Nicholas' church, just up the road in Little Horwood, Patrick Trecarrow. Strange name – Cornish was it? That 'tre' prefix was from those parts, Mrs Priestly felt sure. It was very special to have a vicar along, and surely rather controversial from his point of view. She noticed he was not wearing his dog collar, perhaps in acknowledgement of that fact. His presence, she felt, conferred a sort of distinction on the gathering. To think, a man of the cloth, there in her séance!

The group settled into their chairs around the oval table and Mrs Priestly dimmed the chandelier lights. Then she lit the single church candle in the centre of the table. The fire now threw grotesque, dancing shadows of the guests on the walls behind, all weirdly distorted. The Reverend Trecarrow's looked positively obscene, with a grossly extended snout instead of a nose and thick, fat lips – like some primitive demon of old. Mrs Priestly sat down herself, with her back to the hearth, and proceeded to deal from a pack a single, large laminated card to all those present. Each card bore a symbol. For Mr Holdsworth, Fehu, the fulfilment of desire for wealth and material success. He knew the sign, and looked visibly cheered, sitting more upright in his chair with a new air of assertiveness. Wunjo, or Joy, for Petra Kelly – and how she needed it! The girl sat unmoved, staring vacantly into the fire. The tea room ladies got Laguz and Isa – ice and water, quite appropriate really. Hagalaz, or hail, was Philip Stoner's lot. He sat unmoved. But goodness! It sounded as if it were indeed hailing outside now, the light pattering of rain having turned to an insistent drumming. And what was this for the Reverend? Nauthiz: trouble, need and hardship to come to the individual by fell and indirect means. His eyes flickered up nervously when he saw the card, even without the knowledge of what it meant. When the cards were dealt, Mrs Priestly spoke again, to reassure her newest pupil, "Now Reverend, we've not had you here before," and here she gave from her seat an obsequious bow in his direction, "but it's very straightforward. Simply follow my instructions until the end of the séance, then I will give you some little explanation of what's been going on, and some little tips. Now, we lock hands like *this*, fingers intertwined. Make sure your card is facing up in front of you. The spirits sometimes like to communicate through the runic symbols, you see."

The group members were now locking hands, each with their neighbour. The fire burned lower; the shadows ceased their dancing and settled, tamed for the time being. Mrs Priestly closed her eyes and continued with the same air of didacticism. "And now it is very important – *very important* – that we all clear our minds, because we know that all those jumbled thoughts will spoil the concentration of energy and put the spirits off. So please *empty your minds now*." The room was completely quiet except for the continued drumming of the rain and occasional crackling of the fire. This was the bit Mrs Priestly enjoyed most. After a lengthy pause she started lightly agitating the table from underneath with her knee – not too much, just enough to create a slight vibration that caused the candle glass to rattle lightly and the flame to waver. "There's something here, I can feel it," she intoned. "Who is it? Who is there?" Then, in a much higher voice, "It's me, Trinny, I'm Trinny."

The group knew that at this point they could intervene and ask questions. Philip Stoner detected the obvious fakery but was content to play along. His wife had given strict instructions that he should not rock the boat. So he asked simply, "Who are you?"

"I'm Trinny" replied their host, in her falsetto voice. "I was a little girl from Winslow."

"What happened to you?" put in Barry, an improbable mixture of scepticism and credulity in his voice.

"I got drowned, it was very sad." Philip Stoner suppressed a snort. Good grief, was this the best that the woman could do? "I've got to go now, Mummy's calling, Mummy's calling, calling..." Mrs Priestly's voice trailed off and the room was quiet again. Then she did some more legwork under the table, this time rather more assertively, and feigned a little gasp. "Oh! Someone's here. Oh, Petra, it's Kevin, it's Kevin." Petra slowly stirred from her trance-like stupor and sat bolt upright, staring at Mrs P who continued in her own voice. "He can't speak directly, the vibrations are too weak, but you can ask him a question."

Petra's whole demeanour was reminiscent of some long disused piece of machinery slowly jerking into action. After a short pause, she quaveringly said, "Ask him if he still loves me."

There was a longer, awkward pause, during which Mrs Priestly's brain thrashed desperately. Perhaps this had been ill-advised. "He says he has to go, the vibrations are weak, but he's very happy but he misses you lots and he says you're not to miss him too much."

Philip Stoner stirred in his seat. This was outrageous! Jenny had told him all about Petra. How could the woman play on the poor girl's feelings in this scandalous way? It was too much.

"Going, going … he's gone," said Mrs Priestly, in fading tones. Petra looked distraught, then resigned. The room fell silent once more. Mrs Priestly kept her eyes shut and relaxed. That was rather tricky, but she'd pulled it off. Now for a nice long wait, to build more tension, then just one more.

The group continued holding hands, each staring variously at the runic symbols, the fire, the ceiling. The silence was just becoming oppressive when the self-styled medium spoke again. Philip Stoner noticed that only the whites of her eyes were showing through a little slit. "There's something coming. I can feel it." Her voice was not so high now, and quieter than previously. Another pause. "I can feel it coming ... it is nearly here." Her voice did indeed sound quite different, and began to tremble slightly. Then it rose. "Oh My Lord! It's coming! It's nearly here–" Barry Holdsworth looked up sharply. Petra's eyes widened. The tea-room ladies sat frozen. Reverend Trecarrow assumed an attitude of prayer. "Oh, Jesus, I think it's here." Suddenly Mrs Priestly's voice went down a full octave, becoming deep and sonorous and nothing like any of the variants she had yet produced. It was as if someone completely different spoke: "We are here. We are here now." The candle snuffed out; the fire surged up in a puff of sparks. Now everyone had their eyes fixed on Mrs Priestly. She sat still but appeared to be sobbing to herself.

Then the Reverend spoke quietly but with some authority: "Where are you from?" Silence, then the voice seemed ripped from the medium's body, rising to an inhuman shriek – "We are from the Church, *the Church*, THE CHURCH!!!"

Then all was confusion: the candle toppled over and the glass smashed, the curtains billowed and jerked, the chandelier swayed violently like a great pendulum and books flew from their shelves like missiles. The runic cards blew all over the room in a miniature tornado. No-one was now holding hands; the circle was broken but it was too late. At the centre of it all was the figure of the host, now writhing and twitching as if in the grip of a seizure, alternately sobbing and shrieking, her limbs thrashing. Between the sobs, a babble of voices of all timbres and tones escaped her mouth, while she clutched and clawed at her own throat, seeking air. The shocked guests instinctively sought shelter under the table.

Presently the cacophony subsided, there was a single crash, then utter silence. Trembling, Philip Stoner was the first to emerge, flicking on the light to illuminate the scene. The room was in chaos, as if a storm had swept through it. Mrs Priestly's chair had tipped back with her still in it and was on its back in the hearth – presumably the cause of the crashing noise. Her legs were stuck up in the air in an undignified “V”. Her arms covered her face as if fending something off. A vase of peonies on the mantelpiece had been swept off and, in a final grotesque touch, the flowers were strewn over her body as if in a gesture of commemoration. She was quite still.

CHAPTER 21

The Diary from Hell

I console myself that *the reign of Strife cannot endure for all time, and as the Master says, "The circle revolves, now by Love coming together into one arrangement, now again each carried apart by the hatred of Strife"—and so recurring again and again in their ceaseless dialectic.*

The small hours of the morning at the Tyack residence: Jack was in bed, visited with turbulent dreams of subterranean chambers, terrible screams from the bowels of the earth, foul smoking chimneys and suppurating wounds that would never heal. Briefly he hovered on the threshold of wakefulness, thought about Charlie then sunk back into deeper sleep again. On the bedside table his Cornish stones faintly glowed and faded in a pulsing rhythm.

In the basement of the house was a room which was once used for table-tennis; recently, however, it had been converted for another purpose. While Jack slept on, light streamed from under its locked door and voices could be heard from within.

"And here's a sample of it, just so we all know what we're talking about."

"All right Miguel, let's take it from there."

"We'll go through the last month, get Joanne up to speed."

"I hope so. I just hope this lives up to expectations–"

"No, really, this is the breakthrough. You won't be disappointed."

"Exactly. Then we come back to the schedule at the end. Is that okay with you Joanne?"

Two hours later, four people emerged, still in their evening wear: Joanne and David Tyack, the latter with a sheaf of papers and a book under his arm, a weasel-faced man still holding a three-quarters empty champagne flute, and Miguel Perez, who reached behind him to turn out the lights and close the door quietly behind him as he left. Inside the room, three empty glasses remained on a side-table as testimony to the culmination of what had been a very long evening.

⅄

The sound of a car's engine, followed by the receding crunch of its wheels on gravel, roused Jack from his feverish slumbers. Who was leaving at this time of night? The thought was slowly replaced by his awareness of a great thirst. After a while lying there, waiting vainly to see if he might miraculously get back to sleep, he flicked on the bedside lamp and found his glass empty. There was nothing for it but to get up. He padded out to the bathroom, along the broad landing softly lit by night-lights at floor level. The bare boards were covered with a wine-red runner down the middle. Lying on this runner, barely discernible in the weak light, was a dark, square object directly in his path. Now what was *that* doing there? Jack stooped to pick it up; the cover was soft leather, cool, malleable, strangely inviting. A notebook of some sort. Possessed of a sudden, unaccountable curiosity, he took the unexpected prize back to his room, thirst forgotten. There he shut the door and settled cross-legged on the bed, elbows on knees, the book before him. The bedside lamp threw its close arc of light; the shadows closed in, looming large. Now curiosity was rapidly supplanted by foreboding. He hesitated, gingerly weighting his find in his hand as if some harm might have already come from simply touching the thing. Yet this was silly – it was just an ordinary notebook, presumably something that his father (who liked the old-fashioned approach at times) had dropped.

Then it fell open and, like his father before him, he read on the flyleaf the inscription *Owen Arthur Tyack*. He caught his breath. The chain of causality seemed to close, his heart skipped a beat. It had to be; it always *was* going to be this. How could it be otherwise? He sat quite still, listening, half expecting to be surprised by someone or something, but the only sound in the room was the repeated call of some bird of the night from the garden. Cautiously, he began leafing. He saw yellowed pages crammed with numerous close lines of by-and-large neat italic script. As he progressed through he noticed that in some places the writing did, however, verge into the indecipherable, as if those passages were written under some pressure. Sometimes the script ran horizontally, sometimes it ran up the side of the pages vertically, framing sketches of what looked like mechanical components. Sometimes it broke out into chains of mathematical workings. Jack was reminded of a book in the library at school, reproducing the notebooks of Leonardo da Vinci. The similarities were striking – except that Leonardo's script was written backwards in a foreign language whereas this, for the most part, could be read.

But not with ease. There was page after page of turgid scientific comment and impenetrably cryptic statements, gathered under date headings in a single year, 1899, and a place name. That name was, predominantly, Little Horwood, though sometimes Winslow or other places were given. The text started immediately on the first page, giving the impression of continuity from a previous volume. Jack screwed up his face and read:

> *I can only repeat the process; I was not advised of this. It imparted that such would be the case in the early stages; but how can focussing power be achieved later on? Why was it incomplete? Ah, we have much labour here.*

What did it mean? Some sort of experiment was referred to, clearly. He flicked through more pages.

> *It will have its pound of flesh. These original sorts are too weak; look for purer forms, if necessary catalyse them; it warned of this, and the overcoming of it.*

Oh we work night and day. Christ have mercy on me – ah! I hardly dare blaspheme so – but at least I do not work alone. Alone – it would NOT be possible. Together … we may yet succeed.

…. and though the cost is so high he is right for without doubt it can be achieved despite everything. It can be started. Sustainable Natural Electromagnetism – All around – higher levels – variable magnitudes.

The evil that men do. Corruption is the fuel and the very spark. Each category, one by one, will be needed, and so we continue our search for the right sort. The time we have lost, and when I think of all that flying time has taken out of my life!

Many entries simply had one word under the date in question, *Crypt*. In some places were strange sketches of what at one moment looked like mechanical components, at another like chemical vessels. Further down the page, shockingly, there were drawings of what appeared to be body parts: isolated limbs, teeth, a kidney-like organ, a scalp. Occasionally, brownish stains almost obscured the words; but that did not seem to matter since the pages of script added up to so little. As he progressed further through the diary, Jack came to a point where the writing petered out for a while, to be replaced by a series of small sketches of what looked like distorted winged creatures, resembling nothing that could be seen in nature. Underneath was the single word *Diabolos*. Further drawings of twisted gargoyles made their appearance, rubbing shoulders with more scientific-looking sketches. The writing became increasingly scrawled, quite different from that of the neater, earlier entries. There then followed, on a page of its own, what appeared to be a quotation. At least, it was set out as such and so caught Jack's eye:

...leave this damned art,
This magic, that will charm thy soul to hell,
And quite bereave thee of salvation.
Though thou hast now offended like a man,
Do not persevere in it like a devil.

After this point, the entries changed character entirely, being exclusively short prose paragraphs, more in the way of a conventional diary:

> *November 2nd: there is a falling off in acuity. I feel my faculties diminishing and believe it is close. I have perhaps a week yet still I continue, I know not why. It is nearly over.*

There followed more about 'falling off' and then something only semi-legible that looked to Jack like *claiming what is His*. Then suddenly a clearer entry for November 14th:

> *My every step is followed, my each and every thought is known. It is very near now. Christ have mercy on me. This ever-present dread grows hourly. I see I have no shadow; I dissolve. It is all up with me. It will have its flesh, and more.*

November 15th: went to Barker's but no reprieve. That will be my last human contact. I cannot escape, it is with me always, no – it is IN me now. The terror grows, I walk in fear and dread. I cannot be alone but no-one, save P, will suffer my presence. I am uniquely damned. They all know I am condemned. God would I had never seen It. My final hours are on me – and yet, Jesus save me, I fear that this is only the beginning.

The diary ended at that point. There was just one final statement, set apart in a tremulous hand, undated:

Time runs away
The jaws of Hell are open to receive me.

Jack stopped reading, closed the book and set it down on the bed. He looked up at the window. Were those the first streaks of light filtering through the curtains? No; his clock said four a.m. It was the darkest hour; the room was quite chilly. How he hated the dark, the night, the cold. He continued to sit still, in the circle of light from his lamp, the diary lying there before him, looking so innocent. There was a saying that it was always darkest before dawn; and that would be a good two hours away yet. Was there, he wondered, any dawn for Owen Tyack, after that last entry? He thought not. But what there may have been instead, he didn't dare to contemplate.

CHAPTER 22

AMBER

T*he stones tell me that we are not the only ones in pursuit of this thing. A minor wraith has been released. We must trust that whatever entity has been summoned does not intervene. If only I had acted sooner! All I can do is wait. As ever, tea and tobacco will be the remedies for nervous exhaustion.*

Jack didn't go back to bed that night. He knew there wasn't any point. He remained sitting in front of the diary, pondering what he'd seen. After a while he must have briefly drifted into a light sleep, still in the same position; then he came to with a start. The diary was still there, open at a page on which tiny dark forms appeared to scamper and prance. It was just the light – but had he left it open like that? He honestly couldn't remember. As he became more wakeful he grew aware that he had a very bad headache, probably the result of so little sleep, too much to drink at the party and consequent dehydration. Light was just starting to filter in through the curtains, for real this time. He straightened his stiff limbs and made for the bathroom, to get his long-delayed drink and find something for that head.

Unbelievably, the bathroom medicine cabinet contained no painkillers at all. He wanted to scream. How could that be? The headache had a nasty, persistent feel that suggested it was not likely to clear up soon. Jack thought for a moment. The house was quite silent, his parents presumably being still asleep. He would go out to the garage in town; it was open all night and certainly sold drugs. Beyond that fact, though, he felt he needed to get out of the house, get some air. And his chances of getting back to sleep just now were in any case effectively zero.

Back in his bedroom he threw open the window to dispel the clammy atmosphere. As he pulled on his jeans the pages of the diary, still lying there open on the bed, fluttered and flicked over lazily in the light breeze, as if turned by an invisible hand. He looked at it, curious, fearful. He hadn't yet decided what to do with the diary. It must have been dropped by his father, surely, and soon he would be looking for it, wanting it back. But Jack hadn't finished with it yet. He'd hardly begun to address the implications of his father being in possession of the thing while yet professing to Jack, on being questioned by him days ago, only the vaguest knowledge of their ancestor. At some level, deeper than that of the rational mind, he felt a profound sense of the book's importance – both to the past and to the future. In this room, tonight, the strange events of Owen Tyack's former actions and their consequences for the future intersected, and their meeting point was that faded old journal. From its pages it was clear that a terrible fate of sorts had befallen the man. Perhaps that fate was a just retribution for his actions, whatever precisely they were, but be that as it may Jack knew the spirit of his ancestor did not sleep quietly. The statements in the diary, to be analysed in due course, taken together with Jack's earlier dream-drawings, The Voice, the whispered entreaty in the mine to be saved, saved: undoubtedly these were all connected. What had happened to Owen Tyack while he was lost in the Crown Mines? He reflected on Jim Peters' account of the legend of the Nightmare. An awful story was slowly emerging. Jack thought of the sketched fragments of body parts and shuddered. Richard Attlee had a little quotation he trotted out now and again, "Fear is pain arising from the anticipation of evil." Jack knew that the diary had taken him a step closer to evil – *real* evil, evil with its own, special abhorrent smell and taste.

Resisting for now the urge to leaf through the diary's pages once more, Jack placed it on the bedside table, scooped up a handful of loose change, quietly left the room and descended to the hall. The smells of alcohol and stale tobacco smoke mingled with those of women's perfume; ghosts of the departed dinner guests of last night. He opened the front door and went out into the silent street. Back in his bedroom, the leaves of the diary continued to rustle and flutter in the breeze from the open window. A page turned of itself, then settled, revealing a sprawling, full-page sketch of the strangest creature, a thing of scales, talons, wings and nameless body parts all cobbled together in a ghastly patchwork.

Outside it was still quite dark, the only light coming from infrequent sodium street lamps. In their orange arcs of light, fat spots of rain could be seen starting to fall. Jack looked up and down the road, inexplicably cautious. It was quite empty, except for a lone jogger, hooded against the elements. Some of these keep-fit types really were fanatics! Even his mother wouldn't be out running at this time. He set off on the short walk to the garage, turning his fleece collar up to keep the worst of the weather out. His sense of unease continued. It was not merely the headache; the street itself somehow felt alien, as if it were the *haunt* of something or other. He walked briskly. The jogger, a girl, passed him on the other side, splashing through the puddles that had started to form as the rain intensified.

It took ten minutes, threading his way through the equally deserted high street and across the old lower road past the leisure centre, for Jack to reach the garage. All the while he had an unaccountable sense of a presence of some sort, whether behind him, or above him, or hovering behind walls and hedges to his side he couldn't say. The blood was drumming in his ears when the garage hove into view, its lights twinkling through the gloom in friendly fashion. A van was on the forecourt, filling up. Inside, the shop was warm, like a haven. He could not understand how he had got so worked up! He paid for his painkillers, buying a can of cola at the same time, and swallowed them on the spot, praying for speedy relief. Reluctant to leave the shop's shelter, he then hovered by the door, sipping his drink thoughtfully and staring out at the sheets of rain sweeping slowly down the road. Undoubtedly, something felt wrong. Again he thought about the legend of the Tyack curse; now it seemed rather less absurd than it had before. And yet his family *had* prospered, hadn't it, by any reasonable standard? Then he thought of the diary again, waiting on his bedside table. Perhaps it would be a mistake to keep it?

Absently Jack checked his phone. No new messages. Why should there be, though, at this time? Yet it was strange he hadn't heard from Charlie. He tried to smother the rising sense of disappointment that she hadn't showed up during the party. But that was history now. Anyway, he should make a move. He stuffed the phone back in his jeans and walked out into the rain. On the other side of the road, some way down, was the same jogger again, running slowly toward him. She must be doing a circuit. Their paths would intersect, he saw. He crossed over and headed back towards the leisure centre, waiting for her to come up behind and pass him. But she did not. After a couple of minutes he quickly glanced over his shoulder and saw that the hooded figure had slowed to a walk and was following him at a short distance. Although in a thoroughly nervous frame of mind, he resisted the urge to quicken his pace as he turned up the narrow footpath that ran by the side of the public baths. Intuition told him that she had done so too, that she was closer… Suddenly he felt a vice-like grip on his arm and a voice, so close to his ear that he could feel the breath on his cheek, said urgently: "Jack, I need to speak to you. It's about Owen Tyack!"

⅄

The car was parked in a side road, under a street lamp. The rain drummed on the roof, loud in that small space. Still hooded, the girl sat at the wheel, staring ahead so that her face remained hidden. Why was he there with her, this complete stranger? She had followed him, known his name, pleaded with him so persuasively. But the single compelling reference to Owen Tyack had been the clincher for Jack. He *had* to know what she wanted. The girl pulled down her hood and turned to him. She was pretty – very pretty. Her dark hair was pulled back in a pony tail that curled over her shoulder and her large, almond-shaped brown eyes regarded him inquisitively but with a warm expression. Her whole face seemed alive with energy and animation. She looked as if she were in her late teens, perhaps early twenties at most. Something about her appearance resonated; did she remind him of someone, or had he perhaps seen her before somewhere?

The girl smoothed back a strand of damp hair that had fallen over her face. They stared at each other for a moment before she broke into a wide smile. "I know this is odd, but I had to talk to you, on your own. This seemed the best chance. I'm Amber." She spoke as if she already knew him.

Jack said, "Why did you follow me all that way to the garage? We could have talked outside my house – I saw you then."

She compressed her lips and shook her head emphatically. "No. I wanted to get you right away from there. Then I lost you for a bit" – she grinned – "and fortunately saw you at the petrol station. I knew you had to be around there somewhere."

"How do you know my name? And where I live? I mean … have you been following me?"

"Oh, Jack, don't ask now! I'll tell you everything, I promise. This is urgent, you must believe me. All I can say at the moment is that I need your help. It's about a certain ancestor of yours – I think you know who I mean." She leaned across and clutched his arm again. "We – that is, me and my father – know he's been trying to contact you. But it won't work, not like that it won't. My father needs to see you, to talk to you, because all this is about something much bigger, something really important."

Jack stared at her incredulously. "What are you talking about! What do you mean, 'trying to contact me'? Where … where is Owen Tyack now?" He could hardly believe he was asking the question.

"Oh, don't be silly Jack. Think! Don't you know?"

He rubbed his forehead, thoroughly confused, not knowing what to say. "Well, where is your father, then?"

"Cornwall, not far from Polzeath."

Jack let his head flop back against the seat and stared out into the rain, still cascading down from the sludgy dawn sky against the light of the street lamp. Cornwall. What did this girl know that he didn't? He felt a wave of relief, an overwhelming sense that answers, currently far out of his reach, lay with her, or through her, and her only. Could this be the ally he'd been praying for? "What do you want me to do?"

"Come with me. *Now.* Down to my father's. There isn't much time. I can explain on the way. Please come!" She looked at him imploringly.

There was a long pause while Jack thought. At that moment he realized how utterly miserable he was at home, how slender were the ties that held him there, how little he had to lose. He remembered another dictum of Attlee's, to the effect that the human brain is the most complex structure in the known universe. How presumptuous to try and sum it up in a simple logic of causes and effects! Sometimes, you had to go with the grain of events, and see where they took you. Slowly he said, "I'll need to get some things first."

She nodded rapidly. "I'll wait here. But you must promise me you'll come back."

He looked hard at her. "Can't you drive me – it's only round the corner?"

"No, no. Look, I'll drop you at the end of your road, wait for you there, yes?"

⅄

Five minutes later he was letting himself as quietly as he could back into the house. It was silent; his parents were obviously still in bed. That was unusual for such early risers, but then they'd had an unusually late night. His heart was beating fast

– not with anxiety, this time, but with excitement. How little had he expected this when he left for his painkillers only an hour ago! In his bedroom he shut the window and made to gather some things together. He must be mad, going with this girl on a whim ... When his bag was packed he turned, very deliberately, to the bedside table, where he had studiously avoided looking until now. There was the diary, lying open as he had left it. He looked more closely. The left-hand page bore several sketches, each apparently of mine buildings, unmistakable now with their stubby chimneys and gaunt architecture. Across the top of the page, in confirmation, he saw the words "Crown Mines" written in a neat hand and underlined. Why had he not noticed this before? Then his attention fixed on a small sketch in the margin, remarkably well drawn, showing a naked woman, head in hands, long hair curling over her shoulder, apparently weeping. The tears gathered in an improbable pool on the ground, then ran off to the edge of the page. He thought of Amber, waiting for him outside. With a quick movement he closed the diary and pushed it into his bag, zipping it up tightly. Also on the table were clustered his Cornish stones; these, his lucky charms, he scooped up and put in his pocket to take with him. Then he took a sheet of paper from his sketch pad and scribbled a brief, and no doubt cryptic, note to his parents and left it on the desk. He turned off the light, closed the door ever-so-carefully and padded down the stairs and out.

Amber was still there at the end of the road, waiting in her car. He was almost surprised she hadn't gone. She saw him coming and got out, taking the bag from him as if she were a taxi driver. "Here, let me take that – I'll put it in the back." She opened the boot to reveal a chaos of items within: muddy wellington boots, a rumpled pair of jeans, what looked like a hamster cage (empty) and some small sacks, from one of which had spilled several small and rather pretty stones, not unlike his own. A soft black bag, containing something roughly the shape and size of a football, lay in one corner. Jack saw it and felt a sudden tide of unease rise within him. In a fraction of a second, the sense of a connection with some guiding entity that he had experienced in his dreams, in the library in St Just, at the junk shop, came into focus stronger than ever: the almost palpable presence of another consciousness. It was hard to describe, but Jack felt – as he had done on numerous other occasions recently – that a mind was stretching out to reach him over a vast gulf. He could sense its burning pain and anguish.

Amber slid in his own bag beside the black sphere. She shut the boot and abruptly the feeling passed. She looked across at him and gave a little smile. "Come on, get in or you'll be soaked. We need to get going!" He fastened his seatbelt and relaxed. The decision was made now, for better or worse. Let's see where it took him. His headache, at any rate, had quite gone. The car moved off through the rain, windscreen wipers racing, on the first leg of its journey to Cornwall.

CHAPTER 23

REQUIESCAT IN PACE

It was a beautiful day at the Crown Mines. There was almost no haze and the horizon could be clearly seen, as could every wave and fleck of foam on the wide sea. The perfect day, in fact, for a family outing to this most spectacular of Cornish mining sites. The sun was warm and the two little children careered down the hill at top speed, to the cries of anguished parents bringing up the rear: "Be careful now! Watch the edge! Mind you don't trip!" The youngsters made a beeline for the strange, half-ruined building that was nearest to them, with its mysterious dark slits for windows and its huge wheel partly visible through the ruined roof. With squeals of delight they competed as to who would be the first to get there. But when they arrived, it was only the youngest who stopped, for her older brother had seen something even more alluring below, the wreck of the old pumping house. To this he hurtled on, despite ever more insistent cries from his parents.

Yet it was the upper building that attracted the little girl: its cool walls and temple-like exterior drew her to them, beckoned her in. She edged through the dark rectangle of the door … yes, all was peaceful and still inside – and what wonderful and fascinating things were in there! What was that huge wheel for, that rose so high and whose rusted spokes seemed so strong and unusual? There was something strangely compelling about it. The girl moved further into the building, her eyes adjusting to the gloom. What was that noise? A rhythmic tapping was coming from somewhere, somewhere close to, just behind the big wheel. She walked in further, skirting around the pipes and cylinders. How huge and strange these machines were… Outside, seagulls called plaintively but their cries made little impact on the tranquillity of the winding house interior, with its hypnotic tapping sounds. And now the big winding drum came into the girl's view, with its coils of rusty cable. The noise seemed to be coming from here, was it in those shadows? She moved further round. The light from a narrow window streamed in and fell directly on the part of the drum she could now see clearly. A long bundle of something hung against it. The bundle swung slowly from side to side. It had boots, and it was these boots that tapped so peacefully against the body of the drum. It had a face, and it was over this face, bloated and red, that a grey beard straggled like moss. The bundle had a pony tail, and this pony tail swung lazily with each slow pendulum motion. And the bundle had a neck, and it was around this neck that a loop of rusty cable was pulled tight, drawing up and suspending that chunky figure from the top of the drum.

The girl started screaming, scattering the seagulls that had perched inquiringly on the window ledge, searching for the scraps of food that were usually heralded by the incursion of tourists into their craggy realm.

⅄

Two days later Tom Bradley, Carole Banks and one or two other members of the Woolfe Society were chewing the cud in the bar of the Commercial Hotel in the St Just market square. Socially speaking, Carole still enjoyed occasional drinks with some of the members, although she now took no part in their group meetings. Tom was immersed in a copy of the *Penzance Weekly Chronicle,* hot off the press. Derek Ballard was in the process of draining his pint as a prelude to concluding his thoughts on the proliferation of art galleries in the town. "I tell you, if we get any more of these buggers opening up, I'm putting a brick through their window – just see if I don't."

"It's all very well being like that Derek," put in Carole, "but you have to remember that–" She broke off as Tom excitedly held up his hand for silence.

"Hey! Now you just listen to this, stop press an' all." He was staring intently at a page in the *Chronicle*, and proceeded to read to them:

> *Local man found dead at Crown Mines.*
>
> *The body of a Penzance man was found at the Crown Mines, Botallack, last week. James Peters, 54, was a well-known local historian and expert on Cornish Mining. He had written several books on the subject and was familiar to many*

from his regular lectures and talks in many village venues in the area. Police were alerted by day-trippers that a body had been found in the winding house, one of the derelict buildings on the spectacular Crown Mines site. We understand that Dr Peters was found hanging by the neck from a winch cable in what police described as suspicious circumstances.

A neighbour of Dr Peters', Mrs Tregellis, said, 'It is a terrible shock. He was such a nice, quiet man. He did have very poor eyesight – I wonder if that could have contributed to this dreadful event. He loved Crown Mines, it seems somehow fitting that he died at the place. Jim would have wanted that.'"

Derek Ballard slammed down his glass. "Well I never! That bugger's got his come uppance, I'll say."

"Aye, well he's been a pain in our necks for long enough, that's for sure," put in Tom Bradley, wiping his mouth on his sleeve.

Carole Banks looked aghast. "Really Tom, that's awful. I know he was bit eccentric and, yes, he certainly could be a nuisance, but did he deserve such a terrible end?"

"I'm not saying," replied Tom, "but I reckon Morgana thought he did, an' I wouldn't like to cross swords with *her*."

"But ol' Jim, he did that once too often, I'd say," rejoined Derek. A murmur of assent ran around the group.

Carole said, "Well, he was supposed to be giving a talk tomorrow night at the village hall, on chimney stacks."

There was a pause. Derek smiled crookedly. "I reckon that'll be cancelled, then. No refunds."

"Anyone for another pint?" inquired Tom.

CHAPTER 24

The Magus Calls

"The nature of *God is a circle of which the centre is everywhere and the circumference is nowhere." Very good! Alas, we live in an age of great ignorance and such matters are no longer discerned. I see we are out of coffee again, and other essentials, only four days since last replenishing. Is there no remedy for this excessive consumption? My nerves are bad today. How I long to have my jewel back!*

They were skirting Bristol on the M5 when Jack woke up. Not long after they had left Amersham he'd been overcome by the need to sleep. Of course, he'd had a late, disturbed night and had woken early. But there was more to it than that. In the little time they'd had to talk it was apparent that the mysterious Amber knew so much about him, and the worries that beset him, that rather than appearing sinister or suspicious she quickly seemed to Jack to offer the prospect of help, of sharing some of his burden. Maybe he was being premature but the thought was such a relief it was as if a weight had been lifted, and tiredness quickly got the better of him. Amber, who in any case was preoccupied with driving and not particularly disposed to chat, encouraged him to rest.

With a dry mouth and general feeling of a mild hangover, he sat still for a while and regarded the girl through half-closed eyes. She drove briskly and confidently but without taking risks, focussing on the road ahead and holding the wheel with a light grip. She sat quite still, just occasionally brushing back a strand of stray hair from her face. Jack found himself increasingly fascinated by her slightest movement, her relaxed economy of effort. Without turning she said, "Feeling better?" How long had she known he was awake? Had she been aware he was watching her? Suddenly he felt self-conscious. "Er, yes, not so bad, thanks," he croaked, through dry lips.

"There's a bottle of water in the glove compartment. You know, you've been out cold for about two hours."

"Where are we?"

"Just joined the M5. It's straight down now all the way to Exeter."

He pulled himself into a more upright position and drank a good deal of the water. It was no longer raining and the sun struggled to break through the dispersing clouds. It was not yet nine o'clock and the traffic was light on this Sunday morning. He still found it hard to believe he'd been so rash. But anyway, for better or worse he now had the opportunity to ask more questions of this strange girl. He stared out of the window for a while, watching the panorama of the passing Bristol docks from the high bridge they were crossing, wondering where to start. Again he glanced across at her. She was smiling a little, still staring intently at the road, clearly waiting for him to speak. Presently he said, "What were you doing in Amersham, if you live in Cornwall? Did you come all this way just to see me?"

Amber's smile broadened. "There's no 'just' about it. You're important, Jack! But no, that wasn't the *only* reason. I needed to do two things. One of them, the second, was to find you, speak to you and bring you back down to see my father. As for the first" – here she looked sideways at him, as if weighing him up – "well, I'd just come from the church."

Jack felt his stomach tighten. "Which church?" he asked slowly.

"I think you know the answer to that. Little Horwood. I had something very important to do there, before I could come to find you. I hope you're not easily shocked?" She glanced across playfully, then continued more seriously. "Your ancestor, Owen Tyack, had special connections with that church. He was the vicar, for one thing. For another, he was buried there. Have you been there Jack, seen his grave? I think you have. Did you know that vicars are always buried *inside* the church? But not this one. You see, he'd done something very bad indeed." Now she was frowning. "He discovered something while he was there, something that would have been better left well alone. Anyway, I needed to see his grave, to get something from it." Jack raised his eyebrows but said nothing. "I needed this thing … and of course anything like that has to be done at night, or people will notice." She made it sound entirely matter-of-fact. "Does that bother you?"

He shook his head, disingenuously he knew, but it seemed to matter to her. What sort of a girl was this, who robbed graves at night? Was she simply unhinged? Had he come all this way with a nutcase, to put it simply? Then he thought of the mounds of earth he'd seen around the Tyack graves on his visit to the church with Charlie. He shifted uncomfortably and looked at Amber more warily. "So are you going to tell me what you took?"

"Not just now, no."

He had a feeling it was pointless to argue. "Okay. But I'm not a kid, you know. Why are you so interested in me? And in Owen? Something to do with my family?"

She had moved into the outside lane to overtake a lorry, and waited until the manoeuvre was complete before replying. "Jack, you must have realized by now that your family isn't, well, *normal.* Something happened, something that has changed it. There are very strange things going on in your family. I can't go into the details now – I don't know them all myself, to be honest. My father will explain, when you meet him. You've just got to be patient for a bit longer."

He tried again. "How did you know where I live?"

Again she smiled, enigmatically. "It's not difficult to find out where someone lives, if you really want to. But you needn't worry, I've not been spying on you or following you. Not in the conventional sense, anyway."

He was hardly satisfied with this evasive answer but sensed he wouldn't get much further on that particular point, so he let it drop for now and returned to gazing out at the landscape. The docks had given way to a more rural aspect: neat farmers' fields containing occasional pieces of agricultural machinery, empty vistas of arable land, scattered scarecrows with arms outstretched in beseeching gestures. Ahead in the distance the Quantocks reared, like sentinels, signalling the gateway to the Southwest. What was Amber's interest in him and his family all about? What had she really been doing in that churchyard – assuming what she said was true and she had in fact been there? Everything seemed to centre on St Nicholas' church: the diary, with all its references to Little Horwood; the indefinable sense of something *warped* about the place itself when Jack had visited; the terrible inscriptions on the Tyack tombs; the mysterious photograph in the antiques shop, even – all seemed significant, all part of a single, wider story. But what was it? He ran his hands through his hair and massaged his forehead. Something nagged at the back of his mind, some connection that was just beyond his reasoning ability. So many questions! Well, he might as well continue to try and find out what he could now. He said, "So do you live with your father, then?"

"No. I'm actually in Polzeath town. He's a bit further along the coast, towards Port Quin. You'll be staying with me, no need to worry. You'll be very comfortable." At this, he looked closely at her, but she was absorbed again in her driving and seemed oblivious.

They pulled in at Taunton Services for a break and a refuel. Amber seemed keen to press on and after only the briefest of snacks they were soon back on the motorway, passing through the Quantocks and on to Exeter. It was now a fine, sunny day, the sky beautiful, blue and wide. The murky weather and goings on of the early hours of the morning seemed a world away. Jack started to relax, his spirits lifting until he was almost in a holiday frame of mind. It struck him how easy Amber was to be with. Most people he knew were prone to moods, to flashes of spite, even. She was different. Whether sitting in silence or talking he felt comfortable with her. He began to feel glad he came, clearer in his mind about the decision.

At Exeter they finally left the motorway and joined the broad sweeps and undulations of the A30, the extended dual carriageway that would carry them far into the Cornish peninsula. What traffic there had been largely dropped away, leaving just the odd car, small lorry and van with surfboards strapped to the roof. The weather became alternately showery and sunny, with massed dark clouds on the horizon and shafts of sunlight making dramatic interplay over the moorland that had opened up on either side. Jack checked his phone. Still nothing from Charlie. Well, he had other things to think about.

Now they were driving through a heavy shower. The odd engine house, with black mouths for windows, crumbling roof and stumpy chimney, started to appear, signalling their entry into the county of Cornwall. As if on cue, his mobile signal started to fade, then died. Jack didn't really mind. It simplified matters. He thought back again to the early morning, remembering Amber's reluctance to drive up to his house. He asked, "Why wouldn't you take me back to my house this morning?"

She frowned and looked distracted; the car abruptly slowed, in reflection of her mood. "Your house? No. Not while it was still dark, and with the Messenger abroad. I'm sorry but it wouldn't have helped – and I knew you'd be okay, just for a short while, to go back. But it was good we left when we did. You've been marked, Jack!" Seeing his anguished expression she gave him a reassuring smile. "But don't worry. My father can sort all this out. Really, he's an amazing man."

He began to feel helpless again. "Hang on, what's *the Messenger*? You talk in riddles Amber! Can't you just tell me what this is all about?"

But she just compressed her lips and shook her head in the negative. He persisted. "Look, you said you'd been to the church last night, to get something from Owen Tyack's grave. And then you came to find me, yes?"

"That's right."

"So: the thing you took from the grave is here, in this car?"

She fiddled with the heater for a bit, and he realized she must be nervous. Or was it embarrassment? He found it hard to read her. Then she said, "Yes," in a way that suggested she wasn't going to elaborate. He thought back to the black bag in the boot, and the strange emotions he'd felt on seeing it, as if something, some energy source, were radiating from it. He reflected. Whatever 'the Messenger' was, he didn't like the sound of it, nor of being 'a marked man'. But very possibly he was. The mocking laughter of the mines filled his head, then the blurred image of the headless man in the barber shop. Suddenly he began to feel very afraid indeed, real, naked, animal fear. Now Amber and her mysterious father took on a new aspect, that of lifelines, his saviours in this terrible, whirling storm of subconscious voices, muffled pursuers and intangible threats.

They continued in silence, Amber calmly focussing on the road, Jack alternating between introspection and observation of the changing Cornish landscape. After a series of pronounced undulations, during which they passed small convoys of larger vehicles that had slowed to a crawl as they climbed steeply, the road curved in a wide arc to the right. It was here, at Launceston, that they turned off onto smaller roads that took them closer to the north coast, until they joined the A395 at Davidstow: the so-called North Atlantic Highway. Huge wind-farms appeared, the rotor blades of the turbines either still or barely turning. Jack contrasted them in his mind with the engine houses he'd seen earlier: the difference between the bare functionality of the one and the almost chapel-like intimacy of the other, full of evocation of the past, was vivid. Both, though, were in equal measure testaments of the power of humanity's drive to conquer and harness the elements in its relentless search for wealth and power. The same search, in fact, that dominated his parents' waking lives, day in and day out: Geothermal Ltd. His thoughts turned back to Owen Tyack. Just what was he doing at the church? Those machines in the diary, the descriptions, the endless experiments. What had his father inherited from Owen, beyond his genes? Could there possibly be some greater project here, some strand of endeavour that connected them? Something with its secret in that diary. So where did the mines come in? Again he came back to the question: legend aside, what really happened to Owen Tyack in the Crown Mines? The church, the mines, the diary, a baleful triangle with the Tyack family at its centre.

The sea was near now, although not yet visible. Jack could sense it, smell its spiciness in the air. He tried Amber again. "You said earlier that Owen Tyack had been trying to contact me, and that you knew that. Sorry to be obvious Amber but Owen Tyack died. He's dead, buried, finished. Over a hundred years ago. So what's this stuff about him trying to contact me?" Suddenly he felt impatient with the whole business.

She nodded. "That's right. But death – what *we* call death – isn't really an end at all. It's just a" – here she briefly took her hands off the wheel and spread them in a sweeping gesture – "a sort of *transition*, a stage on a road. It's like a road that reaches a junction, then there are lots of signposts, and other roads leading off. Your ancestor reached that junction like everybody else. But something different had happened to him, something that set him apart." She looked unhappy, her face distorted by a deep frown. "So when he got to that junction, he ended up taking a very strange road, very *dark*, one that led to a place ... well, let's just say somewhere pretty horrific, a place from which there's no escape." She was holding up her hand, already forestalling his further questions. "Honestly, that's all I can say. I don't know the answers myself. You'll just have to wait and my father will explain."

Her father, again and again! Who was this man who knew everything? Jack could see he wouldn't get anything else out of her on the subject. He wondered if he should mention the diary, as a sort of catalyst to the discussion, but decided not to. It still felt very private, very personal, very much his own affair. It was his only tangible link with Owen Tyack; he would keep it to himself, for the time being. And he felt confident that the diary, at least, was something that neither Amber nor her father would know anything about.

He settled back and tried to enjoy the final stage of the journey through the pretty villages of Camelford, Helstone and St Kew. Now the sea was occasionally visible, just to be glimpsed across the fields to the right. The sun had prevailed and it was a fine afternoon. From Wadebridge they passed through a maze of smaller roads until the car descended a steep hill where the road bent sharply to the right. A picturesque bay opened up, the tide low and the beach wide, clustered around with surfing shops, cafés and private houses. A sign said, "Welcome to Polzeath". They had arrived.

CHAPTER 25

Cleaning Up

David Tyack held the note, scrawled untidily in his son's handwriting, outstretched before him, pondering what, exactly, lay behind it. He gave a deep sigh. "I can't understand what he was thinking of. Just to vanish like this. If he had to go, why didn't he at least wait to tell us himself? Don't you think, he could have told us himself?" His wife was sitting opposite him at the kitchen table, armed like her husband with a coffee. From the front of the house came the persistent drone of a hoover, which was being vigorously employed by Katja the cleaner as she made a start on clearing up the party debris of the previous night. The Tyacks had risen unusually late by their standards; but, then, they had a good excuse for sleeping in on this occasion. Joanne shifted slightly in her chair, steepled her hands under her chin and gazed through the patio windows at the garden. She was like a porcelain vase:

petite, cool, brittle and perfectly formed. Exasperated by her silence her husband continued, shaking his head, "I just hope he's all right. He's not been at all himself lately. It's that trip of his–"

"Oh David, don't be so silly!" Joanne snatched the note off him and flicked her glasses down from her forehead to read it better. "Jack's old enough to look after himself and anyway, it's only for a couple of days." Softening her tone slightly she added, "He'll be fine. Honestly."

"I hope you're right. I'm not so sure though. You can never tell with Jack. And why isn't he answering his mobile?"

Joanne frowned and returned to looking out of the window. "You know what he's like with that phone. Half the time it's switched off, or out of battery. There'll be a perfectly reasonable explanation. You really have to let go you know. He's not a child any more. You forget that. Now let's keep our eye on the ball. Jack will be back soon enough. In the meantime, we've got a very busy schedule."

Her husband stared unhappily into the dregs of his latte and looked unconvinced. The noise of the hoover rose and fell in a nerve-jangling whine. "That's another thing," he said. "I can't seem to find the diary. I'm sure I had it with me when we saw Perez and Lovett off. I thought I'd put it in the study but now I can't see it anywhere."

Joanne left off surveying the garden and gave him a look of such piercing intensity, combined with possible elements of contempt, that he almost physically recoiled. "Don't tell me you've lost it?"

He braced himself. "Well, it must be somewhere, I suppose, but it's not in any of the obvious places. I've been looking since I got up–"

"You *fool* David! Can't you see Jack's taken it? That's what's behind this. He's gone off with the diary!"

"Oh come on, Joanne. You don't know that. Why would he be interested in it anyway? It was barely intelligible even to us."

"Why not? He was asking you about Owen Tyack wasn't he? Now he's found it, and taken it." An added note of iciness crept into her tone. "What does this mean for the schedule?"

David Tyack held his hands out and made chopping motions with them, as if attempting physically to cut off the attack. "It won't affect it. Believe me, we've got all we need out of that diary. All the technical insights. Trust me, it won't make any difference."

She looked somewhat appeased. "Well, if you're sure. That's something, I suppose. But you really should be more careful."

"I tell you, I was *sure* I had it, I can't understand it. But if Jack *has* taken it ...." He trailed off, his brow furrowing.

"Well, what?"

"It won't harm the project, it's not that." He reluctantly held her eye. "I … just don't like to think of him with it, that's all." But Joanne was already disengaging from the discussion, her fears largely allayed. David's, however, were only beginning. For him, the diary, so portentously entrusted to him by the mysterious Peregrinus, had taken on a talismanic aura as an object in its own right, aside from whatever knowledge it contained. It had solved his most intractable business problems; as long as it remained in his possession he felt convinced that everything connected with the reactor project would turn out well, that all the long labours would come to fruition. Now it was lost and somehow he knew at bottom that it had really gone, not just been mislaid. What would Peregrinus say, if he found out? Which he mustn't. But in another, paradoxical, thought, he had the distinct impression that this battered old journal had certain properties, *harmful* properties. It exuded the morbid spirit of fear and guilt. For that reason he hated to think of it in Jack's hands, of what mischance might befall his son under its influence. He *had* to contact him. "I'll give Jack another call," he said decisively.

"Do," came the answer. "But he'll be fine."

But David Tyack's third attempt to contact his son only came up once more against his voicemail. He left a terse message. "Jack, it's your father. Phone home as soon as you get this."

Joanne had started tapping away at her laptop, concentrating on the tasks ahead, her previous anger forgotten. Behind her, Katja bustled into the kitchen bearing empty bottles, rubbish and trays of glasses and plates which she loaded into the dishwasher before disappearing into the lounge again to continue her vacuuming. Once more the hoover's whine rose, hectoring and insistent. Joanne pouted and threw an interrogative glance at her husband. "So let's pick up where we left off last night. In practical terms, how long will it take to modify the start-up apparatus, based on the information in the diary? Are you *really* confident of a month?" She smiled ironically. "Or was that just for Perez and Lovett?"

He felt relieved that at least she seemed to be accepting the loss of the diary, yet found it hard to focus his mind whilst there was still no account of Jack. The need for his wife's approval, however, in the last analysis overrode all other concerns. "It's virtually done. We've been taking a parallel approach: checking results at the church but at the same time making modifications at the main site as we go. It's quicker than waiting for the prototype experiments to complete and, after all, it's clear we're on the right track now. There was nothing to lose." He moved closer to her. At some level, surely, she would be concerned about Jack? "Joanne–" He reached out to touch her hair but with a quick movement she pulled back, parrying him with more questions.

"And what about Peregrinus? You said he might still be useful. Isn't he based in Cornwall somewhere? What are your plans for him?" She inquiringly raised a finely arched eyebrow.

"Ah yes. He's moving closer, looking into finding a place near the main site in fact. In Winslow, I believe."

The noise of the hoover stopped, leaving only the background thrum of the dishwasher to break the silence. Joanne appeared to consider for a moment, then gave a curt nod. "Good. There was one other thing–" But at this point she was cut off by a piercing scream from somewhere at the front of the house. "*What on earth?*"

There were several reception rooms in the Tyack residence. One of these served as a library and was lined with the many books, on all subjects under the sun, that the couple had collected over the years. It was to there that Joanne and David rushed to find Katja, standing in the middle of the room like a lost child, eyes squeezed shut, apron-clad and clutching her feather duster in one hand. The room was in chaos, but not from any party. Books had been pulled off the shelves apparently at random and lay tossed here and there on all sides. Several chairs had been overturned and a small leather two-seater had been ripped open, the stuffing welling out like a disembowelled creature. On the desk lay a fine pigskin King James Bible, the wedding gift of pious friends, but only its spine and covers remained. The pages themselves had all been torn out in what must have been a superhuman effort, ripped up into little strips and scattered everywhere like coarse confetti. A terrible smell pervaded the whole room: foetid, cloying, without parallel in the natural world.

Katja, a good Catholic girl from Polish stock, on seeing David appear ran across the room and clung to him like a little girl, sobbing. "There is the Devil in this house, the Devil!" Apparently unmoved, Joanne pushed past her. After surveying the scene with a cold eye she knelt to pick up the nearest fragment of page. A disembodied sentence proclaimed, *The curse of the Lord is in the house of the wicked: but He blesseth the habitation of the just.* She scrutinized it briefly, calmly, as if reviewing a bank statement. Straightening up, she raised her hand to her face, rubbing the fingers together carefully while holding their tips to her nose. An oily film clung to them. She scanned the floorboards, now noticing the dark slick in their centre. She remained still, thinking, for some moments then turned to Katja. "This will be your next job, then, to get this lot cleared up. When you've finished the lounge. Use the author's surname for the books. The order is a simple alphabetical one." And with that, she turned on her heel and left.

CHAPTER 26

PENTIRE POINT

SO, I SENT *Jacob to bring me a* Telegraph. *Although I despise the media of the masses, well – it is an occasional treat. And I read the chatter. Today, this: "When families are strong and stable, so are children. But when things go wrong, the impact on the child's later life can be devastating." And I think of my precious jewel, and say frankly that there I have done well.*

Polzeath is the perennial favourite Cornish town of surfers and certain types of families in the summer months. A ghost town in the winter, for some people it is too crowded, displays too much vulgar 'new money' in the high season. Volkswagen vans, the badge of membership for the surfer, crowd the beach at low tide and you can hardly move along the narrow footpaths for day trippers. For others, though, it is the archetypal holiday destination, with the best beach in the peninsula, and cannot be missed.

Amber lived on one of the steep hills which flanked the main street. Her house was tucked away down a little lane which petered out into a footpath that proceeded to thread its way down past gardens and between other houses until it met the rock pools. It was a wonderful location and from the upstairs you could see a wide sweep of the bay. There was a holiday feel about the small timber building. Above the front door, sloping at a casual angle, was a lozenge-shaped piece of wood with the words 'The Shack' painted on it in white.

Space was at a premium in Polzeath and Amber parked in a tiny driveway, so narrow it was difficult actually to get out of the car. 'Shack': probably a better description than 'house', Jack thought as he shouldered his bag and followed her through the door. He hadn't entirely recovered his energies from having slept on the way down and still felt a bit groggy. The sea air would soon remedy that, though, and already he was starting to feel more alive. Inside, the downstairs space was a wood-panelled rectangle with a couple of sofas facing each other on either side and heaps of fabrics and rugs strewn chaotically in various places. The colours were browns, creams and beiges, all warm, earthy tones. A wood-burning stove stood in the middle of the room, its chimney passing directly up and through a central hole in the ceiling, an unusual arrangement he had never seen before (except in books about how Anglo Saxons used to live). The upstairs was no more than a narrow gallery running around the perimeter, accessed by a ladder at the far end. Next to the bottom of the ladder a door led off into an extension containing, he later discovered, a kitchen, bedroom and tiny bathroom. Along the walls of the main room were several shelves on which were placed ornaments of various kinds: crude vases painted with primitive geometric shapes, objects including shells that had been cast up by the sea, clusters of polished pebbles and larger rocks of many different colours, shapes and sizes – beautiful decorations in their own right. They put Jack in mind of his own Cornish pebbles, in his pocket at this very moment as they usually were.

There was no sign in Amber's living room of a television, nor a computer, nor in fact of any electrical equipment. Her 'shack' was neither tidy nor spacious but, like its owner, it had a charm that Jack felt immediately. It was a welcoming place, all just as he might have expected. Although it lacked the sophistication of the Tyack residence in Amersham he felt instantly at home there. He brushed past a rack of washing that was drying – tracksuit bottoms, a hooded top – dumped his bag on the floor and flopped down on one of the sofas. Amber was going to and fro, bringing in her things from the car, including the hamster cage and the dubious soft black bag he'd noticed in the boot. These she deposited in her bedroom at the back. Finally she dragged in a large bag of solid fuel for the fire. He stirred himself. "Here, let me help you with that–"

"No, it's fine. Make yourself at home! I fancy some juice – what do you say? Won't be a minute." She disappeared into the kitchen, emerging to criss-cross the living room several more times, retrieving various small items.

Jack felt a bit like a spare part, clumsy and inadequate. Amber came back with two glasses of juice and perched next to him on the sofa, giving him her full attention now as if he were the only thing in the world that mattered. "So you like it then?"

"Yeah, it's a great place. How long have you been here?"

"A couple of years. I used to live with Dad but, you know, eventually I needed my own space. So I found this. It wasn't easy as there isn't too much property to be had round here. I know it's small but I love it. Just five minutes and you're on the beach." Her face lit up as she discussed her house. Jack noticed she wore no makeup yet looked good completely natural. He couldn't get over it: where was the brittleness of his mother, the tense, scarcely suppressed edginess of his father? Where was the touchiness that seemed a part of almost everyone he had ever met, so you never knew quite where you were with them, never could quite trust them? Even Charlie, he reflected, had let him down. Amber was different – yet there *was* something familiar about her all the same, something about her appearance, or aspects of her manner. He had known her for less than a day but already he felt sure that what he did know was the real person. Why wasn't everybody like this? If only his parents were more *normal.* His parents ... he wondered what they were doing. They would have found his note by now. Surely his mother would have tried to ring him? He needed to check.

"Can I use your phone?" he asked.

She shot him an impenetrable look, compressed her lips and shook her head. "No, no land line here." She smiled as she saw him toying with his mobile. "You won't get a signal for *that* either. I don't like all this texting and phoning people. It's like you can never be alone, never find your own space. It does you harm, Jack – *it's bad for you!* I really do believe that. Dad's just the same as me," she added quickly, as if to validate her opinion and forestall dispute.

Jack was incredulous. "You don't have *any phone?* What about a TV?"

She shook her head again. "No. Life's too short. I don't have one. If you want to phone someone, the best thing is to go over to Pentire Point" – she waved vaguely in the direction of the sea – "and you can most likely pick up a signal there. It's a lovely walk too. In fact, if you wanted to do that it would work well, as I can tidy up a bit here and get a few jobs done, then we can eat later."

"When do we see your father then?"

"Tomorrow night. We'll have plenty of time to chat ourselves, this evening. Anyway, it's a nice day now, you can take the footpath down to the beach and walk along by the Atlantic Bar. There are some great views."

Amber seemed to have made up her mind that Jack would be going out. He suddenly felt a bit bruised by this. But like she said, there'd be time to talk later and, in any case, he did need to check his phone. "Okay, I'll get going. See you in a couple of hours then."

She smiled cheerfully. "You can't miss the path, it's just opposite. No rush. See you later!"

⅄

It was indeed a nice day. The final dregs of Jack's lethargy fell away as he strode out to the beach. The footpath trickled down past the backs of houses, all at various angles and built in different styles. Washing fluttered in the breeze and occasional Cornish flags flew on poles. Although it was by no means warm, there were several surfers riding the breakers and even some families sitting out by the beach café, eating ice cream. The wide bay opened out to the vast expanse of sea; dark clouds massed on the horizon but for the present it was sunny enough. To Jack's right was a jutting peninsula of headland from which it looked as if amazing views could be had: Pentire Point, presumably. He skirted the beach in that direction until he came to diagonal steps leading up to a road. There he strolled along past the Georgian terraces and the Atlantic Bar until he turned off along a bramble-infested public footpath that marked the way. The path broadened and took him down into miniature sandy coves, across streams flowing seawards, then up again. At first he encountered dog walkers and couples, but these soon thinned out. Now he felt the shadow of loneliness pass over him. Those people he did see were in pairs or small groups but he was rootless, alone, the few connections he did have tenuous and impermanent. A vision of desolation opened up before him. He looked over the cliffs to his left to where the sea churned below and felt its indifference to his empty little personal voyage. Who could he turn to next? He thought of home, of Charlie, of Richard Attlee, of Amber. Who might he really depend on?

He pressed on. Half an hour's further walk along the cliffs and there was the Point directly above him, covered in moss and stunted heather through which granite slabs pushed up at the peak. Standing on that rocky crest gave a tremendous view back to the bay on his left, out to sea and all the way round to his right. A strong breeze hit him full on, challenging him to cast off his melancholy. He squinted to see if he could make out Amber's house among the cluster of buildings to the left of Polzeath but it was impossible, at this distance, to be sure. He found a standing stone that offered some protection from the wind and crouched down behind it to check his phone. Amber was right: there was a full signal now. And a voicemail! This would be his mother ... He listened and heard his father's terse tones: *Phone home as soon as you get this*.

Jack shrunk further behind the stone. Now he had stopped walking the wind was starting to chill him and he felt tired again. He considered. Here in Cornwall, as before, he was at least his own person, making his own decisions. *Sort* of, at any rate – even if he had come down at Amber's behest. The whole control business would start up again if he phoned home now; the very first words would engender guilt, and resentment. Did he really want to go there? Without thinking much further he found himself dialling a different number. A querulous voice answered "Richard Attlee here?"

"Richard, it's Jack."

The voice softened. "Jack! Where are you? Sounds like you're inside a vacuum cleaner."

"Yeah, I'm on a mountain, sort of."

There was the smallest of pauses. "Cornwall?"

"Yes – how did you know?"

"I didn't. A complete guess. I just had a feeling you might – want to go back there. Your father's been in touch, asking after you. Said you'd gone off somewhere for a few days, didn't know where. Is everything all right?"

"Yes, yes I'm fine. Could you do me a favour? Could you tell mum and dad I'm down here and that I'm fine. I can't seem to get hold of them now."

Attlee sounded a little unconvinced. "Certainly, I'll do that. But don't you think you should leave them a message or something? Are you sure everything's all right?"

"Yes, really – but if you could just tell them."

"Right you are then. Oh, and while I've got you there I must tell you I've been knocking up something a bit special in my workshop. I won't say what now but I think you'll be impressed, when you see it."

"Great, I can't wait to see that Richard."

"Good, well come over when you're back and I'll show you. Anything else?"

"No, not for now. Thanks though."

"Well I must get on. 'Bye Jack." Attlee was never one for protracted valedictions, preferring a nice, crisp severance. Even so, Jack felt better for the contact. And at least he'd done the decent thing and got a message home, if only indirectly.

He emerged from his refuge and, taking the full blast of the wind, stood staring at the horizon for some minutes, thinking. Despite his friendship with Attlee, he was well aware that he hadn't been able fully to confide in the older man the realities of his situation. Maybe it was the age gap, more likely Attlee's connection with his parents. Amber and her father seemed more important than ever as a possible source of succour, or at least of information. It was hard to see who else might help him. Exactly who this mysterious, all-knowing man, Amber's father was – that was anybody's guess. Amber had said he would tell Jack "everything". If only someone would! The meeting would have to be pretty special to live up to expectations, raised now so high. Jack stood there for some minutes more, gazing out to sea at a tanker crawling across the horizon. Then he turned away from the mesmerizing view and set off on the descent back to Polzeath.

He kept his head down in the buffeting wind and concentrated on not twisting an ankle on the uneven surface of the path. As he started to descend more steeply, he glanced up and saw toiling along the path towards him a bulky figure in a billowing green waterproof. As it got nearer he could see the man was laden down with what looked like bags of shopping. He was not a walker; clearly he had been to the store in the town. If he was returning to one of the houses Jack had noticed clinging to the cliffs much further round the coast, then he was in for a long walk with all that to carry. But there didn't seem to be anywhere else such a person could be heading with such a load.

As they drew level Jack prepared himself for a casual greeting but when he looked up into the face, fringed by its flapping hood, something stopped him. It is possible to take in a lot of detail about another person in a brief glance, perhaps the requirement of some earlier, animal, phase in our evolution. The man was unusually tall and broad, but it was not this that froze the greeting on Jack's lips. The features were quite out of the ordinary, but in a way that was hard to define: blurred or smudged, as if crudely modelled or melted in some way. There was a brief impression of a wide mouth without any discernible lips and a flat, undefined nose. More disturbing were the eyes – or rather, the apparent lack of them, for there were simply two dark depressions, shadowy hollows, where they should have been visible. The forehead held a deep scar in the centre.

So unsettling was this apparition, its slow limbs labouring with their burden against the full force of the head-on wind, that Jack simply passed by without comment, averting his eyes. Deeply unnerved, after a minute or two he looked back. Was this further evidence of malign pursuit? But no, the broad back forged on stolidly, like a big ship in a gale, obstinately physical, solid. The man had forked off to the right and was doggedly following the coastal path round and away from the headland. My God, what was wrong with him? An accident, perhaps? The poor man, imagine what it must be like for him? Nevertheless, Jack felt he wouldn't like to get on the wrong side of someone like that. But it was wrong to judge by appearances; he was probably decent enough.

Jack continued on his way back to Polzeath, rather wishing the encounter hadn't happened. Just so long as it was not a bad omen for tomorrow's meeting ... The shadows were longer now, the tide starting to come in across the bay in broad, creamy waves. Everything was very clear in the late afternoon light. The town looked beautiful, so picturesque. There was a touch of magic in these parts, it seemed. As he threaded his way up the path and past the houses his thoughts turned back to Amber. She would be there waiting, and they would eat and talk through the evening, probably. That's what she'd suggested, anyway. And would there be answers? He would just have to wait and see.

CHAPTER 27

Portal to the Past

It was a quiet Sunday in Winslow. A few shops were open: a tea room, the paper shop, an estate agent. The antiques – or more accurately, junk – shop on the market square was open too, although it had so few customers it might have spared itself the trouble. Still, it seemed to manage to keep its business ticking over. Nobody in particular noticed when, around midday, a grubby white van pulled up outside it and parked on the double yellow lines, as white vans do. A sinewy figure in jeans and t-shirt hopped out on the passenger side, opened the rear doors and began to unload onto the pavement several boxes and a substantial, ancient-looking trunk. Then he closed the van up, slammed the side with the flat of his hand by way of a signal and off it drove in a cloud of smoke, leaving the man standing there as if he had been beamed down from space. Inside the shop, the assistant put down her book and watched thoughtfully as he looked around for a few moments, apparently summing the place up, then reached inside his jeans pocket for something. To the side of the double windows that formed the junk shop frontage was a black iron stairway that led up to a blue door above. With the agility of a monkey the lithe figure darted up, unlocked the door and vanished for a few moments. Then he emerged again and proceeded to lug up the boxes. He finished with the trunk – no mean feat of strength for one man on his own. Then the door shut behind him.

Inside the flat it was dark, musty and quiet. The living room was long and narrow with a low ceiling from the centre of which a single, naked bulb dangled from a plaster rose. Two sash windows, opaque with dirt, gave on to the street below. There were no curtains, nor was there any carpet, just peeling boards daubed here and there with spots of old paint. The furnishing was primitive: a lumpy sofa covered by a dark red throw with frayed tassels; a lone armchair that listed to one side as if on the point of collapse. In the centre of the long wall opposite the windows was a gas fire festooned with cobwebs and next to it a decayed sideboard. By the latter stood the newly imported pile of boxes and the trunk. A door opposite the entrance led off to a tiny kitchen and bathroom, disagreeably close to each other.

Peregrinus surveyed the room with silent approval. Memories and echoes of the past jostled in his mind, the ghosts of long ago. No, it hadn't changed much in all these years, not even down to the myriad clicks and squeaks of the mice that came from all corners of the building, clearly audible to him. And the calm tick of the clocks downstairs ... but that was new. He closed his eyes. The ghosts were nearer now; they did not sleep quietly. Ah – sleep! Suddenly he realized how tired he was. Going over to the fire he fiddled with the starter, eventually getting it to ignite. He turned up the flame fully and the smell of burning dust filled the room. Then he threw himself down on the sofa and let himself drift off.

⅄

In the junk shop below, the assistant paused again in her reading, almost as if sensing something. She looked up, half raised a hand to her mouth and remained ludicrously frozen in that pose for a few moments, frowning. Then she returned to her book, unsettled.

⅄

Peregrinus quickly became ensnared in the coils of the strangest dream. All kinds of vivid and fantastic images came to his inner eye. He was in a theatre, or some sort of arena. People were everywhere, yet he was separated from them, not a part of the crowd. Huge beasts reared up, decked out with extravagant ornament and fabrics, or so it seemed. A fox ran before him, then an otter; he grabbed vainly at them but they eluded him. A great grey creature lumbered around and shuffled towards him. He knew its name. The people were shouting and it dawned on Peregrinus that he should perform, for that was what they wanted, this crowd. There were rings, and a wooden horse, but what could he do? There was strength in his body, his arms were powerful and sinewy, and yes, he could perform, if that was what they wanted.

The picture dissolved; he was going back further, further. He was trapped in a chaos of bodies. Smoke, fire, the acrid tang of gas in the air everywhere, and coughing, choking, the desperate struggle to breathe. Above, the noise of shells exploding and the whine of something. What was that? A biplane emerged from the clouds, swooping low, its goggled pilot bearing down on them, the machine gun firing, rapid rounds of it, again and again. He was buried in a trench, fighting his way up from a mound of bodies, hauling off severed limbs still in tattered rags of uniform, pawing at flesh through warm, wet fluid. And then the gas again, the terrible fighting for breath ... he would die, there in that ditch he would drown in gas and stench!

The chaos ebbed and was supplanted by a peaceful scene: a country churchyard, bathed in sunlight, the birds singing in the old yew tree and the only other noise the sound of his shears, clip-clipping the verges around the graves. All was harmony; the whole process of the natural world enveloped him. Someone, the vicar, was calling to him from the porch of the church. He must go, he must obey. And now he was in the crypt: dank stone, streaked walls, the smell of earth, and of something else, something less pleasant, cloying and sweet. In the centre of the tiny medieval chamber lay a form, stretched out. If he could only see it clearly ....

But the scene melted into an empty road, stretching infinitely in either direction, before him and behind. The long grasses waved bleakly on either side; not a soul was in sight and the only sound was of the wind. Everything he possessed in the world was with him, he was self-contained, a free agent, independent – and where the sense of loneliness should have been there was only empty space. Yet a fear grew in him, fear of being followed, and he forced his heavy legs to move down the endless ribbon of tarmac. He was nobody, going nowhere. He could not walk fast enough, however, and whatever presence it was that followed steadily gained ground. A roadside chapel appeared; with relief, he entered, seeking repose. Yet, as he stumbled past the empty pews, the sounds of souls stretched out in torment gathered around him. He blocked his ears, but the sounds grew louder and he fell to his knees.

Peregrinus stirred in his sleep and reached out his hand, into thin air and no answering touch. He drifted back into his dreams, and they were stranger still. He was somewhere deep underground, far deeper down than anyone had ever been. There were rocky caverns, spiralling columns, great arches towering above, and fiery lakes. He was curled up, foetus-like, in some secret place. He was half-made, unfinished and unformed. Fire lapped at his limbs, he breathed smoke with fledgling lungs. He could not see but he could hear: many voices filled the secret chamber, speaking no known language yet bearing a vaguely remembered message. When he tried weakly to move his limbs, things restrained him. He was helpless. The voices continued, saturating his being, seeping into his soul with their occult message. His internal organs burned, his skin ran with salty rivulets, the heat was too oppressive to respire ... Again he felt the panic of suffocation rise.

Peregrinus's eyes snapped open and he sat bolt upright on the sofa, sweating. Slowly the fear subsided and he lay back, still and exhausted. The gas fire breathed calmly. Yes, the ghosts were powerful in this place! In the bathroom he rinsed his face in the filthy sink and waited for his senses to sharpen again. All this, he thought, should not be a surprise, not in such a place as this. And his next move, having got here? He gave a little smile. He would go shopping.

⅄

The assistant looked up sharply from her book with a trace of discomposure when the doorbell tinkled and Peregrinus entered. Normally displaying an icy superiority to the inferior species known as 'customers', now she shifted uncertainly on her stool and produced a smile that was more sheepish than disdainful. "Is there anything I can help you with?" she asked coquettishly.

The stranger's intense blue eyes bored through her, then softened a bit. "I'll just browse, thanks."

"Well just let me know if you want anything." She gave a little giggle.

Peregrinus nodded curtly, then began restlessly moving around the front part of the shop, prodding and scrutinizing things: the old crockery, toby jugs, the brass lamps and tarnished jewellery. The second-hand books particularly seemed to interest him. The assistant watched while pretending to read. By the absurd collection of gargoyle carvings he stopped and stroked his chin thoughtfully, looking carefully at each one. The assistant's heart missed a beat. He picked one up, examined it, then slowly replaced it on its shelf. She ventured, "You like those?"

He gave a little grunt, then came over to her. "Have you worked here long?"

"A couple of years. You're new aren't you?"

He flicked his eyes ceiling-wards. "Yes. I moved in upstairs. I don't really know anyone around here." He gave her a smile.

"Oh, *well* … If you'd like me to show you around at all, or help you with anything ...?" She let the words hang for a few moments.

Peregrinus appeared to weigh them. "Thanks. I might take you up on that." He held her gaze briefly, then with apparent indifference drifted off towards the back room. He seemed to be looking for something, preoccupied, but she didn't want to ask him again. She could continue to watch him though – and she turned to a tiny VDU screen on a shelf below the counter. Now he was in the back room, searching, senses sharpened she could tell. What was it? She fiddled with the contrast on the monitor. Now the corridor. Well, well! Twice!

Peregrinus felt stress melt away when he found it. A contradiction had been settled, like something had come home. He reached up, took it down, blew the dust off it, held it, discreetly sniffed it. It was a little metaphor for his life, this process of seeking, then finding, then the momentary release of disquiet that went with the discovery. With contentment he took the object back to the counter.

The assistant nearly fell off her stool in her eagerness to oblige him. "Lovely picture isn't it? Here let me wrap it up for you, just to protect it."

"I'd hardly bother. I'm only upstairs."

"But I must! We wouldn't want to damage it, would we?" While she got out her tissue paper and sellotape he resumed browsing. Next thing she knew he was back, with something else. "I'll have that too."

The fire demon as well! "That's a *lovely* thing isn't it? Those are my favourites, but it's funny not many people seem interested. Are you sure you wouldn't like the set? You see there are seven."

He seemed to consider. "All right. I'll take them all. Assuming they don't cost the earth – no? Okay then."

Finishing with the picture, she produced more tissue paper and insisted on wrapping each gargoyle individually, then putting them all in a bag, just to make it easier for him. He paid and went to leave, hovering by the door just long enough for her to say, "Remember, just let me know if I can help with anything, or if you need showing around the town, or … help with the flat?"

He smiled to himself, then turned to her and said seriously. "Thanks. I'll do that."

⅄

Back upstairs Peregrinus stripped the tissue paper from his finds, located a spare nail head on the wall above the fire and carefully hung the picture there. He stood back and stared at it very intently for some minutes. Then he vanished into the kitchen, boiled a kettle and came back with a cup of coffee. Next he arranged the gargoyles in a pleasing ensemble on the sideboard, the fire demon in the centre, comical and disturbing at the same time. A pity about that snapped horn! He stood sipping his coffee, admiring the overall effect. Just the books to put out now and he'd be properly settled in. Things were looking up.

⅄

"I'm sorry, dear. Didn't he tell you? He's gone. Went last Tuesday. He's taken everything – not that he had much, just that trunk of his and a few bits and pieces." Apron-clad Mrs Frisbee was standing at the door of Peregrinus's lodgings and blinking benignly, feather duster in hand. Inwardly Carole reeled. She had called in on Peregrinus to suggest a walk and was utterly unprepared for this bombshell. Admittedly he'd been out of touch for the last few days – but *this?* She clutched at the hand rail by the doorstep, installed for the benefit of Mrs Frisbee's less mobile tenants.

"Gone? I … he didn't say, no," she stammered. "Was there no message? He didn't leave a message?"

Mr Frisbee considered for an infuriatingly long duration, then said, "No message as such, dear. No. He just said he'd finished his work in Cornwall. Now that made me think, you see. Finished in Cornwall. Ah, I thought; *so he'll be moving somewhere else then*. So I said, 'Are you moving somewhere else, Mr Peregrinus?'" She smiled and blinked at Carole.

"Yes? Well? What did he say?"

"He said yes, that was right. And before I had chance to ask, he said he'd be going East. That's right, The East." Mrs Frisbee spoke impressively, as if announcing an international military strategy. She continued, "So then I asked him if it was anywhere in particular, and he just smiled and said he had a new job. Buckinghamshire was it, is that right? I can't rightly remember, I think it was that. Anyway: he's gone now. He *was* a strange one, I have to say dear, but a good tenant, very quiet. I wouldn't say I miss him though. The plants have picked up amazingly."

Carole tuned out. How could he do this? Just when she'd thought they had broken through to a new level, when she had seemed to be making progress, starting to get behind that outer shell of reserve. To go, without a word of farewell – it was too awful. Too numb for further conversation she wandered off down the street, leaving the landlady prattling away to herself at the door like a wind-up doll. One thing Carole knew: it couldn't just be left like that. No. She had to find Peregrinus, and at least finish the thing properly.

CHAPTER 28

THE PRINCIPLES OF GEODIVINATION

"The antidote for fifty enemies is one friend."

When he got back to Amber's, Jack immediately noticed there had been some attempt to impose order. The rugs that had been strewn everywhere were now turned into throws covering the sofas according to some vague scheme. A large pile of the solid fuel bags had been brought in; surely Amber had not managed all of them on her own? Jack noticed a strange, earthy smell in the air. The stove was alight and starting to warm the room and Amber was in the process of lighting several candles dotted around, padding here and there in bare feet. She had changed into dark leggings and a finely woven, claret-coloured v-neck sweater that showed to good advantage a delicate necklace with pendant stone. When she heard Jack enter she immediately turned and broke into a warm smile. "Hello Jack. Did you manage to get a signal then?"

"Just about, thanks."

"Good! I've sorted us some food, get comfy and I'll bring it out. You're probably starving." He found himself marvelling once more that at this time yesterday he had not even heard of Amber, not seen her and hadn't the slightest intention of coming to Cornwall in the near future. Now here he was, in Polzeath, about to partake of a supper prepared specially for him by, and in the house of, someone who was essentially a complete stranger.

The supper was all cold – salad, fish and pulses. None of these were necessarily Jack's favourite fare but on this occasion he found them delicious. They ate in the lounge with plates on their knees, sitting on separate sofas, while Amber chatted away in her fashion, cheerful and engaging but never pushy or domineering.

"Did you see many others on the walk?"

"Oh, just a few dog walkers, it was pretty quiet." He recalled the grotesque figure on the way back with an involuntary grimace. She immediately picked up on it.

"What?"

"Oh, nothing. Nothing really, just some guy I saw on the way back."

"Well, what about him?" She was wearing an inquisitive expression.

For some reason, Jack did not feel inclined to discuss the incident, such as it was. "Oh, nothing. He looked a bit …

funny, that's all. Gruesome, sort of." Amber said nothing, although Jack thought he detected the ghost of a smile playing around her lips. "Mind you," he continued, "given everything that's happened to me recently I wouldn't be surprised who he was. Could have been anyone."

Amber remained silent, not rising to the bait, looking inscrutable.

They ate in silence for a little while. Amber took a long swig of her juice and picked at the food with delicate fingers. After a while Jack felt he should try the more direct approach. "You know you mentioned about a *messenger* being sent for me, to my house, and it being there the night you turned up? Then you said you didn't want to go to the house with this messenger thing there. Is my family in danger or something? What's it all about?"

Amber put her plate down, rested her chin on her hand and regarded him closely through her large, almond-shaped eyes. The stove spat and sent a shower of sparks up its chimney, as if to prompt her. She said, "Well, there *is* a spirit world. That's a fact, Jack, and I think you accept it now. I hope so. There are some individual spirits that can form a bond with real people, like you and me. The spirit might have had a close relationship with that person when it was flesh and blood. Or it could just be curious about that person. Then again, it could be sent specially to find something out about that person."

"Sent by who?"

"Well, I don't think we should talk about that just now. You'll just have to take my word for it. These spirits, they're not really dangerous. The purpose of a messenger, like I said, is to find out stuff and it might also be to communicate something as best it can. So it might do something, within its *limited* ability, that might seem odd in itself but that might be a warning of some sort. Just a small thing, like knocking some things around a bit, spoiling some arrangement. But I don't think these spirits can go beyond that sort of thing ... I certainly don't think they could harm anyone, at least not directly." She looked uncertain. "So you don't need to worry about your family as far as that's concerned. There are bigger issues, though. My father–"

"–Will explain everything, I know," cut in Jack, irritated.

Amber smiled innocently. "Exactly, right first time! Now, did you enjoy that? Let me take your plate. I think you should sit and meditate – you should, you know, after food, it helps digestion. I'm going to wash these things up, then we can have a drink."

She disappeared into the kitchen. Jack sat on the floor in front of the stove and gazed into the fire while she was gone. Meditate! Yet after a few minutes he found it surprisingly easy to drop into a calm, reflective mode in the low candle light, watching the lazy flames licking the fuel and the sparks rising up into the flue. His irritation quickly passed and by the time she returned he was mesmerized and beginning to feel distinctly relaxed. She had a bottle under her arm a stemmed glass in each hand. She sat down crossed-legged on the floor facing him, set the glasses down and began uncorking the bottle. "This," she explained, "is my home-made elderberry wine. You're very privileged, I normally keep it all for myself." She filled the glasses and held one up to the light, judging its colour with a critical eye before handing it to Jack. The fluid was a ruby red, and cloudy. "Now tell me what you think."

Jack hadn't put Amber down as a drinking type but this was clearly an unusual drink for an unusual girl. He took a small sip, then some more. It tasted quite innocuous, like fruit juice, but he suspected it was really very strong. Sure enough, within half a glass he began to feel even more relaxed, with a warmth spreading from his stomach through his limbs. Amber was talking again. "I'm afraid I still can't tell you why you're down here. Not fully. You will have to wait just a little longer, until tomorrow evening. That's when we'll go over to Dad's."

He smiled ruefully. "That's all right. I'd given up, anyway. Why don't you tell me some more about yourself then? Have you always lived in Cornwall? What happened to your mother?" He couldn't believe he'd asked such a direct question – it must be the drink talking.

Amber sat silent for a while, staring into the glow of the stove. Presently she said, "You know, I'll always be grateful for my childhood. It was beautiful. No-one can take that away from me." She toyed with her necklace as she spoke. "I've got my father to thank for it all, really. And I wouldn't change a single thing, even if I could. Dad brought me up from when I was a baby. He had some help from a … friend, a very special friend. Those two people have been the most important influences in my whole life." She stared at him directly. "What's *your* mother like? What are both your parents like? Tell me."

Jack, who had been feeling rather envious of Amber's description of her childhood, was caught out. Not quite in control of his words he said, "She's not like you. Well, not in personality, although ...." he trailed off. Different as the two were, there *was* a resemblance of sorts. Just physical perhaps? "Anyway, Mum and Dad work pretty hard, at their business. I guess I don't see that much of them."

"But you've got friends?"

"Yeah, of course."

"Well that's the main thing. As long as you've got people you can relate to and spend time with, that's what matters. They don't have to be your parents." She carried on as if talking to herself. "A father and a mother ... would I have changed anything if I could have? No. Never. You know, I don't think we could ever escape our parents' influence. It's the biggest thing in your life. You have opinions and you think they're yours, but they aren't. They're your parents. Or, you think they're yours because they're the opposite of your parents – but that's just the same thing, really, isn't it?" There was a long pause, which might have been awkward in any other circumstances, but wasn't. "Anyway, we managed fine. I wouldn't have changed a thing. Dad managed just fine. And we had Jacob."

"Who's Jacob?"

She laughed. "Oh, you'll meet him tomorrow. Yes, everything worked out okay."

She lapsed into silence. The two of them stared into the stove around which they were seated like votaries, lost in their respective thoughts. It was pleasantly warm in the room and now completely dark outside. The distant murmur of the sea drifted up from the beach below. Amber got up to close the curtains and in doing so she scooped up a bracelet of polished stones from one of the shelves. Sitting back down next to him on the sofa she ran it lovingly through her fingers, as if the touch soothed and consoled. "So you collect stones?" asked Jack.

Amber's face lit up. "Oh, yes. I love them. Dad's a geologist, you know. He taught himself. Now look at this, for instance." He focussed on the bracelet she was holding up. "Jasper, amethyst, malachite, jet – all polished to a high finish. Aren't they beautiful?" She looked at him significantly. "There's more to these stones than meets the eye, Jack. People don't properly understand them. But for those who do, like Dad, they have amazing powers. Look at this." She picked out one of the stones on the bracelet and rotated it so it caught the light. Little flecks of red and white, hitherto hidden, sparkled on the surface. "Haematite iron, or blood iron as the ancients used to call it. This stone isn't a dead thing at all."

"It's not?" said Jack, wondering what was coming next.

"Oh no," returned Amber. "There are emanations from all things. Emanations are given off, emanations are received. This stone, for example, resonates with blood. It can detect the ebb and flow of blood systems that are near it – feelings, in a sense. It can form a connection with other pieces of blood iron too. My father has made a science of the whole field. He calls it *geodivination*. All these" – she swept her hand around the room, gesturing to the many stones on the encircling shelves – "are *seeing stones* of various kinds."

"Seeing stones? You're kidding me. You mean they can spy on people?"

"Well, that's a bit of a negative way of putting it. But I suppose they *could* spy, yes."

In the last few minutes the truth had rapidly begun to dawn on Jack. "It was *you* who left those stones in my hotel room, wasn't it!" He reached in his pocket and drew them out, where they lay twinkling on his palm in the low light. He saw with renewed appreciation just how beautiful they were.

Amber looked sheepish and nodded. "Yes. I'm sorry if you see it as spying but Dad needed to know about you. It was the only way."

"Spying! I can't believe it! Through *these*?" Jack was caught between anger and the absurdity of believing such a bizarre theory.

"Don't be annoyed. Honestly, it was for your own good. I found you in the library in St Just, then waited until you went back to the hotel. Once I knew where you were staying it was easy to find your room."

"But … how did you know I'd take them with me, back home?"

"I didn't. The point was to connect with you in your hotel room. We could absorb enough about you from that. The fact you found them, and took them home, was just a piece of luck – and made my life much easier later on."

"Okay, so how did you know I was even in Cornwall?"

"Ah. The stones work at many levels. To get a true picture you need to have a transmitting stone to work with. But you can also pick up broader movements from a master stone – if you're as skilled as Dad."

In the face of such a cryptic comment Jack really didn't know what to think. *Seeing stones.* Hardly credible ... but on the other hand, it would explain a lot. In any case, he'd already seen enough to know that the tangible world he thought he knew to be so real was no more than a surface layer, behind which was much that was strange and fantastic. Amber was smiling sweetly at him like a small child. "Well they're very beautiful," he admitted reluctantly, his indignation rapidly melting away. He shifted to safer ground. "What about your own necklace?"

She looked both pleased and relieved to move on from a delicate subject. "Oh I'm glad you noticed that." With a deft movement she reached behind her neck, unclasped it and held it out to him. He took it and held it up to the light of the fire. The chain was a gossamer-thin silver cord which carried a single orange stone, about the size of a one penny piece, set in a plain silver mount. Within the stone Jack could see tiny bubbles and dark flecks, trapped like little flies. "It was my eighteenth birthday present from Dad. The stone is amber – my birth stone, you see? Except it's not a real stone at all, it's resin. It's probably forty million years old. Here–" She leaned closer, so close he could feel her breath on his cheek. "These dark specks are insects, insects from a primeval forest. And those bubbles are trapped air, the air of that forest, from all those millions of years ago. Amazing isn't it?"

Jack was beginning to feel intoxicated, no doubt with the wine but also with the ardour of Amber's love of her subject. It infiltrated him like some drug. He asked hazily, "Does it have special properties too, like the other stones?"

"Yes. It brings serenity of mind, and good luck. It's my lucky talisman, I always wear it." Gently she took it back from him and replaced it around her neck, where it sparkled in the soft light of the stove. The conversation lapsed. Only the rhythmic sounds of the sea and the crackle of the fire disturbed the silence.

Then she yawned, and stretched; the spell broke. "I'm so sorry, Jack, I have to go bed. It's been *such* a long day. And for you too ... You'll be comfortable in here," and she motioned to the other sofa. "Let me sort out some bedding for you." She rose to her feet a little unsteadily, disappeared into the bathroom and came back with some linen, a pillow and a towel. She spread the sheet over the sofa, smoothing it in her careful way, and laid out the towel. "Sleep well, won't you? Remember you're safe here. There's spare toothpaste in the bathroom if you need it. Night, night Jack." She padded away to her little bedroom in the extension. Before disappearing she paused and turned to look at him for a few moments, then she went in and quietly closed the door.

Jack remained sitting by the stove. At that moment he could have stayed talking, or simply being with her, all night. After some time the fire burned itself out and only the candles illuminated the room. Eventually he got up, undressed and flopped onto the other sofa, now a bed. He pulled the light sheet loosely over his body. The candle-light threw the shadows of shells and spirals on the walls. He fell asleep briefly, then awoke to find the candles had burned low and were almost out. Their ivory light was replaced by a subdued rainbow glow of colour which seemed to be emanating softly from the stones on the shelves around the room. Then sleep took him again.

CHAPTER 29

KILLING TIME

And the boy. *I should be honest with myself: this is hard to confront. I must hope – no, ensure – that my personal feelings, whatever they may be, do not interfere with the true reasons for his being here.*

When Jack woke up Amber had gone. It was already well into the morning; how had he managed to sleep so long and not notice her leave? He rubbed his head and smiled to himself ruefully, thinking it was probably something to do with all the elderberry wine he'd consumed last night. On the table in the kitchen was a bowl of fruit and a loaf of bread along with a note written in a spidery, childish script:

Dear Jack,

I've had to go out to do a few quite important things today. I hope you don't mind? Help yourself to fruit and toast and stuff in the fridge.

We'll meet at my dad's tonight he's expecting you at 8pm. The map shows where it isn't far. Have a nice day looking around, Polzeath is lovely, key under flowerpot.

Amber x

PS use the shower in my room

Jack raised his eyebrows. So he was to spend the day on his own, that was a bit odd. And find his way to her father's house on his own, too – even more odd. But then Amber was not exactly a normal girl. Well, he would look around the town and maybe walk along the cliffs. The delicious languor from last night still pervaded his body. Feeling hungry, he rapidly consumed some cereal and toast. Then, realising he needed to freshen up, he took the towel she had left out for him and, with some misgivings, entered her bedroom. It was opposite the kitchen and both, along with a tiny separate closet for the toilet, were in what was clearly an extension to the original part of the building. He felt very awkward, as if it was some kind of violation. There was a small bathroom at the far end in an en suite arrangement. Amber's room was very messy, the bed rumpled and unmade, clothes strewn around the floor, some scattered incense sticks on a small table along with little mounds of ash. Also on the table were a few of the beautiful stones she had shown him the night before. An acoustic guitar was propped up in one corner. On the walls were paintings of the coastline and some new-age-type prints of what looked like elves and fairies. Of personal photographs of anyone who might be family or friend, or of

Amber herself, there was nothing. Jack felt a guilty urge to open one or two of the drawers, wanting to find something that would bring him closer to her. He managed to stop himself, feeling ashamed. After all, she had trusted him in leaving him alone there.

The bathroom, though tiny, was amply stocked with cosmetics, soaps and shampoos, and Jack emerged a quarter of an hour later feeling refreshed and fully alive. Pulling on his jeans, t-shirt and a lightweight top, then shouldering his rucksack, he was gloriously free and ready to explore. It was a fine day outside. A warm breeze flowed down every footpath and alleyway. The whole place had a festive feel. Compared to home it seemed so utterly different, an oasis, a separate space, a different world. He went and sat outside the beach café, drinking a Coke and watching the slow breakers rolling in, the surfers in their wetsuits, the languid couples. Then he drifted in and out of one or two shops, buying himself a new pair of flip flops in the process. He considered his plans for the day. Around to the right of the bay was Pentire Point, beyond which he would be going tonight on his visit to Amber's father. It occurred to him that he didn't even know their surnames, a reminder of how suddenly this whole situation had come upon him. It didn't matter for now though; since he'd be going that way this evening, he would walk in the opposite direction along the coastal path, to the left. Amber had mentioned that it was a fine walk and not too far to reach Daymer Bay, where he could get some lunch.

He set off up the hill out of Polzeath, following the footpath as it curved up and round, past the backs of the cottage gardens, until it emerged high above the sea and followed the line of the cliffs near their edge. Exhilarating as this was he soon felt the urge to drop down to pad among the rock pools, which he did at the next opportunity, exchanging his trainers for his new flip flops and then simply going barefoot. He happily splashed in and out of each pool, searching for crabs and shells, feeling like a small boy again. He was so energised and free! At the same time the rhythmic echo of the breakers and twinkling of the sun on the surface of the sea calmed him and eased his anxieties.

And so he made his way slowly along the coastline, with frequent stops to peer at some new type of shell or stone. The fact the tide was far out meant he could walk all the way via the rock pools. After a couple of hours, the sandy expanse of Daymer Bay opened up on his left and he once more joined the coastal path as it descended through the dunes to skirt around the edge of the beach. Beyond, he could see the squat and crooked spire of a church poking up above the sand dunes like a witch's hat. The shop and café were at the far side of a car park which, even so late in the season, was quite full. The obligatory surfers' vans were parked in ranks, their owners either getting changed behind them or shuttling to and from the beach in their wetsuits.

The café was in the back of the shop and didn't amount to more than a few tables squashed into an area encroached on by racks of clothing and rotating stands of postcards and books on local history. But there were plenty of people in there and Jack joined a queue for food. At its head a solid-looking man in shorts and flip flops was ordering, jabbing his finger impatiently at various items behind the counter while all the time keeping up a conversation on his mobile, clearly struggling with the poor signal: "Er hello … Hello? Justin? Are you there? ...Yes …Yes, and don't over prepare. Four slides at the most. Just the executive summary. Got it?" Jack watched him for a while, fascinated, and reflected on his recent freedom from his own mobile, which at this moment lay forgotten in his bag at The Shack. Maybe Amber was right after all, maybe there *was* too much communication. Certainly this character looked far from happy: tense and fractious, while the poor girl behind the counter was reduced to having to decipher his jabbing gestures as best she could.

At a separate till, tourists queued to purchase clothing and souvenirs. It was all in sharp contrast to the tranquillity and serenity of the rock pools. When his turn came, Jack ordered a baked potato with tuna and sat at a small table to the rear, watching the cars crawling in and out of the car park. He ate thoughtfully, reflecting on the impending meeting with Amber's father that evening. What was he to expect? Could this man really be the great guru that his daughter portrayed? Yet even as he framed it, the question seemed to lose relevance. He had come this far, down all this way from Amersham with a total stranger on the strength of a hunch and a sense of trust. And, if he was honest, from utter disillusionment with his home environment. There was little point in questioning it all now; better to sit back and let things happen. And anyway, he felt so very relaxed; the day had so far had a wonderfully therapeutic effect on his anguished thought processes. The morning's glorious walk continued to exert a cleansing and clarifying effect. So he sat and ate, calm and detached from the people around him. After finishing lunch he walked up the lane a short way, exploring. He found a craft gallery set back from the road in a little space of its own, surrounded by neatly trimmed lawns and hanging baskets. Here he looked in and killed time, flicking though some old prints and looking at the prices of various hand-made items such as clocks, teapots and pieces of sculpture.

When he next looked at his watch it had already gone four. Although it was still a beautiful day, the coming evening was prefigured in the lengthening shadows. He had better be heading back. He could have returned along the cliff path, but once again he felt the pull of the rocks and the rock pools. The tide was still far enough out so he set off again along the beach. As he rounded the headland he detected a certain change in the mood of the place: the shadows were blacker, the tide rather nearer than he'd thought, the pools more numerous and deeper than before. He continued, sliding over the wet rocks, cutting his feet on limpets and barnacles, his awareness further heightened. Beneath the layers of sun and sparkling water there lay something darker, he could feel it. He marvelled at the rust-coloured lichen and springy tufts of brown seaweed that clung and swayed in the breakers.

To his right he noticed the rock face giving way to a dark cave, almost as if the substance of the rock itself had been sucked inward by some vortex or hidden channel. He moved nearer and hovered on the threshold, curious. He could see the inside was streaked with curious bands of subdued colours: dark reds, rust browns, yellow ochres, burnt umbers – a kind of muted psychedelic chamber. He wanted to penetrate further, but hesitated. After some moments he took a tentative step forward, then another, and another until he was walking jerkily into the throat of the cave. As he progressed he thought he could hear something very deep, very low; a kind of glutinous or guttural chant. In words, it was hard to frame, but it was as if the idea of the earth itself had somehow found its own voice. It spoke of profound fires in places far below, of pain and greed, of sharp craving and of harsh and heedless self-interest.

Then the sound of a dog frantically barking abruptly intruded, breaking the spell. Jack came to himself with a start and turned on his heel, back to the light, the sound of the sea and the sight of the sky. "Over here Bertie!" a woman's voice cheerfully rang out. A small, brindled terrier-like dog swooped round in an arc, brushed past Jack's legs and ran off in the direction of Polzeath, turning as it did so to look at Jack with a wolfishly smiling mouth and lolling tongue. Taking this as a good omen, he followed the dog as quickly as he could.

He continued more soberly, attuned to the dusky undercurrents of the place as well as the surface lustre. Before long he entered Polzeath. The wide bay opened out before him, populated now with fewer surfers and only an intermittent scattering of the children and couples who had earlier been everywhere. The tide was coming in fast. Now a new emotion overtook him, an unaccountable gloom; not fear, not anxiety, only a flattening of spirits and a sense of futility. In this state of mind he made his way across the beach, splashing heedlessly through the numerous rivulets flowing back to the sea. The café was still open. There he sat outside, sipping a drink and watching the melancholy spectacle of the beach slowly being swallowed up by the incoming tide, the sun sinking to the horizon. He felt empty. All the exhilaration of the early part of the day had evaporated. He thought about Amber, about her past, her friendships, what she really thought of him and what her father would think of him, and about how happy and fulfilled she seemed to be. Why couldn't he be the same? Such reflections continued to chase themselves fruitlessly around in his head as the sun sank behind a low band of cloud. And then the dynamic changed. Suddenly it was not late afternoon, it was early evening. It was as if a switch had been thrown; and for sure, occasional lights had come on in the town and one or two people were emerging for evening drinks. The melancholy lifted: the afternoon was not ending, the evening was beginning. And with the evening came new adventure! He would go to Amber's father's house, he would finally meet this mysterious man, he would see Amber again. He would get answers to questions. He would find a way forward. He turned to make his way up the hill.

When he got back to The Shack it was still empty. He realized he had half been hoping to find her there, in a change of plan. If anything the mess in the lounge seemed worse, the bed linen on the sofa thrown all over the place. Had he really left it in such a state? Maybe Amber's casual ways were rubbing off on him already. A curious smell pervaded the place, as of garages or old machines – presumably the cold reek from the stove. His best bet, he decided, was another wash and change of clothes, to freshen himself for the evening's adventure. Stripping to his boxers he made for the bathroom. As he did so he slipped on an oily slick that was smeared across the tiles of the passageway, nearly losing his footing. With a roll of toilet paper he wiped up the residue, then proceeded to take his second shower of the day.

Twenty minutes later he was ready for off. A glance at his watch showed it was nearly seven. He had no idea what Amber's concept of 'not far' was but he thought it better to get going now if they were expecting him at eight. He pulled on a sweater and a hoodie, then packed his waterproof in a small rucksack he had brought down. With only a moment's hesitation he also took the diary of Owen Tyack, wrapping it in a plastic bag for added protection. It was the time for answers, not for holding things back! And now – he felt prepared for whatever the night ahead held.

CHAPTER 30

Plans to Sin

The silence in St Nicholas' church was complete, as complete as is only found in a quiet parish church in a quiet English village. Light streamed through the plain glass of the aisle windows but they were too narrow to give much in the way of illumination. The brass lectern glinted wickedly, its eagle's beak half open in a silent cry. Shadows gathered in the corners and hung in the rafters like smoke. Spread out on the north wall was that striking anatomy of evil, the painting of the seven deadly sins. Bared teeth grinned, lips curled back, smooth lobes of flesh beckoned, a knife flashed. Pride imperiously straddled the centre stage, a huge and salutary figure surrounded by his clutch of lesser companions. What scenes had he witnessed through the ebb and flow of the centuries? If paintings could speak he could no doubt tell of the annual rhythm of services, baptisms, deaths, Christmases and the rest, an unbroken thread from a distant medieval past to recent times. What else? There were other, stranger things than these, surely – secrets that it had kept to itself through the years, secrets it didn't give up so easily.

Thoughts like these ran through Toby's head while he stood and looked up at the painting, as he had done hundreds of times before, pondering why it was so special. In his head the picture had acquired a talismanic status, something to commune with silently. The others didn't like him doing that, he knew – but as long as he didn't talk about it to anyone they didn't stop him. But it wasn't always easy not to talk … Behind him the door rattled, and swung open. There stepped down into the church the wiry figure of Peregrinus, who paused, looked about him while apparently listening intently, then sighted Toby and purposefully crossed the nave to come and stand beside the youth. For a while they both regarded the wall painting together, Toby barely registering his presence. Eventually Peregrinus said conversationally, "Do you like this painting?"

Toby half turned towards him, struggling to divide his attention. "Yeah. It's *special.* You know?" He put his finger to his lips, enjoining silence. "Special and secret, yeah?"

Peregrinus nodded seriously. "Yes, it *is* special. What's your name?"

"Tob*ee*."

The older man looked at him with sympathy. He was about to say more when from behind the vestry curtain came a voice: "I've told you before Toby not to go chatting to strangers about–" The lean and urbane figure of the Reverend Trecarrow emerged, stooping. He broke off in mid-sentence on seeing Peregrinus standing next to the youth. "Good morning," he said rather coldly. "Can I help you?"

An ironic smile spread over Peregrinus's face. "Do I look as if I need help?"

Trecarrow flushed. "No. Of course, you are very welcome in God's house. I simply meant ...."

Peregrinus waited impassively, letting the vicar's protestations peter out, privately amused by his discomposure. Then he seemed to tire of the game and said, "I've come to see David Tyack. I believe he's here?"

The vicar's whole demeanour changed as suddenly as if a different person had usurped his body. "David Tyack – I'm sorry, he never said … He's expecting you, yes? Then please follow me," and he retreated behind the curtain. Peregrinus paused, put a hand on Toby's shoulder and said to him quietly, "I'm sure we'll talk again soon. I'm sorry we don't have time now." Then he turned to follow the retreating back of Trecarrow. The youth looked after him with an expression of astonishment and something approaching devotion.

Behind the curtain, through the vestry and beyond a further door (normally locked) was a more modern annex to the church, a brick building with a lean-to roof. Originally used as a store room, it was now converted to another purpose and furnished with easy chairs, a desk and a whiteboard on which were scrawled in different coloured inks dates and flow charts. In the chairs lounged Miguel Perez, weasel-faced Nathan Lovett and David Tyack, all deep in discussion. The latter half rose to his feet when, after a deferential knock, Trecarrow entered with Peregrinus in tow. "Ah, Reverend, I should have told you beforehand. This is our right-hand man, Peregrinus. You'll be seeing more of him from now. Peregrinus, I know you've already met Miguel and Nathan – sit down and join us." Hands were shaken all round, and polite noises made. A chair was found for Peregrinus, who accepted it with a modest show of reluctance. Then David Tyack turned back to the vicar. "We've got a bit to be getting on with now Reverend so don't let us keep you. I've got the key here" – he patted his pocket – "so we can sort ourselves out." It was clear that this was more or less a dismissal. Unhappy to be evicted from his own church but realizing that he had no option, Trecarrow gave a curt little bow and withdrew, shutting the door behind him just a little more loudly than was necessary.

Once the vicar had gone the conversation began to flow rapidly. Peregrinus, with a quiet authority blended with his usual deference, started the discussion. "Mr Tyack, you tell me that all the results are ready now, and we are simply 'validating' them. Then these results will be used in the reactor itself, so there will be no mistakes made at activation. We need just one further round of trials with the prototype – am I right?"

It was Lovett who responded. "Correct. Just one more will do it. We'll have to be a little bit careful but I must say that Trecarrow has been pretty invaluable. Without him it would have been *much* harder – who knows, maybe not possible at all."

Peregrinus listened carefully, his fingertips together as if in prayer. "How much does the vicar know?" he asked.

"Just enough," returned Lovett. "His interest in the spirit realm has been the way in with him. I've told him that all this" – here he pointed downwards at the floor – "is in the service of the eradication of vice, nothing else. Our goal is spiritual purity, spiritual purity for everyone. But the worst cases, the most corrupt, must be the stepping stones, as it were, to that purification. As well as getting his cooperation over the use of this place, his ethical sense has been absolutely essential in identifying those worst cases. We've got a lot to thank our vicar for."

"Any scruples?" pursued Peregrinus.

Lovett considered. "A few, at first. Naturally, I suppose. I think he's over those now – the donation to the church has helped, of course. Trecarrow will get a new roof out of us, at the least. As somebody – Thomas Cromwell was it? – said, 'every man has his price'!" He paused and pondered for a few seconds. "You know, the vicar's got so much involved in the whole spirit realm that he actually attended a séance. It went right off track, I gather – gave our vicar quite a shock. I could have warned them, it's not a business to be taken lightly. I know its power and I know its danger. Anyway, he's back on side now, though it took a bit of doing. We may make a psycho-spiritual physicist out of him yet ...."

Here Perez cut in. "There's no need for that. For one thing, we're almost finished with this place now, and that goes for Trecarrow too. And anyway, the whole spiritual aspect is just a means to an end, as I've said often enough. We get the reactor going by drawing on these energies in their pure form, then we're done with that side of it. We shouldn't get so hung up on it!" He directed an accusing look at Lovett, who stared back truculently.

"That's all true Miguel," put in David Tyack, anxious to pre-empt any outbreak of bad feeling, "but it's the spiritual side that's been our missing piece, the solution to the problem that's held us back all this while. It's had its place. Anyway, here's where we are." He addressed himself to Peregrinus. "As you say, we just need this final round of trials, with the help of the Reverend, and I believe we can close down the prototype once and for all. Destroy it, and wind up operations here at St Nicholas."

Peregrinus had been listening intently with eyes half closed. "Yes," he said slowly, half to himself. "We'll finish here. It will have been a long road, a very long road."

"Six years," returned David Tyack. "Six years' labour in that damned crypt!"

"Longer than that."

"Well, yes, I suppose so – if you count Owen Tyack's work here. So far as *that's* concerned, we don't know exactly what errors we repeated, but at least we had the advantage of modern technology. If only we could have spoken to him directly, or to someone who was there ...."

"Over a hundred years ago," put in Perez. "My God, he was ahead of his time! Well, thank heaven we had the diary – the next best thing to the man himself, I suppose."

Peregrinus, hearing this, simply smiled to himself and remained withdrawn in a sort of meditative state. A pause in the conversation ensued while each man speculated privately on the unholy labours of their Victorian predecessor, down in the crypt all those years ago. Eventually Peregrinus spoke again, inclining his head in the direction of the nave. "And where does the boy come in?"

Perez looked irritable. "Toby? He doesn't. He just hangs around here like a limpet. We can't get rid of him. There seems no real harm in him though. You know these types. Always obsessed with something or other. In his case, the paintings." Peregrinus pursed his lips and nodded, appearing satisfied.

At this point, David Tyack roused himself. "Well, we know what we need to do. Miguel, Nathan, I think we ought to get started, yes?"

Perez nodded in agreement: "No time like the present, eh? Come along Nathan, we've got work to do!" He pointed to the floor. "Let's get downstairs." Without further prompting the two men rose and left the room.

David Tyack had noted on several occasions that Peregrinus was one of those unnerving people who seem entirely comfortable in a silence, however many or few people there are in the room. Now he sat there still and attentive, apparently listening carefully to nothing at all, watching his companion calmly. It was as if some social sense, some awareness of basic etiquette, were entirely missing from his character. Yet he was polite enough in his speech and general manner; excessively so, in fact. Very strange. There was something else, too, something truly unsettling. At such times of silence David Tyack got the distinct impression that Peregrinus was somehow, ridiculous as it seemed, *probing* his thoughts. Abruptly dismissing such speculation as paranoia, and more to end this sensation than for any other reason, he said, "So you've found somewhere to live up here. Are you settling in well?"

"Oh certainly. I'm used to moving around, Mr Tyack. You don't need to worry yourself about me. And I know it well enough here."

"Not this church?"

"Perhaps," returned Peregrinus cryptically, in a way that discouraged further inquiry.

"You still haven't told me where you found the diary." As soon as he said it, David regretted bringing the subject up. Why couldn't he be more careful, damn it!

A slight frown clouded the other man's features. "Ah, the diary. You still have it?"

"Yes ...." Peregrinus raised an eyebrow at this. "Well, no. No; I'm afraid not. Of course, we got everything we needed out of it–"

"So where is it now?" The voice was soft, conversational, deferential as usual in its tone.

"I'm honestly not sure. It's probable my son may have taken it. He has an interest in such things – family history, you know. Anyway, Jack's gone away for a few days … I think he may have the diary with him."

"You 'think'. But you don't *know*?"

David sighed. "No, I don't know. Not for sure."

Peregrinus, whose displays of emotion were limited to occasional spasms of intense but restrained enthusiasm, was not an easy person to read. Clearly he was not one to cry over spilt milk, yet even so David Tyack detected a certain discomposure come over the man. His only response, however, was a quiet, "We must get that back."

⅄

In the nave of the church, Toby still hovered, staring at the other painting this time, the one of Adam and Eve. As soon as David and Peregrinus emerged from their enclave he scuttled over and attached himself to the latter, tugging at his arm. "Eh mister! Over here, there's another over here, new one …."

David Tyack rolled his eyes at his companion. "I'm sorry about this." His patience suddenly seemed to snap and he shouted at the youth, "Look, I've told you to *stop* pestering people about these paintings. You're a nuisance! You're *not* to go blabbing and bleating on about them!" He actually raised his arm, more to make the point than with any real intention to hurt.

In an instant, so quickly the movement could not actually be seen, Peregrinus had firmly grasped it. "No!" he said quietly. It was the first time he had contradicted, let alone challenged, his employer, who immediately backed down without even resisting. "You don't need to worry," continued Peregrinus, and turned to the youth. With surprising gentleness in his voice he said, "You can show me the picture. I'd like to see it, if you would?" The two of them, boy and man, went over to the painting together, leaving David Tyack staring after them in amazement and not a little frustration. More than ever, he just didn't know what to make of Peregrinus. He looked over to the north wall. Surveying all was the huge figure of Pride, looking back at him impassively. Did that ambiguous smile condemn or approve? Who knew? Who knew what it had seen in all its centuries of existence? He shook his head and made to join the others in the crypt, leaving Toby excitedly declaiming to an absorbed Peregrinus.

CHAPTER 31

The Lair of the Magus

Jack pulled up his hood for protection against the increasing chill of the evening air and looked seawards. Dramatic streaks of dark cloud reached out from the horizon like the paws of a great beast; behind them the sky was a delicate egg-shell colour. He redoubled his concentration on the uneven cliff path, treacherous at the best of times but near-lethal in the dusk. According to Amber's directions it should not be far now. The sweep of Trebarwith strand opened up ahead, its amphitheatre magnifying the roar of the waves. The path became more grassy than rocky, then began to veer inland. Directly ahead a large whitewashed house emerged out of the gloom, its lights twinkling invitingly. The seaward side of the house plunged directly down, forming a continuous line with the precipitous cliffs as if it had grown directly out of them. This, then, must be it – an incredible place. He left the path;

a gate stood half open and he followed the gravel drive that wound around the side of the villa to a wide entrance portico that offered some shelter from the elements. Nearby stood a flagpole, its rope clinking rhythmically in the breeze. The scent of fragrant late flowers blew in from the garden.

Jack paused at the threshold, unsure what to do. The house really was big, with several floors and cloister-like extensions. It was difficult to get an impression of it as a whole. The windows were unusually small, dotted around the white pebble-dashed walls irregularly, and each was lit with a pinkish light. All in all, the place looked like a huge magic lantern. Like the gate, the front door was partially open; from within came the faint sounds of a piano. Jack felt mistrust vie in his mind with the seductiveness of that open door and the beguiling music. What if the whole thing was a trap, concocted by this man and his daughter? What if they were no saviours but the sinister architects of a plot against him, a plot to … what? He couldn't say exactly, but there were plenty of reasons to be wary, as surely any sane person would be in his position. Yet already it was too late. The music had begun to weave its spell, drawing him in, the sorcerer's siren song. He pushed the door open fully and entered.

Ahead stretched a hallway, plain and whitewashed in a Mediterranean manner, just like the exterior. The effect was both attractive and calming. The principal decoration was a narrow strip of rug that ran the length, richly woven in dark reds and making startling contrast against the white of the rest. Wall lights with pink scalloped shades lit the way.

Several arched openings led off this hallway, none giving any clue as to which one to take. Feeling a powerful sense of enchantment Jack stepped out and, without knowing why, took the third archway to the right. He descended three steps and the music swelled louder: extravagant, sweeping arpeggios, stormy but at the same time poignant and intimate. He came to a small room with simple furniture consisting of shelves, a table and chairs finished in a light wood and a window that looked out on the dark sea and orange horizon. Books were strewn on the floor and table; many were in foreign languages – Jack hazarded Spanish, French, what might have been Hebrew, and certainly Latin. Two doorways were situated on the opposite side of the room. The sound of the piano momentarily slackened and slowed before surging up again in an imploring flurry of rippling scales. Feeling powerless to resist, he moved on and out of the room through the left-hand doorway, the music weaving its profound, subtle spell.

Now he was in another corridor, with a vaulted ceiling. It was only short and terminated in a spiral staircase that wound up above and out of sight. On the walls hung regularly spaced pictures depicting shells, fossils yielded by the sea, maritime creatures, tall ships and mysterious geometric patterns. He pressed on up the stairs, deeper into the house, seeking the heart of the place. As he did so the music faded, as if being left behind, although its notes could be clearly heard still. He emerged into a tiny, turret-like room that appeared to be another study. It was octagonal in shape and in its centre was a similarly octagonal table, strewn with papers and writing materials. Above this table was a skylight and against its panes the rain now pattered. A small, mushroom-shaped lamp on the table provided illumination and a leather chair was pushed back against one wall. The walls of this room consisted entirely of book shelves packed with many old volumes. Opposite, an archway led out and into a sloping passage that curved gently down and to the left. The house was a real labyrinth, no doubt of that!

Drawn by the invisible thread of the music, which now seemed to be coming from the passageway ahead, Jack was leaving the room when his glance rested on something that held him. On the desk was a large, leather-bound notebook that lay open. Next to it were a couple of other books, both very old. One proclaimed itself on the cover to be *Coleridge's Poetry*; the other was an old play of some sort. The double page of the notebook was filled with a neat yet highly decorated hand – decorated, indeed, to the point where it seemed like a work of art in its own right. And immediately he felt conscious of the weight of diary in the rucksack against his back. The entries were separated by paragraph spaces, but bore no dates. His eye fell on the last one. He read:

> *There is so much to consider, to anticipate. I will not risk my precious jewel again. And the boy. I should be honest with myself: this is hard to confront. I must hope – no,* ensure *– that my personal feelings, whatever they may be, do not interfere with the true reasons for his being here.*

And the boy. What was this? What was the meaning of all these books, everywhere, obsessively hoarded like this? After pondering the entry for some minutes Jack collected himself and continued, out of the turret room and down the curving passage. Alcoves on either side held small tables on each of which was a single candle flickering in a pewter dish. Would he, he wondered, ever be able to retrace his steps in this maze of rooms and corridors? The passage straightened; the music grew louder. The notes were stormy again now, imperious, commanding. Louder and louder … then suddenly they faded, ebbing away to a quiet and introspective conclusion, like a tempest that had abated to the gentlest of breezes. A large room opened up before Jack. In the middle, with his back to him, was a man seated at a grand piano.

The room had a comfortable feel. The piano dominated but did not overwhelm it. Beyond, grouped around a stone fireplace, was a set of sofas and easy chairs with a low burr-oak table in their midst, the underneath of which was piled high with books and papers. Curled up on one of the chairs was Amber, reading a book. To the left of the fireplace the wall gave way to a wide window that commanded a panoramic view of the sea, now a near-blackness. The soft furnishings were in pale earth tones and so the overall effect was even more light and spacious than it might otherwise have been. In contrast to the other rooms there were few books here, beyond those under the table. Instead, the shelves held what appeared to be many musical manuscripts, interspersed with clusters of shells and rocks, just as in Amber's house. A niche in the left-hand wall held a life-sized marble bust of a craggy faced, bearded man, who from his vantage point presided over the room. In the opposite corner stood a majestic long-case clock, reaching almost to the ceiling, the woody tick of which now came to the fore as the last chords of the piano died away. The pianist remained motionless, hands still at the keys, while Amber looked up from her book and smiled at Jack. Something held him frozen on the threshold, reluctant to enter the room. Then a rich bass voice said, "Welcome". A pause, and the figure at the piano slowly turned around and then stood up to confront him. "Welcome, I say. Now come in, join us."

The man was on the tall side, though not excessively so, and broad in the shoulder, very upright of stance. His grey hair was brushed back and hung long in the collar; he had a close-cropped iron grey beard that gave his already strong features additional distinction and force. He was wearing a claret-coloured smoking jacket over a white shirt; certainly an aroma of cigar tobacco hung not unpleasantly in the room. The overall impression was of contained authority and self-assurance, with a large measure of the distinguished thrown in. Yet when he spoke his eyes roved here and there restlessly, looking Jack up and down, suspiciously it seemed.

Seeing his visitor was still, perhaps unsurprisingly, hesitant the man repeated, "Come in, sit down, and let us get you some refreshment. Sit over here–" and he motioned towards

Amber. Feeling like an ill-schooled actor making his debut, Jack returned Amber's smile, went over to the sofa and sat down. The man followed and lowered himself into one of the easy chairs facing Jack, continuing to regard him keenly. "I am Professor Benjamin Silverman," he said grandly, as if expecting his name to be instantly recognized. Jack said nothing, in truth not knowing what he *could* say. Instead he carefully divested himself of his rucksack and placed it next to him on the sofa. His host's quick eyes flickered penetratingly over to it, seeming to read a multitude of meanings in that small act. Amber had put down her book. Jack noticed she looked somehow different, troubled, preoccupied. Had she been crying? What had happened, he wondered, to change her carefree demeanour of the night before? Nevertheless when she caught his eye she gave him another broad smile and said, cheerfully enough, "So: were my directions good? Did you find us okay?"

"No problem at all," he replied, suppressing the urge to say something about the inherent dangers of trailing along two miles of rugged coastline in near darkness. "It was all exactly as you said." A wry smile played on Professor Silverman's face, the ghost of some private thought. "How did *you* get here Amber?" pursued Jack, curious as to her movements during the day.

"Oh, I drove over earlier." An awkward silence ensued, Amber clearly being disinclined to say more about where she'd disappeared to for the day, Jack half expecting her to tell him. Meanwhile her father settled back in his chair, crossed his legs and continued to look at Jack with undisguised curiosity.

He stroked his beard and Jack noticed his fingers bore several rings, each with a different coloured, polished stone set in a gold band. After drinking in every aspect of his visitor's appearance, he suddenly clapped his hands together in a gesture of mock decisiveness. "Now! Before anything else, let's have some refreshments. Jack – what would you like?" And, to Jack's surprise, he reached for a little bell on the occasional table beside his chair and rang it. "Ah, here we are, now here comes Jacob."

There was a noise from the passageway whence Jack had entered; a dark shadow was cast, as of someone advancing, and there emerged an apparition the sight of which froze Jack in his seat. It was a man of well over six feet in height, immensely powerfully built and of the strangest appearance he had ever seen. The man was wearing a sort of tunic, all of one piece, that was a dull terracotta colour. His skin was of a remarkably similar colour to this tunic, as if all had been made of the same substance. But what made the greatest impact was the face, a face Jack had seen before: strangely blurred and unfinished looking, with dark hollows for eyes and blunt features. The forehead contained a deep depression, in which some slender object appeared embedded. In a final grotesque touch, the creature was carrying what looked like a napkin or tea towel over one of its arms.

Amber had been watching Jack's reaction with amusement. "I think you've already met Jacob, on your walk yesterday, yes? He'd been helping me while you were out, and you passed him on his way back here."

Professor Silverman, also amused, was now chuckling. "You mustn't be alarmed," he said mirthfully. "He's not as fierce as he looks, don't worry! He will not harm you." He turned to the apparition. "Jacob, I think some of your cordial would be appreciated, for us all." Jacob nodded slightly and retreated back up the passageway with a heavy, shuffling tread.

Jack had seen enough, recently, to be less astonished than he might otherwise have been by this development. Even so, he felt a unique sense of awe and unease course through him, the awareness of being in the presence of a great, tamed power coupled with an intelligence above that of the animal, but less than the human. "What *is* it?" he asked eventually.

The Professor leant back in his chair and put his fingertips together, as if considering the question for the first time. "My servant. My daughter's companion and her best friend – would that sum it up, Amber?"

Amber nodded, serious now. "We couldn't have managed without Jacob."

This strange answer hardly satisfied Jack. "Where did you find him?"

Professor Silverman remained in his meditative pose and gazed at the ceiling. "Find him? I didn't 'find him' anywhere. Perhaps a more appropriate question would be 'where did he come from?'" He paused thoughtfully and continued staring upwards. "Well, to tell you briefly, but perhaps not satisfactorily, I *made him.* Now, Jack, do you like my music?"

Jack struggled with the implications of these words. *Made him* – what sort of person was this man? He had come here expecting answers, not more riddles. But there was the evidence of his own eyes .... He saw the Professor was looking at him from under lowered lids, clearly awaiting an answer to his question. He said guardedly, "Yes, it was pretty amazing."

"Good! I'll play for you again later then. Music is my great passion. I've tried to teach Amber but–"

"Oh, I wasn't very good," broke in his daughter. "Dad tried hard but I don't have his talent."

"You have many other talents, Amber. Many, many others," came the reply.

Jack decided to return to the question of the servant. "What do you mean, that you 'made' Jacob?"

The Professor looked surprisingly grave. "I do mean precisely that. Jack, there are many secrets that are not and never can be understood by most of the people you will ever meet in your life." He stood up and strode over to the bust in the niche, addressing them both now. "Truth is to be arrived at by the lone thinker, not by the broad masses. Many years ago, when Amber was still a baby, I took the decision to withdraw from those masses." He put his hands in the pockets of his jacket so just the thumbs protruded and stared ruminatively at the craggy faced bust. "You must understand that Truth is not appearance, it is *behind* appearance. And I had vowed to follow the Way of Truth. Yet how could I, when every day the pressure of many lives, all going about their trivial business, dragged my thoughts back to the world of phenomena? So I withdrew here. I took the baby with me." He spoke of Amber now as if she were some incidental third party. "That way, I knew I would not be distracted by temptation – not the least of the obstacles to the seeker of Truth, I might say. I studied deeply for many a long night and day, building on my scientific knowledge." He continued to gaze on the bust, and added slowly, as if reading from a script: "*I, a fugitive from the gods and wanderer.*"

"Who is that?" asked Jack, nodding towards the bust, intrigued.

"A great man, who lived many centuries ago, before the era of your Christ. A philosopher. A deep thinker. My inspiration." He seemed lost in thought, the picture of philosophical distraction. Presently he resumed, as if recollecting himself. "But I had a child, I couldn't manage alone. Nor yet did I wish to admit a stranger to my house. Already my knowledge gave me insight into certain secrets, the secrets of life itself! I had immersed myself in the ancient Rabbinical texts; I knew the rituals of animation. The creation of life, Jack: never to be taken lightly." He looked intently at Amber as he said this. "But I made my decision. For one month, I laboured to collect clay of precisely the correct composition. Nothing less would do, yet it was scarce to find. And when I had my clay, I worked through the long night to fashion it, the baby crying all the while. When my work was complete, I rested for a day, and gave what attention I could to my child. The next evening, I performed the animating ritual in the cellar of this place, reading from the ancient texts. The soul I implanted was that of a crow; the *Corvidae* is much maligned and more intelligent than you could possibly imagine. And crows, of course, are plentiful. Then, I placed the wafer of life in the forehead and breathed over my creation, and it took my breath and gave a long inhalation. Its limbs stirred and its eyes flickered." He was now quite lost in the recollection of those many years ago, as if in a dream. "And Jacob was born, the golem of my forefathers."

After a lengthy pause, the Professor abruptly looked up and stared at them defiantly, as if expecting to be challenged on some point of the story. Only the pattering of a now heavier rain could intermittently be heard on the window as the gusts of wind lashed it into horizontal sheets. Jack was divided in his reflections between the extraordinary nature of this self-styled magician's account and a lingering concern as to why, according to Amber, the man needed him there. His thoughts were interrupted by the creaking of the floor – indeed, he could actually feel it give slightly, as if under a great weight – and the next moment Jacob lumbered into view again. The great strength of his limbs and impression of solidity contrasted bizarrely with the tray of drinks which he balanced in one hand, just like a waiter in a café. The creature approached him and proffered the tray, on which were set three identical glasses of a pale green fluid. Jack wanted to recoil, but mastered the impulse and took a glass. A whiff of damp earth clogged his nostrils before Jacob moved on with his tray to Amber. Last of all, the Professor took his glass and nodded to his servant. "Thank you Jacob. You can go now." He turned to Amber and Jack and raised his glass.

Jack watched the broad back retreat. "Does he just carry out your orders?"

"Yes – and more. The golems of old were simple servants and very limited. They behaved quite literally. But I found I had endowed Jacob with something more than that." He smiled at them with pride and took a draught of liquor. "This cordial, for example, is his own creation. I found him one day experimenting in the kitchen. And this was the result. You see it tastes rather good! That is when I knew that Jacob had more than merely literal understanding, but a *creative* faculty too. Anyway: to resume. Now I had my servant. All the things I found I did not have time to do I delegated to him: little tasks, procuring provisions for us, cleaning, tidying, and the like. And more; he became Amber's nanny, so to speak. And so I could pursue my studies."

Jack reflected for a moment on just what kind of a strange upbringing this must have amounted to. Some of the causes for Amber's eccentricity were, indeed, becoming apparent. "Can he talk?" he asked.

It was Amber who answered. "No. The golems are mute. But that's never bothered us. There's too much talk – not enough loyalty," she said, fiercely.

"What's that thing in his forehead?"

"The wafer of life. Jacob is immensely strong, physically almost invincible. Remove that wafer, though, and he's completely helpless."

Professor Silverman ignored this interruption and began pacing up and down restlessly, as if about to embark on some fresh lecture. At this point, something – perhaps the cordial, which had had a wonderfully stimulating and clarifying effect – motivated Jack to ask the simplest of questions, for which he still had no answer: "I'd like to know why I'm here. Can one of you *please* tell me?"

Silverman left off his pacing and looked at him as if for the first time. "Well, that is a fair question, a very fair question. To put it bluntly Jack, I need your blood! As to *why* – I'm afraid there is no quick answer." He sat down with them again, much calmer suddenly. "I shall tell you in the clearest way I can, and you must stop me at any point on which you feel out of your depth." Jack realized that, with both of them, there simply was no point in trying to hurry their infuriatingly drawn-out way of revealing things, which must, he speculated, be a family trait. The Professor would have to tell his story in his own time. He quickly looked over and caught the man staring at him in the most curious way. It was almost as if Jack's very presence had unsettled him - unless, of course, that was his normal way of behaving.

The magus leaned back in his chair and began stroking his beard again, occasionally pausing to fiddle with his rings. Jack got the impression, from the way Amber leaned forward intently, that even she was not fully acquainted with the complete story. Perhaps now he would finally get some answers.

"You need first to understand something of the industrial past of this area," the Professor began. "There has been open, or shallow, mining in this area for thousands of years, thanks to the igneous geology of the coastline here. The ancient Celtic inhabitants of Cornwall worked open seams for tin, copper and silver: all very valuable metals at that time. In the early Christian period Phoenician traders came here in search of just such precious deposits. There are symbols, such as the Chi Rho – a precursor of the Christian cross – that have been found on the beaches here, engraved on stones or ingots. And so it continued through the Dark Ages, this superficial searching for such commodities. But at the start of the eighteenth century came a great change. Humankind began a process that has still not finished, the process of industrialization. And for certain special social, economic and historical reasons, that process began in England. And so you embarked on this path, leading the world. Quite suddenly, more accurate machines appeared; society became gripped by the need for profit as the old structures gave way to a new system: capitalism! This need for surplus, or capital, led to the development of companies and corporations to exploit the riches of this Cornish coast, and using the new technologies these companies drove shafts ever deeper underground, ever further out to sea, in their relentless quest for tin and copper. These were the sacred idols of the age."

He stopped, a look of distaste on his face, and scanned the room, perhaps imagining invisible rows of students taking in his words. Thoughts of his parents' business, Geothermal, filled Jack's head; a testament, surely, to the same remorseless drive described by the Professor. Silverman continued, "If one overlooks the baseness of this money-grubbing, there was no real harm done. All change is governed by necessity; could it have been otherwise? But the next development was more serious. A Cornish man by the name of Richard Trevithick perfected a steam engine, and turned his attention to its application to the mining industry in his part of the world. He was, I suppose, a genius of sorts – but his understanding was only of the world of appearances." He smiled thinly. "I would call him a *technician*; he was no philosopher. But the consequences of this invention and its new application were immense! Now this metal colossus could pump water from shafts hundreds of feet down. Deep mines could be drained. And it was at these depths that the mining companies suspected the richest lodes of tin and copper could be found."

Jack cast his mind back to his researches in the St Just library and the colourful historical account of Jim Peters he had found there. Once more he had the distinct feeling that loose threads were slowly weaving together, in their own good time, to form a final picture. He could dimly sense where this was heading. If only he could see further himself, think further!

The Professor carried on: "Before I retired from the world I was fated to teach, for my crust, the very subject of business and commerce we've mentioned. But then, after I withdrew, I schooled myself deeply in the principles and lore of geology, a true passion." A light of pure dedication entered his eyes. "Yes, there are many very beautiful types to be found in this coastline: sulphide of copper, purple copper ore, sulphide of bismuth, specular iron ore …." He enunciated the names lovingly. "Nobody fully understands the real powers of stones and minerals. But, to return: there was a certain mine that was deeper than any other; indeed, it became famous just for that."

"The Crown Mines at Botallack," Jack interposed, wishing he could somehow fast-forward to the key facts.

Professor Silverman looked pleased. "Exactly! This was a truly remarkable enterprise, with workings three miles out under the sea bed and, of course, to a very great depth. The Botallack miners used their engines and tools to dig far out under the ocean. The mines attracted tourists, and indeed they offered guided tours to cater for them. Now where is it?" He rummaged in some piles of books and papers underneath the coffee table and produced an old volume with a red leather bookmark protruding significantly. He opened it at that page and read out a short passage in a theatrically sonorous voice:

Hell hath no limits, nor is circumscribed
In one self place; for where we are is hell,
And where hell is, must we ever be.
And to conclude, when all the world dissolves,
And every creature shall be purified,
All places shall be hell that is not heaven.

"What is that, Dad?" asked Amber.

"Oh, just an old play. But an especially significant one, for our purposes. It gave me a clue. Now let's leave the Cornish mines for a moment, and talk about *you*, Jack. You had an ancestor by the name of Owen, yes?" Jack immediately tensed. At last! "You may also be aware that this Owen Tyack had a great interest in all things to do with mining, as well as displaying in an unusually pure form the greed that marks all followers of this path: digging, delving, searching always for more. He was a man of great ability, in his own way. He had technical ability, in the manner of say Richard Trevithick, but more than that he had an aptitude for seeing behind appearances that set him apart from the crowd. Something drew him to the Crown Mines, perhaps something beyond simple engineering interest – though I cannot be sure of that. At any rate, he attached himself to one of those guided tours, and descended. I think you know that he was lost down there, and that after a mysterious absence of some weeks he returned to the surface. After which he became a recluse, I believe, in his home town." The Professor's knowledge of what Jack did and didn't know was not a little disturbing. The stones again? Amber's spying? Was he really worth all this effort? He recalled Amber's earlier words, 'You're important, Jack!'"

The Professor carried on: "This episode, in which your ancestor was lost, found its way into a local fable in these parts, becoming picturesquely referred to as *The Nightmare*. Now, that legend speaks of a very sinister encounter indeed in those mines, an experience your ancestor had with a thing of evil, from which he never recovered and which became the source (again according to legend) of a curse that befell the whole Tyack family." His eyes roved around the room as he was speaking, coming to rest unsettlingly on Jack. "That legend is told as something of a joke, but it was of great interest to me. Behind it I sensed a deeper truth, something very strange indeed. Most legends, you know, have more than a grain of truth in them. This one, I was certain, held a clue to something that I had been investigating. The question for me was, and is, *what happened to Owen Tyack while he was lost in the Crown Mines*? Why should this even matter? I had to look more closely! Your ancestor went down into that mine and found something, something that had been waiting for him, I now believe. Something that could only be reached at those great depths." He looked serious. "He established contact with the pure form of evil, what I call the *Shadow*."

The mere word conjured to Jack's mind the dark forms that had clustered and flitted around his dream drawings of the mines. Richard Attlee's words floated into his head, enjoining him to make the visit to Cornwall, to see the mines for himself: *It might just exorcise some of these demons*. Could either of them possibly have envisaged what that trip would lead to? Ever since, it had been shadows, in one form or another, that had seemed to dominate his life. The reflection prompted him to ask, "The Shadow? Is it some sort of demon? The … *devil*?"

"No, not that; nothing so crude. And yet, in another sense, yes! Everything in your mind incompatible with what you think you are, with what you consciously would like to be. Everything you see as foul, wicked, perverted, sick, ill, unacceptable: everything hidden away guiltily, too shameful to be acknowledged. Yet in some ways the Shadow is not 'the other' at all, but a secret, dark part of you, and a source of creative energies at that. It *is* you Jack." Silverman paused, letting these words sink in, watching Jack's reaction with interest and no doubt awaiting questions. Jack, however, mildly rebelling against the role of pupil that was being created for him, decided to opt out of this game and said nothing. Presently the Professor resumed. "So: the realm of this *entity* was, for the first time in this Christian era, penetrated. The immensity of your ancestor's experience stayed with him his whole life, and turned his mind. Whose mind would *not* be turned by such a confrontation? What was it like, such closeness to the pure form of the Shadow itself?" The Professor trailed off, wrapped in private thoughts, a look of yearning on his face. He remained silent for some minutes.

Jack sought refuge in facts. "You said the depth of the mine made all this possible. So that's where this Shadow is, right – in the mine?"

Silverman's expression was enigmatic. "In one sense, as I described, it is *within* – within you and within every person. *Hell hath no limits,* remember? In another, physical, sense it is condemned to dwell in the underground realm, yes: banished there for a term, a vast duration by our feeble standards. Hence the demonic legends that grew up through the ages, in all cultures: Pluto, Balaal, Hades, Moloch, to name but a few – and all below, down, down in fiery depths. Yet here is the thing, Jack: this period of this confinement now draws to a close! I sense a great stirring, a gathering of evil, as if for a final effort. The legend of the Nightmare was, for me, the clue to the coming storm, the storm in which the world may, indeed, dissolve and all places truly shall be hell. Through long study and reflection, and with the help of my stones, I believe I am now in a position to draw some further conclusions."

He stood up and strode over to some drawers that were under the philosopher's bust, stooping to open a wide and shallow one. From it he extracted a broad tray and this he set on the coffee table before Jack and Amber. Then he positioned a little lamp so they could see clearly and sat down with them again. Amber's expression held the trace of a smile, as if imagining what thoughts might be running through Jack's mind. The tray contained numerous hollows, arranged in rows. These hollows contained beautiful polished stones, each one different from its neighbours and all of irregular shapes and sizes. Some were plain and granite-like, though still compelling, while others sparkled with rich veins of blood red or sea green. Some were almost white, while others were black as coal. In the centre of the tray was a much larger hollow: this contained a stone about the size and shape of a large egg. It was richly veined and marbled, with many strata of all colours visible, and it was polished to a mirror finish. Professor Silverman looked at the stones thoughtfully, his chin cupped in his hands. "Did anyone tell you that stones have memories? For," – and here he seemed to be quoting again – "there are effluences from all things that have come into being, for not only animals and plants and earth and sea, but stones too, and bronze and iron, continuously give off numerous streams."

Jack recalled Amber's similar words of the previous day, and her account of her father's development of a new science. If "science" was the word; it sounded to Jack more like a branch of magic. His host pursued his lecture: "These effluences create affinities between similar substances. In the case of rocks, minerals and stones, they not only give off effluences, they also *receive* and *absorb* those effluences. Now, through my science of geodivination, the result of many years' labour, I could open a window onto that fateful encounter between your ancestor Owen Tyack and the Shadow."

Jack screwed up his face. "You can see *the past* – from the stones? Is that what you're saying?"

"Indeed. Some kinds of rock respond to certain types of effluence. For example, this one" – he picked out a small mustard-coloured stone – "sulphide of bismuth, may intercept intentions. Blood iron" – here he picked out a similar stone to the one Amber had shown Jack the previous night – "resonates with blood flows; it is a barometer of life force. Others can detect physical movements; some contain pre-echoes of the future, yet others store impressions of the past. But mark you," he said, glancing up at Jack sharply, as if he were about to dispute the point, "these are impressions only! The stones may give a fractured picture, and not details of fact. They can only be a guide, if the events are far in time and space." His expression lightened for a moment. "And now, Jack, you may understand how both myself and Amber have some knowledge of your doings recently, and I hope you will not hold it against us."

Again Jack thought back to his conversation with Amber. At least all this about the stones was consistent. Almost excessively so. She was now leaning forward over the tray, looking at the stones intently, her finely wrought necklace swinging over them. Amber was so in thrall to her father and his art, all she said and did was like a reflection of him, the very mirror image. And yet there had been that definite atmosphere between them when he had entered, that had persisted all evening. She caught him looking at her and she quickly looked away.

Silverman was speaking again. His serious expression had returned. "So now I began painful investigations into deep strata of the closed workings of the Crown Mines, newly accessible due to the fortuitous efforts of a certain local society. Here Jacob was invaluable to me, for although the mines were still largely flooded, that was no obstacle to him. He laboured many a long night in those black watery depths to find me the stones I needed to confirm my suspicions. We discovered another thing, too: someone else was searching there, someone *different.* Jacob could sense this difference immediately. We'll come back to this someone later, because I think his role in this business may itself be vitally important. But to continue, I matched the stones that witnessed that fateful encounter one-hundred-and-forty years ago. Through my science of geodivination" – the pride in his tone was not concealed – "I could piece together enough impressions to form a fragmentary picture of what may have happened. Owen Tyack entered into an agreement with the Shadow, a pact.

The Shadow wanted to keep him alive for some purpose. It seems that in Owen Tyack, it saw an opportunity to further its aim to free itself. It could use the greed and intelligence of this man for its own ends. And so it gave the man some sort of knowledge: knowledge I suspect to fulfil his need for power, success, recognition and riches. But also knowledge that would *at the same time* – and here I am guessing – if properly acted on lead to its release from bondage."

Amber frowned. "What sort of knowledge?"

The Professor shrugged resignedly. "I do not know. The stones cannot tell me everything. The legend itself is vague, and in any case not reliable as to detail. I suppose it might be connected with the realm of mining, which Owen Tyack loved so much – some kind of privileged insight. I *am* certain, however, of one thing. A pact requires an agreement on both sides, does it not?" His face darkened. "The Shadow never gives freely. There was a bond made; Owen Tyack would surely have had to give something to his new master, in return for this knowledge."

He stood up again and went to the window, staring out into the darkness. Images of the pages of the diary seeped into Jack's mind, chilling him: the strange machines, the disembodied limbs, the alien symbols, all pervaded by the disquieting spirit of fear and guilt. "That thing," said the Professor dramatically, "was *his soul*. The truth is, Owen Tyack exchanged his immortal soul for knowledge in this world. Such are the wages of sin when the canker of greed enters the hearts of women and men."

Jack followed Professor Silverman's gaze, out of the window, over the sea. A moon had risen and was occasionally visible through tattered clouds. The bad weather was clearing. Two small points of light winked out on the blackness of the horizon. There was the sense of a vast organism, asleep. His thoughts turned back to the diary, still there in the rucksack by his side. One of its entries came into his head with stark force: *The jaws of hell are open to receive me.* He thought of his mother, of her constant urging and impatience for progress with Geothermal. *The canker of greed.* There rose in his mind the black cloud of terror, enveloping him; the cloud that had been hovering near him ever since his visit to the Crown Mines, the cloud that engulfed him in his dreams. He now had some inkling of where that cloud might be coming from. It was a place he could never have imagined even in the darkest of those dreams.

CHAPTER 32

A Chink in the Armour

Like many of the stores in Amersham, Guido's coffee shop stayed open late on a Thursday, a happy circumstance frequently taken advantage of by Mrs Tyack and her friends in their regular get-togethers. Tonight, the three women had all just completed yet another fearsome exercise routine, yet more calories had been burned and now they could enjoy their well-deserved lattes (albeit prepared with skimmed milk only). They sat at their favourite window table, unruffled, elegant in their stylish tracksuits, watching the knots of late-evening shoppers eagerly making for home with their booty.

It was Jemima Buffham who was talking. Days after the Tyacks' party she remained greatly impressed with what she had gleaned there of the spirit world; it was a subject that had even ousted the women's network as her chief topic of conversation. "I *still* think there might be something in it, you know," she repeated for the third or fourth time, against the considerable background murmur of customers, for the café was busy even at nine o'clock. "I mean, you could just have a spirit world on its own. You wouldn't need a god, or anything like that. I've often thought that spirits could, sort of, exist in rocks and plants – that kind of thing."

"Have you *really* thought that?" said Maddy, rather cruelly for she was fully aware of the tenuous nature of Jemima's connection with philosophy in any shape or form.

"Yes, yes I have. At any rate, it would be interesting to find out more, to go to one of those séances, for instance."

"Well you can go if you like Jems," returned Maddy, unzipping her tracksuit top to cool off. She re-crossed her legs and took a sip of coffee. "It's not for me, all of that. I wouldn't want to get involved."

"You're not … *scared*?" Jemima's eyes were wide.

"No, it's not that. I just don't believe in it, that's all. And anyway, I'm so busy these days. I don't have time for ghosts at the moment." They both laughed. But Joanne, who had been sitting listening with her usual detachment, only frowned. Jemima looked blithely across at her, the smile trickling from her face.

"Come on Jo, you've been quiet all evening. What's the matter? Don't you think it would be interesting to go to one of those séances?"

Clearly making an effort to engage, Joanne said sharply, "No, I don't. It would be nothing but trouble, believe me. You should leave it well alone, *well* alone. Surely you can find something better to do with your time, Jemima?"

Jemima appeared dismayed, her face falling like a barometer heralding bad weather. "Well, if you think so. I thought it might be rather fun but . . . yes, I see what you mean." She patted her tracksuit pockets, searching in vain for her glasses. "Perhaps the whole thing should be steered clear of, after all, eh?"

Joanne nodded, apparently satisfied, adding, "If you kept up with the news you'd have seen that someone died at a local séance, just recently."

Horror now replaced dismay on Jemima's face. "Died? Surely not?"

Maddy was unperturbed. "Yes, but that would be just coincidence. You're not suggesting it was connected with the spirit world in any way?"

Joanne pursed her lips. "Well, I wouldn't be so sure."

There was an ear-shattering crash from behind her as the waitress dropped a tray; the hum of conversation temporarily ceased, then slowly resumed livelier than ever. Maddy seized the opportunity to smooth things over. "Oops, someone's clumsy tonight. But catering's *such* hard work. That was a wonderful party you had Jo. I thought it went ever so well, didn't you? I hope we didn't leave you with too much of a job cleaning up afterwards?"

"But you had Jack to help," put in Jemima, grateful to move on the conversation. "He did look nice. You must be so proud of him."

Joanne stroked her eyebrow pensively. "Well you say that, Jemima. But Jack isn't easy. You know, he vanished that same night, took himself off somewhere remote without any warning."

Maddy leaned forward, concerned. "But he's okay?"

"Oh, yes. He has these spells though. It can be difficult to deal with. What he needs is a job. I keep telling him that but he takes no notice at all." She sighed and cupped her latte in both hands, as if for comfort. The others were intrigued. They rarely saw chinks in Joanne's amour; Joanne, who surely was competent in all things, adept in business, accomplished in raising her son.

"I'm sure he'll be absolutely fine," said Jemima indulgently. "All boys of his age have these phases. You must find the same with Sebastian, don't you Maddy?"

"Absolutely. Jem's right: it'll pass, Jo. Jack's a fine young man and I'm sure you don't need to worry about him. He just needs a bit of space – there's nothing unusual in that. Tell me, does he have a girlfriend?"

Joanne continued as if no-one had said anything. She seemed to want to confide. "Actually, he does have an interview, at this place in fact. Not much is it?" Absently she motioned to one of the waitresses and stared distractedly out of the window. "Serving coffee all day. But I suppose it's better than nothing."

"Three decaff skinny lattes and some more sweeteners please," said Maddy to the girl when she came over. The waitress gathered up their empty cups, dropping several spoons with a noisy clatter as she did so, then hurried off, embarrassed.

"Can't that girl be more careful!" exclaimed Mrs Tyack with asperity, still staring outside at the last remnants of shopping activity. She was not quite herself. "Anyway," she resumed, "to answer your question Maddy, no he doesn't."

"Is nobody interested? I can't believe they're not. A relationship might do him good."

"Oh, there was someone. A little blonde thing. But Jack's got enough distractions as it is. I put her off – she's given up now, I should imagine."

"Well, you know best Jo," said Jemima. "You *are* his mother after all. Ah – here come the coffees."

"Let's hope she doesn't drop them."

"No need to worry, it's a different girl now." A silence descended for a few minutes, Joanne's gloom stifling the conversational spirit. Maddy discreetly regarded her. She was now staring into her cup, oblivious. Then Maddy caught Jemima's eye; a signal passed between them. Presently she said quietly, "Tell me, Jo, how are things at home? You know."

Mrs Tyack looked up at her slowly. "No, I don't know. What do you mean?"

Maddy swallowed, but persisted. "I mean, between you and David. Is everything alright?"

"Perfectly alright," was the icy response.

"Because, Jems and I, we're you're friends. You can share anything like ... *that* with us. Anything at all."

A pause. "But there's nothing to share, Maddy," returned Joanne evenly, holding her friend's gaze.

"Well, okay; that's fine then. I hope you don't mind me asking."

It was clear that Mrs Tyack would not welcome further questions on the subject. Suddenly she seemed completely assured. But, as Maddy returned her stare, she thought she saw something besides assurance in those strange, grey eyes, something she had not seen before. Were those tears welling up in them, to be hastily blinked back by their owner as she quickly turned her head away?

⅄

Minutes earlier, in the kitchen at the back of the café, a small argument had occurred. One of the waitresses that evening had taken off her apron and was leaning against the dish-washer, pressing her forehead. "I'm sorry Tanya, I'm not going back to that table."

The other girl was mystified. "Come on, Charlie. What's the problem? You were okay with them earlier. I'm run off my feet here!"

"I didn't realize *she* was there then. Look, I'll swap another table with you. I'll explain later." She forced a smile. "It's nothing really, I'd just … prefer not to. *Please* Tanya, it's so – humiliating!"

Tanya could see Charlie was getting in a state, but resisted the temptation to ask exactly what was humiliating. "Don't worry, that's fine. Look, you take table six instead, yes? That's the couple at the back. It's not a problem. But are you all right? You've been sort of, jittery tonight."

Charlie gave a rueful look. "Oh, it's just those women. Or one of them." Voices rose from the counter. "We'd better get on. Thanks Tanya, I owe you one."

CHAPTER 33

SOME ANSWERS AND A MISSION

The funereal chime of Professor Silverman's grandfather clock intruded on Jack's bleak reverie. Midnight. He looked up and saw Amber was regarding him sympathetically. "It's getting late," she said. "Why don't we have a break now and I'll show you to your room? Jacob should have made it up by now."

Jack came back to practicalities. "My room? I didn't know I'd be staying over?"

Amber grinned. "Of course. It's going to be much more convenient."

"But I haven't got any overnight stuff?"

"Oh, don't worry about that, everything's sorted."

Professor Silverman was on his feet. "Jack, you must forgive me. I am forgetting my manners. Please, take your things upstairs with Amber and make yourself at home. We can continue once you're settled. There's no rush – so long as, like myself, you are not one to mind a late night." He smiled and gestured to the corridor.

"No, that's fine, thanks." Jack realized that he was physically tired from so much walking, but after the late nights at the party and then at Amber's place, followed by a long lie-in that morning, staying up wouldn't bother him. He'd already heard enough to fuel an entire night's discussion. He picked up his rucksack – again the subject of the Professor's undisguised scrutiny – and followed Amber out into the corridor.

They passed through the turret room and down the flight of stairs that he had ascended earlier. Leading off from this stairway, on the right, was an archway and it was through this that Amber led him, on up another flight of steps to a square landing with a plush purple carpet and more busts of philosophers gazing down at them from shelves on each wall. They turned back on themselves, up more stairs and on to another, much longer landing with several doors opening from it. Amber, who continued to be quiet and a little distracted, most unlike her chatty self of the night before, stopped at one of the doors half-way down on the left. "Now this," she said, "is to be your room for the night." She swung the door open to reveal a beautifully furnished and spacious bedroom with a double bed. It contained only sparse furniture, but of the highest quality. There was a very large walnut wardrobe opposite the bed, flanked by two cane-bottomed chairs that had a vaguely colonial look about them. The bed itself was immaculately prepared, with the sheets turned back as if in a hotel, and towels and flannels placed neatly on the pillows. Beside the bed was a small table, also in walnut. On the wall above the headboard were two scrolled brass lamps that flooded the room with a delicate light. A small window was set in the opposite wall with curtains drawn across it. What it might look onto Jack couldn't say; he had entirely lost his sense of direction.

Amber nodded in satisfaction. "Good, Jacob has been up here already. He's very thorough, he does take a pride in these little jobs you know," and she smiled indulgently to herself before the distracted look returned. She showed Jack the en suite bathroom, well stocked with all the toiletries he could possibly need, including toothpaste and a toothbrush. Then she opened the wardrobe: inside, there were several sets of spare clothes that looked as though they might be appropriate both in style and fit for him. "Why don't you wash and freshen up and we'll see you back in the lounge when you're ready. Unless you want to go to bed now?"

He felt no inclination to sleep; there was far too much running through his brain. "No, it's fine, honestly. Just give me a few minutes."

"Good. Well, take your time. And remember, make yourself at home. We'll see you in the lounge again in a bit." With that she retreated and left him to himself.

No sooner had the door shut than a sense of bewilderment, of true disorientation, overwhelmed him. He lay back on the bed, closed his eyes and massaged his forehead in an attempt to dispel the onset of a headache. Jack had not, in his wildest imaginings, expected anything like this. What was he to make of this man? A genius – or simply unhinged? And Jacob? Professor Silverman had either tracked down one of the most improbably strange-looking people on the planet, and retained him as a servant, or his story was true. Thinking about it more carefully, though, there was really no way that Jacob could be human. You just had to look at him to see that. Then again, the Professor knew so much about Jack, what he'd been doing, what he knew and what he didn't know, was it really worth continuing to doubt? There was one thing, at least, that Silverman seemed *not* to know, not for sure, and that was of the existence of the diary. Jack turned on his side and watched the moonlight filtering through the curtain. What should he do about that strange fragment of the past? He felt a return of doubt, as if the sharing of the diary would be some form of betrayal: of his ancestor, of his parents, of himself. But in reality there was only one sensible course of action: he would show the diary to the Professor, as he had planned to do all along.

He went into the bathroom, filled the washbasin with cold water and splashed his face. Yes, he would trust this man and his daughter. Patting himself dry he returned to the bed, on which he had placed the rucksack. This he slowly unzipped and withdrew the diary from its protective plastic wrapping. There it lay before him, the antique portal to an as yet unintelligible past. Only now, he realized that it might be more than that; it might just hold the clue to his own future.

⅄

Navigating his way back to the lounge caused Jack more than a few problems. The house seemed to have turnings and corridors everywhere and very quickly he became lost. After several abortive detours into what proved to be cupboards, cul de sacs and empty rooms he found himself on a different landing, with a rush carpet and, again, several doors leading from it. At the far end of this landing were more stairs and these Jack descended, realizing he needed to go further down to reach ground level. Where the stairs turned back on themselves was a square arch to his right, a doorway without a door; here he paused and looked in, curious. It was another octagon-shaped room, perhaps directly above, or below, the one he had seen earlier. Yet more books lined the walls, but these were of less interest to Jack than what was in the middle of the room: the bulky form of the golem Jacob, standing motionless with his back to him, staring out of a tall window. Cautiously Jack entered, coughing so as not to surprise the creature. It did not, however, stir. He circled round it, looking more closely at the face, the smudged features, the curious wafer in the forehead. Very slowly he reached out and touched the skin of the golem's hand, finding it stone cold and ungiving, a crude, cold, hard glove; functional but lacking the finer features of its human equivalent. Jacob remained absolutely still, staring fixedly out of the window through eyes with neither whites nor irises; the most curious eyes. In some remote way they reminded Jack of something. He followed the line of the gaze. Through the window, Professor Silverman's garden was bathed in a pale moonlight, the shadow-forms of shrubs and silver carpet of lawn giving way to the black expanse of the sea behind them. An occasional light from a trawler, or perhaps a warning beacon, winked in the middle distance. In the centre of the lawn a tree was silhouetted, and it was at this tree that the golem appeared to be staring, oblivious to all else, motionless. The minutes passed, bringing no sign of life from Jacob. Quietly Jack withdrew, continuing down the stairs in thrall to a certain compassion. Was, he wondered, the imprisoned crow-soul of the Professor's servant hankering for its former life? Who could tell; who would ever know?

⅄

Eventually he found his way back to the lounge. Professor Silverman was waiting where he had left him, in his easy chair. The curtains had been drawn across the panoramic window and someone had lit a cluster of tall, church candles that burned serenely on the hearth, their beeswax scent aromatically permeating the atmosphere. The Professor was in animated conversation with Amber but broke off as soon as Jack appeared. Amber looked defensive and upset; her father wore an angry expression. Nevertheless, on seeing Jack he immediately composed himself. "Ah, our guest has returned! I trust you found the accommodation to your satisfaction?" He chuckled, as if this was some huge joke. He motioned Jack to the sofa and settled himself back in his chair, still smiling but with his eyes fixed on the diary under Jack's arm. However, he asked with genuine concern, "Jack, I hope you're not too tired to carry on? Amber reminds me of my tendency to lecture. But we have so much ground to cover and I always say there's no time like the present."

"Honestly, it's fine. I'm not tired at all." The moment had come. Reluctantly, almost, Jack set the diary on the coffee table before them, where it lay looking quite at home in its new environment. "I've brought something for you to see," he said. "I'd like you to look at it. It doesn't make much sense to me, but I'm pretty sure it's got a lot to do with what we've been talking about."

The Professor visibly tensed. He hesitated for a moment, then took up the book reverently, his pianist's fingers dancing all over its cover with the motions of a connoisseur. "What have we here, what have we here?" he muttered under his breath, stroking the leather binding as if by mere touch alone he could divine its contents. About to open it, he paused and looked over at Jack, his body momentarily frozen. It was clear that he could barely contain his excitement. "Before I go on, please explain. Tell me how you came by this."

And while the magus and his daughter listened, with the sound of the wind intermittently rattling the large window as a backdrop, Jack proceeded to relate to them both, in as much detail as he could, the circumstances by which he had acquired the diary, the occurrence and nature of his dream-drawings, the history of the Voice itself, his visit to the Crown Mines and the baleful sense of pursuit that had hounded him ever since. While he talked, as much as a personal therapy as from any other impulse, the Professor slowly flicked through the pages of the diary, back and forth, nodding rapidly to himself in response to either some item within or some detail of his guest's narrative. In particular he questioned Jack closely on exactly where he had found the diary, and on the kinds of drawing he produced in his sleep. The Professor then asked him some general questions about his parents: what they did, and what they were like, and then more specifically about their business: its purpose, how long they had been running it, their hours of work, and so on. When he had finished, he very softly closed the book, hugging it to his chest, and sat for many minutes in silent speculation. His face was clouded and he wore a deeply troubled expression. Eventually Jack said quietly, to nobody in particular, "What happened to Owen Tyack? In the end, I mean?" Silence again; only the ticking of the clock could be heard. "And," he continued, the emotion rising within him, "what am I supposed to do? Where do I go from here? I can't – carry on like this."

Presently Professor Silverman replied. His voice sounded different to his usual one, without its customary confidence and authority, quiet and intimate in tone. "What happens to any debtor when the time comes to pay his debt? And imagine that the debt is to the most evil and sadistic creditor of all." There was a further pause, during which Jack attempted to digest this chilling statement, then the Professor resumed. "Jack, I said earlier that there was a pact between your ancestor and a thing of great evil. Evil, that is, as it is simplistically understood, for the Shadow has many dimensions, many forms. I need time properly to analyse this," he tapped the diary, "in full. However, it is quite clear to me now, quite beyond doubt, that knowledge was indeed passed to Owen Tyack and, as I feared, there is more to the legend of the Nightmare than simply a good story. That much is history. The real question for us now is, to what extent is that knowledge alive today? From what you've told me, I am very much afraid that it is indeed alive."

The Professor's quiet manner, his very restraint, inspired more alarm in Jack than any animated recitation of dangers ever could. "Alive in what way?" he asked. There was another long silence during which his brooding host simply gazed at the candles. Where is Owen Tyack now?" Jack presently ventured, feeling that he may never get a clear answer to this most basic of questions.

Silverman roused himself. "His mortal part? In the graveyard of a church in the South East of England. A church you know well: at Little Horwood. Except, that is, for one component of those mortal remains, of which we'll speak shortly. As to his *immortal* part, that resides with the Shadow, for it to use as it will – and I am afraid it will not be kindly. You see Jack, Owen Tyack was just a tool; a tool that came to hand, and a very useful one at that. The Shadow uses whatever it can find to achieve its end, for remember it is not all-powerful but imprisoned below, away from light, hidden from consciousness. Yet Owen penetrated its realm. For you, Jack, it is both your great tragedy and your great distinction that it is *your* family that has become, in some way I can't yet fully understand, the Shadow's cardinal tool." He gave a deep sigh. "Be that as it may, I have still not properly answered your question as to why I asked you here. Let us return to that. But first, some more refreshments are needed, I think?"

He rang his bell and soon Jacob was lumbering in with more restorative cordial. Having completed this task, the golem turned its attention to stoking the fire and bringing in more heavy bags of solid fuel. The bitter perfume of its composite earth wafted in its wake. Haunted still by his earlier encounter with the servant in the octagon room, Jack looked closely at the impassive, crude features as it went about its business. Was the soul within, he wondered, any the less trapped than that of Owen Tyack? What did it think, what did it feel, entombed in that monstrous casing of clay? He looked away, suddenly repelled.

While Jacob was engaged in these chores, Amber rose from the sofa and went to the window. She pushed back the curtains and looked out to some far point. Her father also got to his feet and joined her, the two of them side by side. At the far side of the room Jacob, having finished his stoking, stood against the wall, still as a statue, awaiting further instructions. It was as if the action of a play had been temporarily suspended, the pause button pressed, the characters frozen.

Eventually Silverman began speaking again, still looking seawards. "There is some plan afoot, some great plan bound up with your ancestor's visit to the subterranean realm of the Shadow. From what you have told me tonight, which I trust will be only confirmed and elaborated by my reading of the diary you have brought me, that plan still, even today, involves the Tyack family. Again I ask, what really happened during the Nightmare? We *must* find out the answer to these questions! But how? We can only know for sure by asking one person. There is but one person who can tell us the true intent behind this great mischief. Who is that person?" Here he paused for dramatic effect, watching both his listeners carefully, making them wait before concluding, "It is Owen Tyack!"

Stubbornly, mechanically, Jack rehearsed the basic truth that he clung to, though all the certainties on which it was predicated had long been overturned: "But Owen Tyack is dead."

"His *mortal* part is dead," came the patient answer. "But as we said, his immortal soul is held captive, unable to find the peace we all seek. Yet it is not beyond reach."

"How do you mean, 'not beyond reach'?"

Here Amber interposed, "The spirits in the mine, the Voice, *his* voice in your head, your dream-drawings, your sense of feeling followed .... Already we've seen him reaching out to you. The same thing could work in reverse, surely?"

Professor Silverman spun around to face Jack with new decisiveness. "Exactly!" he exclaimed. He strode over to the philosopher's bust as if to draw power from that brooding presence, beckoning to them so they formed a little group around it. Jack could not help but be struck by the similarity in the features of the two, the marble likeness and the flesh and blood man. Suddenly, the Professor's manner became altogether more direct. "Jack, as Amber says, you've seen enough by now, I feel sure, to be convinced of the existence of a spirit realm, a realm in every way as real as this world of appearances." It was a statement, not a question. "These spirits are not all the same, not all simple things as conceived in the popular imagination. Amber and I know the trials your contact with this spirit world have caused you. Your ancestor's immortal part, a plaything of the Shadow, still has identity; he thinks, suffers, plans. He has tried to contact you many times, saving his precious drops of energy for that purpose alone, bent on his freedom. He sees you, indeed, as his one hope of release. As is common with spirits, the route is the unconscious mind and I believe yours is an unusually highly developed one." The Professor smiled. "Language is of little use here; the analytical parts of the brain cannot help with such communication. One has to appeal to what is popularly known as the 'right brain', the part that deals with whole impressions, the visual, and eschews words. By these means he has tried to guide you to him – first to the mines, where, since they are in surface terms closest to his imprisonment, he could clarify his message. Then to his grave, to his mortal remains, for the same purpose. But so far as saving him is concerned – alas, I doubt there is much that can be done for him in that respect. Yet there may be something that *he* can do for *us*."

"What do you mean?"

But the Professor simply shook his head, and started on another tack. "Owen Tyack's spiritual manifestation is unusual, unusual in that it is focussed, although his spirit is chained. There are few, let us thank the heavens, who meet with his terrible fate. But there are other spiritual manifestations too, the great mass of the unquiet dead, unreconciled to peace on account of the baseness of their lives on this earth; weak, confused, often malign to those of us who still walk the mortal plane. They often cluster around places of ill omen, or where evil deeds have been done in past times. You visited the Crown Mines to commune with one spirit and, unwittingly, stirred up others. That, at least, is my best guess."

"So how can Owen Tyack help us?"

"I'm coming to that. There is in these parts a society, a harmless enough group of enthusiasts who exalt the local industrial pioneers we spoke of earlier, and restore their creations. Now, my stones tell me that those spirits you so carelessly released in the Crown Mines" – he smiled ironically – "have found a new home in these people. It can sometimes happen: the spirits congregate in a certain place, around a certain thing, and transfer to those who come across them. Who knows, perhaps in this case the transference was not a complete accident." He mused, stroking his beard slowly. "I think not, for to me these spirits seem more like *emissaries*. And here our stories intersect. We need to find out what the Shadow's plan is. This is urgent, and I think your ancestor can help us. We need to make contact with him. For that, we need a certain piece of his mortal body, a physical link through which to summon his spirit, for a time, to the surface. For the experiment to work, it should be the seat of the spirit: it is his skull that we need."

Jack thought back to his dream drawings, first of the mines, then of the skull. There could be no other explanation;

the Professor's account made sense. At the mines the captive spirit's message had finally clarified itself in words: s*ave me*. It had scarcely been, however, Attlee's promised exorcism, that much was now obvious. He found his thoughts drifting back to the mute golem. What must it be like, not to be able to speak, to communicate normally? The mine drawings and the snatched phrases – miserable scraps that amounted to all that was possible. Then the pictures of the skull: a pitiful, painful last attempt to lead Jack to a new portal, doomed to failure by its very obscurity.

"As soon as I was ready," the Professor resumed, breaking in on Jack's thoughts, "after long days of practice, to carry out this magic I sent Jacob to retrieve the skull, from the grave at Little Horwood church. Alas, he failed," he smiled ruefully. "Perhaps this was too delicate a task for him." Another connection dropped into place in Jack's mind as he recalled the mounds of earth near the Tyack family graves in St Nicholas' church yard. Jacob's abortive attempts to carry out his mission? "Then I sent Amber to get the skull, and with a second task: to bring *you* down to me. For you, Jack, are also essential to the success of this experiment."

Jack looked at Amber, thinking of the black bag in the boot of her car, and of the fearful emotional charge that had seemed to radiate from it, the very same sensation that had overwhelmed him when he was leaving St Just on the old bus. He said to her, knowing the answer, "And you succeeded?"

She turned away, distressed, and went back to the window. "Yes," she replied in a choked voice. Jack turned back to the Professor, whose face was dark with emotion. "So we can go ahead, yes? What's the problem?"

Silverman replied, quietly enough, "This same Society of which we have spoken has thwarted me at the eleventh hour. The spirits that possess them are clearly inspired by the Shadow. There is no other explanation, for they have acquired the power to enact summoning ceremonies. They have conjured a Messenger."

Jack said, "Amber told me about a Messenger. What is that? I thought it was a harmless thing?"

"A Messenger, Jack, is a more focussed spirit manifestation, normally summoned by group energies to perform some simple task. Typically, that would be to find out information: about a loved one, for example – or an enemy." He sighed heavily. "I believe what has happened is this: the spirits possessing the Woolfe Society know my plans. They want the skull destroyed before we can make contact with Owen, because they do *not* want us to discover their Master's true intentions. For if we *can* discover those plans then there is a real chance we may thwart them yet. Remember the Shadow is itself a prisoner, and must act by feeble proxies in this way. So, they summon the Messenger to track us, putting my precious jewel in danger." His face flushed a darker red, though he continued evenly enough. "First it visited your own house; this much we know. Prying, probing. But then worse. It led them to Amber's house, while she was out, while you were both out. It led them there and they broke in like common thieves, violating our property. The result: they have stolen the skull!" He turned to Amber and made a visible attempt to master himself. "You mustn't worry, it could not have been helped; it was not your fault." Then he addressed them both. "One thing is certain. We may have lost the skull but nothing else has changed. We *must* find out what the Shadow intends."

"But if the Shadow is so all-powerful, can't it just prevent Owen's soul from being summoned?" asked Jack.

"You forget, it is *not* all-powerful! As I have said to Amber, it has no direct jurisdiction over affairs of the surface. Owen Tyack's skull is a thing of the surface; it belongs to *our* world. And that is why we need it to summon back this tormented soul. The Shadow would be powerless to resist – for a time, at least. It knows that by this means we can gain intelligence of its plans."

"So where do I fit in?"

"Ah. For the summoning to work there must be blood relatives of the deceased present. The more of them and the greater their blood affinity, the better. And so we increase the pull of the surface world on the spirit. We can hardly enlist your parents, Jack." And to Jack he suddenly seemed himself like a parent: caring, infinitely wise, torn by a terrible decision. "And so, with the gravest reservations, I must call on you, and you alone." He looked at Jack beseechingly. "And now you have heard the true facts behind this terrible affair and understand something of what is at stake … will you help us?"

The question hung for a moment but in Jack's mind there was really no doubt, no other course possible. He couldn't carry on as he had been and only Professor Silverman seemed to have answers and, moreover, a plan. "Yes, I will help, of course. But is this thing, this 'experiment', dangerous – for any of us?"

The Professor was already looking relieved. "Well, there are always some risks when dealing with the spirit realm. But there should be no physical danger, not if we go about it properly. And your own presence is a catalyst only. You'll need to give a small amount of blood, of course." He paused. "I do have to tell you, though, that if all goes well and we succeed there may be a certain danger to the balance of your mind; to all our minds, but especially to yours, Jack. Who can tell what horrors that unfortunate soul has witnessed, and how they may be imprinted on its temporary physical reconstitution? Nor how it may choose to communicate them – if it can." He smiled in a way that was hardly reassuring, given his words. "But all will be for naught if we do not have the skull. So we need to act, and decisively too. Now: my stones tell me that the Woolfe Society plans to destroy it. This cannot be done by merely smashing it to pieces, as you might imagine. No; there must be a complex ritual enacted to sever the link between the physical object and the spirit that inhabited it. After that, the skull would be useless to us, even if we did acquire it or any of its fragments. The stones say that the destruction ritual is to occur tomorrow night, at the old engine house. If we do not retrieve the skull before then, our opportunity to contact Owen Tyack and hold discourse with him will be lost for ever."

Jack and Amber looked at each other. "And so how do we retrieve it?" asked Jack.

The Professor smiled at them both thinly. "*We* do not. *You* do, the two of you. Tomorrow night. You will take Jacob with you. It will be our one and only chance. *You must not fail!*"

CHAPTER 34

THE STRUGGLE AT THE ENGINE HOUSE

The car bounced wildly along the rough track, despite its travelling at little more than walking pace. The moon was rising low, visible through the ragged clouds; only the last remnants of daylight glowed over the wide horizon of sea and sky. Inside, the occupants jolted from side to side chaotically, the motion doing little to soothe their taut nerves. Amber sat behind the wheel, her knuckles white as she gripped it tightly, her face grave and set firm. Beside her Jack stared at the silhouette of Wheal Owles, the engine house, in the distance ahead, framed evocatively against the deep purple. In the back sat Jacob, crammed into the limited space with his head awkwardly crooked against the roof. As ever, he had not uttered a word during the journey from the Professor's house, for golems cannot speak. Jack looked round at him for a moment, but likewise said nothing. There had been little conversation in the car; he and Amber both knew what they had to do, and as for Jacob – well, he had nodded obediently as he received his instructions.

Professor Silverman's parting words echoed in Jack's mind, doing little to improve his spirits. "You have to remember," he had said as he stood at the door to see them off, "that these people are not as they seem. They are no longer the conservation society acting in a rational way. Their minds are now taken over by whatever it was that escaped from the mine. They are dangerous and we don't know how much they know or are expecting. You must be *extremely cautious.* We are dealing with forces that are rarely seen in the surface world. Take good care." He had kissed Amber and, with absurd formality, shaken Jack's hand, making him feel that maybe he was going to his doom. Yet Silverman had been adamant: the acquisition of the skull was essential to thwart the intentions of the Shadow, intentions that, if left unchallenged, might lead to its release. He had only spoken elliptically of the consequences of that eventuality, but Jack had heard enough to realize that whatever misdemeanours the Woolfe Society had been perpetrating would seem trivial by comparison.

And who, exactly, was in this Society, he wondered? His mind drifted back to his first visit to St Just, to the odd characters clustered in the bar of the Commercial Hotel, to their curious glances. "Our local conservation society." They had seemed harmless enough then. Perhaps they were. He felt a spasm of guilt. If what the Professor said was true and they *had* been "possessed", for want of a better word, then it seemed that he himself had been responsible for that, the day he'd visited the mines. He thought back to the chilling laughter, the dark shadows crowding around the buildings as he looked back at them, remembered his sense of disquiet at what he may have done. Yes, he was conscious even then that he was leaving the mines in a more dangerous state than he had found them. That visit! Nothing had been the same since. Yet he'd had to go, hadn't he?

He was roused from his thoughts by Amber turning the car in the muddy entrance to a field, then pulling it off the road so it faced the right direction for their return. "We may need to make a quick escape," she explained in an even voice. "I don't want to park too near though, we'll have to walk the rest of the way." She switched off the lights and engine; now there was only the moonlight to guide them. They got out of the car, Jacob slowly uncoiling himself awkwardly from his confinement, and made their way along the remainder of the track. At its end it opened out into a rutted turning circle in front of another gate, in which were parked a battered Landrover and several other off-roaders, all unoccupied.

Wheal Owles was about a quarter of a mile ahead of them across a field, perched on a promontory like a beacon. The unlikely trio scaled the gate and struck out for it, Amber leading the way and Jacob bringing up the rear with lumbering, deliberate steps. It occurred to Jack that they had no weapons of any kind. Well, Jacob could be their weapon; hadn't the Professor said he was "all but invincible"? He had a feeling that Silverman intensely disliked violence of any kind, and yet he clearly did not expect the Woolfe Society, in their present condition, simply to surrender the precious skull without any sort of resistance. If the Society was as dangerous as Silverman claimed, they would need guile; that much was certain. But, strangely enough, no-one had discussed a specific plan at all. They were, it seemed, just strolling into a lethal situation. How had he got mixed up in such a business? Jack glanced around warily. The golem loomed behind, a bulky, reassuring shadow, solidly ploughing on.

Now they were close to the engine house. It reared up before them, tall in silhouette, its chimney pointing starkly to the night sky, looking for all the world like some curious ancient chapel. Beyond, the cliffs fell away and there stretched a calm, vast sea. It was a still night. Lights illuminated the arched windows; all was quiet within. Amber led the way around to the right of the building, away from the entrance, where they could hear the faint murmur of the sea against the rocks below. She caught Jack by the arm and drew him close. "The meeting is going on in there now. It's a full session, so there could be up to thirty of them."

"How do you know that?" asked Jack in a fierce whisper, suddenly feeling irritated by always being one step behind in the knowledge stakes.

She held the stone of her pendant out to him and despite the dark he knew she was smiling. "I have an advantage, you see," she said.

"The stones again."

"Exactly." She sounded just like her father.

"So what's your plan? Just barge in and ask for this thing?"

"That's not funny. I – I'm not sure though." He realized that for all her brave face Amber was just improvising. There *was* no plan.

"Look," he said, trying to sound positive. "It's not going to be that difficult. We've got Jacob. These people aren't athletes or anything; from what I saw some of them are pretty ancient. Let's try and get a look at what's going on, then I'll go in and create a distraction. They don't know me, after all. I can pretend I've got lost or something. And while they're distracted you can take the skull. Jacob can watch out for you, just in case."

Amber said nothing but nodded in apparent agreement. Jack's reflections in the car had given him a new sense of responsibility for the whole situation; he felt the onus was on him to do something to rectify it. Without waiting for more discussion he led the way around the exposed seaward side of the building and back to the entrance. A brief, cold wind bit into his face, making his eyes water and sting with tears. Yes, he felt nervous but there was more to it than that, another feeling running below that of nerves, deeper and more visceral.

They paused on the threshold. The door stood partly open; from inside the warm aroma of engine oil wafted out into the night air. By the big cylinder of the engine Jack could see the back of what looked like a woman wearing a dark cloak and hood, her arms raised aloft and head bowed as if in worship. He moved closer, and could now see fanned out in an arc facing her about two dozen people, standing with hands clasped before them in a ritualistic attitude, concentrating on the figure before them. Amber said in a hoarse whisper, "Look! There in the middle." At that moment, the strangely dressed woman moved to one side and Jack saw that on the floor in the centre of the group was an object, a human skull resting on what looked like a silver plate. It was this that was clearly the focus of attention. Amber craned forward to get a better view, fingering her necklace as she did so, pressing the resin pendant into the palm of her hand.

Professor Silverman sat alone in his living room. His cravat was loosened and spilled over his shirt; he still wore his smoking jacket and the stub of a large cigar resting in an ashtray beside him emitted tendrils of smoke. Owen Tyack's diary, the subject of much recent perusal, lay open on an occasional table. A fire burned low in the grate; the fuel had almost expired but tonight there was no Jacob to replenish it. Only a single lamp provided illumination. On the low table before the Professor were his divining stones; the large central stone he had removed and held interposed between the fingertips of both hands. His eyes were closed but the lids flickered and twitched in restless concentration while in his mind shapes massed and gathered, coalescing into vague forms. A scent of hot oil seemed to fill his nostrils. Through a swirl of inward impressions his inner eye now showed the scene before his daughter – not as she saw it, indeed, but as a play of feelings, evil and warped. At their centre he could connect with a formidably strong source of power: the skull of Owen Tyack. Silverman's fingers briefly flickered over the other specimens in their trays, before returning to the master stone. He frowned with the effort of concentration and spoke aloud, though there was no-one to hear: "They have it, I see it! You must go on, but beware. Beware!"

⅄

Morgana Trevose led the destruction ritual, the skull at its centre. Her motions became ever more extravagant, her gyrations accompanied by the hiss of steam slowly escaping from the huge engine around her. The entire group dropped to its knees and they all bowed their heads, remaining in this position for several minutes. Whoopings, squeaks and dry clicking sounds echoed down from the roof space, creating a fretful racket that should have prevented concentration of any kind. The Woolfe Society members, however, seemed quite unperturbed, rising to their feet and following Morgana to a row of trestle tables arranged along one whitewashed wall of the building. The skull was thus left temporarily unattended, a heaven-sent opportunity if ever there was one. Jack was steeling himself to stride confidently in when Amber, seeing her chance, suddenly scuttled out from their cover. "Wait, Amber!" he hissed, certain their plan would be ruined by this hastiness. For a few moments she was completely exposed. In seconds she had scooped up the skull and was making for the door when Morgana turned and, seeing what was happening, gave a harsh, gurgling cry: a cry like no other, with a terrible, wailing quality to it. Her hood fell back to reveal a shocking countenance, all tousled hair, sunken cheeks and staring, cadaver-like eyes. At this point Amber, with terrible luck, slipped on a patch of grease and before she could recover found her escape blocked by two other Society members who had moved with incredible swiftness between her and the exit. She froze, panting, eyes wide like a frightened rabbit while Morgana, with a chilling sigh of satisfaction, advanced venomously towards her. "I think we have found our spy!" she announced to the group in general, as the others also turned to face the hapless girl.

Jack, still watching from the door, noticed how they all wore hungry, fanatical expressions that made them almost unrecognisable. As his mind raced to find a new plan, he was suddenly and roughly pushed aside by a great force. Jacob shouldered past him and burst into the engine house, his arms raised and slicing through the warm air like the sails of a windmill. Immediately the two Society members who had blocked Amber's exit were scythed down by the flailing giant, the others falling back in horror at this towering apparition. They had, however, the presence of mind to grab Amber and drag her and her precious cargo into their midst, closing around her and thus making escape impossible without further conflict. Worse, Jack was dismayed to see others streaming down the upper gallery: the group was larger than he had first realized.

Jack had been fighting to keep his cool, knowing that an impulsive response could ruin them all, but as these events unfolded he suddenly felt consumed by a vast, spontaneous rage and he too ran out into the grim theatre of the engine hall. Seeing him, Morgana gave a start of surprise. Confusion rapidly followed. To the appalling din of chirruping and squeaking noises from the vexed spirits that Morgana had summoned, Jacob set about the main body of the group, lunging, flailing and sending it scattering. From the melee Amber emerged, amazingly still clutching the precious skull. She was trying to pass it to Jack, but more members, aware of its worth, clustered round to prevent her. They would, however, have been in vain, given Jacob's great strength, but for an unfortunate accident. The greasy floor that had already proved Amber's downfall now caused the golem to slip. He fell to his knees, and while he was down Jack watched in horror and amazement as Morgana leapt up onto his shoulders. As he rose to his full height again, clearly disorientated, she wrapped her legs around his neck and clung hard to his head. Her fingers clutched at his forehead, feeling, probing. Jacob gave a great lunge and sent several acolytes flying, clearing the way for Amber to toss the skull to Jack, who was nearer the door. But just at that moment, the giant froze. Morgana gave a shriek of triumph as, still clinging to his shoulders, she held aloft something, something she had prised from the golem's forehead: the animating token of life. Still as a statue Jacob now stood, once more lifeless clay.

And now something extraordinary happened. The Woolfe Society became convulsed in a collective frenzy: paying no further attention to the human intruders, they gave themselves over entirely to wild fury and descended on the stricken golem, who toppled and disappeared beneath the mob as it howled and pounded its helpless victim. The skull and the other two intruders were quite forgotten in all this. Seeing the opportunity, Jack shouted to Amber "Come on, come on!" She wavered, torn between the prospect of escape and the fate of Jacob. She saw the frenzied group tear and wrench at the paralysed form beneath. She looked on in horror as a terracotta-coloured arm, severed at the shoulder, was tossed aside by the mob and came to rest at her feet. It lay there, the fingers stretched out in a supplicating gesture. She froze, stunned, appalled. Jack took the initiative and grabbed her, pulling her to the door, out of the heat, the chaos and the noise. Then the two of them were running, running at full tilt down the slope, across the field and towards the car. At the gate, he paused and glanced back. The engine house looked as tranquil as when they had arrived, still silhouetted peacefully against the night sky. The low moon was now eclipsed by the tip of its chimney, from which smoke languidly wafted, clearly visible against the pale disc, belying the horrors taking place inside.

CHAPTER 35

CURIOUS MOVEMENTS

There were few things that Richard Attlee enjoyed more than inspecting his beehive. A relatively new hobby, Attlee had immersed himself in beekeeping with customary enthusiasm, rapidly acquiring a knowledge of the craft that would have put to shame that of an expert. There could be no doubt that his hive was an impressive sight, nestling in the long grass at the margins of his back lawn. This fine afternoon, in the dappled shade of the beech trees, Attlee approached the task with relish. Moving awkwardly in his bee suit and gloves, he first removed the crown board and then, to the heady music of a concentrated buzzing, began to inspect the frames one by one. He used the Welsh black bee, of course; somewhat more defensive than the gentle Buckfast strain but the honey was better, despite what the books said. His pleasure at the task, however, was tempered with a certain regret. It was not easy to limit these incursions, but limit them he must. No wonder bees got stressed and prone to the dreaded *European Foul Brood*, with all the prodding and interference of modern keepers! To the scorn of other local "beeks", Attlee instead adhered to the doctrines of pre-war French apiarists whose hives were designed to mimic the tree trunk and who left their bees alone for most of the year.

Pushing to the back of his mind the contradiction in which this philosophy trapped him, Attlee continued with his inspection. Yet the sense of focus and calm that normally attended his beekeeping was absent today. Something nagged at the back of his mind, something that prevented his complete engagement. It had all started with Joanne and David's party. Ever since that evening the recollection of David Tyack's strange behaviour had continued to preoccupy Attlee, resisting all his attempts to explain it merely as "stress", or "overwork". He often found himself thinking back, as now, to the ridiculous performance outside his friend's study: the locked door, the odd language, the awkwardness of it all. What was really going on in there? What was David up to, David who used be so frank, so open? The buzzing of the bees surged up, bringing Attlee back to the present. Caution was never misplaced in the beek. After all, old Brady Collins from the village had been stung to death, reputedly, only last year. He fiddled with the hood of his suit, checking its integrity, before slowly replacing the last frame.

The party business was maybe, just maybe, forgiveable had it not been for the equally strange phone call of Jack's from Cornwall. Something was certainly wrong there; the way Jack had spoken, his whole manner, the impression he had given of *fleeing* something. Then the way he had left the message with Attlee for his parents. Why didn't he talk to them directly? In so many ways a rationalist to his fingertips, Attlee nevertheless believed in following intuition. And his intuition told him now that there were deeper connections, darker problems behind all this. As a friend, he had a duty to get to the bottom of them. Thoughtfully, he closed the hive and made for his workshop, divesting himself of the bee suit as he did so. Yes, if he was honest with himself he'd had his suspicions about the Tyacks' business venture for some time now. The party, Jack's phone call – these were more in the way of confirmatory nuggets than anything else. He disappeared inside the large shed-like structure. For a few minutes the sounds of intermittent banging and hammerings came from the interior, then he emerged clutching a tweedy sports jacket in one hand and in the other a piece of paper on which were listed a number of engine parts: the components of another Attlee project that was nearing completion. He called in the direction of the house, "I'm just popping over to the motor shop in Winslow, won't be long". There was no answer. Attlee pulled on his jacket and strolled around the side of the house to his car. The engine screamed like a tortured thing, tyres churned on gravel, and he was gone.

⅄

About half an hour later, Richard Attlee was standing in Winslow's town square. With a practised movement he smoothed back the flap of grey hair from his forehead and scanned the irregular facades of shops and houses approvingly. There was something quintessentially English about the place. He sauntered over to the old antiques shop, peering into the gloomy interior. A funny place, this. Ah yes, it was still there, the grandfather clock he'd spotted months ago. A pity but he'd had to let it go; Miriam would have never allowed another one in the house. Attlee sniffed in a resigned way and moved on. At the newsagent he paused again, the *Advertiser* paperboard outside catching his eye: *Local woman found dead,* it proclaimed. Curious, he went inside to buy a copy. The proprietor was a vague acquaintance. "What have we here," said Attlee, brandishing the paper, "dodgy goings on, eh?"

"Might well be," responded the man, mysteriously. "She died in *strange circumstances*. Read it, you'll see. She only lived across the way there." He nodded in the direction of the houses opposite.

"What strange circumstances?" asked Attlee, only mildly intrigued. He was all too well aware of the local thirst for sensation, to enliven the predictable flow of life in the provinces.

"They think," said the newsagent, lowering his voice, "it was in a *séance*. I'm not sayin' more. You can read it all in there."

Attlee snorted dismissively. "People are always searching for some kind of answer aren't they? Séance indeed! She'd have been better off finding out about the Hadron Collider at Cern." He paid and left, leaving the proprietor staring after him with a confused look.

As he headed for the motor spares shop, Attlee's attention was caught by two men emerging from a car parked near his own in the centre of the square. He looked more closely. Well, well: it was none other than David Tyack, accompanied by somebody – who was that man? Ah yes, Attlee realized it was a face familiar from the Tyack's party, one of David's new cronies. Feeling slightly foolish, and without knowing quite why, he withdrew into a narrow alley so he could see without being seen. And as he watched, a most interesting little episode unfolded.

A door opened in the frontage above the antiques shop and another figure descended the iron fire escape, giving a curt wave of recognition to the other two. This third man, wiry and simian-looking, Attlee did not know but he didn't much like the look of him. At the bottom of the stairs the man stopped and turned to look back, waiting. Afternoon shoppers drifted in little knots to and fro across the square, oblivious to the micro-drama playing out in their midst. After a minute or two, an enormously fat man clad in a straining track-suit appeared in the same doorway and began his ponderous descent. Even at a distance Attlee could see his jowls shaking and clothes stretching with the effort. At the bottom of the stairs the wiry figure continued to wait, occasionally offering brief encouragement to the fat man, as if enticing a circus animal. Above, the door was closed softly by the agency of an unseen interior presence.

When the four men were gathered together they made for a white van parked in the centre of the square. It was at this point that Attlee knew, without a shadow of doubt, that he must follow them. David Tyack was evidently *not* going about his business as usual and, whatever was afoot, here was a heaven-sent opportunity to get to the bottom of it at last. As the van pulled away he sprinted for his own car and, to loud strains of Wagner's *Parsifal* rising above the tortured shriek of the engine, began his pursuit.

⅄

Twenty minutes later and Attlee was beginning to wonder what he had got himself into. He had followed the van at the greatest possible distance consistent with not losing sight of it, yet he could not help thinking how highly embarrassing it would be if he were to be recognized. Furthermore, it seemed there would be no quick resolution to the mystery since they were heading deeper and deeper into the heart of the Aylesbury Plain, through tiny medieval villages, along twisting single-track roads and past mysterious-looking clumps of scattered woodland. What on earth, he asked himself, was David Tyack doing in such a place and with such strange companions? After all, Geothermal Headquarters, the invariable Tyack base, was in Amersham. He was suddenly seized by a terrible sense of foreboding. And so as the afternoon waned and the shadows lengthened, Richard Attlee, jaw set with determination, pursued the careering van along ever smaller and more remote byways into the wild depths of Buckinghamshire.

CHAPTER 36

The Black Feather

The three of them, Professor Silverman, Amber and Jack, sat around the cold hearth in profound silence. The Professor stared into it as though, if he looked long enough and hard enough, he might kindle a fire by that act alone. Amber hid her face in her hands, her shoulders occasionally heaving with emotion. They had both, this strange pair, been like that for the best part of two hours, leaving Jack at a loss how to respond. He re-ran the events of the night over and over in his mind, wondering what if anything he could have done differently. The sense of culpability he'd felt in the car had multiplied many times; just now it seemed as if the whole terrible business was his fault and his fault alone. When they had arrived back at the house, Professor Silverman had taken the skull from Jack, listening to their news of Jacob's demise with drawn features. Amber had been uniformly distraught, crying, despairing, yet her father had made no attempt to comfort her. On the contrary, he'd disappeared with the skull ("downstairs" he had said) for over an hour, leaving his daughter crumpled on the sofa and impervious to Jack's attempts to console her. Then he'd returned to join them but without saying anything at all. And so they now sat. Jack desperately wanted to say or do something to alleviate Amber's distress but both she and her father seemed silently to repel him before he'd even tried.

Presently, without uttering a word, the Professor stood up, walked over to the piano and began to stroke the keys softly. A few quiet notes rang out. He proceeded to play soft phrases for several minutes, occasionally breaking out into a more flowing piece as his mind moved with the music. Then he left off and, completely ignoring Jack and Amber, walked over to a small corner cabinet, extracted a flask of whisky and a glass and poured himself a very large tumbler-full. Having swiftly downed it, he returned to his easy chair and brooded for a few more minutes before saying in a toneless voice, to the room in general, "Do not grieve for Jacob. His work is done now." Jack felt quite sure that this apparent equanimity belied a turmoil beneath. Jacob had been the Professor's companion and assistant just as much as he had been integral to Amber's life: a part of the family, no less. Had Silverman already accepted or even anticipated Jacob's death? It appeared so, for he continued in the same flat voice, "Jacob died protecting you. That was his instinct and his purpose. You must not blame yourselves!" He directed a wan smile at Jack.

Amber said in a choked voice from behind the screen of her hands, "But the *way* he died, what they did to him ...."

"Direct your mind away from those thoughts," replied the Professor quickly, as if not wishing to know any more for the time being. "It's over now. We must be strong, like Jacob, and finish this thing off. There's still work to do and I need your help, both of you. I shall make some tea for us all to help to calm our nerves, and then I shall light a fire." He went off, leaving Jack to comfort Amber as best he could.

In the kitchen, unfamiliar territory to him at the best of times, Silverman clumsily rooted in various cupboards to locate cups. When it was made he poured the tea steadily enough, though an observer would have noticed his knuckles whitening on the handle of the teapot as he did so, his face contorting. Once more he painfully coupled the impressions of the stones with the shocking accounts of the night's work from Jack and Amber, producing a picture as real as if he had been there himself. He saw it, he felt it, he lived it. Of one thing he was certain: the Woolfe Society would pay, pay for this outrage. His mind ran ahead, planning, calculating as he searched ineptly for milk, spoons and sugar, hardly cognizant of his actions. Trembling slightly, he assembled the cups on a tray and returned to the lounge, making a great effort to compose himself.

Amber was looking sightlessly ahead, her tear-streaked face ashen, while Jack had parted the curtains and was looking out in the darkness, having for now realized the futility of trying to comfort her. Her father gave her a strange, puzzled look while distributing the tea awkwardly. Then he knelt by the fireplace and set about trying to light some kindling wood. After several abortive attempts he succeeded in getting a modest blaze going, stoking it with solid fuel from a bag that Jacob had parked on the hearth earlier. The fire's crackle and play of flames improved their spirits somewhat. In as normal a voice as possible the Professor said, "We must be grateful to Jacob. He played his part well, a most essential part – as have both of you. Now we have our prize, though the price is high." He gulped down his tea quickly. "Now I have work to do in my laboratory – to prepare for the experiment, you see. Try and get some sleep. The rooms should be made up." Hastily he left them.

As soon as he had gone, Amber turned to Jack, a little more like her old self now. "I've had enough of it in here. I'm going down to the beach." She glanced out of the window. "It'll be light enough. Are you coming?" Jack noticed with astonishment that dawn was breaking. The events at the engine house, and their aftermath, had consumed nearly the entire night.

"Yeah, why not?" He felt he too had had enough for now of being a prisoner, as it seemed, in the Professor's house. Some sea air would be welcome. Amber silently led the way outside and down the garden, where the trees still were shadows only, then through a small gate in the fence at the bottom. Steep steps led down to a narrow strip of shingle beach far below, treacherous in the dark but there was indeed enough light to see now, for the sky glowed orange in the east. She went on ahead, long familiar with every step, and was standing at the sea's edge, her feet washed by the expiring breakers, when Jack caught up with her. She didn't turn or acknowledge his presence in any way, but just stood there wrapped in private thoughts. He didn't intrude on these, preferring to wait until she chose to speak. When she did, still without turning to him, her question was a surprise. "So, is he what you expected?"

"Your father? Sort of. More than that, I suppose. More – complicated. He seems *difficult*."

"Yes. 'Difficult' is the word. He means well, though."

He sought to encourage the conversation, but immediately came unstuck. "What was it like, growing up with just him? Well, not just him. I mean, obviously you had ...."

"Jacob." She was staring out to the horizon. He watched her shadowy profile; was that a fleeting smile on her lips? "Don't worry, I'm fine now. Dad wasn't often there, to be honest. At least, he *was* there – in the house – but not *really* there. He was mostly in his laboratory, he spent hours down there, always working, always preoccupied with something. He didn't often talk about his work, though. That's where Jacob was important. You see? I didn't need anyone else." The surf lapped at Jack's feet, soaking his shoes. He stayed put, and let her talk, but she had already finished with herself as a topic. "You haven't told me much about yourself," she said, finally looking around at him. Her expression had a shrewdness, visible even in the gloom of the early dawn, at odds with the childlike being he'd first met. It reminded him of her father: the same quick intelligence and resistance to deception. "What was *your* childhood like?"

The question caught him off guard. He realized then that he had more in common with Amber than perhaps he'd realized. "I didn't see too much of my parents either," he said, feeling a release in the very words. "Maybe more when I was small. We did things more as a family then. Then they got really busy with their work, and I didn't see so much of them. Like your dad, I suppose. I guess I've had – 'problems', and that's made life difficult. For them, too, you know?"

"What sort of problems?"

"The stuff I told you about. The voices. All the other stuff."

She nodded seriously. "But that wasn't you. You know that now, don't you?"

"Yeah, I do." He wanted to ask her about her mother again, but couldn't quite bring himself to. What had happened to her? He was fairly sure now that she must have died when Amber was a baby, and the whole area was just too sensitive to discuss. Maybe the Professor had come to Cornwall to forget. After all, he'd said he'd wanted to escape, or words to that effect.

Amber was questioning him again. The sharp sea breeze had blown strands of hair over her face but she made no attempt to brush them away. "You must have had a friend, an ally of some sort? Or is there someone now?"

"There might be ... There *is* someone, but I don't know if she's interested in me. It just never seems to work out."

He shrugged, realizing now, more than ever, how badly he needed allies.

"What's her name?"

"Charlie."

"Nice name." There was a long pause, filled only by the sound of the breakers. "You know, I'm sure she likes you Jack. You'd better not give up." Suddenly she gave a little shiver and hugged herself. "It's *cold.* Let's go back to the house. We've had our sea air. And I want to show you something."

They climbed the steps back to the garden just as a fine drizzle was beginning to fall, whipped by the wind into intermittently denser sheets. The flagpole's rope rattled and flapped like a demented thing. Jack noticed a little shuttered shed-like structure on the lawn, like a sort of beehive. "Dad's meteorological stuff," said Amber, registering his interest. "He loves all that stuff. Rain gauge, barometer, you know." Instead of returning through the front entrance, she led Jack around the side of the house to a small, primitive-looking wing that might have been added on later. It had its own door through which they gladly entered, shutting out the elements. Jack found he was in a very bare space the size of a generous garden hut. At one end another door communicated, presumably, with the rest of the house; at the other, next to the entrance, were some long flat boards laid out at waist height that might conceivably have amounted to a bed, and a very hard one at that. There was no other furniture apart from a simple wooden table against one wall. Amber was standing motionless, her finger to her lips to enjoin silence. She said in a low voice. "Jacob's room."

Jack was shocked. "He lived *here*?"

She nodded. "It was how he liked it. Dad didn't force it on him or anything. Look." Slowly, reverently, she went over to the table. There was a single object on it, some sort of receptacle which Jack identified as an old spectacle case. This Amber picked up with great delicacy, beckoning Jack closer. She opened the case to reveal a single, glossy, black feather. Her eyes filled with tears but she kept her composure. "This was his only possession." Jack stared at the feather, that poignant relic of a past life, and thought of his nocturnal encounter with the golem, gazing out into the garden at the trees. Suddenly he felt convinced of the truth of Amber's statement from what seemed like many days ago, *death is just a transition*. Perhaps, he reflected, that chained soul had finally found its release.

⅄

While Jack and Amber talked, deep in the rock below, in the basement of the house, Professor Silverman laboured alone in his vaulted, crypt-like laboratory. He had exchanged his smoking jacket for a white coat, much stained with brown marks and patches, and was bent low over a large wooden table crowded with intricate apparatus. In the centre of this bench rested a spherical object surrounded by tubes and wires: the hard-won skull of Owen Tyack. Its appearance, however, was now quite transformed, the bone being thinly covered with a gleaming film of something resembling damp skin, while the eye sockets were filmed over with a sort of semi-translucent membrane. The Professor picked up a syringe and from it dispensed over the skull's crown a quantity of blood he had taken from Jack earlier in the day. Crimson rivulets trickled slowly over the parchment-like skin, gathered in the hollows of the eye sockets and then dripped, one by one, into the tray on which the thing rested. The Professor next placed a large, yellowish stone beside the gruesome relic and muttered a few unintelligible words. Standing back a little, he regarded the spectacle before him with a critical eye for a few moments, then turned on his heel and, extinguishing the light and locking the door, ascended the spiral stairs. The laboratory, now empty of human life, was however not left entirely without animation. Through the darkness a faint greenish glow had gathered in a halo around the skull, while the rivulets of blood, though not fed by any new source, continued to flow and drip with their own slow logic.

CHAPTER 37

A Terrible Temper

The sun shone on Little Horwood, turning the village into an oasis of warmth. Light seeped into the dark corners of cottages, infiltrated murky side passages and penetrated shadowy lanes, reviving memories of the recently departed summer. It streamed through the windows of St Nicholas' church and played on the cold, hard surfaces of tomb, wall and bench. In the graveyard, Peregrinus leaned casually against a mossy tombstone, whittling away with his pocket knife at a stray branch he'd found. Behind him bulked the old yew, witness to the slow passage of the centuries, the very emblem of continuity with the past. Its shade lapped the gravel path at Peregrinus's feet; he basked in the sun like a lizard. Perched on an adjacent tombstone and watching him closely, imitating his very posture, was the youth Toby, pretending to carve a branch too but without the aid of a knife. Both of them seemed completely at ease, the older man exuding a rare relaxation. Toby continually looked over at him, as if checking he was still there, pleased to be in the presence of his idol.

The pair were quite content in their silence. Eventually Toby said, "So how old are you, Mister?"

Peregrinus continued seamlessly with his whittling, a look of calm on his face. Casually he replied, without looking up, "Probably older than you think."

Toby seemed happy with this answer, busying himself finding another stick and trying somehow to splice it to the first. After a while he asked again, "Where you from then?"

There was only the slow sound of knife on wood. Presently Peregrinus replied, imperturbably, "Not from around these parts. A long way from here."

"So where, then?"

"Down under, actually."

The youth repeated the phrase carefully, looking puzzled. Then his face brightened. "I know, you mean *Australiar*, eh?"

Peregrinus smiled. "Well, you might say that."

"It's very hot there, yeah?"

Peregrinus's smile broadened. "*Very* hot. I like it hot, you see. And that's why."

A blackbird hopped across the churchyard, from one tomb to another, surveying them with a beady eye. Toby considered further, then looked worried. "You staying here? You won't go back will you?"

At this, Peregrinus raised his eyes from his carving and looked into the distance, at the tops of the low hills just visible in places through the dense screen of trees. His eye darkened, a look of what might have been sadness spread across his face. "I don't think I can."

Toby detected the other's change in mood and said sympathetically, "You want to, yeah?"

"Yes, I'd like that. Very much."

"But you're staying, yeah?"

"Oh yes, I'm staying. At least for now. There's work to be done here."

His worry over, Toby went back to playing with his sticks, without a care in the world.

⅄

Priscilla Malone, retail assistant at *Winslow Antiques Ltd*, moved around Peregrinus's flat with an ease bred of familiarity, tidying small things, doing a little dusting, putting the poky kitchen into better order. Peregrinus himself was out somewhere or other, something to do with his work, and she therefore had the place to herself. She had already worked wonders; the window, for example, now sported a handsome pair of Victorian braided curtains where there had been nothing at all. Various small ornaments from the shop below made it seem more lived in. She was pleased to see that he'd given the fine set of gargoyle carvings pride of place on the sideboard. No need to change anything there; it was lovely to see them in a proper home at last.

In truth, Priscilla did not regard herself as a shop assistant at all, more in the proprietor role in fact. In any case, the actual proprietor only showed up once in a blue moon, which left her with all the responsibility. As for Peregrinus: she'd been lucky there, she had to admit. There was no question they were two of a kind. Obviously he'd fallen for her on that first visit of his, driven no doubt by a powerful attraction. She'd quickly gained his confidence, started to tell him about herself – which had only strengthened the bond. She'd even told him about her worst fault, that terrible temper of hers, and he hadn't minded that. Of him, however, she had to admit she knew less, for he wasn't a very forthcoming type of person. And that was a pity.

There was a knock at the door. That would be him now. She put down her duster, adjusted the cream-and-blue patterned silk scarf (gift of Peregrinus and sure token of his commitment) around her neck and produced an ingratiating smile. Then she opened the door. Standing there at the top of the iron stairway was a stringy woman with glasses who looked in a bit of a state. Her hair hung over her face and she held one hand to her mouth in an awkward, hesitant sort of way. As soon as she saw Priscilla she straightened herself up as if an electrical current had been applied. "I need to see Peregrinus," she blurted out. "I know he's there." Then as an afterthought, very rudely, "Who are *you*?"

Priscilla looked at the woman icily, not appreciating her manner. "I might ask you the same question. He's not here at the moment. What do you want?"

Then, incredibly, without even asking, the woman simply pushed past her and into the flat, scanning the living room questingly. "I need to find him. I know he lives here–" She seemed on the verge of tears.

"I've told you, *he's not here.* And don't just barge into my flat, how dare you!"

"I've come from Cornwall," said Carole Banks absently, almost to herself. "I know he lives here."

"You'd better get back there then, hadn't you," retorted Priscilla, with a sneer. Carole turned to her as if seeing her for the first time, looking her up and down, her eyes finally settling on the scarf. This garment seemed to rouse her in a quite unaccountable way. "We're not through!" she stormed tearfully, the emotion finally bursting out. "It's not over yet. You can't take him away like this, it's not what he wants, not underneath!" She lunged at Priscilla, losing control, her hands scrabbling at the silk fabric around the latter's neck. Priscilla fell back sprawling onto the sofa behind, too surprised for the moment to react.

Although only a slight woman, desperation and despair lent Carole surprising strength. For several minutes the two women grappled together like fiends. Priscilla could feel the scarf being twisted tighter around her neck, her throat closing. Choking, with a spare hand she groped behind her blindly, desperately, seeking anything she could use to defend herself. Her hand came to rest on a heavy, fist-sized object. As Carole continued her wild assault she secured her grip on it and, in a spasm of pure fury, raising it high she brought it down as hard as she could with a nauseating crunch on the back of her adversary's head.

Instantly Carole fell to one side, her body limp and lifeless. Pushing it away with distaste, Priscilla extricated herself and stood up, panting, loosening the scarf so she could breathe freely again. Her right hand still clasped the weapon. She held it out at arm's length: the blood-stained features of the fire demon grinned back at her, the broken horns poking out through a clump of Carole's matted hair. Slowly she set the thing down on the sideboard again, just in the right place where it had been, at the centre of its fellows. A dark stain spread from its base. She looked back at the lifeless body on the sofa and began straightening her crumpled clothes. What had she done?

⅄

Abruptly the sound of knife on wood stopped. Peregrinus froze, apparently listening intently. He moved his head from side to side with rapid, delicate movements as if sniffing the air. Toby detected the change immediately. "What's wrong?"

The older man remained absolutely still for some minutes, holding up a hand to pre-empt further questions. Then he lowered it and sucked his cheeks in thoughtfully.

"So what's wrong, eh Mister?" persisted Toby, infinitely curious.

Peregrinus looked at him from under lowered brows. "A visitor, that's all." He began his whittling again. "But it's dealt with now. Nothing to worry about." He gave the youth a reassuring smile, made a few final flourishes and held up his handiwork. Toby gave a whistle. Peregrinus had fashioned a remarkable carving of a dragon, complete with stylized, zig-zagging scales, coiling spiral patterns and impressive fangs, like something out of Viking legend. It was a beautiful piece of work. He proffered it to his companion. "Here take it. It's yours, Toby. We'll do some more another day. But I have to get back now." He pocketed his knife, swung his rucksack on his shoulder and made for the lych gate, leaving a delighted Toby staring at his gift.

CHAPTER 38

The Experiment

Jack and Amber both slept through most of the next day, not having got to bed until long after the sun had risen. Though not personally in evidence, the Professor had left them a note of rather absurd formality indicating they were to meet him in his laboratory at midnight for the commencement of the experiment. In fact, Jack did not surface until well into the evening, testimony to how much sleep he had to catch up on. That sleep had not been entirely pleasant, being at first full of dreams of dismembered bodies, literal and figurative shadows and flapping crows. In the end, though, oblivion took him and he felt refreshed enough when he woke. He met Amber in the kitchen and together they ate supper and talked about studiedly trivial topics, both keen to avoid the darker matters that hemmed them in on all sides.

At the appointed hour, Jack followed Amber through a crimson curtain and down a spiral stone staircase. They emerged in a poorly lit corridor streaked with damp. At its end was a gothic archway with a wooden door that stood partially open. This they entered; inside, the walls were hewn out of damp rock, coated in a peeling whitewash. Blind arches were set into them, perhaps in imitation of church architecture. The ceiling, too, was ribbed in a similar act of homage. The Professor was at his workbench and acknowledged their entry with a curt nod. "This cellar," he announced in a voice resonant in the small space, "dates back to early Christian times. It was then inhabited by a Celtic hermit; I have found his scratchings and carvings on the walls." He swept his hand around the chamber in a theatrical manner. "Its incorporation into the house convinced me to settle here. These links with the past are essential. Upstairs, we have many rooms for study and leisure; below is a suitable place for my experiments. It was here that Jacob was born." Jack looked across at Amber at this reference, but she merely stared at the floor and said nothing.

Looking around in more detail, Jack observed that the workbench was cluttered with a variety of tubes, retorts and flasks. From the ceiling, low-slung spotlights illuminated within these flasks fluids of various hues and opacities. In the midst of it all he saw what could only be the focus of their night's work, draped with a black cloth for the present: the skull of Owen Tyack, for now a lifeless totem with none of its former power to disturb. Away from this central space the margins of the laboratory rapidly receded into shadow. Set in the far wall, opposite the entrance, was visible in the gloom another doorway, very small, leading to some unknown inner recess. Silverman turned to them and said seriously: "I began my work last night, and many of the preliminaries are already complete. What you are about to see tonight will, I am certain, shock you. You must steel yourselves against it. I repeat, there should be no threat to our personal safety. I am afraid, Jack, there is no other way, for if there was you can be sure I would not expose you – either of you – to such a trial." As he was speaking, Jack noticed quite distinctly a gleam of eager anticipation in the Professor's eye. For all the talk of horror and reluctance, at some level he clearly embraced the horrible experiment; perhaps, for him, it was in a sense the culmination of a lifetime's work and reflection. There could be no doubt, Professor Silverman *wanted* the experiment to happen.

Jack looked at the clock on the opposite wall: half past midnight. The Professor saw his glance and said approvingly, "Yes, the time is of the utmost importance. In popular folklore it is commonly held that the so-called 'hour of the devil' is three o'clock in the morning, and for good reason. At that time, there is indeed a thinning of the barrier that separates the upper and the lower worlds, a brief window when the realm of spirits and the realm of phenomena may enjoy free exchange. It is this window that we need to exploit for the experiment to work." He turned back to the bench to fiddle with some of the apparatus. Amber was leaning against the wall, hands clasped in front of her, watching proceedings with a frown. She shot a glance at Jack and gave a tentative little smile, as if trying to reassure. Neither of them felt remotely confident.

Without turning around, the Professor said, "You may wish to sit down," and flapped his hand in the direction of some chairs. Jack seated himself but Amber remained standing, continuing to frown and, from time to time, play nervously with her necklace. There was not much light in the laboratory, and now the Professor brought up a pair of small lamps, positioning them so they were illuminating the black drape that covered the object of the night's proceedings. He then lifted onto the table, from a shelf below, a tray containing rows of his divining stones. Some of these he removed from the tray and placed carefully in a circle around the covered skull. Clearly, from the attention he paid to this procedure, the precise order of their placement was of great importance. "It is vital," he continued as he seated himself in front of the bench, "that we all pay the *closest* attention to what happens, and more importantly, to what is said – if anything be said. Concentrate on the message only, not on any – distractions." He began to run his fingers over the stones that remained in the tray, eyes closed, face twitching in concentration. Nothing was said as this strange ritual continued for the best part of a whole hour. Towards the end of that time, Jack sat up: he could begin to feel the hairs pricking on his neck, while goose flesh rose on his arms in an involuntary physical response to a change in the atmosphere in the room. He became aware of a dark fear, the same nebulous sense of dread that had oppressed him many times over the preceding months, now beginning to rise again: slowly, very slowly creeping up from the depths of his unconscious mind and seeping into his thoughts like an oily slick. He tried to resist, but the quality of the feeling was this time different, in some horrible way more concentrated, purer. He fancied he could actually smell the fear – a rotting odour, pungent with decay. He felt sick. From across the room Amber gave a small cough and waved her hand in front of her face, as if trying to ward off something.

Throughout all this, Professor Silverman continued to feel and caress the stones, maintaining a fierce concentration. The time dragged on, unpleasantly, interminably. Eventually the Professor let his hands fall to his lap and sat back. When he spoke it was very quietly, almost as if in fear of disturbing something. "The portals are prepared. The gateway is nearly open now, very nearly. We must ready ourselves. Jack, come and stand by me. Amber please stand here, on my other side." They obeyed, the Professor himself now having stood up, and so all three were lined up before the bench. Silverman then leant forward and, with a single swift movement, plucked the drape from the skull and cast it aside.

What lay underneath was a hideous spectacle, drawn from the depths of the worst of nightmares. The process that Silverman had started the preceding night had progressed considerably. What lay under the drape was no longer a skull but in essence a severed head, the skin taut and damp, the features displaying the most extreme emaciation; indeed, the bone showed through in several places. The moistness of the flesh derived in part from a thin coating of blood that trickled down in occasional rivulets from the crown and discharged into the tray on which the fearful object rested. Sickened and horror-struck, Jack was put in mind of a joint of meat on a roasting dish. From underneath the head snaked various tubes, leading to vessels and flasks on the bench nearby. The head was tilted back, its blood-streaked eyes staring at the ceiling. The lipless mouth, a black recess, was frozen open in a soundless scream.

Even Silverman himself seemed shaken by this ghastly spectacle. He swallowed and moistened his lips with his tongue. Amber simply stared. It was ten minutes to three o'clock. The Professor collected himself and said, "The time has almost come to open the gateway. You must place your hands on me, please – we must all be connected. Jack: you must face your ancestor!" Jack forced himself to confront the head, square on. Silverman now pulled from beneath his shirt a large stone that had been hanging around his neck and cradled it in both hands, as if offering it up to the skull. He mumbled something strangely inarticulate and animal-like under his breath, while rubbing the stone; then he released it and let it hang freely. He straightened up and stood back again. All was silence, the minutes passed. Nothing happened. The clock hands quietly moved on towards three. They stood there watching, waiting.

As the "devil's hour" approached, Jack thought he saw the film of dampness that lay over the yellow skin of the head glisten and increase … or was he imagining that? Was the head *perspiring?* At the same time, the fluid in several of the flasks on the bench stirred and bubbled ominously, then died down. Fear hung in the air like a fog. Some further minutes passed. Amber started to say something when with a startling noise the flasks suddenly frothed up again, much more violently this time. Simultaneously, with shocking effect, a thick gout of greenish fluid welled up from the mouth of the head and spewed out to mix with the pools of blood in the tray. Jack wanted to retch; Amber stared with absolute fixation at the head, mesmerized. As they watched, the lips writhed and contorted and more fluid was ejected. Then, even more terrible to behold, the lidless, bloodshot eyes swivelled down from being trained on the ceiling and looked directly at them. Suddenly, a piercing scream, a scream of hideous intensity and volume that nobody present would ever forget, filled the small space of the laboratory. It seemed to come from everywhere, being inescapable: the distilled essence of every nightmare ever dreamed in a single shriek of raw pain.

None of them could withstand that blood-curdling noise. They fell to their knees, hands over their ears. The scream continued for an interminable minute, then abruptly broke off. As they slowly rose to their feet, disorientated, Jack registered the time as precisely three o'clock. The hour of the demon had arrived. The next thing he noticed was how hard it was to actually see the clock: the room had grown dimmer. This was because the two lamps that the Professor had positioned to illuminate the proceedings had gone out, while the ambient lighting had faded to no more than a pallid glow. Through the gloom glowed two greenish points, the twin foci of the eyes of the head, lending it an even more appalling aspect than before. The Professor rummaged around on the shelf under the table and produced a pair of brass candlesticks, complete with candles. These he placed on the table on either side of the head, struck a match, and lit them. In the marginally improved light, the eerie green radiance of the eyes receded to a faint glimmer, visible through milky, clouded pupils; the pupils of a blind man.

Silverman stood back and motioned the others to his side again. His expression was rapt and utterly engaged. There was another spell of total silence in which they gazed on the gruesome spectacle, held by the ghastly greenish stare. Then, quietly, as if from a great distance, came a voice, muttered words blending into a single, rambling lament. Gradually the voice grew louder, becoming a veritable cascade of jumbled syllables, the anguished gabbling of a madman talking urgently to himself. As its volume increased, so the lips of the head began to make quick, twitching movements, which gradually synchronized with what words they could hear, as if in a badly dubbed film. The voice was thin and dry, with a terrible clicking and rustling effect that cracked with emotion as it pursued its monologue. Jack had heard such sounds before; he had hoped he would never have to hear them again. Amidst the jabbering, he could make out fragments of sense, although the continuous nature of the speech made it difficult to interpret:

... my wretched self oh Christ have pity curse that evil day what folly God despises why Lord why but spare me yet my cursed sinful self if only oh if only had I not oh had I not oh had I not if only ...

Against this backdrop of demented rambling it was difficult to even think. Professor Silverman turned to them with blanched features: "God of my Fathers, we have broken in on a hundred years of suffering and self-hatred here. We must give this time to settle!" He lifted a flask filled with a dark, viscous fluid that had been sitting on the table, uncorked it and poured it reverently over the head. The blood trickled down, filled the indentations and creases of the skin, gathered in the deep eye sockets and ran down from them in crimson rivulets. The effect on the agitated spirit was dramatic: the ranting calmed and slowed, like a mechanical device gradually running down. Presently, the ramblings stopped altogether. In a commanding voice the Professor addressed the head: "Who are you?" Several minutes passed in further silence. The nightmarish mask remained immobile. Again the Professor asked, with greater emphasis, "Who are you!"

After a further pause, the black lips writhed back and then the dry voice came, quietly and quite intelligibly, answering question with question, "Where am I?" This first fragment of communication with the spirit had an electrifying effect on the little group. The brief, eerie response was more horrible than anything that had preceded it; there was a terrifying sense of connection at last. Again the voice asked, brokenly, "Where am I? What ... is ... this?"

The Professor edged forward. "Are you Owen Tyack? Is that who you are?"

The mouth pulled back in a rictus of pain. "I was Owen Tyack, curse that name! Curse it!" The green eyes blazed up. The lips and tongue seemed to be struggling to form more words and there was a pause while the mouth continued to work silently. Presently the voice came again, "What is this? Where am I?"

The Professor glanced ominously at the others, then spoke very slowly and distinctly. "My name is Benjamin Silverman. I am a scientist and philosopher. I have used my learning and power to bring you here tonight to my house. I seek knowledge that I believe you have."

The voice of the spirit, when it came again, was initially menacingly quiet, though it rose rapidly in pitch and volume. "Am I saved? Have ... you ... saved ... me? Am I then saved? Is it over? *Over?*"

The Professor swallowed hard, and spoke as evenly as he could. "I have used my art to bring you here, but it is for a short time only. I do not have the power to keep you ... the gateway must close and you must return." A hideous wail filled the room. The eyes of the head flickered and rolled, even the tray on which it rested vibrated with the intensity of its emotion; the candle flames trembled and sputtered. The pitiable cry went on and on before giving way to more jumbled words that made no overall sense at all. The Professor winced and covered his ears, while Jack and Amber turned away and tried with fingers, hands and arms to blot out the terrible sound. When the noise stopped, he tried again. "We know of your suffering, but you must believe me – you can help. You can make amends and help humanity if you will only share your knowledge with us. *You must help us!*" he added, imploring now. But there was no response from the head. The mouth remained open, vacant, the eyes clouded, their green glow burning fainter and, by a strange illusion, as if from a great depth. The minutes passed in silence. After some further time, Amber caught her father's eye. He shook his head slowly and took a step back from the bench.

"What do we do now?" whispered Jack.

The Professor stroked his beard thoughtfully. "We cannot compel the spirit to have speech with us, let alone tell us anything of value. I had hoped that it might repent, and in its repentance give us the knowledge we need. Alas, I fear there is little more we can do …." His voice trailed off and he turned away from the bench, dejected.

Just at that moment, the leathery voice came again, quietly and apparently quite rationally: "What is it you wish to know?"

The Professor froze, then turned again to face the head. His voice trembled slightly as he replied. "You made a bargain, long ago, a bargain with your master, the great Shadow. Tell us of that bargain."

The green eyes regarded them balefully. Again the lips twitched and writhed, the dry tongue attempting fruitlessly to moisten them as an aid to speech. Once more the mouth contracted. "He took my flesh" it said. "Yes, he took my flesh. Curse the day I found him in the mine!"

The Professor glanced over at the other two, almost as if seeking reassurance, before addressing the spirit again. "What happened, when you found him? What passed? Your bargain–"

A long groan cut him off. "Ahhhh! I wandered long, lost, through the stone forest. Then he came to me, the Avatar. He took my soul, the bond was made with blood, that cursed day, oh curse the day!"

"But he gave you knowledge, knowledge!" The Professor bent forward close to the head, speaking urgently and quietly now. "What was that knowledge? Your journal – *what was your mission*? You describe a machine–"

Flecks of foam bubbled around the head's mouth, testifying to the effort of speech. "He told me it would work, yes, it could be done. It … must … be done. The energy, energy for all – was that wrong? I would have great riches. Ah, long I laboured, Satan's work. Christ forgive me! Those poor souls I took – but he drove me on, always on, on, ON!! Oh, the loneliness, with only him, to the end with his help alone." The speech petered out in terrible, abject sobbing sounds. Yet Silverman needed more.

"Tyack, listen to me! Whose help did you have? Hear me; *who helped*? You speak of a helper in your diary. Was it him? Who is he?"

The bloody, weeping eyes gazed back. "Gift of the Avatar, my own helper. He came back with me. He was with me to the end, only him– Beware the helper!"

Jack noticed the Professor glance nervously at the clock, mindful no doubt of the limited time he had, before putting his next question with greater directness. "Listen to me Tyack, what is your Master's plan? Would he free himself? How would he free himself? *I must know!*"

Painfully, the answer came. "Yes. Yes. He would take the upper world. He wants it all. His power stirs. The old hatred. You … must … stop him, stop the helper. Through him he works."

His face a picture of distilled concentration, the Professor made as if to pose a further question, but just as he was about to do so a gust of light wind rippled from nowhere through the room and fluttered the candle flames. Jack had the distinct impression that the skull was actually sniffing the air. It spoke again. "Silverman. There are others in this room. Who are these others?" The eyes arduously scanned the laboratory. "I cannot see. I see dim shapes. Who are the others?"

The Professor looked uncomfortable, and replied "I have my daughter with me."

"And the other? There is another. My flesh!"

Jack fancied he could actually *hear* the sniffing sound from the head, as of air being filtered and gauged. Silverman glanced worriedly across at him before replying, "He is your descendant. Your great-grandson had a child. Here is that child. Your bloodline survives!"

There followed the most terrible of silences yet, minutes in which they could only speculate on what thoughts might be passing through that tortured mind. Then the voice came again, now inflected with an ineffable sadness, "I know him. Jack? Jack!"

Unable to prevent himself Jack moved closer. At last! He said, "I'm here. It's me, Jack."

The spirit unleashed a vast sigh. "*Jack*. Listen to me Jack. You must help me." A note of pleading urgency entered the voice. "Save me, Jack. Only you can do it. Release me from this torture. You must save me. Listen, I shall make amends! Hear me, do you hear? *Can you hear me?*"

Unsure of himself, Jack glanced across at the Professor. He was wearing a most extraordinary expression: there was no sign on his features of the reciprocal suffering or sympathy that he expected to see, only a trance-like look of absorption. Before Jack could respond, Silverman took the centre stage again. "Tell me, what is it like to look upon the Servant of the Shadow? To feel his presence, to abide with him?"

The skull's eyes glowed with demonic strength. The reply, when it came, was both oblique and chilling. "Silverman, you can never understand even a thousandth of my agonies. Never! Do not seek to know!" Despite this unsettling answer, the Professor remained immersed in his trance-like state, lost in reflection. Amber was still standing next to him, completely still, eyes frozen wide as if she held the gaze of the Medusa. Jack glanced at the clock. Even as he noted the time, another gust of wind swept through the laboratory, stronger this time. The candles suddenly blew out, leaving only the green points of the spirit's eyes visible through the gloom. Then through the silence a low, distant animal howl could be heard, accompanied by a sort of background chatter, as of many voices a long way off, all talking together in frenzied tones.

Professor Silverman groped his way along the wall to the light switch and suddenly the laboratory was fully illuminated. They saw the head of Owen Tyack tilted back, its eyes once more trained on the ceiling, the mouth – from whence the howl issued – gaping, lips pulled back over filthy and stump-like teeth. Then the noises intensified, growing nearer and louder. Jack put his hands over his ears to shut out the unbearable cacophony. As he looked at the head, he saw the skin twitch and rise in multiple places, as if clawed by invisible hooks. The features stretched and parted from the skull beneath, while the laughter of many voices filled the room. Suddenly, both the laughter and the babble were cut off, leaving only the terrible howl, which, having reached a peak, gradually faded as if into the distance. Two final words were left hanging in the air, drawn out in a frightful shriek: *"Save meeeee!"*

Silence. The skull rolled onto its side, tattered fragments of skin clinging to it like peeling paint. The green light of the eyes was finally extinguished. The experiment was over.

CHAPTER 39

SILVERMAN SPECULATES

Amber stretched herself out, prone, on the hard planks of Jacob's bed and held out the black crow's feather, sole worldly possession of the deceased golem, at arm's length. She framed it against the naked light bulb, seeking answers in the pattern of its edges, reassurance in its symmetry. Brittle memories of her childhood came back to her and stuck in her mind like shards: near, immediate, defying the gut-churning impressions of the experiment not two hours before. Here at least, in Jacob's room, she might find her own space for a little while, some pause for thought in the horrifying chronicle that was unfolding before her.

The door handle rattled urgently and her father burst in. "Ah, there you are Amber. Are you coming to join us? I have Jack with me in the lounge. We're waiting for you, now." He had his laboratory coat in one hand and the stub of a partly smoked cigar protruded from the fingers of the other. The aroma of stale tobacco smoke filled the air. Amber felt her wounds open afresh. Without moving she said, with unaccustomed asperity, "Give him a chance can't you Dad? We've barely finished and here you go again! We can't just keep on at this pace. It's not fair, not on anyone."

Professor Silverman looked baffled. "Amber, don't be so silly. We don't have time on our side, surely you can see that? We can't just – sit around and contemplate. The experiment was a success; now we must distil its lessons while they are fresh!"

Slowly she lowered the feather and looked at him, the flushed, excited face with its scholarly beard and feverish eyes. "And what's your plan for Jack?" she said. "Send him on some new mission to find out more, just like you did with Jacob in the mines? Is he going to be your next tool?"

Her father continued to hover restlessly in the doorway, still preoccupied with the night's events, uncomprehending. Distractedly he said, "There's nothing we can do for Jacob now, Amber. I'm sorry. I know how you must feel but – we must press on." He looked at his watch, then moved to go. "Are you coming?"

"No. I'm staying here. None of this has got anything to do with me anymore." She turned on her side, away from him.

The Professor paused for a few moments more, then retorted, "We'll be waiting for you in the lounge. Five minutes." The door slammed shut. Amber remained exactly where she was.

⅄

In the lounge, the curtains at the long window were pulled back to reveal dawn sluggishly breaking. Jack was leafing through some of the annotations in Owen Tyack's diary when the Professor re-entered. He looked up inquiringly, expecting to see Amber following behind her father. Silverman briskly seated himself opposite Jack and motioned him to put down the diary. "Well, we must get started. Hardly ideal, I know, with so little rest but the impressions are still vivid in our minds and we should strike while the iron is hot."

"Isn't Amber coming?" asked Jack. He would have much preferred her to be there if more instructions were to be issued – as he had a feeling there would be.

Silverman pulled a face and said dismissively, "My daughter, I am afraid, is 'not in the mood'. I doubt she'll join us. Now, unpleasant though it might be let's cast our minds back to the night's events. In many ways the experiment exceeded all my expectations. But: what information has it yielded?"

Jack pondered. One phrase in particular still echoed in his mind. "What did the spirit mean, 'He took my flesh'?"

The Professor sighed, and said, "We must learn what we can from these scraps and fragments. I hardly expected to glean even those, and yet – if only we had *more* to go on. Well! Let's consider what we do know."

Jack was still profoundly shaken by the experiment. Try as he might he couldn't free his mind from the spirit's chaotic world of pain and madness, its abject plea for help, delivered at last so directly. It seemed just now as if nothing would ever expunge the window of insight on the horrors of the world below, and the ghastly way in which it was presented. "First," continued Silverman, matter-of-factly, "it's clear enough now that the pact was, and is, a reality. Neither the stones nor the legend lie. A bond was made, with blood (which is quite final, by the way) and in exchange Owen Tyack gave his soul. It's also clear that the Shadow is indeed preparing for a great effort to release itself. Remember what the spirit said? *He would take the upper world. He wants all of it* – or words to that effect. I think we may take these things as facts." He sat brooding for a while then shook his head wearily. "However, as to the details of the Shadow's plans – ah, there I still don't understand. Yes, knowledge was passed; yes, knowledge bound up with a machine described in the diary. But to what end?" He broke off again and tugged at his lip for a few moments. "You will remember I pressed the spirit on that very point? You will also remember that it referred to energy, energy that seemed to be connected with some sort of human sacrifice, I should say: *Those poor souls I took.*"

Jack somehow felt, without knowing exactly why, that this issue approached the crux of the entire business. "Is that machine," he asked, "the machine that Owen made, connected with the Shadow's plans for release in some way? Is that what we're saying?"

"Ah, that is the very point, the very point, my boy. As part of the bond, knowledge was given to your ancestor to construct a device conceptually way beyond the possibilities of his time. He struggled to fulfil his side of the bargain and perfect the machine, and in the process people were – consumed, I would say. Why did he do this? Greed! The same canker of greed that drives the whole miserable process of so-called 'industrialization'. Again, remember what he said, about being promised 'great riches'. Furthermore, this machine would produce energy, he said. So some form of *generator* is at the heart of all this, it appears. That leaves us with your question, Jack, which is exactly right: how does the machine described connect with the Shadow's plans for gaining its freedom?"

"Does there have to be a connection?" said Jack, tired and confused in equal measure.

The Professor nodded emphatically. "I am certain there is." He leaned forward in his seat. "There are wider forces at work here. This entity, the Shadow, has been imprisoned for epochs beyond our imagining. It bides its time, and every so often an opportunity comes its way, a chance contact with the surface world that it exploits to the full. In the span of human civilization, anomalies appear. Just think: the great pyramids of Egypt, the Mayan step-pyramids, unexplained eruptions of magical activity, Stonehenge …."

Jack rubbed his head. "Are you saying that those things are connected with what Owen was up to?"

The Professor looked a little defensive. "They might be. At least, that's my theory. Here you have devices, all out of their time, built with privileged knowledge; they could easily be the abandoned instruments of liberation for the Shadow, evidence of earlier failures. Owen Tyack's 'machine', as described in the diary which so fortuitously found its way to us, is the latest in a long line of such attempts. Or, perhaps, not quite the latest."

"What do you mean? How?"

The Professor shrugged. "I don't understand how such devices are intended to work. I think we have to accept, though, that they were all bids by the Shadow for its freedom, thwarted in the past by the complexity of the task and the primitive technical knowledge of humanity at the time. The question for us now is, did this latest attempt die with Owen Tyack?" Here his voice began to rise in excitement, in a manner by now familiar to Jack; he stood up and started pacing. "Everything we know, everything, suggests that it *did not.* The legend of the Nightmare – think about that. What is this 'curse' it speaks of, if not the continuance of this knowledge down through the generations of the Tyack family – all tainted by the original pact, all showing their ingenuity, greed and craving raised to a power by that first promise of riches untold? The curse still holds!" He turned to Jack, who had been feeling worse than ever through all this. "Now look at your parents. They had the diary, yes? That's how you found it. You tell me they are consumed by their work; it takes up all hours, more and more as time goes on, in fact. An energy business, yes? It all fits. Owen Tyack lived out his life in Little Horwood; many of the diary entries were written there and I don't doubt the diabolical device he worked on was constructed there. It wouldn't surprise me in the least, Jack, if your parents have already visited that place of evil omen, located the site of the machine, learned from what's left of it, if anything, and used the lessons to carry on his terrible work."

Jack cast his mind back to the dismal visit he had made that day, with Charlie, to Little Horwood church, and to the ominous Tyack tombs with their doleful, self-flagellating inscriptions. Yes, it was a place of ill omen alright.

"Finally," continued Silverman, "Just look at humanity's advances in technical knowledge in the last century or so. Now more than at any time in the past is a machine of liberation likely to succeed."

Jack considered this. Something was nagging at the back of his mind. "There was something else the spirit said, something about a 'helper', wasn't there?"

"Indeed," said Silverman. "*Gift of the Avatar, my own helper.* He said this helper came back – presumably he meant to the surface – with him, and stayed with him to the end. The diary speaks of the same." Here he bent and picked up the item in question, which now bristled with coloured bookmarks, and began leafing through its pages. "You see: it charts the disintegration of his mind as he approaches the end of his life, struggling as he was to finish work on the device and with the shadow of his fate growing longer day by day. We can read here of the soul bending and cracking as knowledge of its approaching fate overwhelms it." He found the page he was looking for. "Listen: *no-one, save P, will suffer my presence.* This, I am sure, is a reference to the creature that will have been sent by the Shadow to ensure that the task was accomplished."

"He also said to be careful of the helper," recollected Jack.

The Professor sat down again, rested his elbows on his knees and put his fingertips together thoughtfully. "Exactly," he said, quietly now. "'Beware the helper'. We don't know what this creature is but I would be surprised if even now it is not active in trying to achieve its master's purpose. The Shadow's minions – 'demons', as people like to call them in popular lore – can take many shapes. They don't have normal life spans, either; a century would be nothing. They may appear quite human, or they may be entirely incorporeal. Whatever this thing is, we must assume it still walks abroad and it is striving to help the Shadow release itself. It may, indeed, be the seeker that Jacob encountered in the mines, as I had come to suspect. I would therefore suggest," he said with a special precision, "that when you return home, among the other tasks we shall have to set you, you watch carefully for the presence of this 'helper', which may well have insinuated itself into your parents' enterprise. Just because Owen failed, it won't necessarily give up." He ran his hands through his hair and looked at Jack with an expression that seemed to say something on the lines of "so you'd better watch out."

Leaving aside for the moment the matter of whether he would simply obey these 'tasks', Jack returned to another fragment of the spirit's discourse that had been troubling him: "What's the Avatar thing he talked about?"

Professor Silverman looked hard at him, as if sizing up his capacity for comprehension. "The Shadow, Jack, cannot be grasped by any consciousness in this world. It represents itself, shall we say, through a series of *instantiations*."

"What do you mean?"

"Think of a great fire, and think of a tiny insect. Now, that insect could not even remotely approach that great fire; it would be wholly consumed. Even if it could approach it, what would it behold? It could not; energy so vast could never be apprehended in meaningful form by a tiny organism. Now imagine just one spark thrown off by that great fire. To our insect, that spark would itself seem like a huge fire – but one that may at least be compassed by it. So it is with the Shadow and its Avatar."

"So the Avatar is like the spark?"

"Exactly. A fragment of demonic energy by which the Shadow made itself able to interact directly with poor Owen Tyack."

Poor Owen Tyack. The very words struck at Jack's heart. Whatever was at stake, however many lives, whatever the scale of evil planned, the terrible, lonely fate of his ancestor, who had singled Jack out to help him, suddenly eclipsed all else. Could he ever forget the awful, pitiable pleas the spirit had made directly to him, pleas to be saved? How many times had it tried, now? He closed his eyes momentarily, but all he could see burned on his retina was the frightful image of the skull, the mouth wrenched open in its agony. When he opened them again the Professor had once more got up and was standing contemplating the bust of the philosopher. Jack looked out of the window at the restless sea and watched the foaming waves break against the feet of the nearest cliffs. Without looking away he said, "Is there no way the curse can be lifted?"

Professor Silverman looked a little surprised, thought for a moment, then shook his head with finality. "The only way to break the curse, I would imagine, is to release the spirit of Owen Tyack from its imprisonment in the underworld. Whereupon, the pact is negated and his soul may rest in peace. But such a thing is impossible: for him there is little hope, I am afraid. In any case, we must concentrate on more urgent objectives." He seemed to gather himself for a peroration. "You see, Owen Tyack's machine must never be resurrected. It must *never* be allowed to run. There is more to this than the simple murder of innocent victims. The madness and cruelty of the Woolfe Society will be as nothing compared to the chaos the world will see if we cannot stop it. We have a responsibility. *You,* Jack have a responsibility! I think you must see by now that you and your family are bound up with this business in a way that is unavoidable. We must work together, you, Amber and I, but much of the onus, I am afraid, rests on you. We will help you where we can. Of course, you must return to your home and I'm sure your parents are beginning to wonder where you've got to. Go back, discover what you can of their company and their plans: their schedule, who helps them, how far advanced they are with their scheme." His voice was urgent now, his tone deadly serious. "Find the machine, tell us what you learn, and I shall continue my study of the diary to find what answers I can.

Most of all, we must stop the Helper. Stop the Helper and we stop the Shadow itself. There can be no delay!"

⅄

Jack wound the window fully down and let the wind play in his hair and over his face. It was like a release from prison. They were in Amber's car driving back to her house, past the bee centre (he must tell Attlee about that, he thought randomly) and approaching the steep, snaking road into Polzeath. People were about, other cars, life. Could such normal scenes have been carrying on during his days, as it seemed, of incarceration in the Professor's mansion? He felt as if he was plugging back into reality. The beach opened up ahead; a couple of surfers in wetsuits crossed the road, chatting, laughing.

Amber too had her window down, symbolic of their release, and seemed more herself now. "Are you sure," she was saying, "that you want to go back today? You're welcome to stay."

But Jack had already decided. "No, thanks for the offer but I just want to get back now. It's not just this … stuff, either. My parents are going to be wondering what's happened. I'd rather go now. If I can just get my bag from your place I'll get going."

Amber shrugged. "Okay then. But you must let me give you a lift to the station." She laughed briefly. "You know, I think we're both so tired we've sort of got over needing sleep at all. Like a second wind."

"Yeah, I know what you mean. I couldn't sleep now even if I tried."

They had already discussed Jack's "instructions", as relayed to him by the Professor. He hadn't begun to think how he would manage returning home with such a brief: essentially, nothing less than spying on his parents. But there seemed little option and in any case it wasn't that different from what he'd been doing before, only more focussed, more urgent. The reasons, however, were *very* different. Now the whole landscape of family relations had changed for ever, all of the familiar contours swept away and replaced by the dark language of curse and apocalypse. Nothing would be the same again. How exactly Jack would work "together" with these strange Silvermans, as the Professor had promised, seemed problematic. Neither the Professor nor his daughter seemed to be in possession of any kind of conventional technology: phones, email, nothing. But he'd agreed, with some reluctance, to keep Amber's stones on his person and that seemed to satisfy them.

Amber turned off down the small road that led to her house. He looked at her. Considering everything that had happened she was amazingly composed. He knew, though, that it was not only his own family landscape that had changed permanently. "What are *you* going to do?" he asked.

She hesitated for a moment. "I'm not too sure, Jack. It's not going to be the same around here anymore. I've got some questions of my own that need answering." She pulled into the drive and made no attempt to get out of the car. He thought of her alone in the house, after he'd gone, with no Jacob, no friends, her life turned upside down. They were two of a kind. "You've got a key," she continued. "If you're not staying, just let yourself in, get your things and we'll be off. London trains are frequent from Bodmin. You can get your ticket at the station, I don't suppose you need to book."

"Okay." He felt he was letting her down by leaving like this but he knew he had to get away. Inside the house it was just as he'd left it, with chaos everywhere. How much had happened since, though! Too much, in fact, to begin to digest. But one thing, at least, was certain: now he had a plan. He had a plan; he had allies. Going home might not be so bad after all, and this departure was not final. He packed his things, shouldered his bag and, with just one last look at that unconventional sitting room, shut the door behind him.

CHAPTER 40

Accidents Will Happen

"Would you pass the butter, please darling?" Priscilla Malone smiled ingratiatingly. She took a special pleasure in calling Peregrinus that, now. Darling. The word had a certain flavour of ownership about it, whether he liked it or not. And it was possible, she privately admitted, that he did not, though it was never easy to tell. But she was only teasing, and he would know that. They were in the kitchen of his flat, sitting at a folding table. It was a ludicrously small space for breakfast but she didn't like eating in the lounge any more, not after what had happened there. Not for now, anyway, while the memory was so fresh. Any physical signs of the struggle, however, she had carefully removed; all was as before, except for a stubborn stain on the base of one of the demon carvings. But it was not something you would notice. Nevertheless, Peregrinus had now become very protective of the ornaments, grouping them around the fire in a particular pattern that had a touch of the obsessive about it.

Priscilla's toast was going cold but Peregrinus remained unresponsive to her request, gazing past her through to the lounge in a distracted way. "The butter," she repeated, sharply. Rousing himself, Peregrinus reached behind to a shelf and obliged, taciturn as ever. She frowned. "You're very quiet. You're not still thinking about …?" Silence reigned while he regarded his mug of coffee before taking a sip and returning her sharp look.

"No," he replied calmly enough. "We can draw a line under that." The ghost of a smile played around his mouth. "Accidents do happen, after all."

"Then what?"

"There isn't a 'what'." Despite that calm manner something about him seemed strangely uncertain, was it in the eyes? He seemed about to say more, then checked himself.

Priscilla, not one to miss a trick, nor the opportunity to get to the bottom of another's private thoughts, raised an eyebrow. "Well?" she pursued. Peregrinus held the mug to his lips, frozen there. What was he hiding? She persisted, "It's not the … *body*?" She lowered her voice to a whisper.

He shook his head slowly, in the deliberately weary manner of one being forced to address the same point for the thousandth time, which was more or less the case. "I've told you before," he said, "that's all been dealt with. It's a closed book, all done, end of story."

Priscilla felt temporarily reassured. He'd explained enough times that the earthly remains of Carole Banks had been utterly and completely obliterated in that church he was always at. Exactly how, she didn't know, but she knew he was telling the truth on that point, though she couldn't stop herself worrying about it. She relaxed somewhat and once more returned to her question, "What, then?"

He writhed his lips in an uncharacteristic sort of way. There seemed no doubt that he was unsettled. "Have you ever felt," he began, "violated? I don't mean physically. Inside. In here." He tapped his chest.

"Whatever do you mean, darling?"

"As if … as if the inner temple of your being, the spirit, had been broken into and ransacked. By infidels." He was talking to himself, entirely ignoring her now.

"What on earth are you talking about?" returned Priscilla incredulously. What had got into him? If anybody should be cracking up, surely it should be her?

But already his strange mood seemed to be passing. "Never mind," he said quickly, as if dismissing her capacity for comprehension. "It's nothing. You shouldn't worry about what happened. It's all taken care of. As I said, accidents happen and it's history now. Let's move on."

This was more like it. Priscilla hated not knowing where she was. She smiled simperingly. "Yes, you're right. Now I must get changed. What are you up to today? The church, by any chance?"

"No. Everything's finished there. Work's moved."

"Really? So where now?"

"Oh, not too far. Out in the sticks, you might say."

"More so than that church?"

"Yes, I'd say so. Right in the country." Now he was composed. It was as if a completely different person had got the upper hand of the doubtful creature of a few minutes ago. "I'll take you there some time. Quite soon."

She smiled. A chance to get closer to his work, finally. Wonderful! For work was one area of Peregrinus's life that Priscilla had been unable to penetrate however hard she tried, and she hated that. "Oh, I'd *love* that, thank you, darling. I just can't wait."

Peregrinus smiled enigmatically, and said nothing.

CHAPTER 41

A House Divided

Jack stared at himself in the mirror of the family bathroom and cast his mind back to when The Voice had last been his unwelcome companion. A lifetime seemed to have unfolded in the intervening months. He had arrived home the previous evening to an understated (to say the least) reception. Both his parents had been in; he'd phoned them briefly from the train to let them know he was on his way. The smouldering residue of an unresolved argument hung in the air as he'd traipsed through the softly lit lounge, upstairs to the refuge of his bedroom. Not much was said, although he expected more in the way of questions this morning. It was weird: Cornwall had brought him horror, evil and magic in equal measure yet never the feeling he had now, the sense of entering a theatre packed with a hostile audience, all focussed on him and waiting to pounce on his first mistake. All of which was ridiculous, of course; everyone had their own problems to think about. But now his problems *were* other peoples' problems, especially his parents', even if they didn't know it or understand it. Now, he was a man with a mission and a purpose: he was a spy in his own home. He took a deep breath and headed down for breakfast.

Some sort of building work seemed to be going on. What was all that hammering and banging? The noise of drills and shouting came from outside as he went down the stairs. In the kitchen, the patio doors were open and cold air was filtering in. David Tyack was out on the terrace, in his suit, directing workmen who were in the process of screwing things to the walls, erecting poles and climbing up ladders. His mother sat at the table, staring at her laptop in customary pose, her fingers slowly massaging her forehead in an effort to concentrate. Jack slid behind the breakfast bar and reached for cereals while she continued to tap at her keyboard. Eventually he said, "Morning Mum."

Mrs Tyack continued working without looking up. After a few moments came her quiet reply, "Hello, Jack."

"What's going on, with all these guys?" he said.

"You'd better ask your father that," was the tight-lipped response.

Now his father had spotted him and, with a parting volley of instructions to one of the workmen, came inside and closed the doors. The noise of drilling continued to reverberate through the walls, a jarring, hectoring backdrop to proceedings. "There you are Jack. I was hoping to catch you before I left. Your mother and I need a talk with you."

"What's all this outside?" returned Jack, hoping to head off the threatened inquisition. And although he hadn't been absent for long, in the light of day he saw his father looked thinner, older.

"Ah. We're just having some security put in. Nothing major, just a few cameras outside. We've had a burglary, you know, while you've been away." The reproof in his voice was unmistakable, as if it were somehow Jack's fault.

"What happened?"

"Someone broke into the library. They did quite a lot of damage, just vandalism really. Books destroyed." His voice cracked as he struggled to keep its tone level, under control. "Nothing more serious, thank heaven. But I'm not taking any more chances, it's high time we got a deterrent sorted out."

Jack felt a wave of unease sweep over him. "When was it?"

"Oh, the day after the party. The day you left in fact. Anyway, it won't happen again." He compressed his lips in determination and nodded outside, where ladders were being manoeuvred across the patio as if to underline the point. Jack cast his mind back to the break-in at Amber's and the theft of the skull. The Messenger? It was too much of a coincidence not to be; and after all, Amber had said that this mysterious envoy had been "abroad" the same night. In fact, she had refused to drive him to the house on that score. It was a timely reminder (if one were needed) that home was no refuge.

While he turned over these connections, his father had pulled up a chair and settled himself at the table opposite, in front of not breakfast things but papers, notes and several different mobiles, all emblems of his ever-present work. Jack looked at both his parents and then looked around with fresh eyes, at the noticeboard covered in memos, the sheaves of plans and papers on the working surfaces, the sense of restless bustle and process. His mother looked composed and poised as ever, in a smart new tracksuit of an expensive brand, but was her face more lined with concentration, harder now? Perhaps not, but there was no denying that his father looked terrible. Who were these people, his parents? Hard-working professionals who wanted the best for themselves and their son? Or something else, victims of and vehicles for a terrible curse that would bring disaster on themselves and others, if Professor Silverman was correct? At that moment, Jack honestly felt he didn't know. At the back of his mind was the unformed thought that, if only he could secure their approval, approval for who he was and what he did, all would be well and they would once more be a "true" family – whatever that was. But, after Cornwall, *could* there ever be any going back? He felt the weight of responsibility press down on him as he recalled the Professor's words, *the onus rests on you!*

He saw his father was looking at him in a troubled sort of way. He said, "Jack, what on earth possessed you to go off like that? Your mother and I don't want to stop you doing things, but just to vanish, and leave that note … what were you thinking of? And what were you doing down there anyway?"

Jack was prepared for this. With a show of contrition he said, "Yeah, I'm sorry Dad. It was this, er, girl I met. She comes from Cornwall, suggested I went back with her for a bit. A quick holiday, sort of."

Mrs Tyack continued to stare at her laptop screen, yet the fact she had stopped typing was clear indication that she was listening carefully. Then she said quietly, "What 'girl' is this Jack?" Only the fewest words, but they were laced with a chilling penetration that only she knew how to achieve. Then, before he could reply, she added, "And how did you meet her?"

He steeled himself to appear casual, knowing the inherent risks of lying to her. "Oh, it's nothing much. I just met her the first time I was down there and we've kept in touch."

His father came to the rescue, holding out his hands in exasperation. "In the middle of the night, practically? What possessed you to go at that time? You know your mother and I have been worried about you. Why didn't you call? You called Richard." There was both disapproval and hurt in his tone. Jack made a face but, having no real riposte to offer, remained silent. A new note, a curious note of concern mingled with what might have been suspicion, entered his father's voice. "Jack, you didn't ... *take* anything with you, did you? Something that didn't belong to you?"

This was another question, revealing in itself, that Jack had been prepared for. The diary had remained with the Professor, at his request, so he could complete his analysis of it. Jack had been in two minds about that but had agreed, then found he was actually more than glad to be rid of it. His only possible response to his father, then, was flat denial.

Injecting some indignation into his tone, he replied, "No, I didn't take anything. What do you mean?"

His father looked a little abashed. Suspicion, though, still lingered in his face. "Just some documents, documents that we seem to have lost. That's all," he finished lamely.

Jack feigned a look of mystification. "You said we'd been burgled, didn't you?" He shrugged.

Here Joanne cut in again, finally looking up from her computer. "I told you, David. For goodness' sake, stop obsessing about it. It's not Jack after all, it went with the break-in and there's nothing we can do about it now."

A certain look of relief spread over David Tyack's face, although the concern lingered in his manner. He ran his hands distractedly through his hair. "Yes, yes, you're right. I'm sorry Jack. We've been a bit stressed recently, that's all. There's a lot on at the moment, a lot." At that moment, in his father's wild eye, his transformed appearance, his obsession with the fate of the diary (for only that could be the subject of his inquiry), Jack felt a renewed conviction that everything the Professor had said about his parents was true. Now he felt sure that it would be for their good as much as anybody else's that he follow the Professor's instructions as closely as possible. Which left him with only one option for today: his original plan, to make a return trip to Little Horwood and find out once and for all what, if anything, was going on there.

His reflections were cut off by his mother, who had abandoned her laptop and was looking at him directly. With icy composure she said quietly, "Jack, please don't run off like that again. That is not good behaviour." He felt as if he'd been stabbed. "Now what's happened to that job you applied for?"

Here at last he could be open. "I got it Mum. I'm starting on Sunday, an evening shift first." Mrs Tyack seemed to accept this news with silent and limited approval, hardly the enthusiastic endorsement Jack had hoped for. He continued, hopefully, "It'll be minimum wages to start with, but they said I'll have a review after the first month."

But his mother already appeared to have disengaged and was staring past her son through the patio windows at the busy scene of workmen coming and going outside. Presently she nodded curtly and, flicking down her glasses from her forehead and turning back to her laptop, said, "Good. At least that's a start, I suppose. You mustn't stop looking for something better though." He felt crushed, humiliated. The café was no place for him, what if people he knew came in and wanted serving? This thought immediately metamorphosed into a new anxiety as to whether Charlie would also be at the café on his first night – something he had pushed to the back of his mind until now. That really would be awkward. He found himself thinking of Amber's advice, "You mustn't give up, Jack!" Perhaps he should try and see Charlie beforehand, clear things up with her after her non-appearance at the party. That, surely, would be better than having to deal with it all in the context of a new job?

He gazed out at the garden, a barren and desolate scene despite the activity. Nothing looked in good shape: the grass had not been given a last cut before the onset of autumn; the borders were thin and tired. A tall metal pole rose from one of the beds, ugly and disfiguring, the platform for one of the new surveillance cameras. A crow picked at the carcase of a dead squirrel lying part-disembowelled on the lawn. Suddenly he realized there was one presence he was missing, both last night and this morning. "Mum, where's Terry?"

His father made a clicking sound in his throat and rapidly exited through the patio doors to issue more directions. Mrs Tyack, though, without missing a beat at her typing, quietly responded, "Terry has been rehomed." She peered a little more closely at the screen, lips pursed in concentration.

Stunned for a moment, Jack struggled to digest this intelligence. "What! Rehomed, what do you mean? I mean, *why*?"

"Yes, rehomed," said Mrs Tyack smoothly, still without looking up. "He was becoming such a nuisance. He scratched the new sofa, you know. Your father and I simply don't have the time these days to keep a dog. And it doesn't seem that you're committed yourself, Jack."

Terry had been nominally Jack's dog since he was a boy. This was just unbelievable. He searched for words. "But – where has he gone? You can't do this, Mum!"

His mother shrugged, preoccupied. "I don't know. They said they'd find a home for him somewhere."

"*They*?"

"The Blue Cross. Jack, I'm sorry but I'm *so* busy just now. You might help your father outside." She glanced briefly over to the patio, where David Tyack was immersed in conversation with what might have been the foreman. Then, for only the second time that morning, she looked at her son directly. "Failing that, there's still work you can be doing on the job front. The coffee shop isn't much of a start. You can do better, Jack, but you need to get out there and put yourself about. Now, I *must* get on."

Jack had heard enough. He slid off his stool and, not even trying to keep the bitterness out of his voice, said, "I'm going out cycling today. I've got stuff I need to do. I'll see you later." No reply. He left the kitchen, the hammering, the typing, the miserable, cold desolation of it all and slunk upstairs to his room, thankful that at least he had a clear task to be getting on with.

CHAPTER 42

The Poor Souls I Took

Jack was on his bike, coasting down a long, shallow hill, traversing the Aylesbury plain on his quest into its dark heart: the village of Little Horwood. Low skies threatened rain, the clouds massing ominously ahead of him. This time, he vowed to himself, he would get to the bottom of whatever mysteries the parish church might be concealing, "diabolical" mysteries, in the uncompromising language of Professor Silverman. His spirits continued to fall as he drew nearer the place, sapping his energy and making each turn of the pedals harder than the one before it. The air was heavy, moist and humid; a layer of sweat clung to him unpleasantly. He slowed at a cross-roads. Somehow, this time the approach to the village seemed different. Had he taken a wrong turn? He stopped. There was not a soul about. A crooked white signpost pointed to Winslow back the way he had come, and to Milton Keynes ahead. To the left – the direction he thought he should be heading – the sign said "Mursley". There was no mention of Little Horwood at all. After a moment's reflection, more from hope than from any true sense of his orientation, he took the left fork: a miserable little track, poorly surfaced and pitted with potholes.

After several minutes' riding he felt no more confident of his decision. Surely he should see the church tower at any minute now? Sparse woodland lined the road, through which gently rolling fields could be seen beyond. The odd large oak curved overhead, canopy-like. Jack pressed on, all the time fighting a creeping sense of oppression. The road gently rose and he found himself on a small bridge. Here he paused again. Below the bridge was a railway line, the rails rusty and partly overgrown with weeds. Getting off his bike, he leant against the parapet and rummaged in his rucksack for the map. The trouble was, all these roads looked the same. If he could just locate the bridge and railway it would be a useful landmark. But as he extracted the map, his phone jerked out with it and dropped down onto the track below. Damn that phone! How many times had that happened? The last thing he needed now was a broken mobile. He had visions of finding himself stranded, condemned to wander forever in circles in this barren place, unable to contact a soul.

Wishing, not for the first time, that he had the ever-competent Charlie with him, Jack irritably made his way down the path at the side of the bridge and onto the track, to where his phone was lying. He was now standing almost under the arch. In one direction, the line stretched away and was lost in the distance; in the other the rails simply stopped. It was a strange sight, almost as if the line were still under construction and had been temporarily deserted by its builders. The empty track bed curved away in a gentle arc to the right and disappeared in the distance in a shallow cutting as the fields rose on either side. There was a desolate, isolated air about the whole place. His gaze panned bleakly across the countryside, coming to rest on a low hill. A white tower stood on this hill, a water tower probably, intriguing, mysterious. Was it a large tower in the far distance? Or a small tower, nearer? He really couldn't say. Anyway, he shouldn't stand there day-dreaming. Jack picked up the phone and examined it closely. It still seemed to be working; that was something. Relieved, he stowed it in his back pocket and was about to climb back up to the bridge when he was checked by a faint sound, a sound some way off, down the line. He paused and listened intently but only the occasional, dreary caw of a rook intruded on the silence. Again he turned to go when there it was again, now more distinct. What was that? Surely it couldn't be … a whistle? But it was; unmistakably, a whistling in the distance came again, louder, nearer. He stared down the tracks, trying to focus on the furthest convergence of the lines. An uncertain blur appeared far off, shimmered on the threshold of vision then slowly coalesced into something more definite. Now a white plume could be seen, accompanied by a rhythmic pattering sound that ricocheted crisply along the cutting.

Hardly believing it, Jack stepped back off the rails and withdrew onto the embankment. Louder grew the sounds, a heady mix of whistling, puffing and the clattering of many mechanical parts moving rapidly together. Then from under the bridge there emerged at speed an old-fashioned steam locomotive, all red livery and gold lettering, followed by a long train of wooden carriages in matching colours. Jack could feel the heat of it against his face, smell the acrid tang of coal smoke. The visual impression, too, was intense; although the train was moving fast he could see people inside, talking, reading newspapers, drinking from china cups. All were wearing the costume of a hundred years ago: hats, moustaches on the men, white gloves on the ladies and cigarettes elegantly poised. And as he watched, Jack's eyes caught and held, and were held in turn, by one particular face: a hard, set, intense face – man or woman he could not say – that in those few seconds of eye contact seemed to drink in his thoughts and search his soul. Suddenly time seemed in suspension, even the sounds of the train were distant and dulled. Then it had passed. The rearmost carriage was whisking away round the bend, curving out of sight on the trackless line, a solitary red light flashing at its tail. And as Jack watched he saw a sort of shimmering pattern around it. The trees and fields on either side appeared to waver and stretch, then the train shrunk to a point and vanished, as if it had been sucked into a vortex like water down a plughole. The countryside reconfigured itself and all was peace and tranquillity once more.

Again Jack looked at the line curving away, the rails ending and the track bed continuing in weeds and undergrowth. It wasn't possible! Yet it had seemed like a real train, so vivid, so immediate. And the faces, the heat, the smoke .... He looked around but road, bridge and embankment were just as deserted as when he'd arrived. There was no-one who might corroborate what he had seen. An illusion? Slowly he turned and walked up the bank, back to his bike. As he did so, he noticed nestling in the trees just a short distance from the line a church tower, surely that of St Nicholas? How strange he hadn't spotted it before, with it being so close. No longer sure which impressions of his senses he might trust, Jack warily mounted his bike and, glad to get away from the bridge, pedalled off towards the tower.

As Jack entered the graveyard it finally started to rain, heavy curtains of it that quickly collected in the church's decayed cast iron guttering, bubbled over its blocked downpipes and ran in little rivers down the walls. The wind was getting up, too, little squally gusts of it agitating the trees into brief frenzied motions. The Tyack tombstones stood in their grim row of three, weathered sentinels, the churned earth of the nearest more conspicuous than before. Having no desire to revisit any of them and not keen either to get soaked, Jack sprinted for the porch. Once in its shelter he took off his soaking waterproof and hung it on a thoughtfully situated peg. Reaching for the latch of the heavy oak door he paused, wary of what he might find inside on this second visit. Again the Professor's warnings returned to him: *Owen Tyack's machine must never be resurrected. You, Jack, have a responsibility! People were consumed … consumed …*. Again a sense of guilt at his unwitting involvement, the weight of his family's connection with these murky goings-on, swept over him, not steeling him at all but instead depleting his resolve. Wouldn't it be better to leave it all to others, to slink home and try and forget the whole thing? How could such forces be resisted? More likely, though, it was all wild exaggeration; his parents couldn't possibly be involved in such matters, no, not his parents. He stood undecided, the drumming of the rain on the porch roof mocking his hesitation. Then Richard Attlee's words, the ones about following the grain of events, sprang into his mind, renewing his determination. He lifted the latch and entered.

The dank air of the interior met him in a musty wave. Brass lanterns swung gently in the draft that had blown in with him, giving the eerie impression that something was moving in the trembling shadows. Several lighted candles had been placed by someone within a niche in the south aisle, adding to the effect. Only the rain against the windows broke what was otherwise complete silence. He had half expected to find the quirky youth Toby there but the interior was quite empty. Where would he start? The Professor had not been able to offer much in the way of guidance as to where any "diabolical device" might be concealed, and in fact there was in any case no guarantee it was in the church at all. Only

Silverman's chain of reasoning supported that conclusion; there was no evidence – yet. Jack didn't even know what, in physical terms, he was looking for. How would he identify it if he saw it?

His thoughts were interrupted by a harsh grating sound, succeeded by the low murmur of voices. He quickly withdrew behind the pulpit, crouching down where he wouldn't be seen and yet could still have a fair view. Two people emerged from behind a heavy curtain. One was clearly the vicar, tall and spare in dark suit and dog collar. The other was a lithe, wiry individual. Something about the latter immediately engaged Jack; he felt his stomach tighten in an animal reaction. The man was on the small side, his body compact, hard and slight. It was not so much what he *saw*, though, since the shadows were deep, but more an *impression*. Here was someone with some vague oddness, what was it? Mild deformity? Something, some kinship with something *other*, maybe? Jack looked harder. The man appeared normal enough. He was speaking to the vicar in a low voice, unhurried, sure of himself. Jack caught some of it: "–so we can draw a line under things here at last."

"Well, I have to say I'm pleased to hear it," returned the vicar. "And when would you say you'll be gone?" Both men stood talking in low tones for a few minutes by the door, then the wiry man broke off and looked around carefully. Jack had the distinct impression he was actually sniffing the air. He took a half-step towards the pulpit and stopped, a puzzled expression on his face. Suddenly Jack felt exposed, vulnerable; his hiding place was no protection at all, even his breathing might be heard! "Are you alright?" asked the vicar, uncomprehending. The wiry man continued to look puzzled for a minute, then the curtain twitched and a third man emerged, scurrying quickly across the nave like a beetle, distracting him. The wiry man gave a quick nod to this newcomer then, reaching in his pocket, with a wry smile he put a coin in the collection box on the wall. Following which, he held out a hand to indicate precedence to the others, all three filed out and the church was once more empty.

When he was certain they would not return, Jack emerged from behind the pulpit and released his breath in a long sigh. The atmosphere of the place immediately felt better, cleaner, it seemed. Here already, though, was valuable information; what he had overheard of the conversation was suspicious, to say the least. Was, then, the vicar involved in this? As for the other man– Jack stared up at the rays of muddy light streaming through a stained glass window and pondered. Something strange and alien was inside that unexceptional exterior, he felt it. Yet something familiar too. What was it, that uncanny union of the two in one body? Had he found 'the Helper', that malign being sent from the depths to wreak havoc above? Could he really be sure, through glimpsed fragments in a half light? Just an ordinary man in ordinary clothes, chatting to a vicar in an ordinary church; there might be no more to it than that. And what about the third man?

He walked over to the vestry, from whence the three men had emerged, and pulled back the curtain. Behind it was an innocent-enough looking space, with shelves, tables, prayer books and the like. Beyond was a more modern-looking door; Jack tried the handle but it was locked. He felt nonplussed. Back in the nave he cast about listlessly, searching for clues. There was a previously unexamined space under the tower, a dark square into which bell-ropes and weights hung down through slats in the wooden ceiling above. The steady, sonorous beat of the clock echoed soothingly. Nothing here, no leads.

As he returned to the main body of the church he noticed to his right a curious item of furniture, a bit like a dresser but deeper, standing against the wall at an angle, as if it had been moved and not properly returned to its original position. Something about it urged him to look more closely. He went over and crouched down, looking carefully at the floor around this bulky chest. In the dim light he could make out numerous tracks and scrapes on the wooden boarding, evidence surely of much recent activity. And around the back, in the space between wall and chest and set into the floor, could be seen the distinct outline of part of a square. With a great effort, Jack managed painfully to drag the chest away from the wall, inch by inch, causing a wincingly loud scraping sound to fill the church in the process. He rested and looked around nervously for evidence of someone having been alerted to his presence. But peace had supervened once more; he was perfectly alone. Returning to his task, he found he could now see the trapdoor in its entirety. It was quite plain except for a heavy bronze ring, inset to give a flush surface.

Whoever made this ring, some craftsman old, clearly had a certain sense of style for it was done in the fashion of a twisting spiral cord. Still sweating from the effort of his exertion (clearly a two-man job under normal circumstances) Jack now addressed the trapdoor. Although it looked heavy, unlike the chest it moved easily enough, perhaps a sign of frequent use. He swung it back on its hinges and straightened up, regarding the black square below with circumspection. A nasty smell wafted up from the aperture, of dampness as one might expect but with an undertone of something worse. Worn stone steps disappeared into darkness. Remembering the bicycle lamp in his rucksack, Jack fished it out and shone the beam down the hatchway. The steps continued out of sight. The crypt, or whatever it was, was deeper than he had imagined and this, combined with the terrible smell, hardly offered much encouragement to go any further. Here, he thought, was a threshold, in all senses of the term. It was still not too late to back off, go home, try and forget it all, let sleeping dogs lie and leave his parents to get on with their business lives as they saw fit. Below lay knowledge, knowledge that could only (he felt certain now) complete his insight into Owen Tyack's experiments and the ominous pronouncements of the diary. He thought of his promises to the Professor and to Amber and again he realized that his apparent choices were hollow ones. There *was* no choice. Too much was at stake.

The steepness of the steps made it more practicable to descend backwards. A rope hanging from the wall gave a certain limited help as a handrail. After counting ninety steps, and just when he was wondering how far down church crypts usually went, Jack reached the bottom. The stench of decomposition was overpowering now. He panned his light around the confined space and took in the details. The cellar stretched away out of the reach of his lamp's beam. Its roof was low and vaulted in brick, with cobwebs strewn from one wall to the other. Several memorial plaques and engravings adorned the walls while broken tombstones and statues were piled up around the perimeter in a careless, jumbled sort of way. The floor had been sprinkled, recently by the look of it, with a thick layer of sawdust. Further down the crypt bulked the shadow of what might have been a bier, or sarcophagus. Jack found a light switch taped in rough fashion to a column and flicked it. A fluorescent strip flickered on, producing a harsh, cold light that transformed the atmosphere of the place. The first thing he noticed were many small drawings, resembling graffiti, peppering the walls. Most of them appeared to be of a mathematical nature. But more importantly, Jack could now see clearly that what had seemed like a bier was no such thing. Slowly he approached it, his feet sinking softly into the sawdust.

Before him stood a contraption, a most curious contraption, something that had no place in an English parish church, nor in any church in any country on earth. The main body of it comprised a wooden platform about the dimensions of a bed. Surrounding this platform were clusters of wires in multi-coloured sheaths, wires that merged into larger bundles that snaked into a casing beside it, the size and shape of a large dynamo. Next to this, on a crude bench, a row of light bulbs projected from a wooden mounting. A plastic hose of thicker dimensions, rather like something from a respirator or mask, lay to one side and fed into a transparent cylinder, vertically mounted. Clamps and leather straps, the ghastly apparatus of restraint, rested on the platform. Lying on the floor were several lengths of knotted rope. Dark stains streaked the wood; the sawdust was congealed into numerous gruesome clots.

Jack swallowed as he beheld the vile thing. So, here it was. Owen Tyack's diabolical device, the machine described in the diary and elucidated by the Professor with such grisly eloquence. As he looked on, it now came home to Jack just what those jottings and descriptions really boiled down to, and what the prospect of the Shadow's ultimate success might look like. He realized at a stroke exactly the nature of the pitiless greed described by the Professor, its obscene disregard for all the basic values of humanity and of to what, in the end, it was capable of driving men and women. His gaze took in a new feature of the ghastly scene: a pathetic bundle of clothes heaped against one wall – a pair of jeans, some t-shirts, underwear, socks, an odd trainer, a man's scarf. Nearby, the sawdust had been churned somewhat in furrows and ridges. And all in the name of greed, the lust for wealth. Again the image of his dog, Terry, sprang to his mind, evicted and taking up a new life with strangers. Tears pricked at his eyes. He began to understand at last the depth of the Professor's revulsion, to realize what he was fighting against.

Once more Jack saw in his mind's eye the hideous image of the skull of Owen Tyack, again he heard its tortured phrases. *Those poor souls I took*. Suddenly a feeling of nausea overcame him and he retched. The smell was abominably strong, with no apparent ventilation to help disperse it. Fighting the desire to run away, Jack took a step forward and looked more closely at the wooden platform. It had been crafted precisely, not just thrown together as had seemed the case at first sight. Grotesque symbols and letters were inscribed meticulously on its sides in a fusion of occult art and alien science. He came closer. Something odd had happened around the joints, a strange kind of eruption in the wood, almost as if scabs had formed there, the scars of living tissue.

More might be gleaned from further inspection, but Jack began to feel he had seen more than enough. Turning off the light, he retreated back up the stairs, gladly emerging into the comparatively wholesome air of the nave. Trembling, he turned and with relief closed the trapdoor on the horrors below.

CHAPTER 43

Ethics and an Inquisition

Ten p.m. and a peaceful scene in the Tyacks' lounge. As ever, David and Joanne had put in many hours' work that day, and finished late. Weekends, of course, were no barrier to that. Now both were sprawled on their new leather sofas, watching a large plasma screen television. An ostentatious, richly woven Persian rug occupied the centre of the room, replacing the more homely one on which Terry the Airedale terrier had been wont to lie. That had been disposed of, along with his bowls and toys, his scratches here and there carefully expunged. Mr Tyack was still wearing his work clothes, his shirt sleeves rolled up, the neck unbuttoned. A glass of scotch started to tilt dangerously in his hand as he nodded off. Joanne, in black skirt and white blouse, regarded him sharply. She reached for the remote control and turned down the television. "David!" He looked up, startled. "You're nodding off again." She gave a little smile. "You look exhausted. Here, let me top you up." She refilled his glass and sat back on the sofa, legs neatly tucked up under her. Her husband pulled himself up into a vaguely more responsive posture. Mrs Tyack was staring at him keenly. She said, "Nuisance about Katja going, isn't it?"

He suppressed a yawn. "Is she going? I didn't know. Shame – she seemed hard working enough. What was her problem, boyfriend troubles?"

"Not at all. She said she didn't want to work here anymore."

"Really?" He looked more engaged. "We treated her well enough didn't we? Paid her enough, for sure."

"It wasn't that. She said–" Joanne broke off, with a sort of half-snort of laughter, stifled mid-way.

"Go on, what did she say?"

"She said she was frightened. Since the burglary. She just said she didn't feel comfortable here anymore."

"That again!"

"Do you blame her?"

He shrugged and took a sip of his whisky. "I suppose not. These young girls can be very irrational though. I wouldn't be surprised if there was boyfriend trouble at the bottom of it."

Joanne continued to look closely at him, silent for a moment. "Well, if it was that, why didn't she just say so? Or invent a more reasonable-sounding excuse?"

"Who knows? I'll contact the agency; it shouldn't be too hard to find a replacement. Cleaners are ten a penny at the moment." He twisted around half-heartedly, keen to change the subject. "Where's Jack?"

"In his room."

"Ah." David Tyack gave a long sigh and leant his head back on the sofa, so he was staring at the ceiling. "I don't know what'll become of that boy. No drive at all. He's too much of a dreamer, Jo. He should be focussing on doing something useful, not randomly careering about the country. It's a tough old world out there."

Joanne nodded coldly. "Unfortunately, 'sensitivity' isn't a quality that gets results in this life."

They lapsed into silence. David noted for the hundredth time how, whenever he made a criticism of Jack, valid certainly but in the boy's own best interests, his wife seized on it with something like triumph. Her briefest expression of agreement spoke volumes; Jack really could do no good in her eyes. He sighed again. "How are the girls, have you seen them today?"

Mrs Tyack stretched out languidly, the hardness melting away. "Oh, briefly, in the café. They're well enough. Jems is as flaky as ever. Still talking about how much she enjoyed the party."

"Well, that's good to hear. You didn't mention the – burglary to them?"

"Of course not!" she replied, with an acid edge to her tone. She paused for some minutes before continuing more softly, "Tell me David, do you feel happy? With how it's all going?"

Suddenly he felt wary. His face twitched uncontrollably. "Yes, all in all. We're on schedule. It's all coming together well."

His wife's expression remained careful, alert. "Yes, I didn't mean exactly that. Do you *feel* happy with it? Are you *comfortable* with it?"

Again he tensed. Joanne rarely asked about his state of mind, his feelings; it was normally matters of fact that interested her. He said cautiously, "Yes, certainly – well, I think so," and took a generous sip of his whisky. "Why do you ask?"

She looked over at the television briefly, then back at her husband. "So you don't have any … scruples?"

"Scruples? Why should I?"

"I know how much work you've put in, to get the prototype up and running for instance." She was conciliatory, sympathetic almost. She uncurled herself and came to sit beside him, her eyes roving closely over his face as if searching for imperfections. "And of course, we both know the toll it's taken, in many ways."

He returned her stare, but looked much less comfortable. "That was necessary. After all, there was no other way. We *had* to–"

Now she was nodding, reaching out to him and gently smoothing his hair, as if stroking a pet. "Good, I'm glad you still think so. Because in this life you get nothing for nothing. Those people will never be missed, never."

He wished she hadn't raised the subject. It was as if she had an inner window onto his deepest, subconscious mind.

He sighed, trying not to dissemble. "I know, I know. But Joanne – it seems a … well, a shame. And I still think of the risk–"

She cut him off, still stroking his hair, her grey eyes still scanning his face. "You mustn't. You should think of the gain. And there isn't any risk in any case. Low life, low types. They won't be missed. You really shouldn't get dragged down by moralising, David. Remember, I know you too well – you can't hide it from me. You've got to put these scruples behind you. Our work, your work, is going to be a permanent benefit to all of humanity. To the planet. It's too important to let trivial issues get in the way." She was speaking in a low voice, the tone of an intimate whisper, but her words were forceful. Seeing her husband's weak and abashed look – something she knew only she could invoke – she pressed home her point. "Those people were materials. Think of them as fuel, no different to coal, or gas, or any other natural resource."

"I know, Joanne, I agree, I agree. I'm not bothered about their, their *use*." He stared out of the lounge window to the lighted patio outside, on which the trees cast rippling shadows. "No, it isn't that. It's not their use, not that they … died." He spoke the taboo word, the word he knew would inflame her. "It's the *way* they died, I suppose. The manner of it. Do you see? You weren't there, you don't realize."

She drew back. "Then don't *you* be there, in future. Let Perez handle it – *he* wouldn't be so squeamish." He winced at her scorn, regretting his words. Then her angry mood seemed to pass and she resumed her affectionate caresses. "In any case, that phase is finished with now. David, you *mustn't* worry yourself about these side issues. Concentrate on the big picture. It's where your strengths lie." She gave an ironic smile. "And as to my being there – well, you know I never go to church."

There was a long silence in which only the background gabble of the television could be heard. David Tyack slowly relaxed and lay his head on his wife's chest, allowing her to cradle it. Slowly he drifted into sleep again. Joanne held him, gazing across the room and into space. Presently she murmured, although now to herself only, "You get nothing for nothing. You must remember, David: nothing for nothing."

⅄

Upstairs, Jack lay on his bed, inert, caught up in his thoughts. Dark impressions surged and gathered in his mind, of benches and straps, brutal knotted gags, matted hair and congealed blood. He rolled onto his side and gazed emptily at the wall. The terrible truth asserted itself: Owen Tyack's device *had* been resurrected. It was still possible, he supposed, that his parents might not be connected with it all but that was looking increasingly unlikely. If they were, then – but the "then" was too horrible to think about. His parents as murderers? Could it be? He clutched at the remaining wisps of their innocence. Maybe they knew about it, yes, but not details, not actually how it worked, what it was doing.

He rolled on his other side, unable to find repose. Something else from the church stuck in his mind, a small detail, troubling him. The two men he'd seen in the nave, the vicar and his strange companion. What was it? That third individual, the man who'd belatedly emerged from the vestry and quickly left with them: Jack had seen him somewhere before. And where was that? He knew the answer, although he was reluctant to frame it to himself, wishing it would go away. But it wouldn't. No; he had seen that man in this very house, at his parents' party, talking to his father no less. The memory of it, clear and irrefutable, floated into Jack's mind, a concrete connection with home. Just now, it seemed conclusive, utterly final. Again Professor Silverman's account rang true, although he wished it wouldn't.

The thought briefly crossed Jack's mind that, in the face of this murderous criminality, "authorities" should be involved. Instinctively, however, he knew it could never be. He had to tackle this himself, just as Professor Silverman had said. Police? Trials? Imprisonment? Disgrace, at the least, and ruin. He shuddered. In any case, the true causes behind all this were not of this world. This horror had arisen in the dark, private places of the mind. At that level it would have to be combatted. He reached listlessly for his mobile. No messages. He hated the sense of isolation. This house was no longer his home: cold, inhospitable, and worse. Restless, he got off the bed and poked his head through the curtains to survey the black rectangle of garden below, stretching down to the woods at the bottom where the beeches rustled. He closed the curtains and went to sit cross-legged on the bed, reflecting on what his plan was to be. If Professor Silverman was right, the device in the crypt could not be the final thing. If the curse was still alive then his parents would know about this demonic apparatus, for sure, but it would be only a stepping stone, a bridge to something bigger, worse in every respect. Locating and stopping that something was his mission now, and an urgent one. There was one place, in this very house, where he suspected he could get more answers.

Despite his restless mood, Jack yawned. All he wanted to do now was escape into sleep, if he could: deep, dreamless sleep. He padded down the landing to the bathroom to clean his teeth. On his way he passed the model train in its glass case, the model that had been on display there for as long as he could remember. The train! Was he losing his mind? That hallucination had seemed so real – the smell, the sight, the heat … and yet it was as if a veil had been drawn across it and it had completely slipped from his consciousness. Now seeing this model brought it all back. For the first time in years he peered closely at the engine. It looked exactly like the one he'd seen, or thought he had seen. The paint, the wheels – even, now he noticed it, the oval brass plate on the side: they were all the same. He blinked, feeling reality slide away from him, and leant against the wall for a moment. He would ask Richard Attlee about that bizarre episode, an episode *so* bizarre, in fact, that it was surely related in some way to wider events. It was just the sort of thing that Attlee would relish and take seriously, where others would laugh or scoff. In any case, he was long overdue such a visit. The thought of it cheered him a little.

After washing, Jack lay in bed and turned on his television, hoping to take his mind off everything. The images paraded meaninglessly in front of him. A chat show host threw his head back and howled, animal-like, with laughter. On a different channel a man pounded the face of another man with his fists until the other man stopped moving. A third channel showed gritty reportage of bombings, of helicopters and troops in swirling clouds of dust. And so he went on, flicking aimlessly through the stations in quick succession, staring emptily at it all. He felt utterly alone.

CHAPTER 44

MECHANICS OF THE PAST

Jack was familiar enough with the Attlee establishment to ignore formalities and make his own way around the side of the house to the back. Since his recent retirement, Richard Attlee spent much time in his beloved workshop, absorbed in various projects that were all inspired by his ambition to become a renowned inventor. It was a safe bet he would be there now. No mere shed, this workshop was the size of a double garage and nestled at the bottom of the garden, its roof swept by low branches, the walls pressed close by shrubbery as if it had grown out of the borders of its own accord. Over the entrance hung a brass plate bearing the inscription, *Welcome. Now piss off* – one of Attlee's little jokes – and by its side hung a brass bell. Ignoring both, Jack pushed open the door and entered.

Inside, the workshop contained many benches around its perimeter, crammed with tools and machinery: a large lathe; a milling machine; a huge pedestal drill; rows of hammers, screwdrivers and Allen keys in racks on the wall; shelves on which were placed lubricants and semi-machined components; and, on their own separate shelf, a row of malt whiskies. There were also to be seen levelling plates, a bench grinder, a compressor and one half-eaten cheese sandwich. From the ceiling was slung a thing like a skateboard that was bizarrely combined with a leaf-blower, and what looked like a canoe. At the far end was a desk strewn with grubby blueprints and trigonometry equipment, and next to it a couple of grease-streaked easy chairs. A fluorescent strip dangled from the ceiling. Under it was Attlee himself, crouched on the floor in his shirt sleeves, hunched over a petrol engine that was connected to a fan. He didn't look up when Jack entered but carried on tinkering with intense absorption. Familiar with Attlee's quirks, Jack patiently waited. After a while the aspiring inventor said irritably, still without looking up, "Well don't just stand there. Sit down!"

Jack picked his way across the floor and parked himself on one of the chairs, feeling agreeably at home despite this irascible welcome. After watching for several minutes, intrigued, he asked, "What are you making, Richard?"

Attlee straightened his body while remaining on his knees and wiped his hands on his shirt, a sludge-coloured, checked accoutrement that he sported on most occasions. "Ah! Good question. Just a little, er, anachronism, Jack. I've always wanted to get a proper perspective on things, you know. This little device will let me do just that! It's almost finished, too." He flashed Jack a quick, mischievous glance, then carried on tinkering.

Jack waited a little longer, then when it seemed clear that no further conversation on Attlee's part was imminent, inquired, "Is this the thing that you mentioned when I called you?"

Attlee paused in the midst of tightening a nut, then looked up with deliberation. "It is that *thing,* yes. Welcome back, by the way. You and I have a lot to catch up on." More tinkering, and the odd tapping of the recalcitrant nut. "So how did you get on down there? In Cornwall. You still haven't told me properly about the first time. And whether it helped."

The fall-out from Jack's Cornish trips had been so dramatic that wherever possible he'd avoided having to follow up with Attlee about them. Where would he start? Again he thought back to their earlier conversation about "exorcising demons". It had been more a question of invoking them. After rapidly running through several summary-like formulations in his head, he simply said, "There's a bee centre down there, in Polzeath. You'd have loved it." No reply. Then he said, "Richard, do you believe in the *paranormal*?"

Attlee briefly paused in his tapping, then replied, "No, I don't. I believe in the power of the human psyche, though. Now why do you ask that? Do you think you've seen a ghost recently, eh?"

"Not exactly, but I had a bit of a weird experience."

Attlee resumed his tightening again. "Want to tell me about it?" he said, not discouragingly.

Hoping he was not about to invite ridicule, Jack began, "Well, I was cycling yesterday, out around Winslow. I'd stopped on a bridge for a bit, and I dropped my phone." He recounted the business of the train, trying to remember as many details as he could. He was helped in this by Attlee himself, who, in between his tapping and adjustments, made it clear he was listening by interpolating questions at various points in the narrative: "Wait a moment. You said it was very quiet yes?"

"Well, yes. I could hear the train, but it was sort of dulled, now you mention it."

"Now, you said earlier that this engine you saw was red. Am I right?"

"Yes, it was red, red with black stripes on it."

"Good, you're most observant! Now, can you remember about the *rails*? It's an important point, you know."

"Well, they just ended–"

"Yes, yes, you told me that. But did you notice anything about their condition? Were they shiny, for instance? I'm not trying to lead you, just what you remember!"

Jack thought for a moment. "I definitely remember, they were quite rusty and dull, with weeds growing over them."

Attlee had now moved on to unscrewing a filter from the engine, and began chattering on while he did so. "You know, that was a wonderful line, the Metropolitan and Great Central. Used to go all the way out into the Buckinghamshire wilds. It was a great shame when they closed those sections and cut it back to Amersham. People are so short-sighted.

Betjeman mentions it, of course, in *Trains and Buttered Toast.* Anyway: you saw this thing. *But*: it was no mere passive observation. Interesting! There was actual interaction. Let's be quite clear about this: you made eye contact with somebody on that train, correct?"

"Yes, I did. I looked right into their eyes. And they looked straight back at me. It was only for a second but–"

"Alright, I've got that." He appeared lost in thought, and said ruminatively, more or less to himself, "And it just vanished. A shimmering, a distortion … a vortex perhaps? Hmm. The trees, shimmering …." His voice trailed off, then he got to his feet, came over to join Jack by the desk, rummaged around for a bit and then drew out a map from the drawer. This he spread out on the desk and positioned a light to illuminate it. They both stood and bent over the map. "Look. This is the one-inch Ordnance Survey of that area. It'll be similar to the one you had but just more detail. Now if we look here" – he jabbed a finger – "we can see your railway line. It's clearly marked as disused. As I said, it's the old Metropolitan line and used to run from Amersham through Wendover to Aylesbury, Winslow Road and then terminated at Verney Junction, where it met with the London and North Western. The whole place used to be criss-crossed with these lines, before Beeching got to work." He looked up at Jack. "This line hasn't been used in seventy years. There's a preservation centre at Quainton Road, but they don't run trains to there and that's a fact. And you saw a train. And, by your description of it, and that of the people on it, it was from a hundred years ago!" Attlee scratched his nose and appeared to reflect long and hard.

"So what do you think?" asked Jack, reassured at least that Attlee appeared to be taking the episode seriously. "I honestly saw it, as clearly as I can see you."

Attlee nodded and said quietly, while gesturing over the map with precise movements, "Look, I imagine that the train is getting smaller because of the distance and the perspective, and the surroundings seem to shimmer, and then they close in on the train and squeeze it out of existence. Well, that sounds to me very much like the science fiction version of the space-time *wormhole.* Now, wormholes are permitted in general relativity, but they are not big enough for real world objects. The dimensions are smaller than protons so you wouldn't get trains in them – you see?" He made a circle with his forefinger and thumb. "I just mention it, mind you, to show the kinds of thing that are theoretically possible. But nevertheless it's a very odd effect. Very odd. Wait here."

Attlee abruptly vanished up the garden, returning a few minutes later with two cups of tea and a packet of biscuits. They stood standing, drinking tea and staring down at the map, Attlee's jaws thoughtfully grinding on his biscuit. Presently he said, "You know Jack, there are some very interesting features in your account. You said the rails were rusty, for instance. Well, no modern rails are ever rusty. They're shiny. Even rails that are rarely used have a shiny stripe down the middle. But these rails were completely rusty, you said. They haven't been used for decades! And again, just think back. You tell me you saw this *spectacle* of the train yet you said something else, can you remember? You mentioned how quiet it was. Well, that's very interesting. You're not old enough to remember steam engines but the noise was deafening – lots of clanking, mechanical noise, the sounds of wheels on the rails, the exhaust. You *saw* everything, but you *heard* nothing, or at any rate very little. Now let's add to that the other details that you noticed: a particular livery on the train, a livery from a hundred years ago. Not perhaps significant in itself, but then the people in the carriage were all wearing the costume – even the hair styles and beards – of the period too. Then again, with one of these people you established actual interaction, real eye contact. Last of all, there's the extraordinary way the train just disappeared: not round a bend, not progressing out of sight, but 'swallowed up', as you said, along with strange optical effects that involved the trees and shrubbery around." He stopped speaking and turned to look at Jack intently. "You see how very odd this all is?"

Jack felt frustrated. "I know, that's why I came to see you about it. What do you think's going on?"

Attlee smiled reassuringly. "Don't worry, I don't believe you imagined it, and I don't think you're going mad either. Nor do I believe in ghosts, as I said. But suppose, just suppose, that what you saw really *did* take place, not now but a hundred years ago. No, I'm not joking! You know, Jack, I don't think this has anything to do with wormholes. They couldn't accommodate anything on this scale. My other thought is *quantum mechanics*. There is a theory called 'many worlds', where you have parallel existences for elementary particles. Again, we're talking about the atomic level here. One possibility is of a universe where alternative outcomes exist, but you happen to only exist in one of them. The universes keep splitting so there are an infinite number. So you see, the parallel universes could be like our own and could contain trains. In which case, to get to the kind of phenomenon you saw, what we're considering is a possible temporary overlap between two worlds; you get a sort of connection between them that exists for a short period of time, like the two or three minutes in which your experience took place. Then it's closed off again. But it's long enough to get a glimpse into the other world. Do you see? So maybe you had a temporary connection with one of the parallel worlds, which comes out of quantum mechanics. That's a good deal more plausible than the idea of a wormhole in space, which I can't see could possibly ever be big enough to swallow a train."

Jack rubbed his nose. "If all that was true, then what could cause it?"

"I don't know. Some very odd phenomenon of a local nature, perhaps. Show me where you think you dropped your phone, as exactly as you can."

Jack looked again at the map, locating once more the old railway line. He saw marked the tiny hamlet of Mursley, that he had seen signposted on the day. A crooked lane connected Mursley with Little Horwood, just nearby. At one point, the lane intersected with the line, and a bridge was marked. He placed a finger on the map. "I'd say it was here, just at that bridge."

"Hm," said Attlee. "Swanbourne. But there's nothing there at all."

"What *kind* of phenomenon were you thinking about?" asked Jack, a chill creeping over him as the seeds of an explanation began to grow in his mind. "You must have some idea."

Attlee shrugged. "Something like a momentary vast release of energy. Proximate to the event itself."

"How proximate?"

"Oh, within a mile, at the most. But it would require an awful lot of energy."

Jack stared at the map. Swanbourne and Little Horwood, such close neighbours their names almost touched. "What sort of energy?" he asked.

Attlee regarded Jack closely, as if he suspected there might be more to this question than met the eye. "Since you ask, I'm not sure. But it would have to have been applied a hundred years ago, to have an effect on a hundred-year-old train to make it appear now."

"A hundred years ago? So you're saying that some … experiment or machine, or something, close to where I dropped my phone, that released lots of energy and ran a hundred years ago, could have thrown up that train I saw? But why did I see it now? Why when I was there yesterday?"

"Ah, well that's where it gets complicated."

"As if it's not already!"

"Yes, but you'll see all this is just theory. For you to have seen the train when you did, the same energy source would have to be activated while you were there."

"How do you mean? It ran twice?"

"It would have, yes. But this is pure fantasy."

"But just for argument's sake?"

"Well. The energy source operated a hundred years ago, then it runs again, in about the same place, in the present. Just yesterday. What is it that connects the two episodes? It's the energy itself! According to the theory, by doing so, if enough energy was released, two parallel worlds might became momentarily connected. But with a *step,* a hundred-year time difference. A bridge between the two is created by this powerful, no doubt *strange,* form of energy. This bridge even allows you, in the present, to interact briefly with an event from the past."

Jack considered this. "And what would have happened to the original train? Was it destroyed?"

"No, no, not that. That's what I'm saying. It would have just carried on. Nobody would have known anything odd was happening." Attlee chuckled to himself. "Fun idea isn't it? The passenger who saw you standing in the cutting wouldn't necessarily think that anything was odd. He thinks he's seeing a young man in 1900, or whatever, he doesn't realise that he's seeing a young man in the 21st century! But all this is just theory of course."

"So where does that leave the train that I saw?"

Attlee was serious again. "I don't know," he said slowly. There was a long pause, during which Attlee sat down in one of the easy chairs and motioned Jack to the other one. "I have to say, Jack, it's funny you should mention you've been out in that area. It's put me in mind of something. Maybe

I shouldn't say this but I'll tell you anyway." He looked at Jack shrewdly. "Perhaps there's more to all this than meets the eye – but you'd know. Anyway. I've had a suspicion for a while now that your father has been up to something. His behaviour has been most odd, not like him at all. He'd been acting rather unusually at that party you had, for one thing. But there was something else. A few days ago I happened to be in Winslow and I saw your father, with some others who we needn't discuss now. They didn't see me but let's just say that something made me follow them in my car when they drove off." Attlee paused, looking perplexed, scanning Jack's face for a response. Noting the signs of intense engagement, he continued, "Well, I followed them, and it was a strange trip, all through the smallest lanes in those parts." He indicated the maze of tiny roads in the part of the map they had been scrutinizing. "I had quite a job not to lose them, they were driving at a hell of a pace."

"Well? What did you find? Where were they going?" Jack had an awful sense of foreboding.

"I couldn't tell you. Not precisely. They got to a gate, right out in the sticks here. This gate had security, there was no chance of following them once they'd gone through. But–"

"What?"

"I can tell you the *name* of the place. Look here." He gestured at a spot on the map. Jack followed his finger and saw Attlee was pointing to fields near a tiny hamlet. "Verney Junction. This is it. It's a small place, isn't it? Really out in the wilds. You see the same disused railway line you dropped your phone on runs right through it. Anyway …." Attlee shifted in his seat and seemed uncomfortable. "I just thought it was odd. There were some strange features about the whole thing. Would you know why your father was out there?"

The possibilities fanned out in Jack's mind. "I'm not sure Richard. I might have some idea. It's just an idea, though." He thought for a moment longer whilst Attlee stared at the map.

"You're not going out there are you, Jack?" said the older man presently, reading his mind.

Jack replied slowly, speaking as much to himself as to his companion. "I've got to work tomorrow at the coffee shop and I need to speak to Charlie. I don't think there's much time left, though."

"What do you mean, 'not much time left'?"

"Oh, nothing. Nothing at all, Richard."

"Well look, if you need help with anything, anything at all, let me know. I don't know what your father's mixed up in but I wouldn't take it lightly. You know I'm here. Just be careful, won't you?"

"Yes, I will. Of course, Richard."

CHAPTER 45

History Repeats?

Late evening: the head office of Geothermal Energy Solutions Ltd, Amersham, Buckinghamshire. David Tyack was slumped at his desk, the shadow of his former self, drained, physically worn out, mentally unable to rest for even one moment. His mind was dominated by schedules, plans, tasks, the greater goal. He could find no repose; there would, he felt, be no peace for him in this life ever again. On his desk was a bar of chocolate and a cup of coffee, his main forms of sustenance for these past two months. The project was approaching its climax, and its needs swept all before it. Small things like food, rest and a social life – well, they could wait. There would be no homecoming for David Tyack tonight.

This evening he was not alone. Pacing restlessly around the room in habitual fashion was Peregrinus, pausing as was his wont to peer at a wall map, adjust a coloured marker pin, stare suspiciously out of the window, prod and ruffle papers on the printer. His restless energies appeared to be approaching a zenith, even as the other man's waned. David remained collapsed in his chair, hollow-cheeked, eyes feverish, features drawn. Peregrinus was speaking, no longer in the deferential tones of their first meeting. Now he was dominant, with a sureness in his voice. "But you *still* haven't found it," he was saying. "That is the point. You say your son may have it." He paused in his fitful progress and turned to stare directly at the slumped figure. "What progress have you made there? Does he have it? Have you questioned him? You *have* questioned him, yes?" There was urgency in his voice, the pressure of need.

David Tyack hauled himself up in his seat a little, attempting to show at least a semblance of the authority that he knew, now, had been all but entirely ceded to his mysterious helper. "Yes, yes," he replied wearily, rubbing his eyes as if to restore their former clarity of vision. "Yes, I've asked him. He denies any knowledge of the diary, says he's never seen it."

Peregrinus made a reproachful clicking noise with his tongue. "He's lying. He knows. I can feel it."

Tyack stared back at him with what remnants of defiance he could muster. "I think I can read my own son. And how would you know? What do you know about him anyway?"

But Peregrinus didn't deign to answer. Instead, he moved to the window and looked down at the cars ploughing the dark furrow of the White Lion Road, their headlights spreading cones of light from oblique discs. He stood like that, still, burning quietly with his sense of mission. Was, he wondered, this man Tyack equal to the task? Another Owen, perhaps; another one to fail him at the last? No! This time it would be different, there would be no mistakes. Human frailty would not be allowed to get in the way. He turned back to look at the businessman, all crushed at his desk. Where was his fire, where was his fight? They were so nearly there! As he watched, David Tyack hauled himself to his feet and came over to stand at the window next to Peregrinus. He seemed palpably diminished, shorter. The man had shrunk, not grown. Guiltily David said, "What does it matter, in any case? It won't affect our plans now. The Reactor is nearly ready. What difference can the diary possibly make? We've got what we need from it." His voice took on a plaintive, pleading note. "Surely we can let it go now?"

Peregrinus replied quietly, "In one sense you're right. The Reactor can and will run, whatever." He moved closer. Their eyes were level, inches away from each other, on the one side twin burning points of flickering energy, on the other as dead and empty as a cold hearth. "But the diary, that's unfinished business. I want it back, to finish that business. I know your son had a hand in its disappearance. Where is he now?"

"Jack? At the house, I suppose. Look, you're not suggesting–?"

"Never mind." Peregrinus cut him off. "It can wait. I *shall* finish my business, but in good time. All in good time, Mr Tyack." He sidled over to the wall map of the area, eyes probing, darting here and there over its surface. In a more casual tone he resumed, "How is your wife, Mr Tyack?"

The other man's hand went up to his mouth in an absent-minded, childish gesture of pathetic doubt. "My wife? She's fine … fine. Why? Why do you ask?"

Peregrinus ignored the question. "She seems very engaged, very engaged with our project. And that's good. She is a strong woman, am I right? Her character, I mean."

David Tyack went to sit back at his desk, running his hands through his hair, struggling to focus his mind. When had he last slept properly? He couldn't even remember. "Joanne?" He gave a quick, mirthless laugh. "You could say that, yes. Strong, in a sense."

"An unusual woman, wouldn't you say?" pursued Peregrinus, looking at him carefully now.

"Well, yes. Yes, you could say that."

There was a long pause before the next question. When it came it was laced with a new tone, a novel inflection of curiosity and – what? Diffidence? A sudden sense of the vulnerable, for sure. "She's different, an interesting woman. Where did you meet?"

David was scarcely in the frame of mind for small talk. "Oh, at college. Years ago. Why do you ask?"

"Tell me, are you close, you and *Joanne*?" He said the name slowly, with real care, a reverential manner.

David inhaled his coffee, spluttered and choked in part indignation. "Look, I hardly see what this has to do with anything. Can we just concentrate on the business in hand? God knows we've got enough to think about."

Their eyes met again, and it was Peregrinus who looked away first, evasive. With an indifferent shrug he said, "As you wish. As you wish." He looked over at the clock. "Well, I think we both need a trip out to the site."

"What! Now? We were only there this morning! Surely it can wait until tomorrow?"

"Tut, tut, Mr Tyack." The voice had taken on a patronizing, jeering note now. "You know we're approaching the climax of all this. Nothing should be left to chance. Get your car keys. We'll go now."

And despite himself, the other man reached tamely in his pocket, checked the keys were there and, before he quite knew what he was doing, led the way to the door, down the stairs and out to the blackness of the car park on yet another trip to that place of ill omen.

CHAPTER 46

Clearing the Air

Charlie lounged on a bean bag in the living room of her house, her feet up on the sofa. Around her scattered on the floor were magazine clippings of all shapes and sizes; a scrapbook containing further such clippings, neatly glued in, lay open at her side. In one hand she toyed with a pair of scissors. These were mornings as she liked them, a slow start relaxing after a night out with her friends, browsing through the fashion literature for the one part of her studies she really enjoyed. She stretched luxuriously and reached for her tea. She'd have a lazy day now, for the most part, before going round to Tanya's for a bit, then work in the evening.

In the background the doorbell rang. She ignored it and put in her earphones. Charlie lived with her mother in a small semi-detached house in the newer conurbations that had grown up on one side of Winslow, giving the town a distinctly lopsided layout. She had a nice life, mother and daughter being two of a kind and on the whole getting on together well. For a teenage girl, Winslow might have been a bit on the quiet side but that didn't bother Charlie much. She had her friends, and her hobbies, and was quite happy as she was.

Again the doorbell rang, inaudible now to Charlie. Her mother, who was in her bedroom doing her hair and at this moment had it all up in a towel, eventually made it to the door. When she opened it there on the step was that rather nice young man from Amersham, her daughter's friend and some-time companion (though she hadn't seen him for a while). What was his name, John, or Jim? Jack, that was it! "Jack! It is Jack, isn't it? Hello, come in, come in! Wait, let me get you a cup of tea, I only just made one. Come through–" She led him into the cramped kitchen and thrust a mug in his hand, making him at home. But the young man seemed ill at ease, restless. He was gaunt-looking too. He obviously had something on his mind and Charlie's mother thought she could guess what at least a part of it might be. "Go through into the lounge," she said, "Charlie's in there." And she tactfully withdrew upstairs.

Immersed in carefully cutting out a photo, Charlie became aware of a figure on the periphery of her vision. She pulled out her earphones and looked up. Her stomach twisted when she saw who it was. "Oh," she said in a frosty tone. An awkward silence ensued. Charlie had seen nothing of Jack since the party, and her apparent rejection at that event still smouldered painfully. So painfully, in fact, that whenever possible she stuffed any thought of it to the back of her mind and preferred not to think of Jack at all. The whole Tyack family had become tainted in her eyes, so this visitation was not an easy one. Raw anger swept through her again as she saw him; again she felt the hurt and humiliation surge up.

Jack hovered at a distance, as if covering his escape route. Charlie battled with her feelings. "Well come in," she eventually said. "What do you want?" He continued to stand there like a shadow, one hand in his pocket, the other clutching the cup of tea that he obviously didn't want. He seemed unable to speak at all. Eventually she relented a bit, and said, though still coldly, "You look tired. What's up?"

He gave her a quick look and blurted out defensively, "I've not seen you for ages."

Charlie was an open sort of person who didn't like misunderstandings or anything that smacked of game-playing. She gave a little snort. "That's a bit rich isn't it, coming from you? It's not for want of trying. I made a special trip out to your place for that party. You might have at least been there, after as good as inviting me. Or just told me you wouldn't be in after all, if you didn't want to see me. One way or the other, you know?"

Now he was frowning. What was up with him? She looked down at her scrapbook as she waited for him to respond, pretending to be distracted. He took a step closer and, putting down his tea, perched on the edge of the sofa awkwardly. "Hold on. I *was* at the party. I was waiting for you." A long pause. "What made you think I wasn't?"

Charlie pouted. "Your mum told me you weren't there. At the door – she didn't even invite me in. I suppose you know that, anyway. That's pretty low, getting her to do your dirty work for you. Don't try to pretend you really were there."

"I was! I'm telling you. Look, I swear I was there, I was waiting for you!" He looked genuinely very upset.

"If you were there, then why did your mum say you weren't?" And why indeed would she? A genuine mix-up? But her heart told her not. The humiliating memory of her servitude to an oblivious Mrs Tyack in Guido's café came back to her. This was a woman who knew what she was doing.

Becoming more animated, Jack put down his unwanted tea and spread his hands helplessly. "Look Charlie, I don't know exactly what Mum said but I *was* at the party and believe it or not I *was* waiting for you. I'd hoped you'd show up. So when you didn't I just sort of … switched off, you know? I thought I'd come over today because I got that job at Guido's and I know you're there too so I wanted to, to clear the air first. You see?"

"You're saying you really were there?"

"Yes! I've told you. I stayed the whole time, helped with the drinks." He looked very serious. "Look Charlie, I'm sorry about this, I'm really sorry Mum sent you away but that had nothing to do with me. She's – she's not been acting *normal* recently but it isn't personal, honestly it's not."

Charlie looked doubtful. "Let's get this straight, your mum pretended you weren't in and sent me all the way back here with a" – tears of bitterness pricked her eyes at the memory – "a useless bottle of wine because she's not 'acting normally'?"

"Yes. That's right."

She didn't know what to think. But if it was true it changed everything. She switched tack. "Where've you been anyway? No-one's seen you for ages."

"I've just been away."

"Away where? You make it sound like a secret."

"In Cornwall."

She wrinkled her nose. "Why did you go down there?"

He looked desperate, and shook his head wearily. "I just don't know. Honestly, I don't." The look on his face froze the next question on her lips. He seemed almost disorientated. "That place. It's just … I've–" He struggled with the words. Finally he said, head in hands, "Christ, Charlie, I don't know what I've got into. It's all more than I can take."

She could almost feel the emotion – was it anger? Despair? – radiating from him. She felt herself softening. "Are you alright Jack? Look, is it something to do with that church?"

A long silence followed, while he seemed to be locked in some kind of internal struggle. Eventually he said, in a choked voice, "Yes. It is something to do with that. It's Mum and Dad."

"And the church?" Charlie felt totally confused.

"Yeah. The church. It's not what you think. They've got involved with something really nasty there. It's vile."

He was so obviously upset that Charlie forgot her anger. "Well can't you tell me? Are you in some sort of trouble? Can I – help?"

He looked at her through red-rimmed eyes. "Thanks. But I've got to handle this myself. It's something only I can do." He glanced at his watch. "Look, I've got to go now. There's something I need to do. I just wanted to see you that's all." Suddenly he was all impatience, hurrying to be off.

"Wait. What do you mean? You can't go already!"

He made for the door, then stopped. "Look, I'm sorry about all that stuff. You do see it was just a mix up? I'll see you at the café, okay? But I've really got to go." A mirthless smile spread over his face. "I've got to practise for a break-in. Don't worry, I'll let myself out." He turned on his heel and before she could even get up she heard the front door slam.

Charlie sank back in the bean bag and stared in confusion at her clippings, sprinkled randomly on the floor like the strange jumble that was Jack's character. It really did look like he hadn't stood her up after all, and that his mother really was a – *bitch,* to be frank. All of which was a big relief, yes. But what was the bigger thing behind this? Sighing, she spun the scissors round and round her thumb absently. What had got into Jack? And where was he off to now?

CHAPTER 47

A Study in Solipsism

The house was empty when Jack let himself back in. This was no surprise. In truth, he'd barely seen his parents since he got home; just that one morning at breakfast. They seemed to have more or less moved out, their lives swallowed up entirely by their work. It was perfectly possible, Jack reflected, they were now literally living at the office. Or maybe not the office, maybe at some other location. Maybe out in the "Buckinghamshire wilds", as Attlee put it. At any rate, their involvement with the horrible apparatus in the church crypt was now a certainty. Again he reflected that the strange, archaic device in its primitive cellar could not be the end point of all their work. There was something bigger behind it all, and the thing in the crypt was a stepping stone only. Had Richard Attlee given him the clue he needed?

After checking various rooms, just to be sure, he wandered into the kitchen, opened the drawer where various household tools were kept and began rifling through it, his mind still busy with all the possibilities of his predicament. No, his mother would think big, go for the bull's-eye. At the thought anger welled up in him, a loathing that took him by surprise in its intensity. All the years he'd spent, trying to please her, scraping and apologizing, forcing himself through miserably inappropriate hurdles just to get her approval. Somehow, her betrayal in trying to sabotage his relationship with Charlie hurt the most, but it was anger rather than anything else that he felt. He'd finished with her now; now he could see what sort of a person she was, parent or not. Already he felt a weight lifted, the sensation of being cleansed and liberated by his bitterness. "What's wrong with your mum?" Charlie's look had clearly said, though she'd been too polite to say it. That summed it up. What *was* wrong with her?

In an impatient spasm Jack wrenched the drawer off its rails. It crashed to the floor, spilling its contents. He picked out the hammer and chisel he'd been searching for and made his way back up the stairs, stopping on the intermediate landing outside his father's study. Floor one-and-a-half. For a few moments he stood and regarded the locked door balefully. Was it his imagination or could he hear a quiet, dry rustling sound coming from inside? He blinked hard, pushing back the voice of doubt that was struggling to assert itself. Then he set about the lock with the tools, belting the chisel as hard as he could, watching with satisfaction as the splinters flew in all directions, the shattered inhibitions of his old life.

Eventually the lock gave and the door swung slowly open. The study looked onto the garden and light was flooding in via the lattice window, light that amply illuminated what was inside. He was instantly brought up short by what he saw. Jack had been quite familiar with the study until about a year ago, when his father had started locking it. It had been a very conventional room, traditional really, with a tasteful, neo-Victorian style and plenty of books lining the shelves on geology, mining, surveying and the like. Through the open door he saw that this had all gone now, replaced with functional objects such as filing cabinets, scanners, printers of varying sorts and several monitors. The occasional historical etchings of bridges and other civil engineering projects had also gone. In their place, grotesquely, the walls were crammed with a vast array of line drawings of buildings and landscapes, some framed and others simply pinned, taped or glued directly onto the plaster. There was hardly any actual wall surface remaining to be seen. Jack took a step inside. He looked up and saw the ceiling had been treated similarly, covered with a patchwork of the same neurotic sketches. He stood, bewildered, for some moments. Then he slowly moved further into the room to inspect them more closely.

All the drawings looked to be originals, in pen and ink, and they were all done in the same sort of style. Each was very detailed, yet hurried looking, as if produced rapidly in a feverish state of inspiration. All of them depicted what appeared to be a quasi-fantasy world of towering structures, fantastic abysses into which machinery of no conventional design plunged, bizarre landscapes that were seemingly underground, and vast caverns populated with minute figures. Some of the sketches bore tiny writing and formulae here and there, giving a certain, vague scientific feel to them. Together, the pictures projected with an obsessive intensity a surreal world from the depths of madness. And yet there *was* a parallel, for these drawings spoke a language that Jack had seen before. He put down the hammer and chisel on the desk and stared in disbelief. On these walls was nothing less than a projection writ large of the plutonian pages of Owen Tyack's diary. The style, the subjects, even the writing itself were all in keeping.

Here, then, in David Tyack's most special and personal place was a terrifying window onto a mind closed in on itself, a mind at the brink of insanity. Cautiously Jack looked back through the doorway. The silence was too oppressive. Might his father appear at any moment, walk in cheerfully, greet Jack as he used to, settle in his chair and carry on as if nothing was any different? He saw his old life spiral away from him, caught in this vortex of present madness. He collected himself. He still had to find out something concrete, some information about … what? *Schedules* were what Professor Silverman had wanted. He scanned the desk. There was nothing printed, only the same demented jottings. He picked up the top sheet. On it was a strange design, a circle with runic symbols around the periphery and in its centre a star sign, the witch's pentagram of two superimposed triangles. The drawing itself was in brown ink, done with a tenuous, manic line, while speckled across it were small spots and splashes of crimson red. With a shudder he put it to one side and picked up the sheet below. Filling this page was a sketch of a domed building, reminiscent of an Italian church, circular in plan and with its walls full of niches and decorative touches. Attached to this building was a classically styled portico with pillars. The enormous size of the structure was indicated by miniature figures dotted around the entrance. In the background, tiny trees, rivers and ravines completed the landscape, while mathematical equations marched across the top and down the sides of the sheet. Across the bottom was written in capitals, *15 November Inflammo VJ.*

Jack sucked in his cheeks and frowned. VJ. He cast his mind back to his conversation with Attlee the previous day. Verney Junction, the place in the Aylesbury Vale that Attlee had followed his father to, the place "really out in the wilds". The same? Surely, it had to be the location he'd been looking for. Again he scanned the extraordinary drawing; could it really be such a thing, and on such a scale? Horror vied in his mind with simple awe at the sheer ambition of the project. And there was even a date, only two days away. His mind unwillingly confronted the next step in his plan: another journey out, out into the bleak and deceiving countryside that had already yielded such appalling secrets. But there appeared to be no other way. And what would he find when he got there? What was the vast release of energy that Richard Attlee spoke about really capable of doing? Bridging the centuries, if his theory was correct – and what else? A small apparatus, a mere prototype, in a church crypt had conjured an apparition from an earlier era. Jack's mind rebelled from considering the implications of the full-sized version. Again Professor Silverman seemed to be right in his predictions. After a moment's hesitation he folded the sheet and put it in his pocket. The Professor had said the key to stopping the device lay in stopping the Helper. He thought he now knew something about that, too. But how to contact the Cornish magus? He scowled to himself in frustration.

Jack turned to leave that mad room. By the door, where sketches clustered thickly on the walls, he noticed a largely blank space. He stopped and looked closer. A piece of A4 paper had been left empty save for a single, small drawing in its centre. Was it some kind of symbol, oddly elongated? It took Jack a few minutes to make sense of it, then suddenly the parts resolved themselves: three dark holes, pulled tight and distorted, framed by a gaunt oval, and in the centre two tiny slits. What Jack saw was undoubtedly the representation of a face, a face flayed from the skull beneath and then stretched, floating in its own agonized penumbra of pain. Swallowing hard, he turned away from the vile thing and left, shutting the door with its shattered lock behind him.

CHAPTER 48

ALL IN THE MIND

The sky was a dull, metallic orange, the sullen glow of red-hot bronze, not like any other sky. Nor was it suggestive of infinity but of a colossal, closed interior space. Heat pulsed everywhere, off rocks, the dry beds of streams, the very grains of dust and sand that had been blown in heaps by the agency of hot winds. The valley dropped away from dizzying heights to unfathomable depths. Years ago, someone had stood at the head of this valley and looked down on it all in silent amazement: the soaring stone viaducts, the plunging ravines, strange colonnaded structures growing directly out of rocky faces and the dehydrated river beds coiling far below, all of it framed against the glow of that hard sky. And so the landscape continued for miles, with its grottos, temples and slender bridges apparently hovering in mid-air.

At the centre of everything was the Stone Forest. There, the columns clustered thickly in the terrible heat. There the shadows played and flickered, perspectives opened up for miles, only to shift and close, constantly changing, all in motion. Sometimes there would be a clearing where twisted gargoyles perched on pillars, flanking stained slabs on which fearful things were done. At the centre of the forest was a larger space, like an amphitheatre. There hung something suspended, floating in the heat, though it could move here and there if it wished: waiting at the heart of its realm, seeing all, knowing all.

In the hottest, driest depths of the valley was a sluggish stream of blood, a stream that bubbled and popped like boiling porridge. In one of its bends, on a bank, a soul was still stretched on its rack, boiling on its coals, screaming in eternal pain. With the remains of its consciousness it surveyed the body anatomized before it, the bowels sizzling in braziers, organs clawed by unseen hooks, tender places probed with sharp steel. It looked at itself, and it screamed. Yet all was not lost. For, incredibly, this soul had travelled from its confinement, and the agony of its return was tempered by one thing: now, there was hope – just a sliver of it, the barest chance, but hope nonetheless. Now maybe, just maybe, someone was fighting its corner. It had an ally. As the millionth shriek escaped it, it clung to that thought. A plan formed in the sane remnant of its mind.

CHAPTER 49

A PLACE IN THE MIRROR

In the bathroom Jack stared at himself in the mirror, fighting the feelings of betrayal and frustration that jostled inside him. He wanted to bathe clean, wash it all away, strike out afresh. He reached for a towel, turned on the shower and let the water heat up. As the steam began to billow around him he stripped and glared again into the mirror. With a final surge of emotion he slammed his fist into it. The cabinet rattled on its mountings; a broad crack appeared at the edge of the glass and spread inwards. After the revelations of the study, where was he to turn now? It all seemed down to him, either alone or with the (possibly unreliable) allies he had acquired in Cornwall. He slumped over the sink and ran the tap, splashing his face, letting the water run through his hands and down the plughole. As he did so, he felt his temper subsiding. Slowly he raised his head and paused. A new sensation came over him; as the steam gathered around he felt that something else was gathering too, some *presence*, trying to force its way into the room. He refocused on the solidity of the bathroom fittings around him: the cubicle, the bath, the shelves, the towels. Cautiously he stepped into the shower, unsure of himself.

For the next ten minutes, the miracle of bathing worked its magic and when he stepped out again he did indeed feel cleansed, reborn almost. But still something was not quite right. That same feeling. He reached for a towel and wrapped it around his waist. Were those voices he could hear – a single voice? In his head or in the bathroom itself? Surely, in the room? Blinking the steam away he approached the mirror again, curious. The surface had steamed up; with his hand he wiped it clear. The reflection of his face emerged, the dark, ringed eyes and black hair falling in damp locks over his forehead, cheeks thinner than ever. Yet it didn't look quite like him. He looked harder. What was happening?

To the whisper of muted voices the reflection slowly blurred, shimmered and reconfigured itself. Staring back at him through the steam and condensation was the very image of Professor Silverman, filling the space where Jack's reflection had been seconds before. The bearded features looked quizzically out, as real as life. In the background was that well-remembered lounge, the fire crackling in the grate, what looked like the diary lying on a wine table next to a decanter of sherry, the grandfather clock in the background; but all revealed in a sort of oval halo that faded out to mist at the edges. The Professor seemed about to speak, but the image wavered and partially reverted back to Jack's own features before settling once more. Again he tried, and this time his words were clear, though whether they came from the mirror itself or directly into Jack's head was a mystery. Silverman began in the most matter-of-fact way, as if such communications were entirely normal and so preliminaries might be dispensed with: "Jack, I'm pleased to find you in one piece. The stones have brought me news of your endeavours and I have to say there is more danger than I could have possibly imagined. But more of that later. For now, I need details!" His face came close, filling the oval portal of the mirror. "Tell me what you have discovered. Quickly now!"

Jack, still nonplussed at the sudden appearance of this phantom, was unable to marshal his thoughts. "Hang on, how have you found me? I wanted to contact you but .... Is it the stones? How?"

"Yes Jack, the stones, what else? Surely you understand by now? My master amethyst has brought me news of your doings these past days. I have seen how you have pressed forward to find the truth. You have done well but the stones cannot give me details. Yet the details are the key to this riddle. Now tell me what you know."

Setting aside his remaining feelings of surprise, Jack unburdened himself to the mirror of the main facts that had emerged from his investigation. He told the Professor of his visit to the church and his discovery of what could only have been the prototype machine that confirmed their speculations in Cornwall. Then he moved on to what he had found in the study, and the almost certain clear evidence of a larger project. All the time he was speaking Silverman remained absolutely still, drinking in these facts with, so far as could be discerned via the imperfectly clear medium of the mirror, the most intense expression. Jack saved his bombshell for the end. "I was about to leave when I found something on the desk. A particular piece of paper."

"Yes? Well? What was it?" It was as if the Professor had been waiting for something of the kind, and had been fighting disappointment at its not coming to light earlier.

"Wait a moment." Jack went over to where his clothes lay in a heap on the floor, extracted the paper from his jeans pocket and wafted it in front of the mirror. "Just this," and he read the statement across the bottom: "*15 November Inflammo VJ*. This must be the date we need, when they start this thing up."

Silverman became animated. "This is what we want. Well done, Jack! Hmm. *Inflammo*," he repeated to himself in an undertone, before addressing Jack again. "Many of the pronouncements in the diary resort to Latin. That language, along with certain visual features you will have noticed, are affiliated in some fundamental way with the realm of the Shadow. It *must* be a reference to the ignition process of the larger machine, just as you say. But two days! We have less time than I thought. Tell me, Jack, are you any closer to knowing where this final machine is located? What is this 'VJ'? Is that a clue?"

"Yeah, it is. I think I may know. I'm pretty sure it refers to a place near the church, Verney Junction. But further out, right in the country."

The Professor considered. "That would make sense. They'd want it close to the prototype, for convenience, but they'd also need to keep it secret." His voice faded and his face receded in the mirror. Jack could hear him musing quietly to himself, "But how to stop it, where to go now. Where now?" Then with renewed clarity, his voice resolute, he asked, "Tell me Jack, what about the Helper? Have you found him? He's the key here."

"I'm not sure. There *was* someone. That day I went back to the church. I saw the vicar there, like I said, and the man from the party. That man made me think there had to be a connection with Mum and Dad. But there was someone else."

The Professor leaned in close again. "Yes? Who was that?"

Jack thought back. "It was an ordinary looking sort of guy, no-one special. Just a man, a small man. He wasn't wearing anything strange. But there was something about him, something *different.* I can't describe it. I was hiding, I was totally quiet, but it's like he could *sense* me there. It was weird. He was kind of sniffing. He started to come over but he got distracted. I can't describe it but I sort of felt then that this was him, the Helper."

"What else? Did he speak? What did he say?"

"Well it was nothing much, just fragments. I couldn't hear properly. It wasn't so much what he said, it was how he seemed. In control, he was definitely in control. There was just something *odd* about him."

Silverman sat back and took a long, thoughtful sip of something from a stemmed glass. Then he said, "Jack, this is him, I am certain of it." He sat in silence for a while, musing. Presently he resumed, "As we said before, stopping the Helper is the key to stopping the machine itself. This has to be our strategy. That machine you found in the church, they used it to run experiments, to get data. That would have been bad enough: people murdered, and who knows what associated effects. But as we suspected, that's not the end of the story." There was another long pause before he continued. "Jack, I am as certain as I have ever been that stopping the helping creature is the way to stopping this whole evil enterprise. When you described him I think I can be sure that we have identified the same being who helped Owen, who has persisted through a hundred years, biding his time, waiting for his master's next chance to make a bid for freedom. Everything you noticed – the sense of difference, the quiet control, the sense of the animal – points to it. This being, outwardly so normal, is directing events now."

Jack experienced a sinking feeling. He knew what was coming. "And I have to stop him, right?"

"Yes. That is our best chance of stopping the project. You have to get close to this thing, this demon. For that is what it is, underneath. Believe me, I would not ask you if it were not essential. I have not been idle while you yourself have been making progress. The diary has yielded more of its secrets to me, and more about this strange helper in particular. Listen.

It operates by a portal, a link to its master. It opened that portal over a hundred years ago when it began its work with Owen. That was the source of its power. When the first prototype failed, the Shadow claimed Owen's soul and the portal closed. Heaven knows what happened to the creature then. Probably it became a rudderless wanderer for a time, cast aside by the Shadow in its wrath at the failure. But now, the second time around, it will have opened the portal again and its power waxes with its new purpose."

"If this portal is where its power comes from, then all we have to do is somehow break that, yes?"

"Exactly. Now, the Helper will have established itself somewhere, somewhere close to the site of the church. It will be drawn back, you see, to the original location. You need to find its base first. *Do you have any idea where that might be?* Think, Jack. Somewhere near Little Horwood. Do you have any clue at all?"

Jack thought for a few moments while the Professor regarded him keenly. The creature could live anywhere. He shook his head. "I wouldn't know where to start. I just don't know." Silverman's face was in the process of registering intense disappointment when a thought suddenly crossed Jack's mind. There might just be a clue after all. "Hang on. Yes, I might have an idea. Something I saw back in the summer. It was in an old junk shop in Winslow."

"Yes? What did you see?"

"It was a kind of vision. Almost like a hallucination." He thought back to that day with Charlie. There was something very weird about that shop, for sure.

The Professor was nodding rapidly. "Winslow is close to the church, isn't it? Can you go there, make inquiries?"

"Yeah, I could go back. But supposing I do find where this thing lives. What then?"

"You have to break the portal, as you said. I can't help you much more I'm afraid. You'll know when you've found the place, and something tells me that if you do find it, the location of the portal will become clear. As to blocking it, listen carefully. You must take the stones with you, the stones Amber left with you. Make sure you have them with you, yes? We'll just have to trust that all these 'ifs' add up to something and you manage to trigger the link. When it becomes active there will be a field that arises, a type of energy field. *You must place the stones in that field.* Do you understand? I will do the rest; the portal should then close and the field collapse."

"And that will be the end of the Helper?" Jack couldn't believe it was so simple.

"Well," said the Professor, looking slightly chastened, "that is the theory. If not the end then we can perhaps damage its control over the others."

Jack was sceptical. "But there must be a whole team of people working out there."

"You must remember that the Helper is the pivot here. He in turn influences those he chooses. That is why stopping him is so important. All those involved in this hideous enterprise, your parents first and foremost, will be freed from his dominion. Their obsession will weaken."

Jack was about to inquire further when the image in the mirror wavered and shimmered. When Silverman re-emerged he was saying, "It will be dangerous Jack. Remember to keep the stones on you at all times. Are you ready for this?"

"I'll have to be. How dangerous is the Helper though? Is there anything else I should take with me?" The Professor seemed to be saying something important, leaning forward to accentuate his point, but once more the image trembled and his voice faded. "Wait!" said Jack, "What do I do if …?"

"Good luck!" The words floated tenuously from the mirror before the Professor's features vanished and Jack was once more staring at his own reflection. As he looked, the crack in the glass suddenly raced across its entire width and, with a sharp splitting sound, it fell to the floor and shattered into a thousand tiny fragments.

CHAPTER 50

Of Loss and Longing

The smell of incense permeated the air, sweet and aromatic. In the centre of the small, oblong stone chamber knelt a man, head bowed, hands clasped before him rather in a gesture of despair than of devotion. Before the man was a life-sized sarcophagus, made of polished, dark stone. Sculpted with great realism and reposing on its top, in the same stone, was an effigy, the effigy of a woman, hands folded on her chest in the final rest of the dead. On either side stood two tables, draped in black cloths, each bearing lit candelabra and smoking censers from which pungent fragrance rose up and filled the room. The only light was from the flickering candles.

For many minutes there was complete silence. Then it was broken by the sound of sobbing from the man, whose shoulders shook with emotion until it seemed he might collapse on the floor. Again and again he muttered a name, each time with rising intensity, his voice cracking as he did so. Eventually he fell silent again, before lurching forward, head buried in hands, body heaving with a heavy weight of sorrow. The candles continued to burn, the incense spiralled upwards unperturbed. After remaining prostrate for several minutes more, the man rose to his feet, his fingers smoothing his face and beard as if to thereby restore his inner composure. Then Professor Silverman slowly approached the sarcophagus and reverently placed his hands on the effigy, looking down at it intently. And back at him, through lifeless malachite eyes, every feature rendered to poised perfection, stared from the tomb the beautiful face of Joanne Tyack.

CHAPTER 51

The Question of Identity

The room was small, a perfect circle with a domed ceiling. The whole interior was freshly whitewashed and the clean tang of new paint permeated the air. Set into the walls were blind arches, closely spaced in relentless symmetry. There were no windows and from the apex of the dome hung a single light bulb on a long flex, throwing a dazzling white light throughout, the light of the scientist's laboratory or the operating theatre. Strewn across the meshwork of diamond floor tiles were several boxes, some half opened to reveal within piles of blueprints, notes, computer output and minor items of hardware. In the recess formed by one of the arches was a desk, bearing a monitor and more piles of papers.

At this desk, perched on a swivel chair, sat Peregrinus, unfamiliar in a lab coat that he wore incongruously over his usual attire of jeans and t-shirt. He was leaning back, hands behind his head, casting his eyes around this, his new office. He gazed approvingly at the symmetry of the place, his eye pleased by the rhythm of the arches, the balance of the dome above. For Peregrinus, this single room symbolized the closure of a long, restless chapter in his life. Not so much a chapter, in fact, but a fretful chronicle that had itself been his entire life. Here, he had finally arrived; here, he approached his fulfilment. He felt power, life-force flowing through him, the palpable sense of mission achieved. Or very nearly achieved, for he was not quite there yet. He returned to his work, staring at the monitor intently.

Opposite the desk was a door, half open. Outside, the arc of a corridor curved away in both directions, the gentleness of its sweep indicative of a very large building indeed. As Peregrinus continued with his pleasurable reflections he became aware of somebody approaching along this corridor, approaching with a certain tread, purposeful yet quiet, delicate. The somebody stopped, and stood at the doorway. He frowned; the current of moods he might normally sense in others was veiled, hidden from him. That could only mean one thing.

Now his visitor had entered and was standing behind him, watching him as he worked. He waited, then began to turn, discomfited. At the same time a woman's voice said indifferently, "The door was open, I hope you don't mind?" Standing there was Joanne Tyack, as he'd known it had to be. She was wearing her knee-length black skirt and a powder-blue blouse. She stared at him with a mild inquisitiveness that would have seemed rude to anyone else.

"Not at all," he returned, guardedly, gesturing to a spare chair on the other side of the room. "Have a seat." She perched herself on it, so neat, so self-contained. They continued to regard each other from a distance. Peregrinus now became aware of a sensation he'd come across before in the presence of this woman: he felt unaccountably disconcerted, knocked off balance. It was a new feeling, one he did not relish. Yet its very novelty was compelling. How did you deal with such a person? Cautiously he asked, "So, are you happy that everything is in place?" then immediately cursed himself for not waiting for her to speak first.

Mrs Tyack looked down and smoothed her skirt carelessly. "Yes," she said, with an air of not in fact being particularly happy. "Yes, everything has gone well. Or seems to have gone well," she corrected herself, for there were no plaudits to be given just yet. "Yes, you've done a good job, a very good job here. I would hardly have imagined we could make such progress. And of course, the important thing is, we're on schedule." She was tight-lipped, despite her positive words. Nothing about this woman was open, giving. She was a closed book to Peregrinus. What was it about her–? She broke in on his thoughts, surprising him with her next question. "David, my husband. Is it going well for him? Do you think?"

Peregrinus pursed his lips and considered. From the corridor the noise of voices approached, and receded. He didn't want this conversation, he decided; he was on the back foot already. Eventually he said, "I think Mr Tyack is pleased with where we stand, too." He swept his gaze around the room, gesturing with his hand to larger structures beyond.

She smiled slightly and looked down. "'Mr Tyack'," she echoed, acerbically. She glanced sharply at him. "David is very tired, you know."

"Yes. Yes, I had noticed that. But we're so nearly there."

She was nodding dismissively before he'd even finished the statement. She pulled delicately at an eyelash, barely engaging with him. What was the woman thinking? She continued, as if to herself, "He tells me you've been asking about me. Personal questions." Suddenly she was staring at him directly. "Why would that be?"

Peregrinus felt an unaccustomed urge to flee. He narrowed his eyes and met her gaze, trying to penetrate the icy shroud. "No particular reason," he replied. "I was just concerned about you, that's all. With the stress."

Mrs Tyack continued to stare. Presently she said, "There's no need to be concerning yourself about me. All I'm interested in is getting the project completed." It was as if she were reading from a script. "That's all that matters now. I think we agree on that? I appreciate all you've done to make this happen, but we'll leave it at business shall we?"

He felt a confusing mix of resentment and uncertainty rising in him. With matching coolness he said, "It's always business with me, Mrs Tyack. I hope you know that?"

She considered him a little longer, then gave a quick nod, made as if to leave but remained seated. Then it struck him: she, too, was confused, undecided. That manner of hers was concealing something more, much more. There was a whole story there, underneath, trying to come out. Would it? He sat and waited; their eyes held each other's. She seemed wanting to speak, but unable. The tension built, traceable in the tiniest flicker of an eyelid, the quiver of a lip. Then she had gone, leaving behind only the hint of fragrance and a wad of unanswered questions.

Peregrinus stroked his chin thoughtfully, intrigued. Why had she come, really? His thoughts branched down a dozen speculative pathways, each fascinating in itself, just like their object. Then he gave a little shake of his head. He must clear his mind; there was work to be done, final preparations to be made. Every minute counted now. This was no time for distractions, nor could he afford to slacken his mental effort, the effort that kept the whole gigantic project on track. Mrs Tyack would have to wait for just a little longer. How would she feel, he wondered, if she knew about the next visitor he was expecting?

CHAPTER 52

SMOKE AND INFORMATION

Professor Silverman turned up his collar and forged through the fine drizzle to the weather station at the bottom of his garden. Visibility was not good today; the sea blended in seamless union with the sky before his eye had any chance of reaching the horizon. Further along the coast he could just discern the warning beacon of Trebarwith Strand, blinking feebly in the murk. How many vessels, he wondered not for the first time, had it saved from shipwreck over the years? Today, at least, the seas were calm but the thought of being grounded in a storm, then broken to matchwood on the rocks, was a horrifying one. By the white, shuttered wooden box that held his weather instruments the Professor stopped, crouched down and reached inside his coat for the pad and pen with which he recorded the statistics that formed such an important part of his daily routine. As he made his notes, a creaking sound came to his ears on the breeze. He looked up to see Amber coming through the gate, having just climbed the steep steps from the beach below. She was in her shorts and flip flops, while her upper half was swaddled completely in a waterproof, so he could not see her face. He called to her. "Amber! What's this? Walking in this weather?" But she ignored him as completely as if he was not there and continued on across the lawn and into the house.

Half an hour later, the Professor was sitting at the octagon desk in his study, carefully transcribing the meteorological data from his notebook into a large leather-bound journal that he kept for the purpose. Increasingly, of late, he felt most comfortable in this room, hemmed close on all sides by his books. He completed the transcription, closed the journal and transferred himself to a leather armchair. Once seated he reached for a walnut box from a shelf, took out a cigar, clipped the end and proceeded to light it. The plumes of blue smoke curled therapeutically around him while he stared through the skylight at the rain streaming across the glass. Hardly had he begun his speculations, however, when his thoughts were broken by a noise from the passageway outside. Amber appeared again. She was still in her shorts, her t-shirt streaked with wet patches. Damp strands of hair clung to her face. The Professor cast her a quick glance and said, "Did you enjoy your walk?" But she only stared at him. He could tell, then, that she was building up to something. Sure enough, the words eventually came, in a voice tight with suppressed emotion.

"I want you to tell me about Mum." Nothing in her father's face betrayed a reaction to this; he merely continued to puff stoically on his cigar. She continued, a vassal entreating the sceptred king on his throne, "You've never told me the truth about her. I deserve to know. Tell me about her. Please."

Without taking his eyes from the skylight the Professor said, "Don't exaggerate, Amber. It isn't the case that I've 'never told you the truth'. You should know that. It's true that there are certain details, but" – he looked directly at her – "it's all over now, years ago. It would do no good, to you or to me. Why rake over the dead past? You have your future before you."

"What future? What future have I got here, now?" She was crying, from anger. "It's alright for you, you've got your life here. But it's all about you. What about *me*? What am *I* supposed to do?"

Her father made an effort not to get drawn into this emotional storm. Quietly he replied, "Do I restrict you? Do I stop you? You have your own house. You have money if you need it. You have freedom." He spread his hands. "You have a nice life, a good life, Amber. What more do you want?" But she just stared at him, inwardly choked. He continued, "I wonder if I did the right thing in bringing Jack here. I think he has unsettled you. Perhaps I should have–"

"It's nothing to do with Jack!" she broke in furiously. "You *always* evade the question! Tell me about my mother." Her voice rose to a pitch.

The Professor winced and carefully placed his cigar in the ashtray beside him. Amber had been so much more difficult since Jacob had died, that much was certain. "Your mother," he began, "died many years ago, when you were a baby. Of an illness. That is really all there is to tell."

"Her name? Photographs? Letters? There's nothing. It's like she never existed. Why won't you tell me?" She had stopped crying and was suddenly calm, focussed, more determined than ever. But her father just stared defiantly at the floor and said nothing. She tried again. "You met her at university, didn't you? You told me that, years ago." He shrugged in grudging assent. Amber took a step closer to him. "Where was that? Where were you teaching? You could at least tell me that. Or is your whole life just one big secret?"

Sullenly he replied, "You know I taught business studies. I was a lecturer. Let's leave it at that, shall we?"

But Amber wasn't to be deflected. "Dad, I don't even know *where*. It's like your whole past life has just been … erased." She scanned the study walls. "No certificates, even."

Again he shrugged, then said, "Didn't I tell you? I was sure you knew. At any rate it is of no consequence." He rose to his feet, brushed ash off his jacket and gave her a chilly smile. "I was at Southampton. Now, if you'll excuse me, Amber, I have work to do." He swept past her and vanished down the corridor.

Amber waited until he'd gone, then relaxed her tense limbs. She had dreaded this confrontation but something deep inside her wouldn't be denied anymore. As usual, her father had left in his wake stress, frustration and acrid smoke. But this time there was something more, albeit the tiniest thing. Information. She was determined to use it well.

CHAPTER 53

Deus ex Machina

The moon that hung in the darkening void above Winslow's town square was as lustrous and orange as one of Professor Silverman's precious gemstones. It presided over a quiet scene; the late afternoon was turning into early evening and only the odd shopper finishing her business and early drinker making his way to the *George & Dragon* disturbed the peace. Puddles on the pavement from an earlier heavy shower reflected the moonlight. The single streetlamp outside the former residence of Mrs Avril Priestly, deceased, threw a feeble mantle of light across nearby parked cars. A black cat slunk out from a passageway, froze and blinked cautiously, then thought better of it and retreated.

The old junk shop, *Winslow Antiques*, was dark and empty, showing no signs of life across its entire frontage. Jack observed it closely from the opposite side of the square, where he had left his bicycle and was in the process of stowing its lamps in his rucksack. It had been a tedious journey, in the gloom of the late afternoon, but one he knew he'd had to make. But it was bad luck that the shop had closed early. He regarded the bulky shadow forms of old furniture looming in the windows. The place was dead. Well, he was prepared to break in, if he had to. For he felt increasingly certain, following his last conversation with the Professor, that this shop was implicated in the doings of the Helper and his mysterious portal. If he could just get in there, back to the exact spot where his strange vision had occurred the day he visited with Charlie, to where the picture of Owen Tyack at his church had hung and no doubt still did so, he felt sure something would become clear.

Glancing up he saw the sky away to the north, in the direction of the Aylesbury plain, was tinged with a diseased, faintly lurid glow; what the cause was he could not say since only wilds and country lay in that direction. But he had other things to think about now. He slung his bag across his shoulder, set his jaw and, nervously jiggling Amber's gemstones in his pocket, began to walk across the square when a movement opposite stopped him. A hunched, asymmetric-looking figure had detached itself from the shadows at the bottom of the iron fire escape and was now climbing the steps to the flat above the junk shop. Jack watched as it reached the top, where it began a persistent knocking at the door, futile since the windows were as dark and untenanted as the ones of the shop below. Clearly no-one was at home. Intrigued, Jack continued to watch as the figure doggedly maintained its tap-tapping, clearly audible across the stillness of the square. Surely it could see the place was empty? Eventually the knocking stopped. The figure stood there for a few minutes, stymied. Then, judging by its contortions, it appeared to start wrestling with the door, trying to open it. Detecting a familiarity in the whole manner of this individual, Jack made for the shop and quietly climbed the fire escape until he was standing, unnoticed, behind the shadowy form as it continued its exertions. It was swaddled in dark jeans and a black hoodie that was pulled up over its head, but even so there was something unmistakable about it.

"Are you locked out?" he asked eventually, in as conversational a tone as possible.

The figure froze for a full minute, then slowly turned to him, its face still hidden in the recesses of the hood. A voice said from within, "He's not in."

"Who's that, then?"

"'E said to come round, but he's not 'ere."

The voice provided confirmation of Jack's suspicions. "Who are you looking for?" he asked.

"Just 'im. Mr P."

"I know you, don't I? It's … Toby, isn't it? I saw you that day at the church, St Nicholas' Church." Toby said nothing, but pushed his hood back by way of assent. "So what are you doing here, Toby? Who is Mr P?" asked Jack, feeling he might just have had a considerable stroke of luck.

"Oh, he's from the church too," said Toby, brightly enough. "'E's special, we're friends. You his friend too?"

Jack thought rapidly, then cautiously replied, "Yes, I'm a friend of his, too. He lives here, doesn't he?"

"Oh yeah, this is 'is house."

So this was it, the exact place. Its proximity to the junk shop was confirmation. Above the junk shop, where the vision was, and a man from the church …. This 'Mr P' must be the very creature he was after, none other than the Helper. But the flat was empty, the tenants out. What should he do? As he was thinking, Toby had fished something out of his pocket and was holding it up in the gloom. Jack peered at it. "What's that?"

"I got a key," said the youth.

"A key? Well why didn't you use it?"

"Forgot," Toby replied, sulkily.

"He gave you a key? Look Toby, I have to go in there. I've got something very important to leave for Mr P, he's asked me especially for it. It's urgent, you see? But you have to go now. Let me have the key, I'll give it to Mr P and he can let you have it back. Yes?" He hoped he didn't sound too desperate.

Toby's expression was lost in the gloom but his voice exuded suspicion. "You sure, mister?"

"Honestly. Just trust me. Let me have the key and you'll have it back soon. Mr P – well, he'll be really pleased with you." Jack swallowed. He sincerely hoped he wasn't going to get this boy into trouble, but there were bigger things than that to worry about. Stopping the Helper, and thereby the machine itself, took priority over everything else now.

Slowly Toby proffered the key. He watched as Jack took it, then pulled up his hood again and forlornly started to descend the stairway. "'Bye mister, you watch that, yeah?"

"Don't worry," whispered Jack, terrified that they'd already attracted attention. But the square was still quite empty.

As Toby's back receded in the shadows, Jack applied himself to the door. The key fitted easily enough and with a small amount of juggling the door swung open and he stepped inside. The smell of hot dust filled his nostrils in an overpowering musty wave, along with a blast of heat. Fearful of signalling his presence by turning on the lights, he extracted his cycle lamp from the rucksack and panned the beam around the room. Against the opposite wall the source of the heat was apparent: a gas fire glowed, carelessly left on in the absence of the occupant. Above it, his lamp picked out several photographs in frames on the wall. He moved closer to inspect them. They were mainly black-and-white prints. Looking more closely at the largest, central one he froze. This he had seen before: St Nicholas' church, with the three ill-matched men lined up in front of the old yew tree. Now, though, he knew its secrets. In the vicar's gaunt features, haunted eyes and shadowless, bowed body he saw the face and form of his benighted ancestor, Owen Tyack. The aristocrat to his right stared with calm assurance at the camera, a piece of period and social history but no more. But the figure to the left of the vicar, the workman in the cloth cap, diminutive, wiry … Jack peered closer at this man's face with its intense, ageless stare. It was a remarkable face, in a quiet way, radiating force of personality, pure will, a burning fixation. Besides those things, it struck a chord. He saw the inscription once more on the photograph: April 1900. Professor Silverman's words echoed in his mind: "These demons do not have normal life spans. A century would be nothing."

He drew back and pondered. Slowly he played his light over the other photographs. They showed historical subjects, snaps of the Victorian period and last century: old trains, crowds, faces, fashions, nothing remarkable in themselves. He scanned the rest of the room. The beam fell on a large wooden chest in the far corner, much dented and battered and arrayed with extravagant iron hinges. He moved closer. The lid was not fully shut; balancing his lamp on a shelf so it illuminated proceedings he lifted it and peered inside. Piled high in this chest were hundreds more photographs, some in bundles tied with string, others loose. Jack picked up the topmost few and sifted through them. All were old, all black and white. The topmost showed an old aircraft, a Spitfire. The pilot stood by it and gazed out at the camera truculently. The corner bore the date, May 1940. He looked at the next, which depicted the cast of what appeared to be a travelling circus, posing by their tent: the strongman, the lion-tamer, the acrobats with their leotards, the clowns with their painted faces. What was behind all this? The next photograph was brown with age and bore the inscription '1916, The Somme'. It showed three soldiers standing by a trench in a scene of churned fields devastated by war. They were all begrimed with filth and each carried a gasmask in one hand and a bayoneted rifle in the other. So it went on, through other eras, other scenes. Throughout, the same figure appeared, lithe, wiry, with the same fixed, unwavering expression. Indisputably, it was one man.

Slowly Jack returned the photos to the trunk. He stared at the dust dancing in the beam of the lamp. What was his past? A man's life in photographs, spanning a century and more, there in that chest. The same, unageing features, persisting through the decades, never changing. The same spirit, single-mindedly nursing its mission. He surveyed the contents of the chest again. A brown envelope, the flap merely tucked in, not sealed, lay on top of one of the piles. Jack took it and opened it. Inside were two more photos, only this time much more recent, and in colour. He adjusted the lamp to get a better view. Scarcely had he glanced at them when a noise made him spin round, fearing an intruder – or the occupant returning. But it was only the front door, carelessly left open by him, creaking on its hinges. Now sweating profusely in the heat, but also with simple shock at what he had just seen, he sealed the envelope and put it in his pocket. Then he closed the trunk, leaving it as far as possible just as he had found it. He must get on with his main task, to find the portal.

He swept the beam of his lamp around the room again. Something caught his eye as he did so. He went over to the fire once more. It was an old gas cylinder type, and had been pushed back into the cheap wooden fireplace surround. Crudely set quarry tiles jutted out to form a primitive hearth. The fire continued to glow, but it was what was before it, on the hearth, that had caught Jack's eye. There, arranged in a precise delta formation that seemed in itself significant, was a set of grotesque wooden carvings. Carvings that, once again, Jack had seen before; yes, he knew them, like the photograph on the wall above, from his earlier visit to the junk shop. He knelt down to look more closely at them, the hideous heads with their slanting eyes, horns and leering mouths. It was as if their placement on the hearth had been a matter of particular importance. The silence was deep; the only sound was the faint wheeze of the gas fire. Suddenly he felt sure he had found, in this place full of riddles, the most important thing, the thing he had come for.

As if in confirmation of his intuition, even as he looked he saw gossamer threads of silver-blue light shimmer into being and start to stream between the carvings in a mesmerizing tapestry of fine rays, before finally meeting at a focal point in the fire itself. And there before his eyes, hovering in the fireplace, appeared the likeness of slit, a slit that widened to become an oval perforation in the hot air. Disbelieving, Jack stared through this aperture, and found he could glimpse within a fantastic landscape of high bridges, huge viaducts in the distance spanning deep chasms, classical temples on a sublime scale and arcades of stone marching away into the distance. Fascinated, he came closer to the fire, letting his eye focus on the furthest reaches of the strange landscape. What, where was this surreal place? Some trick of the light? From the bottom of the scene, below the lowest edge of the oval, columns of white smoke drifted up, to be fanned by parched breezes within and dispersed. The heat was intense; he could feel his face burning. If he could just get closer still, see properly through this oval portal …. The noise of a door slamming nearby roused him. Before he had time even to get to his feet the lights came on and a woman's icy voice said, "I thought I told you never to come back here."

He stood up and turned around. There before him was someone he had sincerely hoped he would never see again, none other than the junk-shop assistant, Priscilla Malone. She was carrying several shopping bags and wore a mink coat. Her face was at that moment convulsed by a spasm of pure hatred, the lips bared, the eyes burning and twitching, the nostrils flared. Poised, she stared at him panther-like for several seconds. In those moments, Jack had the presence of mind to remember the purpose of his visit. Quick as he could he reached in his pocket and, just as the woman launched herself at him, he pulled out those of the stones that came to his hand and flung them into the fire behind him. There was a puff of smoke and a shocking, throaty rumbling sound. Then she had her hands around his neck and was shaking and squeezing simultaneously with frightening force. Fighting for breath, he felt himself pressed backwards, pushed closer to the fire while his nostrils filled with the burning smell of his own hair. A mighty hand seemed to be pulling him, sucking him in; his vision blurred while the surroundings of the room thinned and wavered. Terror overcame him, along with the incoherent thought that he was not ready to go *there*, not yet.

But Jack was roused too; his fear combined with a strangely precise recollection of the bitterness and humiliation of his earlier encounter with this fiend. With a surge of rage he struggled to his feet and threw the harpy off. She staggered backward into the fireplace with an inhuman shriek. He watched her for a few seconds, crumpled there in the grate, surrounded by dense wreaths of steam belching from the collapsing portal. The fringes of her expensive coat began to smoulder in the heat; venom still sparkled in her eyes. He continued to stare, fascinated and horrified in equal measure by the spectacle. Then, before she could recover herself, he made for the door, almost out of his mind with the fear of her miraculously reviving and blocking his exit. Then he was outside, in the cold night air, fleeing down the fire escape and across the dark square to where his bike awaited.

⅄

In the converted hermit's cell under his house on the cliffs, Professor Silverman worked late into the night, denying himself food and water, concentrating all his intelligence, skill and energy on the matter in hand. He bent low over the charmed space before him, the slab-like bench on which was focussed a small battery of halogen lights. On all sides, the strangest implements lay within reach of those pianist's fingers: bowls of water, blunted wooden tools, trays containing heaps of various amorphous material. Sound, time, heat and cold all receded for the Professor as, clad in his white laboratory coat, he worked through the small hours, intent on one thing only. And under his watchful eye something by degrees took shape, a thing rough-hewn and primal.

Meanwhile, in the shadows at the margins of the laboratory, trapped in a cage against a wall, a form restlessly moved to and fro. All brown fur, glinting teeth and glowing pinpoint eyes it twisted round and round, seeking liberation, its free spirit chained for now. Its release, when it came, would be far from the green fields and earthy burrows for which it pined.

The clock ticked, the hours passed, on the Professor laboured, oblivious to the creature's incessant motion. And so the night waned.

⅄

As he cycled along the Aylesbury road to the Parkway station, dodging potholes and ducking spray from passing lorries, Jack applied himself to channelling his shock and rage into generating more speed, while simultaneously reflecting on his night's work. He had, in fact, done well. The flat, so fortuitously entered, was an Aladdin's Cave of secrets. First and foremost, he'd found the portal, there was no mistaking that, and – who knows? – maybe he had indeed put the thing out of action just as Professor Silverman had desired. At any rate, he'd got two of the stones in there, he was sure of that, and the consequences were spectacular enough. But there was more. Of the identity of the Helper there could now be no doubt. And what he had seen had confirmed Silverman's speculations about the nature of this being. Beyond that, however, something else he had seen now proved to him that his father was not necessarily a weak man who had given way to a corrupt nature. No, his poor father was under the powerful sway of this 'Mr P' no less than Owen Tyack before him. It was not a question of choice; irresistible forces were at work.

A car drew alongside him and hovered there, bringing him back to the present with a jolt. He hadn't considered the possibility of being followed but it would be easy enough for that horrible woman to track him down during his escape. Nervously he glanced across, trying to see into the darkened interior. But the car suddenly sped past and vanished, mocking his fears. He couldn't be too careful though. He pressed on as fast as he could, the sweat starting out on his forehead, gripped by the new fear of pursuit. As he pedalled, new priorities formed in his mind. Whatever happened with the machine, this device of cosmic power, there was an even higher imperative now. Perhaps it was too late for Owen, but for his father there was still hope. He, at least, could be saved. According to Silverman, with the portal closed or damaged the curse would be weakened. If he could find his father, get out to the site of the installation at Verney Junction, then all might not be lost. He had done what he could for the Professor. Now this was his own mission, and a very personal one.

Reaching the railway station with relief, he coasted into its arc of neon lights and took his bike through the barriers to the platform. There was a train due in ten minutes. He leant his bike against a wall, sat on one of the benches and from his pocket drew out the brown envelope he'd taken from the chest. Looking furtively around, he saw there were only one or two other travellers on the platform – as if that made any difference, but now he felt a fugitive once more. Carefully he extracted the photographs and held them under the neon light. There in the first picture, this time in glorious colour, were the now familiar features of "Mr P", once more positioned in front of St Nicholas' church, but with a new companion. Next to him, looking as hollow cheeked and haunted as his great-grandfather more than a century previously, was David Tyack.

Tears pricked at Jack's eyes. With a clatter the approaching train alerted him to its arrival. He reluctantly turned to the other photograph, clutching to a vague hope that what he had seen in the flat had been an illusion. But no. There staring back at him was his own recent passport photograph, mounted on a card with the word "Jack" written neatly in unfamiliar handwriting below it. Suppressing a shudder, he returned the envelope to his pocket, got his bike and boarded the train – but not for home.

CHAPTER 54

UNCOMMON OBSERVATIONS

A heavily creased copy of the *Buckinghamshire Advertiser* lay on the floor of Richard Attlee's workshop, its periphery stained with greasy smudges and a patch of spilt tea. The usual clutter of tools and debris was scattered in its vicinity. In the background a low murmur of voices came from a radio broadcasting some sort of moral debate – just the kind of intellectual backdrop Attlee liked. A trail of oily spots led to the bench at the back of the workshop, over which the man himself was bending in fierce concentration under the arc of a white halogen light. Spread out before him on a clean levelling plate were several small, precision components. Attlee peered closely at one of these through a watchmaker's magnifier that was inserted into his eye like a monocle. He performed some careful adjustments to the device, then, casting the magnifier aside, took it with him through a connecting door at the back of the workshop that led to his adjoining home observatory. Once inside, he screwed the component into the bottom of his telescope, then reached up to open the skylight. Settling himself on the stool at the base of the instrument he began gazing contentedly through it at the heavens above.

Astronomy was one of Attlee's long-standing hobbies. The combination of the vastness of the physical universe, of its infinite possibilities coupled with the application of the principles of physics and mathematics – the two realms of imagination and reason – suited his mind perfectly. He had been known to disappear for whole nights at a time into the observatory, completely engrossed. Tonight, he was viewing what he believed to be a supernova in the galaxy of Andromeda, approximately 2.5 million light-years away from the earth. He held his breath to maintain perfect stillness. It was sobering to think that the event he was witnessing – the death of a star, if he was right – had occurred all those millennia ago, the photons only now reaching the earth, funnelling down his telescope, imprinting themselves on his retina.

In the background, the measured tones of the radio debate trundled on: "I'm afraid the professor has got it all wrong. What we call 'right', in the truly ethical sense, can never be right just for me, or for you, but must by definition be universally and absolutely true. If one reads Kant ...." Attlee shifted his weight on the stool and ever-so-gently rotated the focussing ring he had just been working on. Now it was totally clear. Perfect! He smiled slowly in satisfaction. Just at that precise moment of clarity, the image wavered and abruptly vanished. Attlee scowled. What was this – an aircraft? He made further adjustments, but in vain. The image did not reappear. That was strange; some sort of light pollution, perhaps? He checked again. Yes, a low background illumination had obliterated his cosmic event and other weak stars in that part of the sky. Frowning, he started to fiddle with other parts of the telescope. They really would have to move to Scotland. Orkney, in fact, which had ideal conditions for the amateur astronomer. He peered once more through the viewfinder, but could still see only an odd, diffuse, orange glow. Sitting back in resignation, Attlee's eye now caught the wall-mounted barometer, the needle of which had started jerking in the strangest fashion. It seemed the atmospheric pressure was drastically falling.

Suddenly there was a loud crackle from radio, followed by a deafening blizzard of interference in which the voices became grotesquely distorted. Cursing these irritants, Attlee quit the observatory, went over to the radio and twiddled the tuner impatiently, to no effect. The thing seemed to have gone dead entirely. He sighed. Well, it was no use fretting over it. Perhaps there was some sort of electrical storm. Sitting down in one of the easy chairs he reached for his paper philosophically. As his eyes moved over the text, behind them Attlee's unconscious mind picked away at the tapestry of clues, large and small, that had come before him over the last few days, culminating in the disturbances of tonight. His telescope had been pointing north. What lay to the north, at about the distance of the horizon, that could have been disrupting his observations? A thought began to form, a thought that connected what he had just seen with what Jack had told him only the previous day. He himself had speculated as to the presence of a large energy source, out over there, out in the Aylesbury plain. An energy source powerful enough to link events a century apart; one certainly sufficient to play havoc with his astronomical observations. The thoughts pushed themselves into Attlee's conscious mind, forcing him to put down his paper and pay them proper attention. Jack certainly knew more about this whole business than he had let on, no doubt of that. Did he already know the true origin of these strange phenomena, and had he kept it to himself?

Attlee reached for his jacket. Glancing at his watch, he located his car keys and strode out into the cold night air. He paused half way across the garden, turning to look up at the shocking sight of the sky over Aylesbury and Winslow. Unlike any night sky Attlee had ever seen, it was suffused by a dull orange glow, within which appeared to move towering storm clouds funnelling upwards in endless shifting patterns. Among them seemed to dance small motes or flashes of light with a life of their own. Great heavens! What was going on? It was time to question Jack more closely, and as soon as possible. Attlee made for his car.

⅄

Charlie hadn't had a moment to think since she'd started her shift at six o'clock. For some reason the café was exceptionally busy that evening, mainly with young families all wanting some form of special order or other for the kids. The queue coiled to the door; the howls of toddlers filled the air. "Did you say you wanted chocolate on top of that? Ok, just a couple of minutes–" She looked up, producing a mechanical smile for the spruce young mother. Instead, she was confronted by a dishevelled looking man of about sixty. A grey flap of hair hung low over his forehead, while the rest of it stuck up at odd angles. The collar of his tweedy sports jacket was half raised, as if he'd dressed in a hurry, and in his right hand he twirled a set of car keys restlessly. Murmurs of indignation swept through the queue but the man ignored them, fixing Charlie with a purposeful look.

"Jack," he said, impatiently. "Is Jack here? Where is he? He works here doesn't he?"

"Er, yes but not tonight. Well, he should be, but I'm filling in for him."

"Filling in? What do you mean? Where is he? It's his first night isn't it?"

Charlie felt reticent about divulging details to this eccentric-looking character. "Are you a friend of his?"

"Yes, yes! I haven't got time for that now. I need to know where Jack is." The man's voice lowered to an urgent whisper and he leant forward over the counter. "Can you help me? Did he say anything about where he was going?"

"Well, it was a bit strange. On his first night, like you say." Charlie looked around nervously at the impatient customers. "He phoned me, he was in a rush about something. He said he couldn't do tonight and could I cover for him at short notice."

"How did he seem?"

"It's hard to say really, I haven't seen him much. He seemed pretty wound up about something though."

"Did he say where he was going? It's important!"

"No, he just said he had to sort something out to do with his family."

The man twitched back upright as if he'd received an electric shock and immediately made for the door, leaving a line of indignant faces behind him. Charlie watched him leave, frowning. What sort of trouble had Jack got himself into? If only she'd pressed him harder, found out what was at the bottom of it. But Jack could be so mysterious, when he wanted to be. An impatient voice intruded on her reverie. "Are you listening to me?"

"Sorry about that. Er, was it chocolate you wanted on top?"

CHAPTER 55

Morgana's Small Problem

The town square of St Just looked much the same as it had when Jack had first arrived to track down his demons. Evening was encroaching on a fine day, the townspeople went about their business in a leisurely enough fashion. With the suddenness characteristic of this part of the Cornish coast, however, clouds were massing out to sea, ready within a half hour to sweep in and transform the atmosphere of the place.

Over in front of the Commercial Hotel, standing there on the pavement as if beamed down from another planet, was a little figure, a dwarf of a man. There was something outlandish about this figure, something that provoked distrust. He was no taller than four-and-a-half feet at the outside, though thickly enough set. His pallor was not entirely natural, the impression he gave somehow unsavoury. Again, he was swaddled in a heavy coat that hung stiffly to the ground, and had a hat on his head that made it difficult to see his features. In one hand he carried a bag, something like a briefcase, soft and bulging. Passers by crossed over to the other side, or gave him a wide berth: nobody in St Just was overly receptive to the outré. Ignoring his disruptive effect on the ebb and flow, the small man continued to stand in front of the hotel for several minutes, motionless. Then he set off to his left, around the corner and across the street to a row of cottages that faced the square obliquely.

Morgana Florence Trevose was preparing a rich butternut and marrow soup, one of her favourites. The house was heavy with the smell of cooking, combined with a lingering aroma of herbal cigarettes, one of which hung from her mouth as she stirred the greenish liquid pensively. As ever, cooking was a therapy for all manner of stresses. She pursed her lips defiantly at some private thought. At that moment, what might have been a quiet knock at the door broke in on her thoughts. She frowned. Despite living so centrally in the town, Morgana received few unscheduled visitors. She expelled a cloud of blue smoke from her nostrils and, taking the cigarette from her mouth, carefully balanced it on the edge of the hob before shuffling through to the hall. Perhaps she had misheard. But as she approached the knock sounded again, from the door without doubt, but again frustratingly quietly. Heavens, what was the point in tapping in that half-hearted fashion!

Taking her time, Morgana went to reach for the latch. As she did so, a tremendous blow came from outside and there was a splintering sound. The door swung slowly open. Morgana looked out across the square into thin air, then gradually lowered her gaze. The strange figure that greeted it, complete with hat and bag, stared up at her from hollow craters of eyes. The dwarf was a curious terracotta colour, hair, skin and all, with a pitted face. Beside him lay the twisted remnants of her elaborate and prized knocker, wrenched off its mountings and cast onto the pavement by an inhuman force.

Morgana continued to look with gathering fear at the little figure, then, without taking her eyes off it, backed slowly into her house. Her visitor followed until he was fully inside, whereupon he shut the door with precision behind him. Then he turned back to face her and began to open his bag.

CHAPTER 56

DARK THOUGHTS

Gaia. The world *conceived as a sentient being. Thinking. Feeling. Not just the planet but the whole realm of phenomena. And why not? How we assault and scar our home, yet still she forgives our tunnels, our fumes and fires! We are indeed expelled from Eden and live by the sweat of our brows. Now the final storm gathers. But first, the foundation myth, an old story for which one must go back to the ancient Greeks, and no doubt further: In the great primal struggle Gaia was assaulted by the giants – one giant, let us say, and a terrible one at that. In the battle that followed the giant was overthrown, and banished to the deep places of the Earth, down in her belly, out of sight and out of mind. How the long epochs must have told on him through his endless night of imprisonment! Perhaps he was locked in immobility through the ages. Perhaps he lost his physical being, becoming a dark shadow only, a vessel of malice. But he never gave up his quest for freedom – and revenge.*

Well. To return to the present: the boy is close. I see a tunnel of trees; ahead is the boundary of the place itself, and in the heavens the tempest sings. No ordinary storm, this, if I am weather-wise. I fear Gaia herself rages, knowing what is to come. But he has at least a chance: he has succeeded in closing the portal, for my moonstone, rutile quartz and labradorite have all faded and I guess are far away below by now. We shall see.

Gaia. She is first and foremost energy. The power of all that grows – woods, streams, skies and fertile earth. Comets and stars, too, all of it. How blind I was! With this same great energy the Shadow was locked below, held in perpetual captivity. But how cunning he has been; his great opportunity was the coming of humankind, with its greed, venality and craving. The diary makes this clear; no document was ever greater testimony to that. From where, I ask myself, will this terrible device get its power? Where, exactly, will the energy come from? There can be only one answer: the very energy of the Earth, Gaia herself! This Gaia machine will destroy her. All our mining, pollution, depletion of resources, the innumerable attacks on our parent that she has borne so patiently, will be as nothing by comparison. The fabric of Nature will be torn apart.

But there is worse. Now I am sure of it. How else is the Shadow kept in confinement? Should this machine be successful, the doors of his prison will weaken. He will flex his muscles, his paralysis will finally leave him, he will move once more. And so he will, at long last, find his release and take the upper world. All will be lost.

And the boy. Now he has crossed the boundary. I have impressions of the thing itself, ahead, but through a veil. No-one knows better than I the power of human craving, but to plan on this scale? It hardly seems possible. We have a hard task here. As for the storm itself, I sense something else behind it, some other field of energy. To the stones it feels like a power that comes from somewhere distant, from – the past? Could this be the pathway I have sought for so long?

CHAPTER 57

The Reactor Revealed

Jack was tired from the ride, his legs heavy. Verney Junction was in the middle of nowhere and the nearest station was several miles away. That had meant more cycling, in the wet and the dark, before he'd found his goal, below a beacon of mysterious orange cloud. He'd left his bike at the perimeter fence, over which he had climbed only with much difficulty and at much cost to his clothing. Now he had finally reached this last objective he felt none of the excitement he'd expected, only a great weariness that clung to him and weighed down his least movement. But if his efforts were not to be thrown away, secrecy was essential. Once more he scanned the dark and desolate fields, ready to freeze at the slightest sign of any movement. Ahead, cutting across the blackness, lay the approach road he had been looking for. It was lit at intervals by lampposts, dabs of orange colour suspended eerily in the dark. Away to his left rose the huge dome of the building he sought, looming pale against the turbulent sky. There was light around its walls; the whole structure seemed to be floodlit from ground level. He turned towards the road, pressing on through the wet grass, ignoring the damp seeping into his trainers.

Drawing close to the narrow strip of tarmac, he could now see that the apparent lampposts were in fact no such thing. He approached the nearest: a square plinth of shoulder height set on which, towering over him, was a grotesque form rising against the night sky. With its spreading stone wings, talon claws and hooked beak it might have been the very counterpart of the carvings he'd seen guarding the portal in the Helper's flat. Other statues, all variants on this same theme, stretched away to the left and right like gruesome sentinels. Occasionally one was sheeted over, only hinting at the form within, which somehow made the effect yet more chilling. Jack stood staring up at the statue closest to him, its body framed by the massing storm clouds through which a dusky moon occasionally broke through. Light rain was falling now, a fine mist. Could anything be more surreal?

He shrank back into the shadows and turned to trudge onwards to the domed citadel, following the line of the road, yet at a distance, fearful of whatever talismanic powers the statues might possess. After a quarter of an hour's slow progress, Jack lifted his eyes to find himself in the lee of the building. Its walls described a gigantic circle. Part of its height, he could now see, had been concealed by the depression in which it was sited. The earth had been excavated on a giant scale, some of it having been piled up in a mound around the periphery, like the raised rim of a crater. The floodlighting illuminated every detail. Jack positioned himself behind the rim and drank in the spectacle. The walls themselves were made of stone, finely fitting blocks that glistened in the rain. In tiers of niches around the circumference were statues set in relief, all depicted in the garb of old Rome and each one many times life size. Columns ran between them and met the roof in elaborately carved capitals. As they ascended, their grooves blossomed into strange designs that knotted and twined together like eruptions of exotic plant life. From the capitals, the dome rose up. At the very top was a cupola capped with a needle spire that pointed defiantly to the night sky. To Jack's right was the entrance, a porch with more pillars and cascading plant forms from which gargoyle faces peered. As the road approached this porch it cut through the embankment and, sloping down, ran gently to meet it.

Huddled in the rain and the dark, Jack pondered just what size of workforce had been needed to construct such a building. Where were the workmen? Where were the machines? Yet here it was, apparently complete, intimidating in its sheer size. His eye followed the needle spire upwards. The heavens were uneasy; large cloud masses shifted and gathered directly above, lit from within by a burnished red glow. Dancing flecks of light broke through them, motes that flickered, died and renewed themselves continually. Away to Jack's left, in the field, was a dark silhouette rising from black clumps of trees: some sort of tower. It was strange he hadn't noticed it before. And now, to his right, further off and beyond the line of the road, he saw another such tower. If the reactor building itself was imposing, these sinister outposts disturbed him more. They were, he felt sure, all related to the same larger purpose.

Shifting his weight against the clammy soil he scanned the entrance again. Immediately outside it several cars were parked on the gravel drive. He looked harder and felt the beat of his heart. Yes, there it was, his parents' Range Rover, without doubt. Jack knew the score now as to their involvement in this incredible project, but even so seeing the car there, the family vehicle in which they had holidayed, shopped and visited friends, hit him a fresh blow in the stomach. But this was no time to dither and speculate. He made up his mind and, skirting around the bank, headed for the entrance, keeping low.

It took some courage to step out of the relative safety of the shadows and walk, exposed, across the illuminated car park. But nobody was there; no movement could be seen nor sound heard, save for the moan of a cloying wind that had sprung up and gusted around the pillars like a lost spirit. Momentarily frozen by the majesty of the entrance, Jack looked above, his gaze drawn by a new feature. Set in the centre of the panel above the porch, in a niche, was a statue all on its own. Its very size and central position suggested something special. He paused, held by it. The figure was portrayed in robes. The arms were stretched out in a supplicatory gesture, palms upwards; the face wore an expression of saint-like suffering. Directly underneath the figure was chiselled an inscription in the bare stone, all too visible in the stark floodlighting:

"Owen Tyack 1844–1900"

CHAPTER 58

Attlee Pursues

The trees rose on either side of the single track road and arched above it like a tunnel that vanished ahead into the dark. The car's headlights played over the branches, probing the shadows until the further reaches of the gloom closed in, while strands of fog exhaled by the fields drifted across its path in ghostly wisps. Richard Attlee was driving fast, even by his standards. It seemed unlikely he would meet any other traffic on such remote country roads, particularly at this hour, and he had no time to lose. Strains of a Wagner opera wafted from the car's stereo. On the passenger seat beside him lay an open road map; there were no electronic navigation aids for Mr Attlee, who considered all route planning a form of problem solving and therefore beneficial. Yet tonight he did in truth regret their absence, so urgent was his mission. He screwed up his eyes in concentration and brushed a flap of hair from his sweating forehead. Surely it couldn't be far now? He thought back to the day he'd pursued a careering white van down these same country roads, and tried to remember their configuration, which looked so different now, in the dark.

Ahead the road abruptly branched into two. Without having time to consider he veered up the right-hand fork, then began to curse to himself as it rapidly narrowed then deteriorated into little more than a farm track. Taking advantage of a passing place, Attlee impatiently executed a multi-point turn, taking part of the hedge with him, and jolted back the way he had come. These blasted roads all looked the same at night, and this time he had nothing to follow! Now he tried the left-hand fork, only to find it rapidly curving back on itself, away from the direction he judged he needed to be travelling. This was hopeless. He slowed the car, straining to catch any landmarks through the trees. Nothing. And at this point, as he approached a baleful looking old oak that had broken ranks from the woodland and appeared to be stepping out into the road, the radio began to fade and crackle. The music briefly surged back, then fell silent. As he slowed to a halt the instrument display flickered, trembled briefly and died. It was followed by the headlights, then the engine itself. The silence and the dark were complete.

Cursing again, and frankly unnerved, Attlee groped in the glove compartment for his torch. Thankfully, it worked. Something very odd indeed was going on. He got out of the car and stood for some moments in the road, shining the torch in quick arcs this way and that. Its feeble beam was soon swallowed by the darkness, but reached far enough to illuminate the eerie tunnel of trees stretching away in either direction. A light gust of wind rippled through them, stirring the smaller branches. Attlee's sense of unease deepened. But he must be close; what he needed to do now was get his bearings.

The road was very old and had sunk between high banks from which hedge and tree rose. On his hands and knees, Attlee scrambled up the bank on one side and, at much cost to his jacket and trousers, forced his way through the dense brushwood and out into the field beyond. He felt relief at finally being out in the open. It was now clear that a storm was brewing. The sky directly above was black but over towards the near horizon, just two or three fields away, a metallic orange glow suffused the heavens, revealing great masses of cloud in restless dark plumes. It was the same storm he had seen from his back garden, and now he was closer to it, he was even more certain that this was no ordinary disturbance. Nor did it seem to be moving. He lowered his gaze, pulse quickening. Framed in outline against this disturbed backdrop rose a silhouette from the shadows of the fields: a sinister dome, quite enormous to judge from how far away it must be.

Attlee stood frozen. So there it was. A warm wind had sprung up, billowing out his jacket and blowing tiny particles into his eyes. He frowned. No such wind was possible at this time of year; no *natural* wind, at any event. And now it carried strange sounds to his ear, fell voices calling to each other in a rustling colloquy. Fighting his paralysis, he pushed back through the hedge to the car. The trees closed behind him.

With rapid movements he extracted a rucksack from the back seat and hastily stuffed it with one or two items. Then he locked the car and scanned the lane again. It was quite still, yet he could still faintly hear the babbling voices, hovering as it seemed high in the branches, taunting him. He paused, uncertain, letting the beam of his torch play over the dense canopy as if it might reveal the source of the sounds. Then he slung the rucksack over his shoulder, climbed back to the field and struck out purposefully through the wet grass towards the sinister silhouette of the dome.

CHAPTER 59

NEMESIS

Facing Jack was a pair of tall bronze doors flanked by slender columns. They were shut so tightly that only the barest line was visible between them, nor was there any sign of a handle or lock. Above him the statue of his ancestor looked down from on high. He put his back to the doors and pushed but there was not the slightest give. Standing back he stared at them, perplexed. Outside the porch the low rumble of thunder filled the skies. He wasn't going to be defeated now. Reaching in his pocket, he groped for the sheet of plans he had taken from his father's study; surely they would provide a clue as to another way in?

But as he did so, a harsh scraping stopped him dead. The hairline crack in the bronze wall widened to a pencil's width, then stopped. Wary in the extreme, Jack stood aside, ready for anything. The gap resumed widening; the doors slowly swung open. From inside the jumbled sounds of many wild shrieks escaped, horrible cries of naked terror and pain that froze Jack to the spot. Then there emerged nimbly a small, wiry man, who closed the doors immediately behind him, cutting off the cries, and stood facing Jack, eye to eye.

The face was familiar from some long-forgotten dream, a dark wraith but not entirely strange. For a moment Jack thought he was looking at his father. He looked harder and it was a totally alien face that he saw, inquisitive, simian, with a low brow and hairline. The man drank in Jack's appearance, then said quietly, "I've been expecting you. Thank you for coming." He moved to one side slightly, as if sizing Jack up, getting a better view of him. "We're long overdue this talk, you and I," he continued, in the same deferential tones. "I've been looking forward to it. I knew you were here."

A spasm of great unease swept through Jack, the stirrings of deep and unnamed cravings, coupled with disgust at their existence. "I know you," he said, trying to keep his voice even. "I know who you are. You've got my father in there haven't you?"

The man smiled. "Do you *really* know who I am? Really?"

"What are you doing to him? You've – *destroyed* him!"

"No! I have *not* destroyed him. Perhaps he destroyed himself. But it isn't me. I wouldn't do that." The man continued to stare at Jack, almost reverentially. "Think of me as – a brother," he said. He glanced up at the statue. "The four of us, we're all the same."

"You don't mean that! I'm nothing like you."

"Oh but you are. We're one flesh. You, me. Owen. Your father. Long ago, you see, your ancestor gave his flesh, a little of it, so that I could live. We all share a bond."

The words hardly registered with Jack. All he could think about was rescuing his father, getting him out of there. "Where's my father?" Impulsively he pushed the man, aware of his body as hard as a bundle of metal rods. "I've broken the portal. You won't be able to control him anymore. Not now."

Peregrinus stood aside, quite calm, watching ruefully as Jack scrabbled at the doors. A tremendous peal of thunder from outside stopped him. The ground trembled at the onslaught; the skies were lit by an enormous discharge of white light, framing their joint silhouettes against the doors. Jack could feel a steady vibration through the soles of his feet, as if the whole building were alive. Peregrinus was smiling again now. "This is it, Jack. What we've worked towards. We should enjoy it."

Jack looked grimly up at the doors, and the statue above them. "This thing should never have been built," he said angrily. "Owen never wanted it. He couldn't do it, he *knew* it was wrong, in the end!"

"Owen failed. Your father was failing too – but I helped him to find the path again."

"Why did you want to talk to me?" Jack's voice was trembling, both with anger and with fear.

"You have something I want. Something I need. Where is the diary?"

"I don't have that, and I wouldn't give it to you if I did."

"Well. It can wait for now. We'll come back to that. But listen." His face was rapt. Mingled among the crackles of lightning and crashes of thunder, were those wails of terror on the night air, outside now, coming from everywhere? Stubbornly Jack returned to his mantra:

"Where is he?"

"You won't find him inside. He's over there, see?" The Helper was pointing across the fields at one of the strange, dark towers at its edge. For a moment Jack hesitated, fearing deception. Then he was running, running away as fast as he could. Behind him came the fading cry of Peregrinus, "Your father's finished now. Finished! But you are strong Jack. We can work together, you and me. This is just the beginning. Jack!" Jack was heedless. He sped through the rain towards the tower. As he ran, calling on undreamed of reserves of energy, he saw an incredible scene unfold before him. The towers he had seen earlier were only two of many, circling the main building, some nearer, some far on remote hills. Great arcs of white light, pure energy, were dancing between the tops of each one, and from there to the central pinnacle of the dome, lighting up the congested sky in an awesome lattice of giant sparks. Each arc was accompanied by a tremendous crackling sound. The Gaia Reactor was building to full power.

As Jack neared his goal, from pure fatigue he slowed, then stopped. He saw that the lower part of the tower was shrouded in a dense thicket of woods, dark and dripping. Over to his left, no more than a hundred metres away, was the perimeter fence, its mesh clearly visible in the fitful flashes of light. Rain drenched him, running in cold rivulets down his collar. The one thought dominating his mind was that there in that tower was his father. He struck out for the wood.

⅄

Richard Attlee paused to wipe the rain from his face and settle his rucksack more comfortably on his shoulder. Ahead of him was a wire fence with concrete posts, a high one too: well over two metres tall. They certainly weren't keen on visitors. Within, rising from the fields like an over-sized temple, was the extraordinary building. The strange storm still brewed above, hanging there unmoved for the past hour. Yet now there were huge arcs of light curving from shadowy points at the circumference of the grounds. The nearest such point was over to his left, poking up from a clump of trees, a stark-looking gothic tower. Peripheral energy sources? What in the name of God was going on here?

Attlee scanned the length of the fence in either direction. The question now was how to find an entry point. He stepped up to examine it more closely. Was it electrified? It seemed not. He gazed at the dome. If he was right about things then there would – quite unintentionally, so far as the device's creators were concerned – be another displaced vortex created something like a quarter of a mile from the core, although of course it was difficult to be certain given the huge increase in scale involved. Attlee shook his head grimly. He just hoped Jack had not done anything foolish.

Just as these thoughts ran through his mind, a tremendous blaze of white light lit up the entire scene before him. And there, to his amazement, on the other side of the fence, running with desperate speed, was Jack himself. Recovering himself rapidly, Attlee called out frenziedly, "Jack, Jack! Over here, here to me!" Jack saw him and, using the final dregs of his strength, erratically began to veer towards him, weaving from side to side like a frightened rabbit. "Get to the fence, Jack. I'll help you over. Get out of there!" He willed him on but again Jack stopped, beyond exhaustion now. Another arc of energy flashed above, accompanied by a thunderous crashing sound, illuminating the whole scene for a full quarter of a minute. Behind Jack a second figure was thrown into relief, a lithe, animal-like creature chasing him down. "Over here, over here!" shouted Attlee, his voice cracking. On the wind came the voice of the pursuer: "Jack, wait! We can work together–"

Jack vacillated between the two men, paralysed. And as Richard Attlee looked on, the air around him seemed to tremble and shimmer, the trees waver and bend. The entire landscape was briefly sucked into a point like water down a plughole. Attlee could only continue to stare, helpless, transfixed, disbelieving the evidence of his eyes. Then the phenomenon passed and he once more saw the sheets of rain falling steadily in the flickering light, the dome rising behind and the silhouette of the simian pursuer framed against it. But of Jack, nothing whatever was to be seen. He had vanished utterly into thin air.

⅄

The lights were low in the lounge of the house on the cliffs. A fire burned languidly in the hearth, summoning shadows that danced across the walls. Faint draughts from the storm outside caused the curtains to rustle and sway; the clock ticked on with its slow, woody beat. In the circle of light from a green-shaded reading lamp sat Professor Silverman in his favourite armchair, hunched forward, staring intently into his master divining stone, his face set in concentration. There in the depths he perceived a tiny, doll-like figure, spinning endlessly, growing ever smaller in the grip of the vortex that drew it down, down and away from the world of phenomena he despised so much. The Professor continued to watch until only the merest dot was visible, then sat back and returned the stone to the tray by his side. Reaching for his glass of ruby port, he stared into the fire. The trace of a smile played around his lips. Then he closed his eyes and gave himself up to dreams of other realms.

Epilogue

In the sweltering realm of the Shadow in which the soul of Owen Tyack suffered, something happened, the tiniest change. A sound, first – could it be the distant rumble of thunder in skies that had never heard it? On the horizon, were those the outriders of dark cloud masses building, building in skies that had never seen clouds through countless millennia? Did the hard bronze glow of the vault above tremble ever so slightly; did a spot of *rain* drop from out of it onto the dusty terrain below, ground that had for eons been dry to any fluid but blood? The Soul shifted its phantom body a little, panting on its bed of pain, and felt a faintly cooler breeze play over it. A change was coming, far off, slowly – but coming.

Every minute was an hour in that place. Many passed. Then it came again, a cavernous rumbling above. Almost imperceptibly, the ground trembled. Fine cracks spread like veins at the roots of the great viaducts. A single stone toppled from the crest of a temple perched high on a rock. At the centre of the stone forest, the floating thing, connected by the finest webs to the outreaches of its kingdom, twitched and flinched. Then a great flood of exultation swept through it, causing every consciousness in that realm to stop, and take heed. The hour of liberation had arrived.

⅄

To be continued in Book Two....

Proof

Made in the USA
Charleston, SC
20 May 2014